THEORY OF MAGIC

UNEXPECTED MAGIC #3

Patricia Rice

Theory of Magic

Patricia Rice

Published by Rice Enterprises, Dana Point, CA, an affiliate of Book View Café Publishing Cooperative

Cover design by Killion Group

Book View Café Publishing Cooperative

P.O. Box 1624, Cedar Crest, NM 87008-1624

http://bookviewcafe.com

ISBN: 978-1-61138-599-1 ebook

ISBN: 978-1-61138-600-4 trade

Author's Note

Those of you familiar with my magical Malcolms and scientific Ives know that I'm playing with possibilities more than I'm using magic. Centuries ago, flying would have been magic and scientifically unfeasible. Today, we know airplanes aren't magic at all.

So in Duncan's book, I'm toying with the possibility of strong empathy. Neural scientists have studied empathic receptors and human behavior for decades. I won't go into a scientific essay but Google "empathy scientific studies." It's fascinating!

For those of you curious about Duncan's eye condition, the simplest explanation is in **Wikipedia**. Keep in mind, of course, that in 1830, physicians had utterly no idea what was wrong with his eyes or whether they'd ever be better. Since this is fiction, I get to make my own choices on what might happen.

I want to recommend a truly fun site if you're interested in a better understanding of the area of St. James that I write about in this book: **http://www.british-history.ac.uk/survey-london/vols29-30/pt1** If you poke around, you can see it rather sounds like a modern urban neighborhood in transition.

And just for the grammarians out there—as in the previous series, I know the plural of Ives is Iveses, and I don't care. If my family refers to themselves as Ives in the plural, that's how it comes out on the page. My characters are dictators!

One

Early November 1830

CLENCHING HER LARGE HANDS in the billowing skirt of her ample lap, Harriet Christie Russell Townsend tried to appear content studying the flowered walls of the empty parlor of her stepfather's rented London townhouse.

Inside, humiliation crept down her spine, filled her lungs, and crushed her heart. She could not, simply *could* not, do this again. Ever. She would rather walk in front of a run-away carriage.

She'd probably break its wheel.

It didn't bother her so much that not one gentleman sent her a posy after last night's ball. After all, since she had never been to London before and had no acquaintances, she'd not danced a single step and had decorated the wall all evening. In the few weeks she'd been in the city, she had felt like a prize pony being walked around the arena for her stepfather to sell to the highest bidder.

But Townsend had vowed that Mr. Lively would ask for her hand today. She had an attractive dowry, and the gentleman had a need for funds. He had all his teeth and hair and even though he was a bit on the skinny side, he might have made a decent husband. So even if they'd looked like Jack Sprat and his wife, she'd have someone to talk to in the evenings, and perhaps, eventually, there would have been children.

She was so desperately lonely and bored that she would not mind settling for children and a home of her own.

The case clock ticked away another minute. She needn't look. She knew Mr. Lively was already over an hour late. Had she been another woman, she would have been furious at his lack of respect.

But Harriet knew, deep down in her suffocating heart, that he wasn't coming, that he didn't want her, and that like everyone else, he was rejecting over-tall, big-boned, homely *her*, even with all her money.

A few minutes later, a maid crept in to hand her a hastily scribbled note from her stepfather.

Lively ran off with his mother's pretty parlor maid rather than marry you.

Lord Townsend really hadn't needed to add that last phrase. It just served to grind her pride into smaller particles of dust—no doubt as he'd intended. He had made it clear in many ways over the years that he had never wanted to be stuck supporting an ugly duckling for the rest of his life.

THE TUG AT ASH'S POCKET would never have happened had the thief not targeted him as *weak*.

"Poisonous hunch-backed *jackanapes*," Duncan Ives, Marquess of Ashford, Earl of Ives and Wystan, roared, furious at this insult to his pride.

With that warning, he yanked his ebony walking cane up as hard as he could between the thief's legs. There was nothing wrong with his damned arm, so the blow was strong.

It was his lack of vision that prevented him from disabling the man so badly that he'd never have children.

The thief howled in anguish anyway, which gave Ashford another locator. *"Paunchy beef-witted blood sucker!"* He balled his fingers into a fist and swung hard enough to hear cartilage crunch. The thief staggered backward, if Ash was any judge of sound at all. Behind him, his footman gasped.

"Nab him, Smith," Ash commanded, hearing his victim hit the shrubbery.

He waited while his footman and the maimed thief scuffled in the park hedges. The footman was new and barely trained, another of his sister-in-law's charity cases. Ashford growled in exasperation as he heard the thief splash through the water basin and the footman pound off along the gravel path to pursue him *around* the damned water—no doubt to keep his new boots and livery dry.

The dawn silence was broken only by bird song and a distant wagon rattle. Not until then did Ash realize he was now out here by himself.

He had not been left on his own since he'd been blinded.

He'd seen no purpose in exposing himself to the humiliation of his disability in public, until his brothers had started squawking like chickens every time he refused to go out. Intending only to show them that he wasn't a coward, Ash had forced himself out the door in the early hours, when all his aristocratic neighbors slept—and thieves apparently still lurked.

This was only his third morning walking in the gated park. How would a damned thief get in without a key?

Standing there abandoned, Ashford realized the better question was—how would *he* get *out*? He had only his walking stick to guide him, and one bush was pretty much the same as another. He could follow the circular fence forever and come out on the wrong side of the square and end up in a real thieves' den. The busy commercial thoroughfares around St. James Park weren't the polite residential streets of Mayfair. The thought of stumbling blindly past the clubs on Pall Mall filled him with revulsion.

To make matters worse, drops of rain spattered against his new top hat and coat. And Smith had run off with the umbrella.

So now he could stand here like a senseless Greek statue and let the pigeons land on his head until someone rescued him, or he could stagger like a drunk along circular paths and pray he found the right gate.

The depths to which the mighty had fallen had been a nagging theme in his head these past months. If it weren't for his stubborn pride—and his immense, annoying family—he'd have cast his whole damned life aside and become a hermit.

Then blown out his brains in boredom.

A light scent of lilies approached, along with the confusing sound of heavy footsteps. Ashford clenched his walking stick in defensive mode.

In the growing light of dawn, he thought he might actually see the movement of a silhouette. Shocked at actually *seeing* motion, Ashford froze, straining to determine the full outline of what appeared to be a less-than sylph-like figure.

"I'm sorry, might I trouble you to explain how this umbrella works?" The contralto was sweet, almost sensual, and very definitely feminine. "I am wearing a new hat, and I fear we're about to be drenched."

"Of course, madam," Ashford agreed, as if he could actually see her blamed umbrella. He might have spent most of his life in a wolf den, but as the heir to a marquisate, he'd had a few good manners beaten into him. One aided ladies who asked for assistance.

She pressed the umbrella's handle into his fingers, then exclaimed in shock, "Your hand, sir! It's bleeding. You should wrap that immediately. Do you have a clean handkerchief?"

Of all the damned things she could have noticed . . . He handed her his walking stick so he could hold the umbrella pole with one hand and push up the clumsy ribs under the canvas with the other. "It's just a scratch, madam. I'll be fine. Thank you for your concern."

Her voice sounded young, but if he was actually seeing her silhouette, she had a tall, matronly figure. Besides, he found it hard to fathom why any young woman would be about at this hour. They'd all be sleeping in after last night's frolics. Could it get any more humiliating that the best he could do was stir some old woman's maternal instincts? He hoped to hell that Smith returned soon.

"It's Miss, my lord, Miss . . ." Oddly, she hesitated before continuing, "Miss . . . Christie."

"Christie? With a *y* or an *ie*?" he asked, because he knew she was lying.

She hesitated again, and he almost heard the wheels in her brainpan whirling. "Does it matter?" she asked, then returned to the subject at hand. "Cuts like that attract infection. Really, if you haven't a clean handkerchief, I can use mine. It's not very large but it will do until you return home."

She still held his walking stick. Irritably, Ashford pulled out his clean linen and wrapped his bloody damned fingers.

"I saw you hit that thief," she said in what sounded like admiration. "I am ever so grateful that you chased him off before I reached this spot! But your man has run off with your umbrella. Here, why don't we share this one? Where are you going?"

"I will not melt . . . Miss Christie with or without a *y*," he said, grating his teeth against his hatred of helplessness. But then he realized what she'd just said—she was out here alone with thieves running amuck. "But you should not be walking alone. Where is your maid?"

"It's a long story," the smoky voice answered with a sigh. "Shall we walk? I'm heading towards Carlton Terrace, but I assume you live closer to the park? I could keep you dry with this umbrella you so kindly opened for me."

Ashford understood the fine art of manipulation. Normally, an insult to his intelligence set off his temper, but he couldn't blow up at a woman who needed his protection as much as he needed her eyesight—and who refused to admit her weakness any more than he. He amazed himself when he offered his arm. She was nearly as tall as he, and he was no small man.

He wasn't even certain she knew he was blind, no more than he knew if she were young or old. "You are correct, I'm one street past Warwick." When she wrapped a long-fingered, gloved hand around his elbow, he used his stick to prevent walking on her gown. He let her steer him, and returned to finding out why she was here. "I always enjoy a good story. Is yours sad or happy?"

"Hmm, a bit of both, I'd say." She sounded more thoughtful than pleased. "It seems my . . . cousin . . . is to be married shortly. It is a very happy occasion."

Ashford suspected that she lied every time she hesitated, but he'd never see her again, so it hardly mattered. He was escaping the park in the company of a woman. How long had it been since he'd escorted any woman other than his brothers' wives? He sincerely hoped this one was at least remotely attractive and not a gray-haired matron.

"I am happy for your cousin, then," he said solemnly. "And how does this lead to you walking in the park in the rain without a maid?"

"Well, that part is mostly silly," she admitted with a lovely rich laugh. "I wanted some thread to finish a hem, and thought if I hurried, I'd be back before my cousin had her chocolate."

That part *almost* sounded honest. "You do not stay abed in the mornings as your cousin does?" he asked with actual interest, attempting to determine the lady's place in the world. He enjoyed a good mystery.

"Oh, no, I've always kept country hours. We've only just come to the city for the short session. Usually, we stay home, but of course, my cousin wishes to visit the shops for her trousseau."

Ah, there was the sadness. She had an expressive voice. "And you are helping her sew her trousseau?"

"Well, no, I was taking out a hem for myself. I am rather above average size, so my cousin has her gowns made with large hems and seams. Then when she's done with them, I can let them out!" She sounded quite proud of her accomplishment, although he still suspected she was enjoying embroidering her web of lies.

"I see. And running errands for yourself means you cannot borrow her maid?" Although he didn't know how much was truth, he actually understood the predicament she described. It wasn't uncommon for impoverished relations to live with wealthier branches of the family as companions and general servants. "Where does the sad part come in?" He leaned over to open the gate that she nudged him toward.

"Well, I fear she will no longer need me as a companion once she marries. I can always go home, but I was so enjoying the city. But that's not exactly sad, is it? It means I have an opportunity. Would you know how one goes about looking for a position as a secretary or companion? I am very experienced."

Her ingenuousness made him want to laugh. Since very few things made Ash laugh these days, he was feeling more in harmony with the world than usual. Surely, she could not be very old to be this unaware of how life worked, even if she normally lived in rural ignorance.

He kept looking for more shadow or light, but they were in the gloom of the buildings now. Flickers of motion were the most he could catch. That was more than he'd seen inside the house, but not enough to be useful, and just might be an indicator that his head was about to explode. The doctor had feared some such for a while.

"If we are lucky, my sister-in-law will be martialing her troops by now," Ash said with a modicum of maliciousness on top of his frustration, "and you may ask her. She generally trains servants to work in big houses, but she knows a great number of people. Perhaps she could ask for you."

It should be inspiring to see how Lady Aster dealt with this new stray he brought home. Goats and hounds and orphans hadn't daunted her.

"Oh, that would be above all wonderful, sir," his companion said with what sounded like genuine excitement. "I hate to impose upon a stranger in such a manner, but another such opportunity might never open. And to think, it all came from being foolish enough to walk in the park in the rain!"

Ash heard Smith's asthmatic huffing and puffing approaching. He could abandon the little liar here, or continue with the charade. In dire need of amusement, he chose the latter.

"Smith, run ahead and warn Lady Aster we're to have company. Come along, Miss Christie. You may miss your cousin's hot chocolate, but I can give you a cup of tea before sending you back out in this mist."

"And tend your hand, sir," she answered. "That must come first."

He thought she honestly meant it. He despised being treated as an invalid, and still he laughed at her prim command. "Of course, Miss Christie. We must see that my knuckles live to punch another day."

Two

HIS HAUGHTY LORDSHIP was laughing at her, but Harriet didn't care. She was much too utterly astonished at her temerity. *What had come over her?*

She'd only meant to help a gentleman emanating distress, but as soon as she'd given herself a new name and assigned herself the role of companion, she had grown bold. It was as if dropping her stepfather's name had removed a dark curtain. She was certain that was a sign that she had done the right thing, even though she was shivering in her shoes to be walking along on the arm of an actual *marquess*—a rarefied creature she'd never so much as caught a glimpse of in all her life. Well, perhaps as a babe, but she wouldn't remember that.

The imposing gentleman hadn't introduced himself, but Harriet didn't doubt his identity. Her stepfather had a habit of ranting against reformers like Ashford and had actually been delighted when the marquess had suffered the accident that had left him blind and helpless. No one had seen the rakehell marquess since the fall from his horse, but she'd heard enough to be intrigued.

And now that she'd met him, instead of regarding a debauchee with appropriate horror, she was captivated. He stood even taller and broader than she. His size was all muscle, if she was to judge by the arm she gripped and his graceful stride. He possessed the famous Ives thick black hair and masculine, square jaw—even though one side of his handsome visage bore a ragged red scar from eye to temple. No dashing dueling scar there, but if he couldn't see the damage, it hardly mattered. He was a wealthy marquess and carried himself with the arrogance of his position. She understood why he'd had so many women in his bed. He even set her battered heart aflutter.

Had she been properly introduced as a lady, she would have been horribly intimidated by a ravishing, aristocratic rake and would have had nothing to say. But as a poor relation looking for a position, she was too far below his notice to be of consequence—even if he could see, which he couldn't.

That he couldn't see how unprepossessing she was also added to her freedom to be herself, she suspected.

It also helped that the marquess emitted waves of sadness and loneliness as strong as hers. Unfortunately, he was also a volcano of suppressed fury. She supposed he might have a lot to be angry about after losing his eyesight, but he possessed everything else a person could desire, and wrath was such a wasted emotion!

She ought to run the other way, but he had connections far beyond anything she could conceivably wield. His company couldn't be more harmful than walking in front of a carriage, as she'd considered doing yesterday.

As a dyed-in-the-wool Tory, her stepfather would have an apoplexy if he knew she was consorting with the enemy. She vaguely understood that Wellington and the Tories represented educated landowners like Townsend and her mother's noble family. However, Ashford had radical ideas and supported Earl Grey and the Whigs, who demanded equality for the common man, possibly even criminals and sailors. She couldn't imagine why one would support criminals, and she probably ought to be ashamed to be seen with such a decadent profligate.

Instead, she held her breath in hope and trepidation as a footman ran ahead to open the impressive double doors of one of the grander old houses. She really did mean to enter this stranger's house alone—a much more interesting way to die than being run over by a carriage.

She'd never been a risk taker, but then, she'd lived an extremely sheltered rural life and had never had the opportunity to do anything even remotely daring. This was her chance to be impossibly foolish.

After the marquess's manservant held their umbrellas for them, his lordship placed his large—bruised—hand at her back to assist her up the granite front stairs. She shivered at the physical contact.

All thoughts of herself fled the moment they stepped through the front doors, into a fantastical world of utter chaos.

Harriet blinked and attempted to adjust to the whirl of activity. This wasn't a narrow, modern terrace house like the one her stepfather had rented. The front doors opened onto a wide corridor that led the length of the house. To each side there were formal public chambers and an enormous staircase leading to the family rooms above, although paltry candle sconces were the only illumination.

This was an *old* house, one laced with a dizzying array of inquisitive spirits almost lost in the confusion of people and activity. Harriet had to rub her forehead to sort through the incoherent chatter, both spiritual and actual.

Deliberately shutting out the voices in her head, sealing off any emotional influences, she turned her concentration outward.

Ladders blocked the staircase where workmen painted and papered. Carpenters and plasterers carried buckets and lumber over soiled canvas that would have protected carpet had there been any. In the large, dim parlor off to the left, female voices prattled excitedly. Deep male voices carried from a room behind the staircase.

A giant hound raced after a black kitten. A maid flattened against the wall to avoid spilling the tea tray she held. If Harriet did not mistake, childish voices rang from overhead.

How in the name of all that was holy did a *blind* man navigate this circus?

"*Dammit*," the aristocratic gentleman abruptly roared into the chaos. "What slubber-de-gullion allowed that wretched, beef-witted hound in here?"

More footsteps on the stairs above, whispers, and then a boy darted down to chase after the dog.

"In here," Ashford directed, as if he hadn't just roared curses with the vehemence and volatility of a Shakespearean actor. He slapped his walking stick against a door frame to ascertain its location. Then he steered her toward their left, into a chamber containing three women so different that there could be no possible blood relation between them.

"Aster!" the marquess thundered. "Tell the brats to lock up their pets before the maid scalds herself again."

"Tell them yourself, Ashford. They're your brats and that's Theo's dog."

Stunned into dizziness already, Harriet thought she might fall over her own feet at such a defiant retort to a *marquess*! Good heavens, had she said any such thing to Townsend, he would have locked her up with bread and water for a week. Or thrown her out in the snow.

"Very well, then I'll leave you to introduce yourselves," Ashford replied with acid sarcasm. "I thought Miss Christie might be the solution to a few of your problems, but I'll let you sort that out."

In the blink of an eye, the polite, laughing gentleman from the park and the roaring lion from the foyer transformed into a cold aristocrat. He stalked away, spine rigid, shoulders back, just as she'd always envisioned men of power would do.

The old Harriet Townsend cringed and wished she had never been so idiotic as to involve herself in this mad escapade. The new Miss Christie was a bold wench, however. She swallowed hard and waited to see what would happen.

Since the three fashionable ladies currently occupying the parlor were studying watercolor sketches and fabrics in the gray light from the front window, Harriet could only stand dumbly and hope to be acknowledged. She knew for fact that she wasn't invisible, no matter how hard she tried to be.

With interest, she noticed the . . . *telescope?* . . . in the front window.

"Have a seat, Miss Christie." The outspoken copper-haired lady finally acknowledged her, gesturing at a sofa with once-pretty slipcovers that had been torn and muddied. "Moira needs to run to the shops, and we must make a decision on the upholstery fabric now. Ashford has another gathering planned at week's end, and the animals and twins have nearly destroyed everything in here."

"If pets and children are involved, I'd recommend leather," Harriet—Miss Christie—said daringly, refusing to cringe. Yet. "Not fashionable but practical."

"Better yet, keep the menaces in the country where they belong, and then you can use the pretty satin you prefer," a slender blonde proclaimed, gesturing at the sketches.

Opening her emotional awareness again, Harriet/Christie sensed the confusion and dissatisfaction of the copper-haired lady and the dark lady who had yet to speak. But her awareness was too vague to determine if the ladies were equal in status. All three dressed in expensive fabrics. None of them seemed concerned with the marquess's opinion. She didn't know a great deal about his family, but she hadn't heard he had a wife—although he apparently had children.

"Have you asked Ashford?" she asked, more timidly than she liked, but she was, after all, being intrusive.

All three women stared at her. Oh well. In for a penny and all that. She might not always be bold Miss Christie, but timid Harriet offered a tentative smile. "I cannot know the circumstances, so I apologize. It just seemed if this was his parlor, then either he or his wife should be the final arbiter."

"My word, Ashford has gone out and found his own general!" the copper-haired lady exclaimed in awe, dropping the sketches and hurrying forward, hand extended in greeting.

A *general*? Harriet almost glanced over her shoulder to see if someone else had entered the room. Speaking up was all it took to be a general?

"It is our place to apologize for ignoring you, Miss Christie. I am Lady Aster Ives, Ashford's sister-in-law. Our dark beauty is Mrs. Celeste Ives, another of his much put upon in-laws. And the annoyingly blond English nuisance is my cousin, Moira McDowell. She has a brilliant gift for beauty, but apparently not for practicality."

"This is a *formal* parlor—for entertaining prime ministers and important men," the blond Miss McDowell exclaimed. "They will expect fashionable elegance, not these horrid slipcovers you threw over everything!"

"Fashionable salons have telescopes these days?" Harriet asked, unable to hide her doubt.

Lady Aster laughed. "That's Theo's. He's testing different lenses. It's naughty fun looking through it at night when no one draws their draperies."

Harriet frantically tried to remember if she'd drawn her bedchamber draperies at night.

"Aster is wanting to go back to her husband and charts." The slender, mahogany-haired lady with the bronzed complexion finally spoke, drawing Harriet back to the conversation. Her musical voice, with its foreign accent, conveyed amusement. "Miss Christie is correct. Even though he cannot see what we are doing, Ashford should be consulted. It is his money and his home, after all."

Harriet had seldom had the opportunity for feminine company. It was immensely refreshing to be with people who were amused by their problems, instead of frustrated and critical of all suggestions. She sensed Lady Aster's impatience and desire to be elsewhere underneath her geniality, but she was the person to whom *Miss Christie* must talk about a position. She had to walk a narrow path here—which shouldn't be difficult after a lifetime of experience in treading cautiously.

"Please correct me if I am speaking out of turn," she said with her former humbleness—another quality she'd learned after years of being ground into dust. Humility didn't quite suit her emerging persona, which was, admittedly, a work in progress. "If I may be blunt, Lady Aster is in an *interesting condition* and has need of a . . . general . . . to take some of the decision-making from her hands. Was that too bold?"

The blond Miss McDowell shrieked and flung her sketches aside to hug her cousin. The dark-haired Mrs. Ives smiled serenely, as if she was already in the lady's confidence. And Lady Aster turned pink beneath her cousin's hugs.

"How did you know?" Lady Aster asked with interest, studying Harriet as if she were a fascinating new fabric.

Harriet had never been able to explain her *feelings*, not any more than she explained the voices in her head. But avoiding mentioning those matters had given her lots of experience in fudging the truth. "You seem to glow with it."

The lady raised her eyebrows in disbelief, but she nodded without questioning. "It's true, I'd rather be back in Surrey with Theo, only there is likely to be a vote on the current administration during this session. Ashford needs to be here to represent his party and someone needs to direct his household. Moira has no authority, and Celeste has her own home and business she should be attending."

"Lord Ashford brought me here because I told him I was looking for a new position," the bold new Miss Christie said. "I have many years of experience as a nurse, companion, and secretary. I can be . . . a little overbearing," she claimed, lying through her pretty white teeth—Harriet's best feature.

"How would you make the decision on this room?" Mrs. Ives asked in her lilting accent. She seemed to be regarding Harriet with interest, as if she knew she wasn't telling the whole truth.

Harriet would make the decision the way she always had—by sensing how everyone around her felt, judging who had the most interest, and finding a compromise. Doing so would give her a dreadful headache and possibly let in nattering spirit voices, but it was a price she would pay for this opportunity.

"If it were up to me," she said judiciously, "and Lord Ashford agreed, I would decorate this room as Miss McDowell suggests, in the finest elegance for special guests. And I would keep the door locked and keep out children and pets. And then I would decorate a room on the family floor for them in leather and cane and indestructible fabric."

Miss McDowell beamed. Mrs. Ives looked even more thoughtful but nodded agreement. Lady Aster—opened her eyes wide in surprise, nodded hasty acceptance, and squeezed Harriet's hand.

"Yes! I've only recently had excess rooms to decorate and so hadn't thought of actually banishing family from an entire parlor. Excellent! Bring us references, and you're hired!" Lady Aster beamed and hurried toward the door.

Shocked, Harriet cried after the lady's retreating back, "As what?"

"Lieutenant general," Miss McDowell said with a snicker as Lady Aster vanished into the din of the corridor without answering. "Can you keep accounts? I am very bad at them. I could start my own business as a designer of interiors if only I knew how much to charge."

Lieutenant general? "Yes, I've kept accounts for years," Harriet said, without lying. "And I have a fine hand for correspondence. I've been told I have a good reading voice," she added, thinking of the blind marquess, even though she would do well to stay out of his way.

"All excellent qualities," the exotically lovely Mrs. Ives said. "But it is evident that you are a lady and not a common servant. The problem with that is that without Aster and I on hand, this is an all-male household. Moira goes home to her family in the evenings. Unless you have your own flat . . . ?"

Of course she didn't. She lived nearby and could walk easily. But the whole point of this episode—the blinding revelation that had come to her as she'd made up her tale— was to escape her stepfather's house for these next six months. She didn't wish to see him become truly desperate and hold some poor man at gunpoint to force him to marry her.

Apparently noticing her dismay, Miss McDowell interrupted. "What if we bring in Aunt Nessie? Then I could stay here, too. My work would be done much faster. Ashford refuses to navigate the stairs, so we could take rooms above. The twins and the servants are on the third floor and shouldn't be any problem, although the twins really should be in school."

"They were sent down for brawling and something to do with snakes in pillows," Mrs. Ives said with more amusement than disapproval. "For some odd reason, they lack discipline."

"Their uncles often stay here. They are no help and should probably be banned from the house if we are to move in," Miss McDowell suggested. "Or Miss Christie and I must repair to the attic with the servants."

"Nessie won't make it to the attic," Mrs. Ives said. "I believe if we tell Aster what we wish to do, she will happily allow William and Jacques use of her townhouse, and she and Theo will stay here those nights they are in town."

Harriet assumed William and Jacques were the useless uncles. Her head spun too much just trying to follow her part in this quick exchange.

"Is it settled then?" Miss McDowell demanded. "Aster remains our general for major decisions. Miss Christie will be our lieutenant general to carry them out . . ." She hesitated and swung to meet Harriet's gaze. "Will you be able to face Ashford and tell him exactly what we want? And force him to listen if he begins yelling?"

"I found him to be very r-reasonable," Harriet said with a slight stutter. The marquess had, after all, punched a full grown man in the face and nearly brought him to his knees. And then turned into a cold aristocrat in a heartbeat. He was not precisely an *easy* man, but he'd been thoughtful.

The tall Mrs. Ives shrugged her elegant shoulders. "If he terrifies you, then we are no worse off than before, and Aster will find you another position. Bring us the reference, and we'll send for Nessie. You are now captain of a very leaky ship. Or I suppose, officer of a rebel army."

Terrified at what she'd just done, Harriet nodded and wondered if all the inhabitants of this house were as mad as she.

A voice in her head chortled *FINALLY!* in what seemed to be delight. Harriet rapidly slapped the mental door shut against the intrusion.

Three

"MARY, I HAVE DECIDED to stay with Cousin Deirdre for a few weeks," Harriet told her maid several nights later, with all the confidence of the almost-independent. She'd just received word that *Aunt Nessie*, the chaperone, would arrive in the Ives' household on the morrow. Her heart thumped with the audacity of what she planned next. "Why don't you take the time to visit your family while I am gone? You've earned a bonus for your attempts to create a silk purse out of a sow's ear."

She produced a small bag of coins for her startled maid. After a few minutes of argument, Harriet had brushed aside all of Mary's objections, and the maid was happily giggling over this opportunity to see her mother and siblings again.

Later that night, Harriet surreptitiously packed a valise with her older gowns. A companion could not look *too* elegant, and the plain cloth and design suited her better than the London finery the modistes had dressed her in these past weeks. Who needed silk when they were writing accounts anyway?

This modern townhouse lacked the spirit to answer her silent question, possibly another good reason to leave. Maybe she needed to develop the courage to listen to the voices in her head, especially the ones who delighted in her decisions like the one had in Ashford's home. But she feared that way lay madness.

Knowing she might never be allowed to return, she prudently added her mother's silver-backed brushes, the locket containing the watercolor portraits of her parents, and every other personal item she couldn't bear to part with. She could buy her own shoes in six months, so she wasn't much concerned about material goods.

She had already written a glowing reference from Miss Harriet Townsend about Miss Christie and sent it to the marquess. Now, she forged a letter from Cousin Deirdre for her stepfather's perusal. She'd leave the letter with her note of explanation on her stepfather's desk. Townsend could plot her marriage just as well without her and would probably be relieved at her absence.

***

"You've installed a *chaperone?*"

Lord Theophilus Ives, Ashford's heir presumptive, made his location known by falling into the squeaky leather chair on the other side of Ash's desk.

Ash could hear the hubbub in the corridor and understood the source of his younger brother's puzzlement. The house already exploded with people, and now, apparently, the new assistant and her chaperone had arrived.

He bounced the useless pen in his hand. "Your wives are plotting. We're to order our loutish brothers to stay at Aster's for the duration while the women repair this tomb. I'd be happy if they could just rid the place of river stench and coal smoke. But they have brought in Miss McDowell and an assistant and Aunt Nessie as chaperone so they can fluffify the place."

"Fluffify?" Theo repeated in amusement. "Well, I suppose that will give Aster the opportunity to do the same at Iveston. Has she drawn the new assistant's zodiac chart yet?"

"I'm sure she's discovered Miss Christie's birth date, determined she's some amazing combination of heavenly harmony and universal accomplishment, and Celeste has analyzed her voice and announced her to be the perfect specimen to do whatever in hell she's doing." Ashford said in sarcasm, refraining from mentioning his theory that Miss Christie was a liar. That little mystery he preferred to resolve on his own.

Unconcerned by Ash's opinion of Aster's proclaimed astrological prophecies, Theo settled into his chair and produced documents to be signed, judging by the the paper rattling. Ash knew his heir would rather be staring at moons with his new high-powered telescope glass, but Theo had been the one who had told them they must unite against their common enemy. He was doing his part by handling the farm business as Ash no longer could.

Theo was doing his best, even if he knew nothing of land. And they had yet to define the enemy who had caused their tenants to riot or who had hired men to cause Ash's "accident." Beyond learning that the earl of Lansdowne hated everything they represented and that he consorted with their Tory neighbors, they had no evidence of the earl's involvement.

However, there was strong oral evidence that their neighbors, Sir George Caldwell and Lord Henry Montfort, had hired the villains who'd aimed at Ash's horse. But Lansdowne . . . had too many black marks against his name to be ignored.

Since they'd recently halted the earl's outright theft of Celeste's inheritance, Lansdowne had every reason to despise them on a personal level as well.

"Once we have the vote, you can go back to rural splendor," Theo said absently. "In the meantime, I have a list from your steward asking your priorities."

Ash snorted at the polite title for the rough-speaking old soldier currently in charge of the fields he'd once rode. "That's not Browne's phrasing. How many men does he want to hire now and which fields is he threatening to abandon and how many epithets were employed?"

Rather than indulge Ash's desperate need for entertainment, Theo simply began reading the prepared list.

Ash stifled a yawn and listened to the women running and up down the stairs. He wanted to see what they were up to. He couldn't, not any more than he could see what Theo and the steward were doing to his land. He fretted over not knowing what the devil was happening in his own domain. He'd walked that land since he'd been a boy in nankeens. It killed him to be unable to discern matters that only he understood required attention.

He gritted his teeth and returned to the moment. Aster had reported some faradiddle about hiring the lost companion as a lieutenant general. That had made as much sense—and maybe more—than anything else the females had done lately. Having women in the household was such a new experience that he hadn't found a way to object to their annoyances. Yet. An unrepentant liar would ultimately have to be tossed out, but not until he understood her intentions.

"Tell Browne he can hire ten men for the harvest, and I want the lower field harvested first." Ash stood up, found his stick, and limped for the door. "Palmer, Whyte, and Birchcroft will be here this afternoon with a report on how much support they think the Whigs have. Have Erran here so he can tell us whose arms we can twist to put the reformists in the majority."

Ash assumed his brother's silence indicated he was grimacing in distaste. Theo despised politics precisely because of what "arm-twisting" entailed—trading favors instead of making decisions based on what was best for all. But Theo was an idealistic scientist with his head in the Milky Way.

Ash knew how small minds worked and relished the diabolical challenge of turning mankind's ignorance and greed into his favor.

Following the sound of women's voices, he swung his stick across the corridor, attempting to avoid paint and painters and any other obstacles in his way. Mostly, people had learned to dodge when they saw him coming. Someday, maybe he'd grow so small-minded that he'd enjoy that too.

First, he needed to accept that his eyesight would never return. The silhouette he'd seen in the park had disappeared, perhaps a figment of his own demented hopes brought on by his ability to see occasional flickers of light.

The doctor had told him that the ability to see light meant his eyes were unimpaired, but some internal pressure caused his sight to narrow to dots of light, akin to looking down Theo's telescope the wrong way. So far, no physician they'd consulted had enough experience to offer any hope of correction.

At least his limp justified carrying the despised walking stick. Gripping the knob harder, he stopped outside the parlor. He could hear Theo following behind him. His antisocial brother's coat brushed against the wall as he took his favorite position lurking rather than walk into the women's gabfest.

"What does the new assistant look like?" Ash demanded, listening to her smoky contralto weave into the conversation. Except for a timid hesitancy, she spoke as if she had the same status as the powerful Malcolm ladies who'd hired her. Companions often had aristocratic backgrounds, even if they were poor.

Theo hesitated. "Tall," he said with caution.

"I can tell that," Ash retorted. "You may as well say not small. How old is she?"

"Hard to say. Around Aster's age, perhaps? Not a giggly adolescent. Not a stout matron. Just a pleasant young woman."

Young. Excellent. So he hadn't looked a complete blockhead being led through the park. Impatiently, he demanded a fuller picture. "Hair? Features?"

As if Theo ever noticed such things while his new bride was around. Ash hated knowing nothing of a member of his household.

"She wears one of those dreadful caps with lappets that women use to hide their hair when it's not all curled and puffed. I'd say she's blond and blue-eyed, good English stock." Theo sounded proud of his descriptive abilities.

Ash might as well ask the twins what they thought—the result would be as useless. Asking if her figure was as lavish as he suspected would reveal entirely too much of his depraved—or deprived—state of mind. "Find out more about Townsend and his household. Erran read me Miss Christie's letter of reference, but one young woman recommending another young woman is meaningless."

"You have reason to doubt her when *Aster* doesn't?" Theo asked in a voice that probably meant he was lifting his eyebrows in surprise.

"I believe in cold hard facts, not Malcolm magic. Townsend is one of Lansdowne's flunkies. He could have sent her here to spy on us for all we know."

Since the vile earl had set rioters loose and done his best to rob his own family in his efforts to maintain control of the current administration, Theo grunted in agreement. "I'll let Jacques deal with that. Might as well find some use for his prowling around backstreets."

Their bastard half-brother had a penchant for drama and a way with words that Theo didn't possess. Ash nodded approvingly. The whole family working together instead of going their own ways might actually be helpful, once they had the knack of it. "Good thought. Go ahead and take Aster back to Iveston to safely hatch the next generation."

The generation that Ash wasn't likely to produce hung unspoken like a large polka-dotted rhinoceros between them.

"We might have girls. That's the Malcolm legend," Theo warned.

"Between you and Erran, we're bound to have a boy sooner or later. I have the twins, and that's enough for me, even if they can't inherit."

"That'll teach you to marry women before you tup them," Theo said crudely.

Just *finding* women to tup was his current problem, so Ash didn't lend that nonsense the dignity of a reply. He had not yet reached the degenerate level of bedding servants or sending them out to pimp for him.

He might make an exception for a spy.

Four

HARRIET NESTLED A TABBY kitten in her lap and petted its tiny head, delighting in the purr. "Such a little beauty!"

The older lady the others called Aunt Nessie nodded her mob-capped head. "Yes, a duty. Raising kittens takes as much responsibility as children, but they each have their own rewards."

Startled, Harriet opened her mouth to correct the grandmotherly lady, but Miss McDowell shook her head so hard, her ribbons whipped in the wind. She pointed at her ears, and Harriet gathered Nessie was hard of hearing.

So she just beamed and played with the kitten. "I've never had a pet."

"Clever hat?" Nessie asked, glancing up from her knitting. "The things ladies are wearing today are an utter disgrace. I trust none of you indulge in those sailboats adorned with fruit baskets."

Miss McDowell nearly choked on laughter, and Harriet was left tongue-tied.

"Now that Nessie is settled in, we should repair to our own chambers. The painters will be here first thing in the morning, and they won't use the right colors unless we watch them every minute." Miss McDowell hugged her aunt and gestured Harriet to the door.

Miss McDowell had insisted that she be called Moira since she was one of the younger of half a dozen siblings. The familiarity seemed odd to Harriet, but then, she had no close relations with whom her name could be confused. The few long-ago times she'd met her cousins, they had been distant and formal. She let the other women take the lead until she knew how to fit in.

Reluctantly, she returned the kitten to Nessie and followed Moira down the upper corridor of the family rooms. The workmen hadn't been up here yet. The walls were papered in dark rose bouquets, and any lighter colors had dimmed with age and smoke. The carpet was beyond repair. Candle sconces and a few oil lamps were still used for lighting, although she had noticed a gas light at the front door.

"I thought it would be quieter for us to use the back rooms overlooking the garden," Moira explained, opening the door to chambers across from each other. "These rooms might have once been part of the master suite, but the whole house has been altered at some time or another. Since Ashford won't be using this floor, I see no reason to change it—although I suppose we should move the sewing mechanism."

"This is perfect," Harriet said, admiring the tidy chamber, which included an odd machine attached to a table. "This is a machine that *sews?*"

"Lord Erran tinkers. Celeste has basted some of the drapery hems on it, but I cannot begin to tell you how it works."

A household with telescopes and machines that sewed! Harriet was beyond fascinated. "It might be interesting to learn. Let's leave it here."

She studied the remainder of her new home. Her only bag had already been carried up and left beside the bed. The narrow, old-fashioned tester had no curtains, and the room was a little drafty, but the walls were a plain apple green and the bedcover was done in dainty bouquets of flowers. Cautiously opening her mental door, she sensed fond maternal spirits in here, nothing too intrusive. "It even has a writing desk so I can work on your accounts!"

"First, you will have to teach me to write down expenses and give you receipts," Moira said dryly. "The accounting for the formal parlor is already completely out of hand, but we can start anew on the ante-room once the parlor is done. Ashford's chambers have already been finished, so we'll have to make decisions about the dining chamber next."

"How long do you think it will take?" Harriet asked, trying to hide her desperate need to know.

Moira shrugged. "Depends on how many people interfere. Don't worry. Aster always has need of help somewhere. Prove yourself useful, and you'll have a position for life—if you can tolerate chaos."

Harriet's sedate life had never included chaos. It sounded rather exciting. It had never occurred to her that she had the power to seek her own entertainment!

"If I am not being too bold for asking—why is the house of a marquess in such disorder?" She bounced just a little on the mattress, testing the bed's strength. It seemed solid enough.

"They're Ives," Moira said, opening the muslin draperies to look out. "They haven't had a woman to take care of them for twenty-five years. Aster says they were raised like wolves. Men simply do not grasp domestication on their own, so Aster, and now Celeste, have a long uphill battle ahead of them."

"And hence the need for a general? To order the troops? How many Ives are there?" Harriet thought she began to understand, and wondered if she had what it took to command men. Servants, yes, but a marquess? She didn't think so.

"Depends on which ones you're counting. Ashford, Lord Theo, and Lord Erran are the legitimate branch. After that . . . I've seen at least three full-grown half-brothers, an uncle, and the twins born on the wrong side of the blanket. I've been told there are more. Aster is currently playing the part of general over three different houses. From what I've seen, she really does need a lieutenant to carry out her orders." Moira grinned. "Dream on that. I'll see you in the morning."

A lieutenant—over half a dozen grown men and more. Harriet almost giggled at the thought. *I can't even* talk *to my stepfather*, she thought. *How will I command a half dozen strangers?*

THESE ARE GOOD MEN, JUST STRONG-WILLED, a spirit said reassuringly inside her head.

Oddly, the voice was louder and more distinct than her mother's had been back home. Most of the time, the voices were muddled and unclear, and she simply closed her head to the headache they created.

But if the voices said *good* things . . . she might try listening. She needed all the encouragement she could find in this frightening new world she meant to carve for herself. After spending a lifetime thinking she must have a man to look after her, she needed to adjust to the notion that she might be able to take care of herself.

Looking around the narrow room that was only a fraction of the size of her rural chamber, Harriet dropped back against the bed and inhaled the sweet air of freedom. She need only hide for six months, until her twenty-fifth birthday. She couldn't believe her luck in stumbling across this haven.

Her own narrow, stultifying life had suddenly opened wide—exciting and terrifying at the same time.

"WHERE THE SORRY DUNGHILL are the hog-grubbers taking the furniture?" Ashford roared, having just walked into an armchair at nose level. The workmen carrying it scurried toward the vague rectangular light of the open front door, out of his way.

The lily fragrance arrived, on his left, from the ante room.

"To be upholstered, my lord. Lady Aster's kittens shredded the new slipcovers in the salon. May I help you with anything?"

She sounded more nervous than she had in the park. Good. It was nice to know he still wielded some authority here. "I cannot entertain thirty gentlemen in a wardrobe!" He pounded his stick on the floor to show his frustration since he had nothing at hand to fling. "Where the devil will I put them if there are no chairs? Aster said she had this house in hand."

"She does, my lord," the lady said. "She has rented some sofas, and we're moving in chairs from elsewhere in the house. All will be ready before your guests arrive."

It was maddening not to know what she looked like. He amused himself by touching his cane to the top of her head to better judge her height. When she surprisingly didn't run screaming, he ran it down the length of her arms—no billowing sleeves there—to the ample curve of her hip and gown stiff with petticoats. She stood still instead of smacking him away, as he deserved.

"I am large and unprepossessing, my lord," she said in that rich low voice which tingled his spine. "If it matters, I am wearing a blue muslin which I am told flatters my eyes. But I am wearing it because I've already splattered it with ink, and I expect to splatter more while working on Moira's rather haphazard accounts."

Ash almost smiled. "You read my mind like one of Aster's witchy Malcolm family. I trust you're not related or she would have crowed the news."

"I am aware of no relation to Lady Aster," she said stiffly. "Although I should be proud of it, if I were. You do comprehend how tirelessly she works for your family?"

"And we're a thankless lot, granted. Carrying the weight of the world distracts from domestic issues," he said with the arrogance of his station.

"Which should be left to the ladies, understood," she said noncommittally.

He ignored the jab behind her politeness. Now that he had her where he wanted her, he could test her. "I am told you write a good hand. I have pressing correspondence that needs attention. Can you spare a moment?"

"You have no secretary?" she inquired with honest curiosity.

"I threw an inkpot at him, and he took umbrage. Stupid man. I would have bought him two new suits in apology." He leaned forward just enough to catch another whiff of her fragrance.

"I'll remember that, my lord. I'm wearing an old gown today, and two replacements would be very pleasant. What must I do to earn them?"

He could swear he detected laughter instead of fear in her voice. "Do not argue with me, to start with. I do not like to explain myself."

"Of course you do not," she said soothingly. "Tyrants generally don't. Where is this correspondence, my lord? I will endeavor to see how quickly I can earn two new gowns."

His lips twitched at her insolence. "My study. We will leave the door open to observe all propriety."

"I generally have no fear of improper advances," she said with dryness.

He could hear her petticoats swishing as she followed him down the corridor. "Why? Do you carry a pistol and shoot your suitors?"

Her chuckle was low and sensuous and roused a part of him that he'd thought dead. Ash nearly walked into his own damned door.

"Had I any inopportune suitors, I'd no doubt break their fingers or crack their toes. I am not a lightweight, and as a female, I have not been trained to fight fair."

Did she think him a *eunuch*? Or just helpless? Ash's dangerous lust for knowledge got the better of his good sense. Once they crossed the threshold into his study, he swung around, caught Miss Lying Christie in one arm, and dragged her up against his chest.

She was a rare handful, and his cock rose to full mast with those high, firm breasts crushed into his waistcoat. She smelled of aroused woman as well as lilies and tea, which made him even hungrier for a female caress. He traced the outline of her face with his fingers, as he'd been longing to do since they'd first met. A beautiful oval, with strong cheekbones, a nice narrow nose, and a wide brow. He wished he could see her eyes, but her lashes were full and long.

She did not protest his pawing, as if she understood his need to know her appearance.

Unable to resist the incredible pleasure of long-denied feminine proximity, hoping for a reaction from her, he pressed his lips to the line where her jaw and throat met. The muscles were firm, and her skin was like rose petals. Or lilies. Impetuously, he found her plush mouth.

Still, she didn't fight him. Her lips responded, presumably out of a curiosity as strong as his. She held herself stiffly, though, as if debating whether to break his fingers. But she kissed him back. And the more he asked, the more she gave, until they were both hot and gasping. Miss Christie was not an experienced kisser, but she was a quick student.

The clatter of paint cans and ladders down the hall forced Ash back to sensibility. His cock protested, and he had to hastily take a seat behind his desk, amazed she had not slapped him into the next room. Or crushed his toes. "I should apologize, Miss Christie."

"But you won't," she said in a tone he could not quite decipher. "You are already telling yourself that you were doing the poor spinster a favor, and I practically asked for it."

Ash leaned back in his chair and frowned in contemplation. "No, not that precisely. We *both* asked for it. And seemed to enjoy it. But it was ungentlemanly of me to impose on a lady under the protection of my roof."

"If you would please to remember that from henceforward, I might be able to help with your correspondence. But should there be any repeat occurrence, my lord, I shall have to remove myself from your presence."

She did not offer to leave the house, he noted with interest. She had said she had a home to go to. But she was not eager to go there. Or *could* not? Or had that been another of her lies? Not that he had proof yet that she'd actually been lying, just instinct.

"With the understanding that my correspondence is often of national importance and of confidential nature, I bid you read the names of the correspondents on these letters so I know which to answer first." He pushed the stack of mail across the desk.

SUSPECTING THAT THE MARQUESS heard more than most, Harriet tried to slow her ragged breathing as she picked up the letters he thrust toward her.

He'd *kissed* her! As if she were some foolish debutante caught in the garden at her first ball. Worse yet, she hadn't protested because she'd *liked* it! Her blood had boiled when his mouth had come down on hers. She still frothed with pleasure. Ashford's lips had been hungry, forceful, and tender all at once, making her long for more—unlike the limp fish lips she'd experienced once or twice in her younger years.

She had to stop thinking like that. He was a marquess, and she was a deceitful nobody. Taking a deep, calming breath, she read off the names on the letters he'd handed her. Some of the handwriting was atrocious, and she had difficulty translating, but Ashford guessed much from her stumbling attempts and directed her to lay them on the appropriate stack—to the left for his immediate personal reply, to the right for someone else to answer.

Almost at the bottom of the stack was one from Townsend. She recognized her stepfather's handwriting before she'd even read his name. Not giving it a second thought, she dropped that one in her lap and read the next. Ashford had no way of noticing.

"Start with the one from Earl Grey," Ashford commanded. He had his chair turned to face the wall and not the desk. She assumed that the placement was meant to make it easier for him to drop down into the seat without fumbling. It was certainly easier on her nerves. Even though she knew he was blind, she felt as if he could see right through her. She rather he glared at the wall.

She had spent the latter part of her life living lies. She was still uncomfortable with them. It took a great deal of self-confidence to carry off a true lie, and the Harriet she'd been didn't possess any. She hoped Miss Christie was stronger. The letter in her lap burned a hole in her skirt.

She read Earl Grey's letter aloud—an *earl*. She was reading the private correspondence of one of the most powerful men in England—and he was asking Ashford's opinion. The same Ashford who had just kissed her. She was in well over her head.

From this letter, she gathered that the upheaval brewing in the Commons to overthrow Wellington's administration was vital to the reformists. The unrest among men throughout the kingdom could lead to a revolution as devastating as the one in France had been in her parents' time. And Ashford and Earl Grey were fighting for the reform necessary to prevent the kingdom's destruction. She was in such awe that she nearly lost track of his reply.

"Tell him we need a dozen more votes, preferably two dozen for safety, unless he can bring Lansdowne's faction around. We cannot promise that the Irish and Scots contingents will arrive in time."

"What will happen if Wellington's party wins?" she asked, swallowing her trepidation in favor of an overwhelming curiosity.

He sent her an impatient look, even if he couldn't see her. "Slavery will continue. Men who have gained wealth through their industry but still have no vote will rise up in revolt just as the Americans did for being taxed without representation. Workers will burn manufactories in justifiable rage at their inhumane treatment. Shall I go on?"

"And the decision could depend on Irishmen or other rural representatives who never come to London?" she asked, understanding finally why her stepfather had actually left his comfortable study in Somerset. He was part of this process.

"Exactly. It's not as if we can change minds that have already been made up." The marquess tapped his walking stick on his knee. "There was a letter from Bryghtstone, wasn't there? Pull that out next, please."

Apparently she was to remember his responses and write them out later. That gave her mind more to occupy it than how strikingly handsome he looked with his scarred visage turned away from her. Perhaps that was another reason for his chair placement.

They had almost reached the bottom of the left hand stack when two young boys raced into the study. Harriet could not call them *small* boys, for they were tall and husky, but they didn't look to be above ten years of age. She'd heard them racing about in the schoolroom and on the backstairs, but whoever had responsibility for them usually kept them out of the front where the workmen were.

"Mr. Baker said we are to take our hoops around the park ten times, then name all the trees and shrubs around the basin. Can you go with us, please? You know the names of *everything*." Both boys spoke as one, sometimes in unison, sometimes talking over each other.

"Hugh, Hartley, there is a lady present," Ashford said sternly.

Two identical youths turned and bowed to her. Both looked much as Ashford would have at that age—dancing dark eyes, with too long arms and legs, angular features, and patrician noses they must grow into. Only the dark auburn curls gave a hint of their mother.

"I'm Hugh," the more jovial one announced.

"I'm Hartley," the more somber, mature one said.

"They're lying," Ashford warned, standing. "Hugh is the eldest and actually interested in naming trees. Hartley would rather chase squirrels. You will join us, Miss Christie. Bring the right hand stack, and we'll work through those as we walk."

She liked that he knew his sons so well that he could tell them apart by their voices, especially since they were bastards most men would ignore.

ADMIRING MY GRANDSON DOESN'T MEAN YOU MUST GO ANYWHERE HE COMMANDS.

The spirit voice confirmed what she already thought—or perhaps that was just her new persona standing up for herself. Harriet remained where she was. "I will answer the letters we've already discussed while they're fresh on my mind. You will enjoy the day with your sons."

Ashford gestured commandingly and grasped her elbow. "You need fresh air as much as we do. If you don't trust me to lead you while you read, then leave the letters here."

Put that way . . . She still could not go with them. With her mental door open, she heard his loneliness—and his dread?—but she simply could not be seen in public. She didn't think anyone had missed her yet, but she couldn't disguise her size if anyone had. A public park and the marquess at her side—out of the question.

Harriet removed her elbow from his grasp and slid her stepfather's letter into her pocket. "Your sons need time with you—alone. I have work here to do."

She could sense Ashford's roiling anger and frustration far better than he expressed it aloud. He was *hurt,* presumably because she might think him incapable of walking and talking at the same time, or that she did not wish to be seen with him. The marquess existed on the volcanic edge of explosion, simply looking for insults.

That could not be good for a man with the reins of the kingdom in his hands.

Five

"BRYGHTSTONE WANTS TO ENCLOSE his woods and treat them as his own personal fiefdom, as if he were some medieval baron preventing the peasants from poaching his private stock," Erran said with disgust, plunking his boots on Ash's desk.

Ash was still disgruntled enough over the afternoon's disastrous outing with the twins that he growled at Erran's disrespect. He listened for the boots hitting the floor before he replied.

"Aster's family says the workhouse in his village is full, since he's turned most of his fields to sheep." Ash was a farmer. He understood the desire to cast off the uncertainties of crops and concentrate on the easiest profit, but a man of position had responsibilities to his community. "Lansdowne must believe he doesn't need more votes if he's denied Bryghtstone's request."

"More likely, Lansdowne has asked for cash in return for favors, and Bryght hasn't any. Promise him income, and you've gained his vote."

"Have you always been this cynical or has marriage made you wise?" Ash asked his newly-wed brother in amusement.

"I've always been this cynical," Erran said with a verbal shrug. "Why else would I become a lawyer? Once, I was naïve enough to think justice could be had in courts, but now I see the entire court system is corrupt and needs reform. Celeste keeps me from setting fire to wigs."

Ash laughed. "Perhaps I need a woman as sensible as your wife. In the meantime, we can't let Bryght deprive the village of possibly their only source of putting dinner on the table by granting his ridiculous request. Tell him we'll introduce him to a few wealthy ladies instead, and if none suit, we'll promise him ground floor investment on the municipal water works we'll be building near him, in exchange for his valuable time and knowledge of the area, of course."

Erran snorted. "Which will ensure he won't protest if we need to run the canal through his property. Excellent. I'll learn horse-trading yet."

"Only if you join the right clubs and learn the idiosyncrasies of the men with whom you're trading." Ashford twirled his stick. "I suppose I can pay your membership. It's not as if I'm spending time in them any longer."

"We can go together. You can introduce me around," Erran said with a verbal shrug. "I'm seen so seldom that half the town thinks I'm one of father's bastards. But I need to call it a night and return to Celeste. She's sent her brother and sister off to school, and she's moping."

He could hear Erran shove back the chair to leave. After today's fiasco, Ash wasn't making any promises to attend his old clubs. He nodded dismissal. "Give her my regards. And ask her to nose around, if she would, and find out more about Miss Christie. For all we know, she's one of Lansdowne's spies."

He hated saying that, but Miss Christie's refusal to attend him in the park had added to his misgivings.

On top of which, he was pretty certain Theo had told him he'd received a missive from Townsend. Miss Mysterious Chris hadn't mentioned it.

AFTER SPENDING A PERFECTLY LOVELY DAY feeling helpful, Harriet sat in her lonely chamber and fought tears. She crumpled the letter in her hand and let the old rejection swell and spill over, until she held her middle and rocked with the familiar agony of it.

She *had* to cast out the old Harriet, who cared what people thought of her, the weakling who yearned to be loved. She had been taught in so many ways—by her stepfather, by governesses, by the village ladies and their sons—that she was apparently too different, too large, too proud, or too clever to be loved, or even respected. So she *had* to give up these megrims and learn to live on her own.

She could not let Townsend's letter return her to a weakling. She knew she had value, if just given a chance. She could make her own life, find a place where she might possibly be useful.

And she would learn to be proud of herself, do as she saw fit, and stop expecting people to love her for it.

It was this wretched letter that had brought back all the insults she'd suffered over the years.

Her stepfather wanted to trade his pocket borough votes for a man who would marry her! That was immoral on so many levels, she could not quite put her mind to it all. Shame washed over her that an intelligent man like the marquess might read such a letter. What kind of beast traded his family like livestock? If he ever found out who she was, Ashford would regard her as contemptible by association to such a man.

It made her sick to think of what Townsend may have said to persuade her other suitors to court her.

ARE YOU DONE FEELING SORRY FOR YOURSELF YET? The maternal spirit clucked unsympathetically. *WOULD YOU CARE TO LOOK AT IT FROM YOUR STEPFATHER'S PERSPECTIVE?*

It was hard to keep her mind closed while weeping, so she'd asked for that. "If Townsend had written that letter in an effort to help me," Harriet argued, "I might find it in my heart to forgive him. But he merely sees my money slipping from his hands."

YOU ARE FORTUNATE TO HAVE YOUR OWN MONEY, the voice in her head reminded her. *AND THE BARON HAS PAID YOUR SUPPORT ALL THESE YEARS. YOU CANNOT BLAME HIM FOR WANTING REIMBURSEMENT.*

Arguing with herself had to be a new form of madness, but anger was more bearable than the agony of self-pity. "I can't touch my trust fund until I am twenty-five. He has claimed all the income over the years. I keep his accounts," she whispered, unable to convey her hurt without physical expression. "I know to a farthing how much I cost and how much my mother's investments and property earn. I could support a village on the difference!"

DOES HE GAMBLE OR WASTE THE PROCEEDS? YOU SHOULD NOT JUDGE HASTILY.

No, he lined his own pockets. She ought to shut out the voice, but that was the coward's way out. Harriet rubbed her head and tried to reason with herself as well as the invasive, judgmental spirit. Had she really thought it interesting to hear the voices more clearly? She had attics to let, if so. "Townsend is greedy and dishonest. He intends to dupe some poor man into deeding my mother's property to him in exchange for me and the investments. Townsend likes land, and mine is productive."

The spirit didn't have an argument for this one.

She'd *known* what her stepfather was doing. Humble Harriet had been willing to accept such a marriage bargain as the price of having a family. But this . . . She flung the letter across the room and let anger well up. This was *humiliating.*

She had no good means of expressing her anger in the city. In the country, she might have gone for a good long walk. Here—she couldn't even stride quickly, even if she dared to go out on the street, which she didn't.

THERE ARE ALTERNATIVES, MY DEAR, the kindly voice said. *LOOK AROUND YOU.*

She was angry enough to tell the voice to jump in a lake, but someday, the voices might be her only companions. With a sigh, she looked out the window to the walled garden below.

Outside the wall was the mews and a tavern. She was still trapped—she didn't dare let herself out the back gate. These were not the safe environs of the country. Perhaps a stroll in the garden would help.

A figure ran back and forth along the short garden path, and she frowned. Who could be out there at this hour and what could they possibly be doing?

Needing diversion, she donned her pelisse and crept into the hallway. Light shone under Moira's doorway, but Harriet didn't wish to intrude upon the lady's private time. A floorboard groaned under her weight, but this old house creaked in the wind. She doubted any would notice. She took the servants' stairs down to the back door.

A footman glanced up sleepily, but she simply walked past him.

At this time of year, the sun had set hours ago. The only illumination was a lantern someone had left on a post. In the garden, she was nearly bowled over by a mangy hound who ran straight into her skirts and across her feet before darting under a hedge. A second later, a shirt-sleeved boy followed, but instead of running into her, he halted and looked wide-eyed in surprise.

"Miss Christie, sorry, I didn't know you were here."

Harriet sorted through his array of emotions. Ashford had been correct about his elder son's confidence and the younger's immaturity. This was the younger son, Hartley. He had a soft heart that was easily hurt. She related too well, but she had no means of understanding the difficulties of a little boy.

"You should be wearing a coat. Was that your dog I saw a moment ago?"

His shoulders slumped. "No, miss, he's just a stray. I'll go in now."

"Not because of me, please. I'm out here for a stroll. If you don't mind keeping me company, I'll fetch a blanket I saw just by the door and you could wrap up in it."

"Like a mummy!" he cried, immediately enthusiastic. "I'll fetch it. Keep an eye out for the puppy, please? I think he's hurt."

Human contact was far better than brooding over what she couldn't change, Harriet concluded, glancing around the garden. By this time of year, most of the roses were spent, but in the flickering lamplight, she could see one or two blooms struggling to survive.

She could hear the puppy sniffing around in the bushes. If the cook had an herb garden out here, she wouldn't appreciate a dog watering it. But Hartley had been sad until he talked about the dog, so she didn't say anything when the boy dashed back down the steps, wrapped up in an old horse blanket.

"Have you found him?" he asked, immediately setting off down the path.

"I think I heard him near the rosemary."

"Hugh is the one who knows bushes," Hartley said in disgust. "I'll never learn them. Mr. Baker should ask me about *dogs*, but he wants to show off Hugh to Papa a'cause he'll be the one to run Iveston someday."

Harriet raised her eyebrows at this perspective. "One day is a long time in the future, since I'm sure your father will be around until you're both old and fat."

Hartley laughed, presumably at the thought of being old and fat. "I'll be like Uncle William and raise dogs to save people. But Papa is mad at me now and will probably send us back to our mother. I hate living in town."

That was quite a great deal to process all at once, but far more diverting than her own grievances. After watching the marquess return dripping wet earlier today, she'd heard several variations of the afternoon's adventures. "Your father is angry with himself, not at you. He knows you didn't mean to knock him into the pond."

"He yelled and cursed. And then he made us come home and told us he's sending us back to school. I hate school. They don't have dogs there." Hartley crouched down and held out his hand.

Harriet smiled, realizing the boy had taken the opportunity to steal a sausage from the kitchen when he'd fetched the blanket. Wise child.

"I always wanted to go to school," she said. "I wanted to have friends. Don't you have friends that you miss?"

He shrugged, broke off a piece of sausage, and flung it under a bush. "I have Hugh and my dogs and Uncle William."

"Yes, but I assume your Uncle William has friends who help him sell his dogs, doesn't he? He can't just raise them and keep them."

Hartley pondered this while the stray poked its nose out to sniff the sausage. "Maybe. There's one or two fellows at school who aren't too bad. But I hate Greek. Dogs don't understand Greek."

"But I'd wager the Greeks loved dogs. What if there were books in Greek that told you how to treat an injured dog, but you couldn't read them?"

"Then I'd pay someone to read them." He broke off another bit of sausage after the dog nabbed the first one and scooted back under the shrubbery.

"Only if you had lots of friends, so you could sell lots of dogs and make lots of money. Growing up is hard because you don't know everything that's out there in the world. Not knowing can hurt you."

"I still want to go back to Iveston," he said stubbornly.

"Well, I'm sure you will for the holidays, won't you?" Harriet admitted to curiosity about how one lived between two different parents. High society was well beyond her limited scope.

"Maybe, if Papa isn't still cross." He darted a look to her. "You're sure he's not mad at me? He yelled and cursed something fierce."

"I have a feeling he does that frequently, does he not? He's a grown man and can't cry, and he's too busy to chase stray dogs to feel better. So he just shouts to let out all the bottled-up steam. I'm very sure he loves you and wouldn't want to hurt you. He simply doesn't understand how he sounds."

That was the impression she'd received, anyway. Ashford had been very angry that he hadn't been prepared for Hartley's stumble. But it was the same anger she'd felt in his study—frustration, mostly at his limitations. She didn't know how deep the pond was, but the boy could possibly have drowned. The inability to save his son would surely drive Ashford to madness.

"He never says he loves us, but men don't do that," Hartley said with assurance. "That's mawkish stuff for women and girls. Could you ask him to send us to Iveston? We hate it in town."

"I'd rather tell him that you'd like to return to school. Don't they have grounds to play in? Perhaps if you asked if you could take your dog?" Harriet didn't know why she was interfering, except that she really had longed to go to school and knew education was important.

"I want to fix hurt animals," Hartley said. "They don't teach that at school. Uncle William can teach me."

"I don't think what I say to your father matters," she said honestly. "You must ask him yourself. But you must do it by showing you know you could be an important man someday, an asset to your family. Little boys who hate Greek will not impress him."

Little girls who whined because they had no suitors weren't very impressive either, she realized. How did she set about impressing a marquess? Or others?

The puppy finally belly-crawled from the shrubbery to sniff at the sausage in Hartley's hand. The boy dropped the treat just before sharp teeth could connect, then rubbed behind the dog's ears while it ate as if starved.

"I'll be an important man?" Hartley asked. "How? I'm a bastard nobody."

Oh, ouch, so that was why he hated school. Harriet pondered a moment. "First, anyone who says that is very ignorant. Ignorant people and cowards think they can make themselves look bigger and cleverer by bullying others. You'll have to ask your father how to deal with bullies because I'm not good at it." Actually, she was extremely bad at it. She preferred hiding.

Hartley nodded wisely and held out the last piece of sausage. "I can beat up bullies but girls can't. Why do you say they're ignorant? I *am* a bastard."

"For many, many reasons. Just think about it. Your father is a very important man who loves you, so he will do everything he can to help you be whatever you want to be. You're intelligent, you're kind, you will have many friends as well as a large family to help you. Does that sound like a *nobody* to you? Perhaps your bully is jealous of how much you have."

"Huh. Maybe he thinks just a'cause he's got a title, that anyone else is a nobody. But that's stupid. Uncle William and Uncle Pascoe are very important somebodies, and they're bastards, too. Dogs don't marry, so they're all bastards, but they save lives." Hartley pulled the mongrel into his blanketed lap to examine its paws.

"See, I told you that you're clever. *Who* you are is much more important than what you are. Why don't you give your friend there the blanket to sleep on and go on up to bed? He'll be here in the morning now that you've fed him."

"I'll fetch him some water first," Hartley agreed. "Thank you, Miss Chris. Do you like puppies? I can have Uncle William bring you one."

Miss Chris. The nickname warmed her all over, and she nearly wriggled in pleasure like the puppy.

"I like puppies very much," *Miss Chris* said boldly. "And in April, when I have my own home, I would very much like a puppy *and* a kitten. Perhaps you can visit me when your term is over."

She left him to tend the dog while she considered what she'd just said. She had never made any plans for her financial freedom after her birthday. She had always assumed she'd be married well before the ancient age of twenty-five. But now . . . the date was only six months away. Would it be a terrible awful thing to live alone if she could have pets and friends?

Not having to hide from Townsend and his mean-spirited household gave her a whole new perspective on the world.

Six

"CHRISTIE!" ASHFORD BELLOWED for the third time Thursday morning, furious that he had to leave his lair. He groped his way past furniture that had no place in the corridor, to the front parlor where he heard the women chattering.

"Does everyone always run when he shouts?" the damned woman asked in that seductive voice, which told him she knew he could hear her.

"It depends," Aster's cousin, the blasted decorator, replied. "Aster tells me that shouting is the Ives' principle means of communication. They generally do not expect an answer, but if you have need of his attention, now is the time."

If Ash wasn't so frustrated, he'd laugh, knowing his sister-in-law had formed that theory from astute observation. "The witch doesn't know everything," he countered, entering the salon by shoving an object from his path with his stick. "Miss Christie, if you expect to live another day, you will answer when I call."

"Murder would lose you no end of votes," she replied impertinently. "And I might respond with more promptitude should you send a servant with a polite request to come at my convenience. We are in the midst of arranging your furniture so you needn't stumble through your own home. Perhaps you might tell me if your request is more important than my task."

"I have a duke and two earls arriving shortly, two more stacks of correspondence to attend, and my son tells me you advised him to go to a school with *dogs*!"

"Oh, dear, no good deed goes unpunished."

He could hear her sigh of exasperation. He shouldn't enjoy disrupting her day so much, but Hartley's demand had made it impossible for him to concentrate on work. It seemed fair payback if she was the cause. His son had called her *Miss Chris*—indicating a certain level of familiarity.

"Moira," his secretary-general said, "if you don't mind, I'll take a little break while that handsome footman helps you shove chairs around."

The scent of lilies approached. Today, she wore fewer petticoats and apparently boots. She walked like a country girl, with long stomping strides and not mincing little steps. He despised going outside, but he wanted to see more of her. Ashford held out his arm. "Call for your pelisse. I have need of fresh air."

"I am not dressed for the street, my lord. If you wish to traverse the mews, I'll be happy to accompany you."

"By Beelzebub, must you argue everything?" he asked in impatience, waiting for the footman to fetch her outerwear. He actually preferred the privacy of the garden, now that she mentioned it.

"Previously, no," she muttered, "and see how far *that* has taken me. So if doing what I'm told accomplishes nothing, why shouldn't I do as I think best? I can scarcely accomplish less."

She took his arm. Since she now wore gloves, he assumed she was properly attired for the outdoors. He let her steer him past the confusion of furniture into the safer haven of the back of the house. He didn't mind her subtle nudge that told him left or right, or a gentle squeeze to be cautious where he stepped, not when applied by this Valkyrie. He might have punched a man who presumed so, or been humiliated by some petite princess he felt obligated to protect, but he was coming to respect that Miss Chris was a force all her own.

Townsend's letter had returned to the stacks. Theo had read it to him. Ash had no way of knowing if Miss Christie had simply not noticed it or had deliberately not mentioned it. Perhaps the pathetic Miss Townsend who must be traded off for votes was her friend— but how would Miss Chris have known the letter's contents?

And hadn't she said Miss Townsend was already about to be married? She was still a liar. He needed to know more of the lady who was teaching his sons rebellion.

"Hartley summoned the temerity to confront you?" she asked, keeping her voice neutral.

"It takes courage to talk to me?" Ash thundered in surprise. "Why?"

"If you would keep your voice to a low roar, my lord, you might not send the servants into hiding."

She took her hand from his arm to unfasten the door latch on her own, presumably because the footman had fled.

"Puling cowards," he muttered, using his stick to find the steps. "And you're changing the subject. Why is my son afraid of me?"

"Oh, perhaps because you swore and yelled at him yesterday. He is just a little boy, and he's a bit out of sorts from some incidents at school. You should probably talk to the twins separately about what got them sent down. They may be intrepid, but underneath all that bravado, they have feelings that can be hurt—just as you have."

"Balderdash. Women have feelings because they're helpless. Men have choices. My sons chose to misbehave, presumably in retaliation for some slight. That's what boys do."

"And men thunder and sulk and seek revenge or build up constituencies to support them against other men who have treated them badly. I suspect a great deal more could be accomplished with less posturing and more intelligent discussion, but I realize this is asking too much."

"I am neither hurt nor seeking revenge. I am merely putting the best men into office to move this country forward. I am asking about my *son*."

The late autumn day smelled of coal smoke and a hint of burning leaves. Ash tried to remember the layout of the garden. Wasn't there a potting shed that concealed a corner of the garden from the house? He ignored Miss Chris's nudge toward the gate and steered her to the right. For a brief moment, there was a battle of wills until she gave in and turned down the path he'd chosen. Ha, he'd won another round.

"There is nothing I can say about your son that he cannot say better. Hartley is more sensitive than Hugh. He is more interested in animals than Greek. He is being bullied by a titled idiot calling him a useless bastard. And he wants to return to the country. There, that is the utter extent of my knowledge—all of which you probably already knew."

He did. He hadn't put it together as succinctly or as quickly as this woman who had lived here less than a week. That alone ought to make him wary, but she had succeeded in distracting him, and his mind had found a new outlet. "He needs schooling," he said, defying her to argue so she wouldn't notice that he was literally leading her down the garden path.

"Of course he needs schooling," she agreed, throwing him off balance. "But he also needs love and attention to feel important. Animals give him that. And apparently, his Uncle William. Hence, his desire for Iveston."

Ash stumbled over a broken paving stone, righted himself, and caught his hand on the brick shed. The garden wall would be just a few more steps away.

"William acknowledges no one except his damned animals. I don't want Hartley to turn out like that." He maneuvered her past the shed, where the gravel was worn down to the dirt.

"Then find Hartley a school with animals, as he requested," she retorted. "And this path ends here. We must turn around."

"I am not yet prepared to return to the pandemonium of my house. Your presence is infinitely saner." He turned her so she faced him. Daylight made it easier to see her silhouette, he confirmed triumphantly. She had gorgeous curves in all the right places.

She stepped back, as he'd known she would. "My presence is irrelevant. You have said yourself that it is improper to opportune a woman under your roof."

Able to gauge the height of her delectable jaw, he caught it in one hand and brushed a kiss across her lips. "Ah, but out here, there is no roof."

Out here, he could *almost* see shadowy movement, if he turned his head just right. His heart took ridiculous leaps of joy, which he ignored. He preferred to follow his cock in this instance.

"That's specious reasoning!" she protested, stepping away again. "I will have to leave your employ."

He knew when she hit the wall. Her shadow blended in with the bricks, but he still had a good idea where she stood. He placed his hands on the ivy on either side of her head. "A few kisses will make us both feel better. None will ever know."

He lowered his head and tasted her gently, not forcing her. The women he'd seduced over the years had always been experienced. They'd liked feeling helpless at his aggressiveness and had been eager for romps—except for his ex-fiancée, of course. Margaret had been cold as a marble statue when he'd tried this with her. He'd thought a little experience would teach her to enjoy kissing. He could see that had been arrogant.

Miss Chris was inexperienced, but she responded with enthusiasm and an exciting warmth that even the most skilled of his lovers had not possessed.

When she was practically melting into his arms, Ash used his tongue to ply at her lips. She gasped, and he was inside, stroking her, pushing into her magnificently crushable bosom at the same time. For a brief, exhilarating moment, she allowed him this blissful state. He could almost believe he was his old self, with a willing woman in his arms.

When she started to resist, he dared to drag his hand over the curve of her breast, hoping to tempt her more. She wore heavy wool and a thick corset, but still, she shuddered at the touch. She would be so beautifully responsive if he could just—

She placed both hands on his chest and shoved. She was not a small woman, and she did not hold back her strength. She might have succeeded with a smaller man. Ash held his place, but dropped his arms, releasing her. He wanted her to be as willing and ready as he.

"Then I will remember not to walk in the garden with you again, my lord."

She stomped off, leaving him to find his own blind way back.

It had been worth it, he decided in satisfaction. Miss Christie was no helpless servant. She was a passionate woman and appeared to be exactly what he needed to release this frustration eating at him.

He just needed to find out who she really was so he could formulate the necessary argument to persuade her to his way of thinking.

HARRIET'S AGITATION MUST HAVE BEEN EVIDENT when she returned to the salon. Even the spirits swirled incoherently in her head. Moira sent her a questioning look and suggested tea. Tea couldn't erase the delicious taste of Ashford from her lips. Never had she been kissed with such hunger and passion. Or *experience*, she reminded herself.

Her heart was breaking, and she couldn't even explain to herself why she must leave this most desirable position. How could she possibly explain to anyone else? She couldn't. No one who could *see* her would believe the handsome, commanding marquess of Ashford would have an interest in her, even if he was blind. He might have a rakehell reputation, but not with unmarried ladies, and certainly not with ugly spinsters.

Was that the problem? Did he not believe she was a lady? Or a maiden? Had she done anything to convince him otherwise? Since she wasn't who she said she was, she certainly couldn't argue her case effectively.

So, she should leave. And go where? It would be April before she had money of her own. She didn't even know when she could expect payment for her services in Ashford's household.

She struggled with the dilemma the rest of the morning.

To her utter dismay, the marquess joined them for luncheon. She swallowed hard and tried not to watch the chiseled lips that had seduced her, but he'd deliberately taken the end of the table at her right. She couldn't ignore his impressive size or provocative proximity or forget how it had felt when he'd touched her. Her breast burned in memory.

"Miss McDowell, I trust the salon is arranged. I need to borrow Miss Christie this afternoon. My lamentable correspondence continues to pile up," he said, locating his teacup where the footman had carefully placed it.

"What about your two earls and a duke, my lord?" Harriet asked, without the sarcasm he deserved.

"They are unfortunately unable to deal with my correspondence," he said, with just the right wry humor. "But if you would sit in the meeting with us, you could take notes. The next batch of letters will no doubt reflect today's discussion."

He sat there as aloof as any employer, concentrating on finding the prepared sandwiches on his plate. They'd been cut to be devoured in two bites, so he needn't deal with floppy bread or slippery ham. Viciously Harriet considered exchanging plates just to see if she could embarrass him as he had her.

But she'd been embarrassed so many times before that she could not convince herself that the crime deserved the punishment.

"I know it is not always obvious," she said frostily, "but I am a *lady*. A female, as you will. You cannot expect me to sit in on a closed meeting with four gentlemen, even had I the ability to understand a word said."

"Yes, but I am an Ives, and as you have no doubt been told, I have little care for what society believes about females, ladies or not. I am only interested in what they can do. These particular lords are morons, and I am quite certain even a monkey is perfectly capable of understanding far more than they utter."

Moira spluttered her water. Harriet had to bite into a sandwich to keep her mouth from falling open in shock. By the time she'd finished chewing, the marquess was looking satisfied with himself. Having gained control again, Harriet replied with the same frost as earlier. "You are incorrigible. I will have Lady Aster begin searching for a chimpanzee to act as your secretary."

One of the spirits in her head was frantically trying to convey panic and the other was laughing in approval. No wonder she thought of herself as two people. Even the voices in her head didn't agree.

She shut out the headache they caused and turned to Moira. "Please, if you would, could you ask your cousin if she might know of a quiet companion's position in some rural abode? It need not be for a long term, but it would be preferable if the house did not contain any insolent males."

With that, she rose from the table and left the room before the marquess could even find his feet. Or his tongue.

She needed a good country walk so she might work off the steam boiling her blood. No one had ever infuriated her so much.

Well, to be perfectly honest—which she hated to do under the circumstances—no one had ever paid enough notice of her to deliberately infuriate her. Perhaps it was all this unaccustomed attention that was leaving her a little . . . frazzled.

If only she did not feel the marquess's pain and frustration so much! Perhaps that was it. She *felt* what he did and had begun to express it in the same way—even more reason to leave. She didn't want to turn into a witch on top of being ugly and unlovable.

Although if she gave that much thought, perhaps becoming a witch was just what she needed, were such a thing possible. She'd turn Townsend into a toad and simply take over one of her properties without a qualm.

Until the miraculous happened, however, she had to hide.

Seven

JACQUES IVES-BELLAMY paced Ash's office Friday morning, stopping every so often, presumably to examine the paintings on the walls. Ash would ask his half-brother to describe them, but the news Jacques had brought was more pertinent.

"I have a letter right here on my desk from Townsend offering to trade his daughter's hand in marriage for his help in defeating Wellington's administration. And now you tell me the wench is *missing*?" Ash rubbed his brow, hit the scar, and scowled. "Do I really need to hear this?"

Jacques began shuffling through a bookshelf. "You told me to look into Miss Christie's reference, which came from Miss Harriet Townsend. When I made inquiries, I was told Miss Townsend had recently left to stay with a cousin. So I hung about a bit in the local pub, lifted a mug or two with some of the kitchen staff. They gave me the name of her cousin."

Ash had *known* the lady was lying. He wasn't certain if he was ready to hear it proved. With a low growl, he leaned his chair back and followed his half-brother's pacing. The office had no window, but he thought he saw a flicker every time Jacques walked past a lamp.

He'd mentioned the flickers to his physician back in Surrey. Dr. Joseph had said that merely proved his impairment was neurological rather than ocular. Ash translated that to mean it was in his head, not his eyes, and did not feel comforted.

"Go on," he said, trying to imagine where this might be going and failing.

"Her cousin lives a few hundred miles away, so I was reduced to sending letters. Keep in mind that Miss Harriet Townsend is an unmarried female of twenty-four, and it appears she took no maid or family carriage on this journey."

"Which she made directly after writing her companion a reference," Ash said, following his train of thought. "And after Miss Christie told me her employer was in London to buy her trousseau, presumably for an upcoming wedding. Runaway bride? Have you had any responses to your letters?"

"The cousin in question is visiting a friend in Cornwall. I have not tracked her down," Jacques said in a tone that expressed his annoyance. "If Townsend is attempting to marry off his stepdaughter, when Miss Christie says Miss Townsend is planning a wedding, there appears to be some discrepancy in their stories. Perhaps we should ask the baron where his stepdaughter has hared off to so precipitously."

"Most likely, she objects to being traded for votes," Ash said with cynicism. "Pity. We could have offered to marry Miss Townsend off to Bryghtstone and gained his two boroughs."

"Townsend?" Aster asked from the doorway. "Why does that name sound familiar?"

"It was on that letter of reference you brought me from Miss Christie." Ash had given up any attempt at privacy. The townhouse contained too many people and was too blasted small. He really ought to sell it. Except it was an excellent size for finding his way around. Perhaps he ought to sell off his relations, instead, as Townsend meant to do.

"Townsend, yes," Aster mused aloud. "I didn't pay attention to the signature. I'm pretty certain the name is in my files somewhere. I shall have to look."

She was gone in a breeze of exotic scents. Aster favored the jungle her father had sent home in his youth, Ash had learned. He thought her soap might be sandalwood today. And her perfume was decidedly un-English.

"Let's wait to see what Erran has discovered about Lord Townsend. Then perhaps we should invite him over to tea to discuss his vote." Ash leaned back in his chair and plotted the entertainment such a visit might provide. Now that he thought about it, it was interesting that Miss Chris had not provided a reference from the baron.

"VISITORS WAIT IN THE ANTEROOM," Moira said, pacing the smaller front chamber adjacent to the foyer and drawing room. "They must be shown Ives' wealth and grandeur."

"At the same time, they are likely to be dripping wet or covered in snow," Harriet pointed out. "A tile floor, perhaps, with a good wool Axminster carpet."

She had no difficulty speaking in housekeeping terms since that was all she'd had to occupy her mind for years. If she could just stay away from the mad marquess . . .

"The Axminster looms burned a few years ago," Moira replied, her thoughts obviously traveling onward. "They might have some limited stock left, or we could buy second-hand and save a few guineas. Or look at Turkey carpets. I like the idea of marble tile. We'd need the carpet first, to determine the other colors."

Harriet sat at a writing desk, jotting notes. Lady Aster whirled in, trailing a smocked and aproned young girl missing most of her fingers on one hand.

"Muster is our new housemaid. She'll be keeping the fireplaces clean and lit this winter. I need to show her around, but first, Miss Christie, we need to talk about your previous employer."

Harriet had learned that Lady Aster and her family trained and employed workhouse women while they toiled tirelessly to support the labor bills the conservatives refused to consider. Little by little, she was grasping the importance of Ashford's position and was in awe of what the women of his household could accomplish.

Mention of her *previous employer,* however, meant her new position here might be in more jeopardy then she'd feared. She tried not to look nervous or guilty. "Miss Townsend? Is there a problem?"

"She is the baron's stepdaughter, is she not?" Aster sent the maid to the next parlor with a gesture.

"Yes," Harriet said in puzzlement.

"What is her full name and her mother's name?"

Harriet didn't know how to reply. Lady Aster appeared to be emanating distress and excitement equally. "Russell is her father's name," she said, offering as little as she could.

"Ah, yes, the Russell is familiar. That will help, thank you! Did you know your former employer appears to have gone missing?" Aster started from the room after her new housemaid.

"Gone missing?" Moira called after her. "Aster, come back here!"

"Later," the copper-haired lady said with a wave. "Let me do the research first." She cast a look back at Harriet. "You said your birthday was in April, did you not?"

She had given the lady her correct birthday when she'd first arrived. Moira had explained that drawing zodiac charts was her cousin's hobby. Harriet nodded and lifted her eyebrows questioningly, but the lady merely looked satisfied and swept out.

Harriet had the distressing notion that she should have lied about her birthday as well.

Despairing over where she could hide next, she apparently grew so quiet that Moira noticed. The slender blonde stopped her chatter to pat Harriet on the back sympathetically. "Sometimes it is difficult to adjust to a strange place, is it not? And this place, admittedly, is stranger than most."

"I fear I am out of my depth," Harriet agreed with a sigh—the bold Christie had left the room. "I think, perhaps, I should just go home. I only meant to find a place where I could be useful."

"You have been so marvelously useful that I fear I cannot bear to ever part with you!" Moira cried. "Tell me what we must do to keep you until you learn to endure our eccentricities. I truly have hopes of opening my own shop someday, with your help, of course."

Harriet let Moira's fantasy distract from her worries. "Your family would allow you to open a *shop*?"

Moira waved a dismissive hand. "What else will they do with me? They have six daughters, and my father's estate is entailed to his only son. Emilia has a large dowry from our grandparents, but my annoying sister is in no hurry to marry and help us out. We're all Malcolm gifted, which threatens the wealthy gentlemen who might want wives for mere ornamentation. My mother spends her time helping our father with politics. I am nothing."

"Malcolm gifted?" Harriet was fascinated with the idea of a large family. She'd had no notion that one could feel lost with so many others around.

"It is why Aster keeps charts," Moira said, returning to measuring the windows. "Our ancestry dates back to a family of so-called witches centuries ago. Or further back, to the Druids, if one believes our old journals. Aster has a gift for prediction based on the stars. I merely bring happiness by matching my designs to the people who will live with them—which is why it's so frustrating working here!"

That was almost too much for Harriet to absorb at once, but it certainly distracted from her own fears. And here she'd just been wishing she was a witch who could turn people into toads!

She let the impossible about witches and Druids pass by while she concentrated on Moira's emotions. The lovely blond lady truly was vexed.

But how did one match room designs to people to make them happy? "You cannot give the marquess the design he needs because he cannot see it?" Harriet guessed.

"Possibly." Moira made a mark on the woodwork with her pencil. "But if I could make the people around him happy, that might improve his humor. Except look at all the people around him! And none of them actually live here. How do I work with that?"

"You cannot," Harriet said, thinking of the crowds of people passing through these rooms, and the marquess living here essentially alone while his family led their lives without him. "You will have to expand your abilities to encompass strangers. What will make them happy to be here so they'll deal more pleasantly with Ashford?"

She could not believe she'd just said that. She actually believed Moira could make people happy with draperies and upholstery?

But Moira visibly brightened and hastened down the ladder to pick up her sketchbook. "That might work! I've never done anything like it. Usually I need only please a bored lady or her children. But the marquess's guests . . . Perhaps my instincts were right . . ." Her voice trailed off as she sketched.

Harriet really did not wish to give up this wonderful new life she could see sparkling in her future like an inviting green-land path filled with fairies and . . . Druids. Here, she didn't mind being plain and lumpish because in this fantasyland, people listened to her anyway. She could say what she thought and not be told she was a stupid cow. She could be regal Christie or the amusing Miss Chris.

And even though it was about to break her heart, she couldn't dither any longer. She had to leave, tonight, if possible. If Ashford was looking into her reference, she would be out on the street soon anyway.

Eight

ASH SAT IN HIS BEDCHAMBER playing with fire.

It wasn't as if he had much else to do while everyone else slept. Perhaps he should find a woman desperate enough to marry a mad blind marquess just so he had a woman to read to him on sleepless nights. Although right now, he'd prefer a woman for a far different purpose.

He struck one of the new lucifer matches Erran had brought over and could see the sparks drop to the hearth. Erran had said the flames could be explosively large and dangerous, but all Ash saw was a vague glimmer against the perpetual darkness.

If he stood close enough, he could see the coals burning in the grate. He added more lumps from the bucket and thought he saw the fire flare.

Of course, that could just be wishful thinking.

The old stairs creaked overhead. He tilted his head and listened to the wind howl and almost dismissed the sound as part of the orchestra of noises a house like this produced. Windows rattled, doors shook, stairs creaked.

But this was a steady, methodical squeak on the back stairs when all the servants should be in their beds. If that was Hartley out to feed another damned puppy . . .

But no, Hartley was faster and lighter on his feet. Only one other person in the household would be creeping down those stairs at this hour.

He should let her go. Last spring, he would have said good riddance. If she was a spy, she'd learned nothing new. If she was out to steal the family jewels, she'd discovered there weren't any.

Except, in these last months, he'd had ample time to lie in his lonely bed and examine what was left of his life. When he'd been whole, he'd taken a great deal for granted that he could no longer expect to ever have again. Women and bed play were part of that loss. They had been his release from the tedious duties of his life, a vital pleasure that he missed almost as much as his sight.

And here was a woman who didn't flee screaming from his ruined visage or his tantrums, and she was about to run away, if he did not mistake.

Carrying the lantern he didn't need, Ash crept into the corridor. His damaged leg ached after a long day, and he stumbled, no doubt startling whichever footman guarded the hall. It wouldn't do to have the servants gossiping, but he didn't want to send the mouse he was about to trap scurrying out of his reach again.

Holding a finger to his lips to indicate silence—hoping there was actually someone to see him do so—he whispered *tea* in a command that caused rustling by the garden door. A moment later, he heard boot steps descending to the kitchen. Excellent. Living in the back of the house had its conveniences.

He covered the lantern and listened for the woman creeping down the stairs to turn the landing and squeak the last few steps. When he was certain she was in reach, he opened the lantern.

She stopped moving, as he'd hoped she would. He didn't want her to think she was being attacked, but once satisfied she knew precisely who confronted her, Ash took her arm and almost yanked her down the last few steps. He rather enjoyed that she was large enough to fight back against the strength he often forgot he wielded. Tip-toeing around frail delicate misses was a nuisance.

Her valise bumped against his legs, but he didn't want to leave a lantern lying about to be kicked over. She'd have to carry the bag herself.

"Let me go," she whispered.

"You're deserting me," he accused, leading her past his bedchamber and toward his study.

"I told you I would," she said, tugging her elbow from his grip. "How can I feel safe in a household where you feel free to drag me about?"

"And kiss you," he said in satisfaction, shoving her into the study and closing the door. The footman would wonder where he'd gone and might come looking, so he locked the door for good measure. He wished he could see Miss Chris's face as he did.

He wished he could see her face, period.

"I am not a lightskirt," she said unhappily. "You may lie to yourself and pretend that I am the kind of woman men notice, but I am exactly what I say I am, a spinster who hoped to be useful, but not in the way you have in mind."

"You are a liar, Miss Christie. I can hear it in almost every word you speak. Not only that, I may be blind, but I am not stupid." Ash followed the sound of her voice and reached for her hair.

She'd covered it with what was probably a deuced awful bonnet of plumes and plums. He yanked it off and threw it in the direction of the grate. At last, he had his fingers in the glorious thickness of her hair. He began plucking pins. He could vividly imagine such silk gleaming in the firelight, and it calmed his raging soul.

She did not smack him away. She was no lowly servant, terrified for her place in his household. One of the things he liked best about her was that she knew how to stand tall and argue with him. Her kiss had conveyed her loneliness and hunger as well as his own. He dared to continue.

"You have a lush figure of the kind men drool over in their dreams," he informed her while she irritably grabbed her pins from his hand. "If even a blind man can tell that, then the male population of London must have lost all their wits not to be following you down the street with their tongues hanging out."

"I have not *met* the male population of London, but I am well aware that I am taller than most." She dodged from his marauding hands in her hair.

Undeterred, Ash located the river of silk again and drew his fingers through it. "This is blond, isn't it? I can feel the length and thickness but can't tell the color. How blond is it? Whitish, gold, bronze? I want to picture it draped over your magnificent breasts like Lady Godiva."

This time, she did smack him, on his hands. "Don't be ridiculous. What is it you want, my lord? Surely you did not come out of your lair just to molest me."

He shrugged and wrapped her luxurious tresses around one hand so she could not escape. "I may have. The nights are tedious without company. You said you wished to be useful. You could read to me."

"I may be a maiden, but I'm not a lackwit," she retorted, dropping her valise to pry his fingers loose from her hair. "It is not reading that you want."

"Well, no, but I would settle for it. The footman is about to deliver tea. If you'd like to hide behind the coatrack, I'll let him in."

"I won't fit behind a coatrack," she said indignantly.

But he heard her traipse to a corner of the room, out of view of the door. Ash unlocked it and opened his lantern again to indicate his position. With his bulk, he blocked the area where Miss Chris hid and encouraged the servant to simply leave the tray without hovering.

He locked the door after the footman's departure, set the lantern on his desk, and fumbled until he'd found his chair. "Tea, Miss Christie. Now let us sit and converse about your folly in thinking you could go anywhere at this hour of the night."

"There are carriages for hire," she said stiffly, stepping toward the desk and pouring the tea. She served him first, nudging his hand with the cup so he knew where she'd placed it.

"I'm sure the drunks in the clubs and gambling hells along Pall Mall would be happy to fetch one for you," he countered. "I shudder at the thought. You are not familiar enough with the city to know where a lady is safe. And without a maid, you will not be seen as a lady. That is all irrelevant. I cannot believe I have made you feel so unsafe that you must sneak out in the middle of the night. So tell me the truth for a change."

"I cannot," she said with a sigh. "Then you would feel compelled to do whatever you consider to be the right thing, and you would become involved in what is none of your affair. It would all be quite calamitous and unnecessary, so I thought to depart before that happened."

"And that will happen if you stay here? Even if I promise not to kiss you again unless you ask?"

"I am not likely to ask!" she said in outrage. "And yes, calamity is likely to happen if you continue with what appears to be an investigation of my reference. You will not find Miss Townsend to confirm it."

Ash sipped his tea and considered all he knew and all she didn't say. Jacques had already told him that Miss Townsend was unavailable, even though her stepfather was offering to sell his votes in exchange for marrying her off. Miss Chris mostly likely knew why and where she'd gone. Interesting.

If he really wanted Townsend's vote, he could simply send this impostor anywhere she wanted to go and avoid whatever explosion she feared. That would be politically expedient.

He didn't want to be politically expedient. He wanted Miss Chris. He either had to believe his instincts had deteriorated with his eyesight, or that his secretary-general was worth the drama she was about to unfold.

If no one would read him a good story, then he could enjoy a good drama. "The reference was a fraud?" he suggested.

She sat so still, he thought she might have evaporated. But finally, she reached for her teacup, muttering to herself as she did. He almost smiled. He hadn't completely lost his ability to coerce and persuade despite his rustiness.

"Will you promise upon your honor as a gentleman not to reveal what I am about to tell you?" she demanded.

"If you are a murderess, I cannot make such a promise," he pointed out, just to point out her ridiculousness. "But if you are an innocent, I promise to keep your secrets. Who wrote your reference?"

"I wrote it. Miss Townsend has run away," she said angrily.

THAT HAD SEEMED THE SAFEST EXPLANATION she could manage at a moment's notice—and it was the truth. Miss Townsend had most certainly run away.

Harriet sat back and waited for Ashford's reaction. She wished he didn't look so delightfully rumpled and almost approachable in wrinkled shirtsleeves and without a neckcloth. The lamplight wasn't sufficient to do more than throw shadow on the muscled chest revealed beneath the shirt, but he was impressive in any light. His dark curls fell on his forehead, almost obscuring his blank, unstaring gaze. As usual, he'd turned the scar away from her view, so all she saw was his angular cheekbone and jutting jaw—probably too strong-boned for true handsomeness but appealing enough to have her wish circumstances could be different.

GOOD LOOKING, IS HE NOT? one of the spirits said wistfully. *BUT HE'S JUST AS STUBBORN AS HIS FATHER. YOU MUST BE MORE STUBBORN.*

More stubborn than the marquess? She wished she knew how, but again, she felt reassured that she was taking the right course. Or half her mind thought so, anyway, depending on her degree of sanity.

She really should quit dropping her defenses like this. But it was rather interesting not to have headaches, as she'd always suffered before, when she left her mental door open. Was it this house or the people around her who allowed her to relax and be herself?

Ashford sipped his tea while apparently working his way through the implications of her revelation. She almost held her breath but realized the folly. No matter how much she tried to fool herself, she couldn't live here. Sooner or later, Townsend would realize she'd fled, and he'd raise a hue and cry. It would be horrid.

"And Townsend is such an imbecile as not to have noticed his stepdaughter has gone missing?" Ashford asked with a hint of incredulity.

"As long as he believes he can find her when he wants her, he does not care. You read his letter. She is a pawn on his chess board. I cannot blame her in the least." Her tired mind had difficulty trying to think about herself in the third person, so she spoke about timid Harriet with the voice of the bold Christie.

"So knowing Townsend will have your head on a pike when he finds out his heiress has fled, you have taken this opportunity to search for a new position? Very enterprising." He didn't sound totally convinced. She could almost hear the cogs in his formidable mind spinning, looking for his own advantage.

"Yes, my lord." She was completely telling the truth, from top to bottom. She *had* written the letter. And her stepfather really did not notice if she was in the house. She had just left out the fact that *she* was the heiress.

Thank goodness he couldn't see her face to judge her expression.

"Do you know where she has gone? Is she safe?"

"She is with friends and safer than with Townsend," she acknowledged truthfully. She felt the ladies of the household were her friends.

"Amazing," he continued. "The truth really is stranger than fiction, is it not? It's rather like one of those gothic tales women read, with a runaway heiress. If only I were poor and could take advantage of that . . ."

She wanted to both laugh and cry. She had been terrified that the intimidating marquess would roar and thunder and humiliate by raising the entire household. But the impossible man was probably imagining Miss Townsend as a sylph-like romantic heroine in need of rescue. "Now who's being ridiculous? If all you want is someone to read tall tales for you, tell me which volume you'd like, and I'll gladly read it to you this evening. But in the morning, I must leave."

"Where would you go?" he asked with seeming interest, while staring at the wall and drinking from his cup.

"To one of Miss Townsend's properties, I assume. Dorchester is a few days away. I'll come up with a story by the time I arrive."

More truth. She had done the bookkeeping, but those were just numbers. She had no real idea of the location of her properties or what condition they were in. She hadn't been to Dorchester since childhood and couldn't precisely say what roads she must take to get there. She'd been left in the dark the better part of her life. But she knew the steward's name and the village, and she'd work it out, somehow. She had to.

"You're lying again," he said, making her squirm. "I don't know about which part, but you have no idea what you'll find when you reach wherever you're going."

How could he be so certain? And she really wasn't lying about her plans, just about her certainty of explaining herself once she arrived.

"Lying will not do, Miss . . . is your name really Miss Christie?"

"It is." That wasn't entirely a lie either. Calling her by her given name was not acceptable had he known what it was, but perfectly suitable as a surname.

He frowned. "Are you related to Townsend then?"

She swallowed a bit of panic. "To Harriet's family," she said, again, without lying.

He narrowed his eyes as if hearing the half-truth but nodded acceptance. "All right, Miss Chris, if you will find an interesting volume on the shelf over there, we will discuss your predicament in the morning, when we've both had time to think on it. I recommend you reconsider telling any more lies, though. I know it when you tell me one." He gestured at the ceiling-high bookcase in the corner.

Bold *Christie* wouldn't crumple into a weak-kneed, weeping infant. A strong independent woman didn't have that luxury. Feeling defiant, she set aside her cup and studied his shelves, deliberately taking out a female writer. "I have not read this one, Germaine de Staël's *Corinne*. I did not even know it had been translated from the French."

"It is politics concealed as a woman's travels," he said. "I should be interested in hearing your interpretation."

By all the heavens above, *this* was what she'd hoped to find someday—a husband who could be her friend, with whom she could enjoy a cup of tea and a pleasant conversation.

She should have sought out a blind man from the first. With a sigh at her own foolishness, she turned the lamplight to fall on the book and began to read.

Ashford was not only endangering her virtue, he endangered her battered heart. And she knew how badly that would work out.

Nine

"CHRISTIE! BY ALL THE BILIOUS BLOWHARDS OF HADES . . . where is that insolent female?" Ash shouted the next morning, stomping down the corridor from his suite to the front rooms. If the woman had slipped out when he wasn't looking . . .

He was never *looking*. She could escape any time. She'd made that quite clear last night. When she chose to finish reading, she had simply shut the book, said good-night, and walked away. He had no hold whatsoever over her, which drove him insane.

"In the kitchen," Moira muttered through what sounded like a mouthful of pins. "If you have a moment, I'd like to discuss—"

"I don't have a moment," he grumbled, only momentarily relieved that the elusive Miss Chris might still be about. "What is she doing in the kitchen? She knows I won't find her there."

"I don't believe she knows you wish to find her." She must have removed the pins to spit this out. "I told her I didn't need her this morning, so she is teaching mathematics to your servants. It's not as if she has designated duties, and she likes to be useful."

Ash could hear her amusement but refused to rise to it. His life had become too boxed in to argue over vagaries. Had he eyes, he'd simply go to the kitchen and terrify everyone into doing as he wished. That he must send a servant was demeaning—and even he understood the irrationality of that thought. Most men preferred sending servants.

He couldn't read his correspondence. He couldn't walk down to see whoever was speaking in the Lords when he wished. He couldn't even go to his damned clubs without looking like a pathetic has-been. What the devil was he supposed to do on his own without a nanny watching over him?

Tup a woman came to mind, which brought him right back to the eminently tuppable Miss Christie—a damned lady he couldn't have without marriage. Not that he was considering marriage anyway. It was too . . . humiliating . . . not to even know what his bride would look like.

Besides, Miss Chris was an enigma to be solved. He had refrained from asking too many questions last night for fear he'd drive her off.

He needed to study the situation in the new light of her creative untruths.

Why the devil was she teaching mathematics to the servants?

The knocker rapped as he reached his study. Bored, knowing the staircase hid him, he waited to hear who it might be. He grimaced on recognizing his Uncle Pascoe's voice. "If you're here to dump your toddlers on us, it's too late," Ash called irascibly, stepping from his hiding place. "The twins have taken their tutor out to visit schools with dogs."

"Schools with dogs?" Pascoe asked with interest. "That has possibilities. A dog trainer might manage my brats." He approached, carrying the scent of damp air and pipe tobacco.

Ash recognized the silence of the second pair of boot steps as his brother Erran. "Have you brought interesting news or just more complaints?" He led the way into the study, taking his chair and leaving the others to find their own.

The memory of Miss Christie in here, reading to him in that delicious voice of hers, was marred by the presence of male intruders. She had left too soon, after his comments on Madame Stael's lascivious life had grown too rude. He was fairly certain she'd been as aroused as he, but he hadn't tested that theory for fear she would run off.

That her previous employer had run away from her idiot of a stepfather, and Miss Christie had taken advantage to find a new position, made a certain amount of logical sense and fit with what he knew as truth. He still didn't fully trust the not-so-little liar. He needed more information.

"A little of both," Pascoe said with good cheer while servants stirred the fire and delivered a tea tray.

The moment the door closed, Erran spoke. "Caldwell has brought Margaret to town."

Ash snorted. He had no sympathy for his traitorous neighbors, especially since evidence pointed at Caldwell being behind the accident that had caused his blindness.

He'd known the baronet was in financial difficulties. He'd offered to help. But Sir George had delusions of living in the past. He'd wanted Ash to follow his suggestions for their adjoined lands. Ash hadn't been drunk enough to let him run Iveston into the ground as Caldwell had his own property. They had not parted company on friendly terms.

"I suppose now that Montfort's son has run off to France, Margaret has no suitable suitors left." Ash hated saying that of his former fiancée, but he knew her desperate situation.

Roderick Montfort was the sort of man Caldwell would prefer for his daughter—a drunk who could be led by the nose. Presumably under the baronet's advice, the young dolt had led a band of miscreants to terrify Theo and his wife, which was why, when caught, he'd fled to France—probably the most intelligent thing the sot had ever done. "So, how does Caldwell's arrival concern me?"

"The obvious, as always. Sir George wants to increase his acreage, and your land is the best to be had in the county. He has three boroughs in his control. He may be ready to return to our side if you and Margaret make up."

Ash almost laughed at the notion, except he knew Erran was serious. For the good of the country—marry a cold fish like Margaret? One who had slipped out of his life the instant he'd actually needed her? One whose father had threatened his life in order to stop him from investing in modern farming practices? Not even for the good of the country.

"You must admit, whatever Miss Caldwell lacks in human compassion, she makes up for in social and organizational skills," Pascoe pointed out. "If you're truly not interested in marriage, one of convenience might be beneficial."

Ash grimaced in distaste. "Marry her off to Bryghtstone. I'm aware of the extreme importance of replacing Wellington, but I'd like to believe I'm a little more valuable than a pawn." Even if he was now blind and incompetent went unsaid.

"The baronet wants land and preferably an influential title for his daughter, not a sheep farmer hundreds of miles away. Margaret would be wasted on Bryght."

Ash knew his brother was right. That didn't make his argument any more acceptable. Maliciously, he suggested, "What about Townsend's offer? If I'm to lower myself to marry a baronet's daughter for a vote, how would a baron's daughter line up as a political wife?"

"Since Miss Townsend has never been presented, was in town for only a few weeks, and no one seems to have seen or heard of her, one assumes not well," Pascoe said dryly. "Although she is said to have a dowry that might make Bryght happy, and if she's invisible, all the better. But that's not the only reason we're here."

Ash nearly laughed, entertained that he knew more about the missing Miss Townsend than his well-connected family. It almost made him feel like his old self.

The conversation turned to political strategy. Ash usually enjoyed the challenge of out-plotting master plotters, but the bloom had left that rose today. He needed to put an end to the dreary argument. The moment a servant returned for the tray, Ash sent for Miss Chris.

"You still haven't hired a secretary?" Pascoe asked in astonishment. "You can't ask the lady to join us as if she were a man!"

"Miss Christie does not cringe when I throw inkpots," Ash said coldly, although he lost his urge to fling things in her presence. He didn't need to mention that.

"She's not a gray-haired old lady," Erran warned.

"I know," Ash responded with too much satisfaction. "I'm tired of listening to your voices. Hers is more pleasant. And if I must write this letter, I can trust her to do it properly. Unless, of course, the two of you wish to lounge about, pondering what I should say and writing it for me."

"Specious argument, Ash," Pascoe said. "You could dictate to us as easily as the lady."

"We'll see about that." Ash heard the reluctant stride of his errant companion and rose to greet her. "Miss Christie, if I might ask your aid—these gentlemen would have me write to our more senior members asking for proxy votes. Could you take notes and compose the missive?"

He heard a rustle. Seats shuffled. Judging by the location of her lily scent, she had taken the chair in the corner behind him, just like any good menial. He sat when he heard her do so, admiring her performance. She had their attention, even if they were annoyed as hell at her dawdling. Unlike any true servant, his mystery lady had an intriguing habit of thinking before she spoke.

Into the increasingly irritated silence, she asked in that seductive voice that brought a smile even when she crossed him, "Wouldn't a personal messenger impress the importance of this session on them better than a letter that might sit on a desk for weeks? I thought a vote in the Commons was imminent."

"There's my best student," Ash said proudly. It had been worth the performance to hear their audience's stunned silence when she said exactly what he had. Their hours over correspondence had not gone wasted.

"You are playing games again," she scolded, although she didn't change her dulcet tone. "I was about to explain subtraction to the children, and you disrupted the lesson so you might make a spectacle of me for reasons of your own. I understand your impatience Mr. Ives, Lord Erran. You need to find new entertainment to occupy his lordship."

"By Jove, she's rumbled your lay, Dunc," Pascoe said in disbelief.

Ash heard her set the writing desk down with a loud plop to make it clear that she was done. She swept out in a lovely summer breeze.

"A Valkyrie," Erran said, while Pascoe just whistled admiringly. "What is that abomination she wears on her head?"

"I'd wager it's a disguise to conceal the gears and cogs operating in her brainpan," Ash said, laughing. "Miss Chris conceals unexplored depths."

"She just scolded you like a truant," Erran said. "And you didn't sack her!"

"Could you sack anyone who sounded like that? Your wife has a lovely persuasive voice, but does it contain the depth of feeling my secretary-general just expressed?"

"Celeste modulates her voice to *disguise* her feelings," Erran explained. "Miss Christie lacks that degree of sophistication."

"For which I heartily give thanks. It's tiresome being coddled like an infant." Although he ought to ask himself how she always knew exactly the right thing to say, but this was a case where ignorance was bliss. "Now, gentlemen, let us begin the task of finding messengers to persuade senile old men to give up on Wellington."

And then he would have to consider the task of dealing with Lord Townsend's request that he find a suitor for the heiress he no longer had, before Ash's archenemy, the earl of Lansdowne, discovered Ash was concealing a scandal and the key to valuable votes.

CHRISTIE STILL HADN'T SLOWED HER heartbeat by the time Moira found her.

The three Ives gentlemen had been exceedingly hard to read. *Impatience* and *irritation* hadn't precisely explained what they wanted. Only Ashford had offered any emotional hints as to the basis for their argument. Fortunately, she had listened to his earlier complaints and felt his eagerness for her to repeat what he wanted, even if he had not said it aloud. She thought she'd replied correctly.

"No, I can't go to the shops with you," Christie answered Moira's request regretfully. No matter how much she would love to explore London's temptations, she must resist. After a lifetime of obscurity, the necessity grated, but she need do it only until her birthday.

"Why not? Ashford is consulting with still more boring officials this afternoon and can have no need of you. We need to decide on wall color. Seeing what is fashionable can be very useful. I'll buy you a ribbon for your hat!" Moira gathered her sketches into her portfolio.

"As if I need another ribbon," Christie said in genuine amusement. "Really, I need nothing. And you are the color expert, not me. Just remember to bring back bills of sale."

"You never go out!" Moira protested. "You are worse than Ashford, without his excuse. That cannot be healthy."

It probably wasn't, but she could take no risk that Townsend might see her. She had hidden in the kitchen all morning playing at schoolteacher and quite enjoyed herself. That Ashford had called her bluff by dragging her out to entertain his family grated, but how could she object? Until they had the discussion about her leaving that he had promised last night, he was concealing her as certainly as she hid herself now.

They were *supposed* to be discussing her fate, but politics always came first with the marquess. She'd thought and thought all night and had come up with no better solution than to retreat to the country, where she could hope to hide more successfully than a street away from her stepfather.

She wasn't entirely certain how she felt about Ashford knowing even part of her secret. Last night, she had hoped that she might have his aid. After this morning's performance, she feared he might use her—Miss Townsend's—secret against her if she roused his temper. She had best come up with a better escape plan.

Of course, after Moira departed, she was very aware that she'd been left in the anteroom with a gaggle of men arguing in the study. It seemed wisest to return upstairs to the company of Aunt Nessie and her kittens until she and the marquess had reached an understanding.

It was disappointing that she'd never really see London and must return to living without family or friends, but once she had her independence, she could decide what she wanted to do with the rest of her life. A few months to read and plan was no bad thing.

By the time she heard the twins return that afternoon, Nessie had taught her basic knitting. Harriet longed to run up to the schoolroom and ask what schools the boys had looked at and how they liked them, but that was presumptuous. The Christie part of her personality must be a bit of a snoop.

Below, she heard male voices raised in farewell and the front door opening and closing. She nearly bit off her tongue waiting for Ashford to start yelling for her. Surprisingly, he didn't. Had he forgotten her then?

She should be so fortunate. Before she'd completed her second row of stitches, a maid scratched at the door.

This servant hobbled badly as she entered, and probably shouldn't be running up and down stairs, but the little maid beamed as if her world were perfect. "His lordship requests your presence at tea, Miss."

"Wordsmith?" Nessie asked in puzzlement. "Presents? I once received a lovely book of poetry from a suitor. I wonder where that volume is now?" She glanced up at the maid. "Might I have a bit more milk with my tea today? The kitten is growing."

"Yes, Miss Nessie," the maid said, bobbing. "I will bring your tray."

"That's the thing," Nessie said in satisfaction. "I shall pray to find the volume."

Biting back a smile, Christie addressed the maid, hoping if she kept her voice low enough, Nessie wouldn't hear her. "Tell his lordship that I am taking tea up here while Miss McDowell is out of the house."

It pleased her entirely too much that he recognized her as a lady and not a menial, but she was not about to sit at the table alone with Ashford. That was simply asking for trouble. Her eyes nearly crossed remembering the suggestive comments he'd made while she was just *reading* last night. The man had an extraordinary effect on her that she simply could not act on, even though she understood he encouraged it. *Someone* had to be the mature adult around here.

Christie knew the moment his lordship had been informed that she was disobeying his command. His bellow carried up the stairs. Perhaps she could go up to the schoolroom and eat with the twins. Then she could pretend she hadn't heard him.

Really, if this was how the Ives men normally communicated, it was a wonder they ever accomplished anything.

The pounding of heavy dog feet on the stairwell distracted from her musings. Hartley's latest acquisition had a hound nose and floppy ears, but the enormous paws of a St. Bernard. The mutt wasn't supposed to be inside the house.

"Chuckles, come back here!" Hartley shouted frantically from above.

Oh, dear. She froze in indecision. Her stepfather would have had an apoplexy if she'd chased a dog through the house.

Judging by his roars and the slam of a hard object against a wall, she thought Ashford might already be having an apoplexy.

Warily, she set aside the knitting and stepped into the corridor. She had to dodge one of the kitchen cats and the hound happily racing down the threadbare carpet in a game of chase. At least there were no vases or statues adorning these barren upper corridors. Hartley crashed down the stairs on the dog's trail, not so much as acknowledging her as he raced by.

The look of determination on his face strongly resembled his father's—who was still roaring on the floor below.

She had no experience in handling chaos, much less fury or determined men. Perhaps she should just slip out the back and never be seen again.

No, she couldn't let the poor boy suffer the consequence of being young and bored. If she was to give up being Hidden Harriet, she must learn to deal with others. Taking a deep breath to calm her rattled nerves, resolving to take this one step at a time, she followed hound and boy down the front stairs.

The other twin caught up to her before she was half way down. "He'll send us back to mother for certain this time," Hugh muttered. "I told Hart not to bring the damned dog in."

"Apologize for your language, please," she corrected, lifting her skirt and hurrying.

"Apologies," he said. "But Papa is already in a rage."

"That's because of me. He'll have to throw us all out." The front door knocker resounded, and she winced.

Below, furniture toppled. "Thou loggerheaded miscreant!" Ashford roared, fury escalating.

"Don't let him out!" Hartley cried as some servant evidently headed to answer the door.

Christie and Hugh ran the rest of the way down the stairs.

Ten

As it often did since his accident, Ash's head pounded with the savagery of demons wielding pickaxes against his skull. Why the devil he'd ever thought politics would relieve his boredom eluded him. If he couldn't make one infernal woman obey, what was the point?

Or control his own damned household, he amended, hearing the thunder of dog's feet and feeling a cat brush past in the direction of the kitchen. He edged up to the wall to avoid any unseen encounters. The dog raced over his boots, colliding with the pedestal table at the bottom of the stairs. A lamp crashed.

"Hartley!" Ash howled. "Miss Christie! Get yourselves down here now!" Grimacing as the pickaxes rattled his brain, he gripped his walking stick and edged through the field of debris left in the dog's wake.

The door knocker sounded. The dog changed direction, nearly toppling Ash again. Cries and pounding feet warned Hartley descended. From above, Miss Christie shouted, "Don't let the animal out!"

She ought to be shouting to let the animal go. The beast didn't belong in a house this small, or any house at all. It stank and was probably riddled with fleas.

The knocker sounded again, louder and more impatient while the footman dithered.

"No-o-o-o!" Hartley screamed as the footman must have finally decided the guest was more important than a dog.

Ash stepped away from the wall to halt the proceedings. Leaping from the stairs at that same moment, the boy bounced off Ash. Thrown off balance, Ash spun and caught the wall to steady himself. Ash heard Hugh pound by on his twin's heels.

The front door opened. Female screams erupted outside.

From the piercing shriek, Ash was pretty certain the female was his untrustworthy ex-fiancée, Margaret. Still hanging on to the wall, he almost relished the scene.

"Excuse me, my lord," Miss Christie murmured, brushing past him where he'd frozen in place.

"Christie, dammit, get back here!" Feeling abandoned, he shouted at her as if she truly were a male secretary.

"Sir George Caldwell, Miss Margaret Caldwell," the new footman announced.

"Excuse us, we have a dog to catch," his disobedient secretary said to the guests beneath Ash's furious curses.

He blamed well wasn't facing these unwanted intruders on his own, not when pain was already loosening all the gears inside his head so he couldn't think straight.

He swung his stick at the door, encountered skirts, and rudely stomped past, forcing his guests to dodge. "Catch the dog," he shouted at the footman. He hadn't learned all the voices of the new servants, but this one was a hair's breadth from being sacked.

"*Ashford*," Caldwell protested as Ash shoved past.

"You can't go out like that," Margaret cried in horror.

Like what? It didn't matter. He heard Hartley's cries of fear and anguish and the dog's yelp over the rattle of carriage wheels and horses.

He halted helplessly at the bottom of the street stairs, unable to go further without risking his neck like a stupid beast. He swung his stick in fury, connecting with the footman's knees. The lackwit hadn't gone far in pursuit of the dog. The servant yelped and crashed to the pavement. Ash's backhand swing hit a gas lamp and glass shattered.

"We've caught Chuckles, my lord," Miss Chris called from a distance. "Smith, he's hurt. We need some help carrying him."

Smith—the footman he'd just crippled. Ash swore and reached down to help the man up.

"Thank you, my lord. I'll be fine, my lord," the footman stuttered, while Margaret screeched like a bloody barn owl from above.

The footman's hand was wet, probably with blood since it wasn't raining for a change. He'd probably cut his hand on the shattered glass.

"Christie, his hand is bleeding!" Ash shouted his fury. "By Beelzebub, Caldwell, don't stand there like a lamppost. Help the lady, or at least poor Smith here." Having only a cacophony of noise to guide him, Ash strode in the direction of his sons' high-pitched cries.

"He's hurt," Hugh called.

"The horse hit Chuckles!" Hartley cried, nearly weeping.

"Ashford, we're over here. Give me a moment," Christie called somewhat breathlessly. "The animal won't hold still."

Ash trod determinedly toward her, waving his stick to beat people back, if nothing else. He could sense a crowd gathering. Nothing so entertaining as a blind marquess stumbling about after a worthless mutt.

"This way, Ashford," Miss Christie murmured from nearby. To his relief, she caught his arm to guide him. "The boys can't get a good grip on the dog, and I can't lift him. What happened to Smith? He's all bloody and your visitor is yelling at him."

At seeing her shadow move, Ash bent his head in near-giddy relief to speak for her ears alone. "Never mind that. Let's remove the circus from the street. How much further?"

"Half block, this way. The twins are holding him down on the corner. Please don't yell at the boy. Hartley knows he was wrong, and now the puppy is paying the price. Does your head hurt? You're looking particularly fierce."

He was feeling like a doddering old man. He despised feeling weak, so it was gratifying to know that she thought him fierce. Christie grounded him, letting him know exactly where he was and what was happening. With her information, he could kneel and lift the overgrown hound without making a complete ass of himself. In the gray light of late afternoon, he could almost see the dog's form against the stones.

Hartley apologized profusely all the way back to the house. Ash focused on the woman guiding him and the unhappy animal in his arms. When they reached the steps, Christie exclaimed over the hapless footman while Margaret scolded like a shrew and Caldwell harrumphed and generally made himself as useless as the mutt.

"Hartley, help your father take Chuckles out back," Miss Chris commanded. "You will have to tend his paw while I look after Smith. Can you do that?"

"Yes, miss. I know a lot about dogs."

"Then you ought to know better than to bring untrained ones into the house," Ash scolded, ignoring his guests and following his son down the corridor.

He was being abominably rude and savoring every moment of it.

***

"SURELY THE HOUSEKEEPER CAN LOOK after the footman," the slender blond lady in the height of fashion said with a curl of disdain on her rouged lips. "If you're the twins' governess, you should be keeping them out of this sort of trouble."

Harriet bit her lip and seriously debated calling herself either the housekeeper or the governess and disappearing into the woodwork. Unfortunately, the new *Christie* was a malicious wench. "One never knows when medical attention will be required," she said with her haughtiest rounded vowels. "My mother taught me that a *real* lady always learns to look after those who need it, whatever their station."

She deliberately wrapped her handkerchief around Smith's hand before leading him away.

Her mother had said many things—all from her bed where Harriet had waited on her until she died. It comforted her to know she was following her mother's edicts, even if she did so with spiteful intent. She certainly didn't have any other notion of how to deal with irate, aristocratic guests.

"Marie, please," she addressed a hovering maid, "take our visitors to the salon and bring them tea. I'm sure Ashford will be back directly."

One hoped he would do so *after* visiting his valet. The magnificent madman had stormed into the street in waistcoat and shirtsleeves, his neckcloth unfastened, and his unruly curls looking as if wrens had nested in them overnight.

Absurdly, her insides were melting in admiration and laughter. She'd just participated in a scene all London would talk about, and she felt more alive than she had in her whole life. Obviously, insanity was contagious.

After making certain that the nearly weeping, apologetic Smith had been adequately tended downstairs, Christie washed her hands, removed her blood-spattered apron, and climbed to the garden to check on Hartley.

To her surprise, Ashford was still there, holding bandages in place while Hartley tied them so the dog wouldn't chew them off easily.

"My lord, you have guests!" she admonished. "And you need to see your valet before you can go to them."

"That's just Miss Caldwell," Hugh said in scorn, taking his scowling father's place in holding the dog now that Chuckles wasn't struggling. "She was supposed to be marchioness, but she was too much a coward."

Even bold Christie didn't know exactly how to respond to that. Shock hit her first. The lady waiting in the salon would make the perfect marchioness—her delicate ice-blond beauty would balance beautifully with Ashford's brooding dark height. But the boy's description of her as a coward—

"Well, not everyone likes dogs," Christie said sympathetically, dodging the riptides of this topic.

"Or likes boys, or blind men," Ashford added, rising. "Or much of anyone except herself."

He towered half a head taller than she, and she felt a little giddy when he offered his arm. Really, she belonged out here with the boys, not with a sophisticated marquess. A dull farmer was more her style.

"Do not turn coward on me, Miss Chris," he sneered.

"You do that on purpose," she said, finally opening her mind to the undercurrents beneath all the anger and pain. "You drive people off deliberately. You're standing there, daring me to take umbrage and pack my bags."

"I'm not that stupid," he countered, pressing her hand to his shirtsleeve and turning toward the house. "You are more likely to beat me with a rose cane."

"Possibly," she admitted. "But I'll excuse you this time. I have some headache powders. I will mix them up while you change."

"Mix them in brandy, and I might even take them. I'm not changing for Margaret."

With that ambiguous remark, he released her arm and continued down the corridor without her aid.

Eleven

WITHOUT STOPPING TO CONSULT with his wretched valet, Ash stalked down the long passage from the back of the house to the front salon, whacking his stick back and forth, giving his guests plenty of time to flee.

That they did not told him more than he cared to know and added to his festering pain, anger, and humiliation. He halted in the salon doorway, glad he could not see himself in the mirror the women had said they'd installed on the far side of the room.

"I didn't think to *hear* you cross my portals again," he said, with wicked reference to his disability. "To what do I owe the honor?"

"Now, Duncan, we are neighbors. You needn't be so rude," Margaret admonished in a high soprano that now grated on his ears.

Living on neighboring estates, they'd grown up together. She used his childhood name, as his brothers often did. She was six years his junior, so other than considering her a nuisance, he hadn't paid much attention to her until adolescence.

He couldn't precisely remember why he'd thought it wise to betroth himself to her after that. Knowing Margaret, it had probably been her decision, and their parents had approved, and he'd just gone along because he knew someday he needed an heir. She'd been content with a betrothal and had been in no hurry to wed, which had suited him.

"I've always been rude, Margaret. You just failed to notice." Ash could hear her in the direction of the new sofa under the window. He assumed the baronet was beside her, so he addressed him there. "Caldwell, I'm amazed you have the audacity to show your face in my presence. Did you really think blindness robbed me of all my senses?"

"I don't know what you mean," the older man said indignantly. "We've had our differences, but nothing has changed."

Ash thought his brainpan might incinerate in fury. To avoid whacking his stick against his guest's thickheaded noggin, he gripped a table just inside the doorway. His fingers struck a book. Setting aside his stick, he lobbed the tome back and forth to keep his hands occupied.

"Did you think me so disabled that I'd not discover that it was you who encouraged Roddy and his rioters to terrify Lady Aster? Or that once we caught the scoundrels, did you really believe they wouldn't admit they'd been hired to *shoot* at my skittish horse to make him rear? *Why*, Caldwell? Was my marrying your daughter not enough? Did you think I'd hand over my entire damned estate if I was incapacitated?"

Margaret gasped. Good for her. Ash didn't think she was much of an actress, and he had hoped she wasn't involved.

Caldwell harrumphed. "If you convict me on nothing but the hearsay of a bunch of drunken louts, you are a rotten magistrate. You were the one carousing in the village with the whores while ignoring my daughter. If you'd been home where you should have been, the horse would never have thrown you."

Ash was aware he was no innocent. He also knew he wouldn't have fallen off his horse even if he'd been in a drunken stupor. His memory of that night was hazy, but he hadn't gone headfirst off Zeus into the rocks without cause. Zeus only reacted badly to gunfire. The malfeasants they'd caught had admitted they'd been ordered to shoot if he crossed the bridge. They could not, however, give him the name of the man who had paid them to do it.

Only his neighbors, Caldwell and Montfort—and politically, the earl of Lansdowne—would benefit from Ash being laid up in bed through the fall session.

He'd spent these last months wanting to throttle the wretch responsible for his blindness. He now knew he'd never do so.

In a fit of frustration, he flung the book at Caldwell's head. "If I'd had proof, I'd have you and your cohorts up in chains," he roared. "As it is, I prefer to have no further business with you or your partners in crime."

Apparently the book did not connect. He heard it bounce on the floor.

He would have bowed out then, but Margaret spoke. "I regret taking you up on your offer to end our betrothal, Duncan. It was childish of me. Could we not set grudges aside and try to make amends?"

In shock that she even dared suggest they could repair what she'd cast aside, Ash wanted another book to heave. Or a good crashing vase. He groped behind him for his stick. A soft object pressed against his fingers, and he grasped it in puzzlement. A pillow?

The scent of lilies and woman wafted around him, telling him he wasn't alone. *Christie* had handed him a pillow?

He wanted to laugh out loud, but his head was still ready to explode. "Will your father cast his pocket votes for a new administration if I agree to marry you?" Ash asked with a viciousness Margaret didn't deserve. "What's the going price of my title these days?"

"That's absurd," the baronet sputtered. "One cannot buy votes!"

In satisfaction, Ash flung the pillow in the direction of his guest's voice. He thought he heard a feminine snicker behind him. The wench really shouldn't encourage his filthy behavior, but he didn't intend to stop because she watched.

"Of course one can buy votes," Ash retorted in fury. "Lansdowne bought yours long ago. I'm assuming you're so in debt to him now that he can't be persuaded to provide a suitable husband for Margaret, so now you're crawling back to me."

He couldn't tell where the pillow had landed, but Caldwell sputtered and fumed incoherently. Ash wiggled his fingers behind his back and another pillow brushed against them. He was fairly certain he heard one of his sons racing down the corridor, possibly in search of more.

Uninterested in why they were aiding and abetting his misbehavior, Ash simply dug his fingers into the pillow and kneaded the stuffing, while trying not to take off heads.

"No one buys my vote!" Caldwell shouted. "I am here for my daughter's sake, and because you need help with your estate that your star-gazing brother cannot provide. I did not come here to be insulted and have objects thrown at me."

Ash wished he had an inkpot to respond to this insult to Theo's valiant efforts to manage a task to which he hadn't been trained.

"Flinging things is *all* I can do now, thanks to your cohorts, Caldwell! Leave my house and don't darken my door again. Margaret, I hold no grudge against you, but Lady Aster could have been *killed* when those reprobates invaded our property. I will not have my brothers and their families insulted and harmed for the sake of a few acres of miserable land!"

"That's easy for you to say," Caldwell shouted back. "You own half the damned shire!"

Ash flung what felt like a long, hard bolster at the baronet. This time, judging from the fits of smothered giggles behind him, he was

fairly certain he connected. "I give you good day, sir, Margaret."
With a formal bow, he stalked out, hoping the mischief-makers
dodged from his path because his head hurt like a thousand furies
and he'd forgotten his stick.

MY WORD, NO WONDER ASHFORD roared and rattled invisible
sabers, Christie marveled, hiding in the ante-room with Hugh as the
guests huffed irately and departed. His *neighbors* had caused the
accident that had blinded him! That they'd had the audacity to
return to discuss another betrothal . . . Even brash Christie couldn't
imagine such cheek.

She would wonder at the Caldwells' level of desperation, but she
was more concerned about the marquess. He was hurting. She could
feel his physical and emotional pain as her own, and it was beyond
anything any one human should endure—striking heart, head, and
soul. Tears lined her eyes, and she hugged herself, almost breaking
into sobs of anguish until she saw Hugh watching her worriedly.

"Tell the kitchen to send up tea," she whispered to him as the
door rattled closed after their visitors. "Your father is fine. He
simply does not have enough outlet for his energy and cannot run
off the excess as you and your brother do."

The boy continued to look anxious but nodded as if he might
understand. Once he was gone, she grabbed the fallen walking stick
and followed Ashford down the hall. He was counting steps and
using his fingertips to brush against the wall to verify his position.

She pushed the knob of the cane into his palm. "I have the
headache powder mix on your desk. You were supposed to go there
first, *after* you changed your clothes."

He grabbed her upper arm, dragged her into the study, and
slammed the door. Before she had any inkling of what he meant to
do, he pushed her up against the panel, held her shoulders pinned—
and kissed her.

He kissed hungrily, needfully, as if he'd devour her in one bite if
he could. Christie's lonely, empty soul responded with all her
neglected desire. She dug her fingers into his shirtsleeves, and the
heavy muscles rippling there added to the incendiary explosion of
her insides. Ashford made her feel *small*. Every particle of her

existence thrilled at his proximity. She opened her mouth and welcomed his invasion.

This was no gentle, seductive kiss, but the violent passion of a man pushed to the brink. He released her arms to cup her breasts. Christie squealed against his ravishing mouth, but then the caress of his big hands on her breasts dissolved her lower parts, her knees turned to jam, and she couldn't stand on her own.

Oh my dear lord, she prayed as pleasure spread through her in ways she would never comprehend. She *wanted* what he was doing to her—she wanted *more*. She didn't protest when he pushed closer, rubbing at the place where all this molten fire was gathering. She nearly wept with frustration that he could not untangle her clothing to touch more of her. She'd always hated her huge breasts, but now she understood their purpose, and she *ached*.

She could *feel* his hunger, felt him relinquishing his fury and enjoying the moment—

"Tea, my lord," a maid said through the closed door, scratching at the wood and asking for entrance.

Ashford shoved away, panting, looking as overheated and desperate as she felt. She hastily adjusted her bodice while he retreated to his desk.

"The headache powder," she said, although she wasn't certain she said it loud enough to hear. She shoved the cup she'd left on his desk in his direction.

She opened the door, staying behind it while the maid bustled about, clearing a place for the tray. The gleaming silver pot and sugar and creamer pieces appeared so formal and . . . *elegant*. And here she stood, rumpled and sturdy and more like a common rotund Brown Betty teapot. She wanted to weep with the futility of the desire rushing through her blood and pooling in her lower parts. What on earth had she been thinking?

After the maid whisked away, closing the door after her, Christie flung a few coals on the grate to give herself something to do and steady her confusion. Apparently, she was such a nonentity that no one thought twice about closing her into a room alone with a dangerously unstable man.

The dangerous man looked even more rumpled than she did. His shirt was still damp from their escapade with the dog. It clung to a massively muscled chest, revealing a dark shadow of hair. Blood stained his unbuttoned waistcoat. His black curls fell across his scarred forehead as if he truly were a spoiled, bad-tempered brat who had just thrown a tantrum in front of his neighbors.

But he radiated pain . . . and desire. She couldn't mistake the feeling. Perhaps men just lusted over any woman available.

She hadn't noticed him lusting after ice-cold Margaret.

She shoved the cup at his hand again. He threw the contents back as if it were whiskey, then spluttered and gulped and flung the cup at the wall. It shattered into tiny slivers of cream porcelain on the Turkish carpet.

"I'd rather have the headache," he grumbled. "Give me brandy."

"Not with headache powder, my lord." She supposed it was convenient that she had the powders for her own headaches. She gathered her last remaining nerves and poured his tea the way he liked it, one lump and no milk. "I'll give you the cracked cup. Be careful of the chip. The brandy crystal is too nice to break."

He glanced bleakly in her direction. "Why the devil aren't you running fleeing into the night?"

"It has started to rain," she said prosaically.

He grunted what might have been a laugh. "Why pillows, then?"

"Because you just missed the front window with the book. Those are hundred-year-old panes. I would hate to see them shattered." She sat down across from him and poured her own tea. She *deserved* tea after these past hours. She also deserved two lumps and a good deal of milk—and a biscuit, but the maid hadn't brought any.

"Not precisely the best example for my son," he said without reproach.

"No, you weren't," she agreed, even knowing he'd meant Hugh handing her the ammunition. "But if you hadn't thrown things, it was very possible Hugh may have. I'm not certain he completely understood who was to blame for your accident."

Ashford's rigid shoulders slumped, and he reached for the tea she pushed at him. "He shouldn't have to know the depths of human greed and depravity, but one day, he'll be the steward Theo doesn't want to be. I can't keep him innocent forever."

"It can't be easy raising children," she said noncommittally. This was not her battle, after all—even though she'd enjoyed joining in from the sidelines. "As magistrate, could you not have the offenders up on charges? Someone should be made responsible for injury of such extent."

"It's never that easy. Hearsay is not the same as solid evidence. I know the people, and I know the situation, and I've heard as much as I'll ever hear, and it just isn't enough for a court of law. Did George look guilty when I made my accusation?"

"I had to hide behind the door and could only see him in the mirror, my lord. I thought he might turn purple and have an apoplexy. Miss Caldwell seemed shocked, though."

He nodded, looking slightly relieved. "She needs to marry and crawl out from under her father's thumb. George is land rich, but his pockets are always to let."

"Why would he harm you if you were betrothed to his daughter?" she asked, sorting through all the revelations of this past hour.

"My brothers and I surmise that the intent was to disable me to prevent me from interfering in the elections this summer, as well as allowing Caldwell an excuse to take over the estate in the interest of *helping*. He and Montfort have been protesting my new agricultural practices for years. Their laborers hear what I'm paying mine and demand more for their work. Caldwell and his cohorts probably also assumed any form of incapacitation would prevent me from what I'm doing now—rounding up votes against Wellington's Tories. I wasn't able to stop them from filling their rotten boroughs during the election, but I can gather undecideds now. My neighbors are opposed to anyone but landed aristocrats running the country."

"I've heard some of that ranting," Harriet acknowledged. "I've just not heard it put quite that way. Presumably, your neighbors thought they were saving the country when they tried to incapacitate you?"

"I doubt that they thought it through more than that, anyway. I'm known as a bruising rider and have yet to break my neck, so killing me was not likely and would have cramped Caldwell's plans to take over if I married his daughter. He must have had an apoplexy when Margaret walked away." He sipped his tea and grimaced as if his head still hurt.

Christie drank her tea and pondered the situation. "Townsend once said that a man only need buy a round or two of drinks at the local pub and mention the name of the merchant causing trouble, and everyone with a grievance against that merchant would form a mob and strike against him. I suppose it's easier than the courts since mere complaints are seldom actionable. So men riot instead of working out their problems."

Ashford rubbed his temple but nodded. "He is not entirely wrong. Let us hope he's not in the practice of using that method for punishment."

"He's not a bad man, just a selfish one," she said with a shrug.

"Which could be said of most of us with the coin to buy a round. Wealth buys bullies, but it does not buy compassion or diplomacy."

"We are speaking in generalities, my lord. Not all men are alike. Unfortunately, most have a bad habit of imitating each other. Gives new meaning to the phrase 'do unto others as you would have them do unto you.'"

"Because they're quite likely to do so," he said with a snort of laughter. "I apologize for taking out my temper on you just now. You deserve better."

"You'd not have me treat *you* as you just did *me*?" she asked, then wished she could bite back the retort. Pushing him up against the wall and kissing him would not be entirely a bad thing, in her estimation.

"On the contrary, feel free anytime. Just be prepared for the consequences," he said, and even in his blindness, he conveyed his meaning with his look.

She melted just thinking about it.

Twelve

THE NEXT DAY, HIDDEN HARRIET reverted to form and cowered in her room.

Apparently word of Ashford's public tantrum had spread, and all his family seemed to have descended on the town house. He certainly didn't need her adding to the melee.

She was studying the sewing machine and wondering if she could make it work when the twins rapped at her open door. They entered when she looked up.

"They're saying father is *mad* and not fit to serve!" Hugh said indignantly.

"I should let Chuckles loose and see how *they* react," Hartley said. "Could we not throw more pillows and make them leave?"

Harriet sat back and studied the boys. They seemed sincere, just a little confused. "Should you be listening at doors and who is *they*?"

Both twins shrugged in their unbuttoned coats. Hugh wore his neckcloth neatly tied, but Hartley's was half undone, as was his waistcoat. Except for the auburn hair, they looked like miniature Ashfords in both his personas—dignified aristocrat and furious brat.

"We decided Papa *needs* us to listen," Hartley said, completely oblivious to the deceit of eavesdropping.

"Some of Father's guests," Hugh answered her second question at the same time, sounding worried. "Uncle Theo and Aunt Aster are arguing with them. Uncle Erran and Aunt Celeste look as if they might chew them into bits. Father is tossing pillows back and forth and not saying much."

The boys had reason to be concerned. A non-talking Ashford was building up steam. Or perhaps it was helium. Whichever, it wouldn't be pretty when he exploded. Again. Yesterday's public performance had shown how far beyond society's strictures his temper could take him.

"I don't think there's anything I can do," she said.

"Papa said he has three secretaries, and they're all quite capable and aren't mad. You're his secretary, are you not?" Hartley asked eagerly. "Could you not tell them Papa is perfectly sane?"

"People are far more likely to believe Lord Theo and Lord Erran. If they haven't convinced his visitors, I doubt that I can."

The boys looked disappointed. "We thought you might have some idea," Hugh said, taking the lead again. "London is boring and we won't mind going back to Surrey if we must, but Father has been better since coming here. He will be horrid if he's sent back before the vote."

Horrid was a pale word for what Ashford would be like without the diversion of politics. If his guests wanted to see him insane, they should stay around to see the result of *that* ridiculous decision. She thought it might be akin to attempting to geld a wild stallion. Someone would die, of a certainty, and she didn't it want to be Ashford.

"Perhaps I can distract him enough to prevent him from throwing inkpots," she said, not wanting to disappoint the boys. No one had ever come to her for help before, and she hated to let them down.

They crept down the front stairs, although she doubted if anyone could have heard a tribe of savages beating drums over the noise issuing from the front salon.

"The issue is that our party has enough difficulties. We cannot *look* as if it's being run by raving lunatics!" a stranger's deep voice rose over the others.

"I'm not the one raving at the moment," Ashford said dryly. "And if you would have let your son run into the street to be crushed by a carriage, then I'd change parties too."

"You beat up your footman in the street and flung books at a woman!" another voice argued coldly. "You cannot keep a servant. They all claim you've run mad. Go back to Surrey, Ashford. We'll bumble along without you."

Overhearing this, Christie's fury rose so swiftly that she thought she saw red. She had to place a hand against the wall to steady herself. She could not imagine what Ashford might be feeling. My word, if he had a pistol, he'd be using it now. And deservedly so.

Hurrying to his study, she snatched up the writing desk. Holding her finger up to the boys to warn them to stay quiet, she strode determinedly back to the salon. Ashford's brothers were speaking while the marquess remained ominously silent.

The twins watched her with hope shining in their eyes. She scarcely knew what *she* could do and so had no idea how the boys could help. Her only hope was to open herself to the emotions of his guests for a clue of how to deal with them, while diverting Ashford's temper and giving his brothers a chance to clear the air.

She sensed that these were men who respected power and despised weakness—like Townsend. She knew how to deal with that. Taking a deep breath and concocting the most enormous lie she could think of, she strode into the salon and dropped the writing desk on Ashford's lap. "The messenger from the king cannot wait longer, my lord. I've replied as you've requested. You might wish Lord Erran to scan the missive for correctness before you sign."

She took the document—she thought it was an invoice to be entered in the household ledger—and waved it at Lord Erran. Ashford's younger brother had the Ives' jutting cheekbones, but his nose had been broken at some point, and he was shorter and broader than the marquess. Standing with his fingers hooked in his watch pocket, he radiated the part of intimidating barrister in his sophisticated dark suit.

He looked startled but accepted the document. He glanced at it quizzically. Christie rode over any question he might ask by tapping another invoice on the desk in Ashford's lap.

She could feel the marquess's fury ebbing beneath his maniacal humor as he realized what she was doing. It wouldn't do for him to start cackling. "Sir George's debt has come due. While I have your attention, might I ask if you wish to call it in? You were talking of using the funds for the new railroad, I believe."

Lord Erran hastily ducked his head to examine the invoice as if it were really an important document.

"What the devil . . . ?"An iron-gray-haired gentlemen who'd been pacing behind the sofa glared at her. He radiated confusion and a cold cynicism.

"Pardon me, sir." She bobbed a curtsy. "I'm one of his lordship's secretaries. The only way for me to make myself known in this extremely busy household is to be forthright. This meeting seemed likely to last too long, and really, His Majesty cannot be left waiting."

Lord Theo, the brown-haired, slimmer, more ascetic-looking brother, started to look amused. Beside him, Lady Aster was hiding a grin behind her teacup. Really, since they couldn't actually sack someone who wasn't a true employee, they could do little more than show her the door. And Christie thought perhaps they might not object too terribly to the interruption.

Lord Theo held out his hand. "Let me see Caldwell's marker. That's a year old, isn't it?"

The Ives were apparently as adept at prevarication as she was.

The younger lords seated on the sofa watched this exchange in amazement. "You have a female secretary, Ashford?"

"Splendid, isn't she?" Ashford said with a lazy drawl, swinging his stick to bat at her skirts. "Theo is too busy to nag, but Miss Christie keeps a tight ship. Dodges inkpots well, too."

To show her annoyance at his inflated self-importance, she picked up the sharply whittled pen on the desk and jabbed his hand with it, although her action was blocked from the rest of the room by her size. "You have yet to fling an inkpot at me, my lord," she said with the stiff objection of a loyal servant.

"Pillows, perhaps?" the gray-haired gentleman asked. "Books?"

Ashford grabbed the pen from her hand before she could fling it at his attackers.

With as much dignity as she could muster while the Ives brothers and their wives snickered, she said, "I am a valued *servant*, sir. His lordship treats me with respect. He has an unfortunate impatience with those who offer insolence, however."

"The footman was insolent yesterday?" the more affable younger gentleman asked.

Christie could sense that his earlier concern was ebbing. "Of course not. Is that what this is about? Smith is a recent hire and has not learned to dodge his lordship's walking stick. He fell and hurt himself. You have only to ask him. The dog was the true culprit in yesterday's unfortunate incident, but one can hardly blame a dumb animal."

"Caldwell claims he and his daughter were *attacked*. He's talking about pressing charges," the pacing man insisted, still not convinced but less furious. "The entire town is buzzing about Ashford's tantrum and the street incident. Our party is vilified enough as it is. We don't need this sort of misbehavior."

"If Grey wants me to withdraw my leadership, have him say so," the marquess said in a deceptively languid tone, grasping the document with which Erran was batting his hand. "I believe I've been insulted quite enough this morning. Miss Christie, if you would show these gentlemen out, I need to confer with my brothers about this debt before Caldwell spouts any more feeble nonsense."

The inference that Caldwell was blackening Ashford's name in an attempt not to pay his debt finally registered on the strangers, Christie noticed.

She dipped a curtsy. "Gentlemen, I'll have Smith bring your hats, shall I?"

She heard the twins racing back up the stairs.

The rest of Ashford's family rose to hasten the guests' departure.

Christie shivered with cold sweat as the unsatisfied visitors harrumphed and made their farewells. She hid in the study while the strangers questioned Smith, who held the door for them. She waited until the door shut after them before she sank into a wingchair and tried to pull herself together.

She didn't *do* things like that! What on earth had come over her?

"Christie!" Ashford's roar rattled the rafters.

"I quit," she shouted back, having reached the very last thread of her nerves. "I plan to join a circus."

Laughter erupted down the corridor. Not Ashford's, she knew. Tears sprang unbidden to her eyes. She had not meant to make such a fool of herself. It had just happened. She'd felt Ashford's pain and humiliation even more than his controlled rage, and she'd lost her own temper and wanted to kick the men causing it.

Perhaps she *should* have kicked them. Then they could have called her lunatic too. Now that she thought about it, she was angrier than she had ever been. How dare they accuse a brilliant man like the marquess of being *insane*?

Cowering behind the study door, she listened to Ashford stamping in her direction. His brothers were laughing and repeating apparently humorous parts of the conversation. How could they be so oblivious to Ashford's hurt? They thought him invulnerable, perhaps. He hid behind arrogance as she hid behind doors.

"My lord," Celeste Ives called sweetly, "please leave poor Miss Christie alone. It does not do to hunt her like prey."

"My dear, your voice does not influence my clodpoll brothers," Christie thought she heard Lord Erran say. She had no idea what he meant. His brothers couldn't hear his wife?

"Oh, Ashford is swayed, all right," Lady Aster replied with humor. "He's simply like an angry elephant who can't stop once he's on the warpath. Do elephants have warpaths, or is that Indians?"

Ignoring his family's inanities, Ashford stomped into his study and found her instantly. "I do not need you to fight my battles," he thundered.

For a blind man, he had an excellent sense of direction. She stayed huddled in her chair. "I quit, so it doesn't matter."

"You can't quit. You were never hired. One cannot hire *ladies*. Where the devil did you learn to act like that?" He leaned against the door jamb, properly leaving the door open while his family was about.

"Lying is what I do," she said with a shrug. "Townsend would demand to know who had let the sheep escape, or if I knew who broke the clock, or whatever had enraged him that day. And I would say I did, because he couldn't strike me. The house belonged to . . . my cousin and her mother . . . and so did the servants. After . . . my aunt . . . died, and he tried to marry . . . Miss Townsend . . . off to the local farmers, I told the village she had a contagious disease. They believed me and not him. Storytelling was my only entertainment."

His shoulders shook with what she hoped was laughter. "By Jupiter, you should pair with Jacques. Your stories are better than his. The *king's* messenger! That flummoxed Birchcroft so badly that he couldn't speak."

"That was rather the point." She couldn't unfurl from her tight ball of nerves. He was too close. Her lies were mounting so rapidly, she couldn't keep up, and she was reaching a breaking point. She was too aware of what they had done yesterday—and that his brothers were just down the hall. And she didn't want to *pair* with his playwright brother. "When Townsend had one of his real rages, I had to make up huge tales to distract him. And it sounded as if your brawl was bigger than anything he could generate. The king was the largest distraction I could summon short of the city being on fire."

"You don't like lying," he said, abruptly sobering.

"I lack the confidence to be good at it. No one with any real sense would believe such outrageousness." *Harriet* lacked the confidence, anyway. *Christie* was becoming much too good at tale-telling.

"You convinced that lot of imbeciles," he argued.

"Because they couldn't believe you'd hire a liar," she suggested. "Lying is the only way I can make myself heard. It's not as if a mere secretary could tell your guests what she thought," she continued, "not any more than a plain female could tell Townsend anything."

"You should have been born a duchess," Ashford asserted. "They have the power to command."

"Duchesses aren't born," Lady Aster said, entering the study and interrupting before that thought could travel to what marchionesses could do. "She's *my* lieutenant general, so leave her alone. Miss Christie, you were simply brilliant. We shouldn't have worried when we heard the news that Ashford had lost his wits."

"You knew I didn't have wits to lose," the marquess suggested.

"No, but your temper is notorious." Lord Theo came up behind his wife and circled her waist. "We feared you'd shoot someone." He nodded amiably at Harriet. "Miss Christie, we thank you. Whatever we're paying you, it isn't enough."

"She quit," Ashford reminded them. "If you actually paid her, she'd take the money and run."

Christie wanted to run right now, before they could demand explanations. She glared at the mad marquess, who grinned devilishly, even though he couldn't see her glare. The damned man knew exactly what he was doing.

"I am glad I am entertaining you, my lord," she said irritably—totally out of Harriet character now. If they were not blocking the door, or if there'd been a window, she'd leave this minute.

Blessedly, the front door knocker sounded.

Not so blessedly, she heard her stepfather's familiar bellow the instant the door opened.

Thirteen

TIRED OF IRATE GUESTS, ASHFORD ignored the shouting new visitor. He had servants to guard the door against such interferences.

"I must leave this *instant*," Miss Chris whispered, catching him by surprise.

From the urgency in her voice, Ash was pretty certain she'd just turned a whiter shade of pale. Theo had said she had an English coloring, so he could picture the roses fading from her cheeks. He'd touched those cheeks—they'd been petal soft and warm. He didn't want her to be afraid of him.

"Why?" he demanded, not understanding. "Because I have made you angry? That won't be the first or the last time. You're doing quite well in learning to fight back."

"No," she said without an ounce of her earlier vigor.

He heard her stand. Her petticoats rustled within his reach. He could grab her . . . but outside the study door, an eager audience awaited.

"I do not wish to involve you and your family in my problems," she said in a rush. "Let me pass, my lord."

Something he wasn't seeing was very wrong, but his brothers weren't warning him, which meant they were equally puzzled. Ash stiffened and listened closer. Their latest visitor was as loud as the nodcocks who had just left, but Ash didn't recognize the voice. Could Miss Christie?

He shifted to block her escape until Smith brought the salver with the caller's card. Theo took it.

"Boswell Townsend, baron," Theo said in a low voice that would not carry to their guest. "Did you tell him we'd marry his daughter to Bryght in return for two votes?" he asked with humor.

"Send our guest to the anteroom, Smith," Ash ordered, pulse accelerating. Only he understood that Townsend's heiress was actually missing, and Miss Christie might hold the clue to her whereabouts. He had to think as quickly as she had a few minutes ago. This was his problem to address, not his brothers'. "May I have your permission to explain your situation to my family, Miss Christie?"

"I just told you I didn't want to involve anyone else," she said with irritation. "He cannot see me back here. I'll take the back stairs and be gone."

He heard the whisper of a lie again. A half-truth?

"Townsend," Aster whispered in understanding, obviously connecting lines in her strange museum of a mind. "I've just started looking for that name, now why . . . Oh, the missing heiress."

Theo's annoyingly prescient wife was always around when she shouldn't be. Ash listened for whatever inane Malcolm angle she'd take on the baron's arrival.

"I knew Miss Christie's chart did not add up to being a companion." Aster explained, placing her hand on Ash's chest and shoving him up against the jamb so she could peer around him into the study. "Miss Christie . . . *Townsend*, perhaps?" she called into the study. "I recall a member of Sommersville's family of similar name. I'd have to look it up, but that would make far more sense with your zodiac. You may tell us all about it upstairs."

Ash almost fell over. Miss *Townsend*? Could *Miss Chris* be the missing heiress? No wonder he'd heard a half-truth in her story. And then the rest of Aster's comment sank in.

Sommersville—a bloody damned duke? His shocking secretary was related to one of the most powerful dukes in the kingdom?

No, this time, the dangerously prescient Aster had to be wrong.

Theo chuckled. Ash debated bashing his own head against the jamb in frustration. Bashing Theo's would release more tension, but even he realized Theo wasn't the one he wished to throttle.

She'd *lied* to him. He'd known she was lying . . . but . . . she'd made a total ass of him. Rationality did not play a part in his fury. He could toss Townsend into the Thames without a qualm, but *Sommersville*? The man was a giant among men—and not just by size. If he wasn't such a recluse, His Grace would have been leading the Whigs instead of Ash.

Miss Lying Christie rustled in the direction of the connecting door to his chamber, apparently intending to flee.

He panicked.

Despite her lies, he knew this was one woman he didn't wish to drive away. Lose an heiress and Sommersville's relation? Anything could happen to the fool woman. She didn't have an iota of understanding of how to go about in the city.

"Christie!" Ash raised his voice just enough to get his command across. "You will *not* leave. If you leave this house, I will personally track you to the ends of hell. You would not wish to be responsible for the Tories remaining in office, would you?"

If it was possible to hear confusion, he heard it in her silence.

"Aster, Celeste, do what you must but don't let her go." Ash debated alternatives but if he was to get to the bottom of this farce, he came down on the side of privacy first. "Theo, Erran, make yourselves scarce but don't leave yet. I feel an episode of inkpot-flinging coming on."

"Don't you dare," Miss Christie whispered in horror. Was her name even Christie? "Just tell him I am gone."

"Not a chance," he said in his best threatening voice. He had found a new direction for his rage as it fully sank in that the brilliant Miss Chris, possible relation of a *duke*, might be the woman the baron had meant to trade for votes. How stupid was this rank villain? "You stay, he goes to hell."

"I only need six more months—" she cried in a low voice.

"It was my fault that you went outside yesterday," he argued with deceptive calm. "If he heard of it, I'll take the consequences. It could be about something else entirely. Now, out." He pointed his finger at the connecting door to his chamber.

"Rude," Aster admonished, brushing past him.

His sister-in-law had no conception of *rude* if she thought that was the worst he could do. Respect and manners had little to do with men of his rank. A marquess could throttle a nobody like Townsend and heave him in the Thames and there was little anyone could do about it.

He heard the women rustling and a door opening and closing. Instead of leaving, as requested, his brothers shoved into the study and closed the hall door.

"What is the meaning of this?" Erran demanded.

"That I may need your legal services or I may not." A furious mind was an agile one, Ash decided, as he worked through all the possible scenarios he could perpetrate here.

"Don't you dare," Theo responded, pacing the room. "We don't need any more drama to prove you're insane. I'll move to Northumberland and leave you to rage around the Hall until you drive off all the servants again."

"I wasn't the only one to do that." Ash wasn't really concentrating on Theo but on how he would deal with Townsend. If Miss Chris was actually Miss Townsend . . . Could Aster's instincts be that accurate? If so, a man who would treat a brilliant—if amazingly annoying—liar as if she were a good horse to trade deserved to be thrashed. He was in the perfect mood for thrashing.

"Do you intend to tell us what this is about?" Erran demanded in the low bellow that presumably brought courtrooms to their knees.

Ash had heard Erran all his life and wasn't impressed. "Not yet. Go away and let me take care of this."

He was actually starting to anticipate the challenge. And it wasn't just because he wanted to ram Townsend's head up a chimney. No, it was suddenly all about the deliciously devious possibilities of *keeping* Miss Lying Christie.

"Right," Theo said with annoyance. "Let's be good little boys and go listen with the women. We can dismantle his bed and hide the pieces while we're at it." Theo shoved Erran from the room.

Brothers, always there when you needed them. He snorted at the notion. Grateful they didn't feel it necessary to treat him as if he were a pathetic invalid, Ash opened the study again and gestured for Smith to show their guest in.

He settled behind his desk in his favorite position and waited.

"My lord, thank you for seeing me." The baron's thunder diminished once he was introduced to the presence of a marquess.

Ash assumed his mundane surroundings weren't the source of Townsend's sudden obsequiousness. Ash had inherited the title only two years ago, but he'd been his father's right-hand man since adolescence. He'd had a lifetime to learn that men cowered before wealth and power. Ash wasn't averse to making this worm crawl.

He wished he could see him. Judging from the height of Townsend's voice, Ash decided that his caller wasn't particularly tall. Christie probably towered over him—mentally as well as physically—which would annoy a small-minded man. "Have a seat, Townsend, and tell me what I can do for you."

Christie's tale of telling the village that Miss Townsend was diseased rose in his mind—could she have been speaking of herself? Of course she had. Only someone who had no fear of losing her position would be so irresponsible. He would throttle *her* later.

A chair groaned under a heavy weight. Out of meanness, Ash pictured Townsend as short and rotund, probably balding. He could hear his caller shift his weight to remove his handkerchief and assumed he was wiping his brow. Definitely nervous.

"I've been told my daughter was seen entering your premises yesterday," his guest said in what passed for a polite tone, although Ash recognized the bluff behind it.

Daughter. Dashitall . . . Ash took a calming breath so as not to breathe fire. "Is that so? I didn't realize you had a daughter. Is she a friend of my sister-in-law's then?"

"Stepdaughter," the baron said dismissively. "Same thing. She doesn't know anyone in London. I can't think of any *good* reason she'd be here when she's supposed to be with a cousin in Somerset."

"You've lost your stepdaughter?" said the spider to the fly.

"Females are unreliable. I want to see her."

"Well, that's more than I can," Ash said, wondering if the baron even realized he was talking to a blind man.

It took the man a few seconds. "I beg your pardon, my lord. Perhaps if someone in your household could fetch her, I'd be appreciative. She belongs at home."

"As far as I'm aware, we have no Miss Townsend here." Which wasn't a lie since Miss Lying Christie had failed to identify herself correctly. Ash was still playing all the angles of that dilemma through his need to not give her back to this imbecile. "I don't know who I'd tell them to fetch. I'm still wondering how you lost her. If I remember correctly, you wished to find her a husband, and you offered your vote to the Whigs if we could help."

Townsend should have had no difficulty marrying off a member of the duke's family. Was the man a total half-wit . . . or up to no good? With a fortune involved, the latter seemed as likely as the former.

"Yes, yes, of course. She's very obedient, simply wants a home of her own. She'll make some man an excellent wife. As I said, I thought she was with a cousin, but my butler and the neighbors swear they saw her yesterday in some altercation with a boy and a dog and that she followed you into this house on familiar terms." A hint of irritation slipped past his polished tones.

Dammitall . . . That was his lying lady, all right. "Ah, that would be Miss Christie, my decorator's assistant. Your butler must be mistaken." Ash thought he heard a snicker or a sniff from the direction of his chamber. Perhaps both, since all the women probably had their ears to the crack. Not the best time to throw inkpots.

"Harriet isn't anyone's assistant!" Townsend responded with indignation. "She's a proper lady. I spent a fortune turning her out in style."

"I can't see *style*, Townsend. I don't see how I can help you."

"She's large!" Townsend raised his voice in frustration, as if talking to a deaf man. "She's unmistakable. She's bigger than me, bigger than our footmen, wears the most hideous caps, it's hard *not* to recognize her!"

Ash stiffened, imagining how a sensitive female would take these insults—as Miss . . . *Townsend* must have taken them most of her life. Appalled that his invaluable lieutenant-general had been treated so reprehensibly, he fisted his hands where his guest couldn't see them. He might want to wring the lady's neck, but Townsend needed to be flung through a window.

"Where is your decorator?" the baron demanded, unaware of how close he was to being tossed against a wall, since there were no windows.

"I had meetings today. The decorator isn't here." Ash thought he ought to be given awards for keeping his temper. Apparently toying with mice didn't involve ripping their heads off. Interesting. Or maybe knowing Miss Chris might be listening had a calming effect. He could wait and throttle *her* instead. "I don't know how large you are, but the lady in question is smaller than I am, has a lovely voice and is kind to children and dogs. Does that sound like your stepdaughter?"

"We don't have children and dogs, how the devil would I know? Send her in, and we can find out, can't we?" Townsend's studied nonchalance was starting to slip dangerously into sarcasm, a tone he probably used to belittle anyone who annoyed him—like Miss Christie.

That realization raised Ash's temper another degree.

If her name was Miss Townsend, could Christie be a given name? Because he couldn't think of her as a Harriet.

"Do you think your stepdaughter would simply walk over here to help my decorator?" he asked as if deep in thought. "How odd. Is she prone to straying, do you think? I really can't recommend her as a wife to any of my colleagues if she's prone to being mislaid."

Definitely muffled hoots from the other room. He suspected it wasn't from sheltered Christie, who wouldn't understand the ambiguity of that remark. Still, she was clever and caught on quickly. He expected pillows flung at his head at any moment. Yes, she was definitely influencing his temper because he was enjoying himself again.

Townsend sputtered and wiped his forehead. Ash could almost hear his guest sweat while he controlled his annoyance. Ash spent the silence wondering if it was fine for barons to have tantrums, and if it was just blind marquesses who weren't allowed to bellow.

"Perhaps you would allow me to inquire of your servants, my lord," Townsend said in a more unctuous tone.

"Valuable, is she?" Ash asked. This man had treated a gem like a lump of coal for most of her life. A little torture was good for his character.

"An heiress, my lord. Her mother's family were eccentrics who locked their lands and investments into trusts for the females of the line. Her mother left me as executor of the trust, but the chit has almost reached the age to inherit. Can you imagine a flighty female handling valuable property? She must marry before that happens, so her husband can supervise it properly."

Ash frowned. Aster's family tended to lock up wealth in trusts for the females, but he was fairly certain there was no relation between sensible Christie and the insane Malcolms. They would have known about her, for one thing.

Except Aster *had* known about her, once Townsend's name was personally associated with her instead of the unknown heiress. He fought a pang of foreboding. Whatever Aster knew had to wait.

"Ah, I see your concern," Ash said, nodding knowledgeably. "Well, I'll have the servants keep an eye out for her. What is her full name, anyway?"

"Harriet Christie Russell Townsend," the baron said with surliness. "I did everything proper for her when I wed her mother. Does your decorator go by those names?"

Relieved that there wasn't a "Malcolm" anywhere in the lot, Ash returned to tormenting his visitor. "No idea, but I'd look in Somerset or wherever, if I were you. Your heiress probably has a beau there."

"She doesn't have a beau!" Townsend shouted. "She told them all she's dying of consumption! The woman is a goosecap, but she's an heiress. If you think you can keep her and trade her for more votes than mine, I'll report you to Wellington! He'll hear me out."

"Oh, he knows about the mad marquess," Ash said, toying with his inkpot as his anger returned. Christie was the very last thing at the far end of the spectrum from a *goosecap*. This was the brute who had turned her into a timid mouse who lied and hid in corners. Really, throttling, hurling, and stuffing wasn't good enough.

"You can't tell Wellington anything he doesn't already know." Ash continued playing out the line to bait this obnoxious shark. "I wouldn't talk to Earl Grey, either, if I were you. He's tired of hearing the complaints about me. He's an intelligent leader who accepts that madmen can still deliver votes. I'd like to count on yours, Townsend."

"Find Harriet and get her betrothed, and I'll think about it," Townsend said, shoving back his chair to stand.

"Excellent. I'll do that. You won't need to negotiate the settlements, will you?" Ash asked with deceptive disinterest, concealing his roiling temper.

"Of course I need to negotiate the settlements!" Townsend said in outrage. "What kind of fool do you think I am?"

"A very large one," Ash said, hefting the crystal inkpot. "If you cannot recognize kindness and an intelligence superior to your own, perhaps you should not be her executor. Good day to you, sir."

Ash turned his scarred face to the baron, offered his most ferocious scowl, and shouted, "Smith, the baron is ready to leave."

"*You have her!*" Townsend shouted, not understanding the trap. "I'll bring the law down on you! You cannot kidnap anyone you wish just because you have a title."

"*And you cannot sell off a woman just because you want her money,*" Ash retorted, flinging the inkpot with all the force with which he used to throw punches.

In satisfaction, he heard Townsend squeal like a pig. His accuracy was improving.

Fourteen

SHE'S BIGGER THAN ME, *bigger than our footmen, wears the most hideous caps, it's hard not to recognize her* . . . Townsend's words struck straight through her soul.

Harriet wanted to sink into a puddle of . . . ink . . . and ooze through the floor.

She felt the justifiable confusion of the marquess's family behind her, and their sympathy as they finally understood. After Townsend raced from the house, Aster and Celeste tried to hug her and remove her from the door. The Ives men tried to politely push past her to reach Ashford.

Harriet could not, would not tolerate their pity.

Slipping into her *Christie* persona, she used her bulk to prevent them from entering the study. Then she summoned her courage, straightened to her full intimidating height, and charged in to confront the conniving marquess on her own. She closed the door with a loud snap. She was shaking with fury and tears and could barely see him in the windowless gloom. No one had turned on the lamps.

"Had I thought throwing inkpots would make a difference, I would have thrown one myself," she said angrily, taking the chair and not caring if her old gown was soaking up ink.

"I threw it for you." Apparently not noticing her distraught state, Ashford tossed a pen back and forth with amazing accuracy. "Had I any pots left, I'd throw one at you. You *lied* to me, Miss Christie *Townsend.*"

"I lie to everyone, Lord Ashford," she retaliated. "I told you I lie. You said you know when I lie, so you knew I was lying. I was trying to protect you and your family . . ." Her voice shook with tears and humiliation and she gestured with her handkerchief, even though he couldn't see. " . . .from a horrible scene like that. He won't stop there. I must leave at once. I have come to say farewell and to thank you for defending me."

Ashford appeared unmoved. He continued tossing the pen. "Tell me, Miss Townsend, what should a man look for in a wife?"

Set to leave, unprepared for this tactic, she sank back down in confusion. He was looking for a *wife*?

She'd deliberately shut out the pain of Townsend's destructive emotions earlier. She had to warily open up again to sense Ashford's mood. He roiled with understandable fury beneath his deceptive placidity, but it was fury laced with... *anticipation*? And confusion? Her anguish receded beneath curiosity—and just a wee bit of worry. What was the madman plotting now? Why was he not roaring for her to pack her bags?

"I should imagine it depended on the man," she answered evasively, until she had a better understanding of where this was going.

"Just so," he nodded approval. "It would be senseless for me to wander the marriage mart, seeking the latest diamond, don't you agree? Aside from the fact that I couldn't see if she simpered or smiled, I don't need her wealth."

Harriet Christie had only sampled a few of society's rarified events, but it was easy enough to imagine this formidably large man with his scarred scowl stalking among the frail gossamer-clad young misses in a ballroom, scattering them hither and yon in terror like unarmed villagers before a dragon.

Even though she was shaking in her shoes over her fate, she sympathized with the image. She would miss this complicated man when she was gone. "You could throw a flowerpot and choose the one who caught it."

"Yes," he almost hissed in satisfaction. "Other than pot catching, what else should I look for?"

She really couldn't see where this was going, but thinking of the twins, she said, "A love of children? Kindness?"

"Excellent." He tapped the pen point on his desk, dulling it. "But in case you had not noticed, a wife must appeal to her *husband* before there are children. Men are notoriously thick-headed about choosing wives. What would a woman say they needed to look for?"

She frowned and stood to leave again. "This really isn't relevant, my lord. I was not lying when I said I have properties in Dorset. I will have control of them after my birthday in April. I apologize for causing you any grief, but if you could provide transportation, I think I can hide until then, and I will cause you no more trouble."

"You have already caused me no end of trouble, Miss Townsend. *Sit down.*" He pointed the quill at her. "Now tell me, what would a *woman* say a man needed to look for in a wife?"

Desperate to be helpful after she'd caused so much ugliness, she tried to understand what he asked but couldn't. Since he was still sitting, she sat down again. "I don't think I can help you. I should think only a man could know what a man wants in a woman."

"Exactly!" He turned to face her. "You are a woman of immense understanding. I know precisely what I want. I just wanted to see if you agreed. Courage would be a good start, don't you think?"

"Most women aren't brought up to be courageous," she pointed out, heart sinking. If men wanted courage, then she would never marry.

"Don't be ridiculous. Bearing children requires courage. Watching husbands ride off to war requires a stiffer upper lip than most of Parliament possesses. In my case, it mostly requires the courage to not stand in my way if I choose to make an ass of myself. That means handing me pillows instead of books and not complaining about flung inkpots." He sat back as if satisfied with his conclusion.

Harriet started to feel a little fluttery in her bafflement and responded in the same foolish vein. "You will most certainly hear complaints about flung inkpots once it is discovered what you have done to your new wallpaper. Might I suggest repainting in deep blue? Then the black splatters might look artistic."

She saw a flash of white teeth through the gloom that she hoped was an appreciative smile. She couldn't even be properly angry with this charming lunatic. No wonder he had lured so many women to his bed! That thought brought her abruptly back to reality.

"A wife who occasionally pricks my inflated arrogance would probably be a good thing," he suggested.

"You have spent the better part of your life expecting everyone to roll over and sit up at your command as if they were dogs," she agreed. "I cannot imagine there are too many women willing to tell you to jump in a lake instead."

"*You* would," he said with certainty. "When it mattered, you would fling inkpots back at me, wouldn't you?"

Since that was precisely what she had wanted to do, and hadn't, she swallowed hard and tried to think that through. "Me? I told lies to the entire village rather than tell my stepfather to jump in the lake."

"You had no choice," Ashford pointed out. "He provided your bread and butter and the roof over your head. Sniping from behind bushes is not the work of a coward but of a brilliant rebel with too few troops to fight an army."

His words tingled all the way down as she considered them. Could she trust this madman meant what he said? She'd *always* been brave? It wasn't just her freedom as Miss Christie, the companion, that had given her boldness? Lying wasn't brave as far as she could tell. It had just been easy. Maybe he really was mad. But he had her attention.

"The question is," he continued relentlessly, "why did you lie to *me*?"

Ah, there was the temper rising again . . . and hurt? The man kept throwing her off balance. She didn't even know to which lie he objected. "Because that is what I do, my lord," she answered callously. "It is the only way I know to survive and to protect others. And I fear you lie as well, my lord, making promises and telling half-truths to get what you want."

She could sense his dissatisfaction with that reply, but he was apparently willing to let it ride—for the moment.

He steepled his fingers and nodded thoughtfully. "Very possible. People like to hear what they want to believe, and a politician gives them that. Sometimes, it's the only way to achieve what is best for all."

"It is arrogance to assume that *you* know what is best for all!" she protested.

"Well, I am in a better position than most to know," he argued. "I'm educated. I've wielded a position of power for years. I'm in communication with the men who run the government as well as men who run industry. *And* the laborers who work for both. Whereas someone like you, Miss Townsend, has knowledge of nothing more than your housekeeper."

"Sadly true," she admitted, losing track of the direction of this inane conversation. "But that does not mean I cannot read, see what is around me, learn, and understand how people will react. My knowledge is of a different sort. I can sense your ambivalence, you realize. You are talking yourself into something as much as you are trying to persuade me. What I cannot understand is what and why."

"I think you know *what* I want, but you're denying it. You would also understand *why*, Miss Townsend, if you had my experience in recognizing desire. I want you rather desperately. I see an opportunity, and I wish to seize it, but I find I want you to want the same. It's another one of those humbling experiences I've suffered since my fall."

She didn't know whether to laugh or throw inkpots. Surely he could not be offering her *carte blanche.* He knew she was a wealthy lady and didn't require that kind of protection. She was six months away from freedom.

"Perhaps I should explain what a woman would like to have in a man," she said dryly, looking for firm ground to stand on. "Humility works better than arrogance most of the time."

He laughed hollowly. "Given my experience, that doesn't happen overnight. Once upon a time, I had women groveling at my feet, hoping for any piece of me I might throw their way—money, power, position. I have a great deal of all that to spare and everyone, including myself, knows it. Humility doesn't happen in my position. Besides the twins, I have a daughter in Manchester whose mother lives very nicely on what I provide. There are many others who would happily follow her example. I have had no experience in women requiring anything resembling humility of me."

"I understand, my lord. You cannot claim to be a saint, and neither can the women willing to take money instead of offering love." She almost sympathized with him. Give an adolescent boy wealth and privilege and one could expect little other outcome, and now he paid the price of never knowing faithfulness or a partner to share his burdens.

Ash shrugged. "I took what they offered and have no reason to regret it. Except now here I am, unable to leave the damned house, looking like a ravaged beast, and incapable of remembering a single woman in my past who would make half the wife you would."

Wife. Harriet stared in astonishment. He flattened her with his honesty—not *flattered* but laid her out flat like a carpet.

Unable to see her shock, he waited for her to speak. Why were men so insensitive that they could not tell when she was upset? She struggled but no words seemed sufficient—or even correct or honest. She couldn't even tell if that was a proposal. She rather thought not. His lordship certainly wasn't emanating *love.*

She stood up again. "You could leave the house if you liked, my lord. You *choose* not to. You have guests and it is probably time to dress for dinner."

Ashford rose just as quickly, leaning both hands against the desk. "Stop running away! Use that courage I know you possess and think about what I've said. If you have demands, let me know them. I expect no less."

"You have not even said plainly what you really want," she said crossly. "You have spoken in circles like a good politician. I am very good at guessing what people want, but once in a while it is important to me that I *hear* it."

"I want you to marry me, with a license and a vicar, as these things are done!" he shouted. "Is that plain?"

The words she'd longed to hear from anyone, for years, and they still weren't what she wanted. She held back tears and straightened her weak spine. "I am tired of being bossed around by bullies," she retorted, letting all those years of neglect and the feelings of inferiority well up and spill over. "In six months, I will have the independence to do anything I want. I could buy any husband I liked. I have no wish to be shouted at, pushed around, and dominated by a man who knows no other way to act. Grovel, Ashford, it will be good for you."

Heart pounding so hard that she might faint, Christie fled. She could not believe she'd *said* that. She was as mad as he!

She'd forgotten that his entire family occupied the next room. Well, not the entire family. Apparently there was a daughter in Manchester, and of course, the twins were in the attic. She saw the rest pouring from the bedchamber into the hall, and this time she truly fled—up the stairs and into her room, where she locked the door.

"WELL, THAT WENT WELL, OLD MAN," Theo said. "Smooth with the ladies, I can see that now. I should have taken lessons."

Ash groped for the inkpot, then remembered it was gone. He needed to install an entire line of them.

He could see the flash of the lantern being lit and debated returning to his seat or fleeing as Miss Chris had. Humiliation was a concept he was becoming all too well-acquainted with, and he despised it. "You must have the ears of a dog," he said as witheringly as he was able. "That's a solid door, and you should know better than to listen."

"That was Celeste. The women claim this house sits on some kind of ley line that enhances their gifts. Celeste thought she heard pain and insisted that someone listen. Erran devised a contraption that he could press against the door, and we took turns. We caught enough."

"Ley line," Ash said in disgust, sinking back to his chair. "The women are all about in their heads. I hope they've gone to assure Miss Townsend that she's safe here. Erran, what's the penalty for harboring an heiress against her executor's will?"

"Assuming she's over twenty-one, none that I know of," his less talkative brother asserted with a verbal shrug. "Single women above the age of consent have far more freedom than married ones."

"It's just not done," Theo countered. "Women belong with their families until they marry."

Both Ash and Erran snorted at this simplicity.

"Miss Townsend is an heiress and a *lady*," Theo, the astronomer and idealist, argued. "And since Aster is usually correct, we must assume she's also a relation to the duke of Sommersville. The scandal will be immense. You'll have Birchcroft and probably Grey here as soon as it becomes known that you're keeping her against her family's will. We cannot just usurp her without ruining her reputation as well as yours, Dunc. Not that you need to do much more to prove you're as mad as a hatter."

"Fine, then. If she won't marry me, how do we keep her?" Ash didn't intend to give up, but the argument deflected his brothers from digging any deeper into his wounded pride.

Miss Townsend expected him to *grovel*.

He wasn't accustomed to not getting what he wanted. Admittedly, he'd not wanted any other woman enough to consult her about her preferences. His Miss Chris wanted *independence*? He ought to let her have it and good riddance, but he was a fighter. He needed her—just as she needed him, he was convinced.

Perhaps courting her would suffice, except he couldn't seek her out if she hid in her room. Groping his way upstairs and hunting her chamber would lead to many things, but groveling or courting weren't among them.

"We'll send someone to locate her properties," Erran concluded. "Aster can find a companion to go with her. And we may need to write the duke."

"Like hell. We don't need to involve Sommersville in this too." Ashford had no intention of letting a duke come between him and Miss Townsend when he was perfectly capable of handling this on his own. Did they think blindness had made an idiot of him?

He stood and crossed the study to his chamber door. Miss Christie *Townsend* wasn't going anywhere unless he went with her. A man as desperate as her stepfather could find many ways to coerce her. "Jones!" he hollered at his valet. "I need dinner clothes."

"My lord, yes, of course," his much-maligned valet agreed, appearing like a magic genie. Since Ash hadn't bothered dressing for dinner in months, the man sounded over-eager. "Are we expecting special guests?"

"I am going courting. Just make me presentable." Now that he'd made up his mind, Ash didn't intend to waste a minute. All he had to do was persuade the stubborn female out of hiding. "Let the cook know I'm going out," he added, with malicious intent.

After all, Miss Townsend knew he was as much of a liar as she was.

Fifteen

"MISS TOWNSEND, WE MUST TALK. Open the door, please."

Through her fury, fear, and humiliation, Harriet Christie recognized Celeste Ives' captivating Jamaican lilt. Even though the last thing in the world she wanted was to face the Malcolm ladies, she opened the door. As she did so, she realized with a wince that she'd fallen victim to the lady's magical *gift* for compulsion. It was too late to slam and lock the panel.

Besides, she desperately needed to talk.

Preferably, she needed to talk with someone who wasn't an arrogant, obnoxious tyrant. Until a few weeks ago, she could have sworn she didn't have a temper, but since coming here . . . Anger was apparently contagious. Clutching her elbows, she paced as the prescient Lady Aster and voice-compelling Mrs. Ives bustled in.

They filled the narrow chamber with petticoats. Short, rounded Lady Aster wore a gown that shimmered with blues and greens and made her fiery copper curls gleam like a flame burning from her excess energy. The more sedate Mrs. Ives settled gracefully on a chair. She was tall, slender, and wore a delicate apricot gown that enhanced her bronze coloring and sleek dark hair. Christie was painfully aware of her towering plainness beside the gorgeous Ives wives. For a change, she was too angry and confused to care.

"It's quite amazing," Lady Aster said, lighting a lamp without permission and opening her satchel of charts. "I had started on your chart using the time and birth place you gave me, and it seemed oddly familiar. And none of the signs were lining up as they should. A stubborn Taurus, maybe, but combined with a strong Leo moon—that does not compute into a meek companion. You would bite the head off any silly chit who crossed you."

"I've never bitten the head off anyone," Christie said irritably, sitting on the bed so her guests could have the chairs. "Not until I came here, at least."

"You certainly bit off Ash's," Lady Aster said, laughing.

"That's this house," Mrs. Ives said soothingly. "It enhances our gifts, I've discovered. I used to use my voice simply to charm people into giving me pretty dresses or dolls. Now I can *hear* emotion in voices and persuade people to do what they need to do. I'd never so much as raised my voice until we came here, and now I've even caused a riot!"

"You still don't raise your voice. It's your persuasion that works. The demonstration at the factory was a peaceful one and turned out particularly well," Lady Aster said, pinning a chart to the wall. "The workers were all women and children, and they were being horribly mistreated. Celeste persuaded them to walk out and refuse to return until management agreed to shorten their hours so they could see daylight occasionally. It was a rural village, with very few workers available. The company had no choice. They quickly capitulated and had to raise wages and allow time off for childbearing."

"Once people act together for the common good, they can accomplish great things," Mrs. Ives explained. "I didn't do anything. The women did it all."

"Leadership is necessary." Lady Aster pounded the final tack in her chart with an air of satisfaction. "And Miss Harriet Christie *Russell* Townsend has buckets of that quality in her chart."

If her head hadn't already been spinning, Christie thought it might be on backwards now, after this inexplicable and excited chatter. They weren't angry that she'd lied? That she'd brought a furious Townsend into the house? "I have never led anyone, anywhere, ever," she protested.

YOU HAVEN'T HAD THE OPPORTUNITY, the elderly voice in her head said reassuringly. AND YOU'RE CERTAINLY LEADING MY GRANDSON A MERRY CHASE!

Harriet didn't trust the voices. She'd have to declare herself lunatic if she did. She rubbed her brow and tried to straighten her thoughts.

"Because the conditions weren't right," Lady Aster said, echoing the voice. She held up the lamp and pointed at the chart. "But the sun and Jupiter are now in your ascendant, which gives you the accomplishment, fame, and wisdom to manage whatever happens next. The moon was there last week, giving you the boldness necessary to walk away from your past. And of course, here is Venus coming up on the part of marriage. With Scorpio rising . . . you are perfect for Ashford! He really needed a Malcolm. I can't imagine how I was so blind."

"A Malcolm?" both Christie and Celeste asked, although Christie thought her question might be different from the other lady's. "What is a Malcolm?" she clarified. Moira had tried to explain, but her tale was worse than anything Christie could make up.

"A family of witches," Celeste said with a laugh, verifying Moira's explanation. "Or Druids, depending on which aunt one asks."

"A family of women with different abilities," Lady Aster corrected. "Ones who can trace their ancestry through oral history. Our early journals are written accountings of stories repeated for generations."

"Different *abilities*? I think you mistake me." Christie examined the chart on the wall but could make neither heads nor tails of it. "I can sew, but that's about the only ability I possess. Painting and music are beyond me."

Lady Aster removed a thick tome from her satchel. "Did your mother keep journals?"

Christie tilted her head to admire a delicately tinted lion claiming a large area of the circle chart. "She died when I was twelve and was ill for a long time before that. I believe she wrote in a journal when she was feeling well enough."

She had not thought of that for a long time. She had a sudden desire to run home and look for that book of her mother's words.

"Did she encourage you to write also?" Celeste asked. "Both my parents did, and it turns out they both have Malcolm roots. It's all quite fascinating once you learn about it. We're sisters through the blood."

"I doubt writing in journals means we're related," Christie said prosaically, returning to sit on the bed.

The voice in her head cackled in delight.

"It is a common pastime," Christie continue doggedly, ignoring the voice. "I kept one for a while, but my life was too boring, and I lost interest. Just having you to talk with is exciting to me."

"If Ashford has aught to do with it, we will all become quite close, so we may as well use our names and not our titles. Do you prefer to be called Harriet or Christie?" Lady Aster asked. "I am actually named Azenor, but my friends and family call me Aster. And Celeste really cannot be called anything else. Her voice is beyond celestial."

"No one has ever asked how I would like to be called," Harriet Christie said. "I do not exactly feel like a Christie—except when I'm acting completely out of character. It was my grandmother's maiden name. Ashford calls me Miss Chris. Maybe I could be Chris."

"The person who came to us was bold and called Christie. Let's try Christie and see if you don't grow into it." Aster found the place she wanted in the book she was studying. She pointed at a page. "Here's your family. Your father's name was Russell, was it not? And your mother's maiden name was Winchester? Did your mother choose your name?"

"I was told the girls in my mother's family were always named some variation of Christina and the boys were named Harry. Apparently, my father agreed to calling me after both, since *Christie* also honored his mother. I don't know if they knew then that they'd not have another child." The memory brought sadness.

"Yes," Aster said in satisfaction. "That's the family I'm thinking of. The Winchesters are related to the duke of Sommersville. The first Malcolm in the duke's family, several generations ago, was named Christina. Her son was a gifted healer. You'll find their journals in Wystan."

Duke? Healer? Harriet—*Christie*—opened her mouth, but nothing came out. Her spinning head had apparently fallen off.

"You offer too much at once, Aster," Celeste protested. "You always knew who you were, but those of us who had no notion need time to adjust."

"I believe the Winchesters and Russells were distant cousins," Aster continued, "so it's possible Christie has several lines of Malcolm blood, as you do. It's not so very uncommon given the intermingling at our level of society. But the branches are growing in many directions, so it's difficult following the genealogy."

"Family I do not know and who do not acknowledge me are less than useful," Christie said. "Once my father died, my mother and I lived in rural obscurity. I cannot remember any of my mother's family visiting after she married Townsend."

Aster flipped pages in the book she'd produced from her satchel and found what she wanted. "Viscount Russell was an only son. His parents died shortly after your father did. A cousin inherited the title and estate—he may not even know of your existence."

"He does," Harriet said with a shrug. "We choose not communicate."

Undeterred, Aster continued. "On your maternal side, the current duke of Sommersville prefers his northern estate and seldom comes to town. He was a famed physician in his day—quite possibly a Malcolm ability. Men are unfortunately erratic in keeping up with family. So if your mother's family was not the visiting type, and haven't asked him for anything, then he no doubt assumes all the various cousins are fine."

"Which we were," Christie said with a shrug. "My mother was too ill to travel or consort with dukes, but she never lacked for anything."

"But the relationship to a duke makes you perfect for Ashford," Aster declared. "We won't tell him about the Malcolm connection; it will only annoy him. And if you exhibit no unusual abilities, he cannot mock you as he does us."

"He mocks, but he listens," Celeste corrected. "The man is a deep well with a boiling stew at the bottom. One never quite knows what will come out next."

He'd certainly mock if he knew she heard his great-grandmother in her head! Besides, she wasn't marrying a bully.

"Has he always been that way?" Christie asked, hoping against hope that things might be different. "It seems to me he's festering with frustration at his inability to act on many, many things. If he does not find some outlet soon, he will turn explosive."

"You understand him very well already," Celeste said in approval. "Most women would merely see the trappings of wealth and power and not understand what he has lost. To understand him as well as you do, you must have a latent gift you simply don't recognize."

"I would love to have a gift of any kind," Christie said in despair, wondering if she must exhibit eccentricity to fit in. Telling them she heard voices wasn't a *gift,* but it would be eccentric. Ashford would hate it though. And why should she care if he hated her voices?

PERHAPS WAIT, the voice recommended judiciously. THESE MODERN WOMEN DON'T BELIEVE IN GHOSTS.

Ghosts? If she told them she heard ghosts as well as voices in her head, they'd lock her in Bedlam. Appalled, Christie hurried to reassure the ladies. "At the risk of being repetitious, I am *not* special. I am an overlarge, boring, nonentity who has never met her very distant, noble relations. I am amazed that Ashford has not thrown me in the street. Perhaps I'm simply a new toy that he will tire of when a more exciting prospect comes along."

The voice cackled in delight again.

"Since I disagree with your basic assumptions that you are overlarge or boring, I must also question the rest of your argument. For the sake of the kingdom, I think we must take the risk that you are what Ashford needs," Aster said. "Surely you understand the desperate need for reform."

The petite lady didn't think Christie was overlarge? Or boring? She'd had those notions beaten into her head for so long, she didn't trust a second opinion. She couldn't go past that disbelief to reach the even larger one of Ashford needing anything at all, much less a woman with voices in her head. It would be lovely to be needed and useful, but independence was a far more achievable goal.

A rap at the door interrupted. Celeste opened it to a maid who conveyed her message in a whisper.

"Excellent, thank you. We'll be ready." Celeste closed the door and announced, "Ashford is dressing for dinner and claiming he is going out."

"Why would he say that?" Christie asked in annoyance. "He won't go out. He refuses to be seen as less than perfect, and the more he stays hidden, the less he will go out. It's not healthy."

She looked up when both of her chatty companions stayed silent. They stared at her as if she'd turned into a unicorn. "What?" she asked. "Does one not call a marquess a liar or a hermit?"

"Your understanding of his behavior is quite extraordinary," Aster said. "If he's actually staying in, let's surprise him and appear in our most elegant attire."

Christie laughed. "If anything, he knows *you* too well and that is just what he's expecting. I have no elegant attire. I will remain here."

"The plot thickens," Celeste said with a trill of laughter. "He's trying to trick *you* into coming down! You do not actually need visible elegance, you know, since he cannot see you. You need *sensual* elegance—a nice perfume, a velvet wrap, your hair . . . Why do you hide your hair under that dreadful cap?"

Christie yanked off the cap and admired the rosettes and frilly lace. "Because it's pretty and I am not."

Both women shook their heads in combined exasperation. Christie could *feel* their incredulity. Nervously, she ran her hand over her stringy mop, tugged back in an uneven bun. "What?"

Celeste smiled. "Do you really believe we all climb out of bed looking perfect? Very few people are actually beautiful. Most of us learn to make the best of what we have."

"Don't you have a ladies' maid we can send for? You have lovely gold locks. They just need trimming and arranging."

"I sent my maid to stay with her family for a while. She simply braids my hair in the evening, though. I don't go anywhere, so there is not much need for fancy." Beneath their scrutiny, Christie started to feel like a bug under glass. She had nothing that could be made the *best of*.

Celeste removed Christie's hair pins. "We will tell Ashford it is a glorious pale yellow gold with strands of ivory and bronze. Aster, do you know if we have scissors and a curling tong anywhere?"

"I am not going down to dinner if he's dressing and pretending he's going out," Christie protested, brushing Celeste away from her hair. "He's looking for trouble."

"And we're here to provide it," Aster said cheerfully. "You said yourself that he is bored and it is unhealthy for him to stay inside. For the fate of a nation, we must keep Ashford entertained. Have you not noticed that his tantrums disappear when you're around? He actually smiled earlier. You are the key."

"I am not the key to anything! I *yell* at him!" But Christie felt their sincerity. How could she say no if there was any chance she might be allowed to stay and help the marquess recover? And she desperately wished to be friends with these women.

Now that Townsend knew where she was . . . Did she need to run? Would it be better for Ashford . . . and thus the kingdom . . . if she stayed?

Perhaps she could lead Ashford a merry chase—as the *ghost* claimed. She must be running mad. And he was very bored. Two such combustible elements were an explosion waiting to happen. But perhaps . . . just perhaps . . . she could persuade him out and about again. At which point, he would tire of her, and she would be free to go home—to Dorset.

She could spend the rest of her life on the wonderful memories of a dashing marquess following her through London.

Sixteen

SITTING BEHIND HIS DESK, Ash heard the women descend, chattering like birds escaped from a cage. With grim satisfaction, he could tell that Christie was among them. She'd freshened her perfume, and his unruly cock rose to attention as they passed the open door of his study on the way to the dining room.

His fury now was as much anxiety as anger, which only served to make him more determined. As long as he was making an ass of himself, he might as well satisfy his curiosity. "Is Miss Townsend still wearing her cap?"

Theo was closest to the doorway and replied, "No, but the sconces don't give enough light to tell a great deal. We really need gas lighting in here."

"*I* don't," Ash said. "Wait until I am elsewhere to install it. You can describe her once we join them."

"Not likely," Erran said. "Theo could describe a moon on the other side of the universe better than he could describe his own wife. Let the women do it."

"I'm starving," Theo said without disputing Erran's claim. "May we join them now? Do you think they will all run screaming, from your presence?"

"Of course not." Ash shoved Theo into the corridor, out of his way. "It's just that Miss Townsend has the irritating habit of staying upstairs when I am present."

"That may be because she's a proper lady," Erran observed. "And you no doubt have done something to distress her."

He'd kissed her. And he would kiss her again, because she liked it and deserved to be kissed. His brothers weren't stupid. They'd know that. Ash concentrated on entering the dining room without stumbling over chairs or footmen. Between his leg and his eyes, he was half the man he'd been.

How the devil could a blind man court a lady? For courting was apparently the road his lust was leading him down.

Ash followed his nose to Christie. She was still standing, as were the other ladies, waiting for the footmen to seat them. He grasped her chair back and held it for her. "I am out of practice, Miss

Townsend," he murmured, delighted that she stood tall enough for him to reach her ear without burying his nose in her hair. "But I believe I can manage chair shifting."

"Thank you, my lord," she said stiffly. He could sense her lowering slowly so he had time to arrange the chair beneath her petticoats.

His sisters-in-law had had the sense to sit her beside his place at the table, on his good side. Ash claimed his seat with one hand while pretending to balance by placing the other on Miss Townsend's shoulder.

She wore a damned shawl. It was thin, and he could feel her shoulder beneath it, but he had anticipated—had spent this last half hour thinking about—finally touching warm flesh. Sulking, he took the chair.

"I am glad you could come to the table tonight," he said. He was accustomed to watching for smiles and flirtatious looks to determine a woman's reactions to him. Now, he was forced to listen to both words and intonations to judge his success or failure.

"It would be rude of me to ignore the ladies' requests," she said primly. "You should entertain more often."

"You wouldn't come down for strangers for fear of being recognized," he argued. "That ridiculousness must stop."

"Miss Townsend is your guest, Ashford," Aster said from across the table. "Quit badgering her. Your valet has outdone himself this evening. Is that a new waistcoat? The indigo almost matches Miss Townsend's eyes."

Wickedly clever woman, she'd just told him that Christie had dark blue eyes! One more detail to add to the image he pieced together. The glittering chandelier allowed him to see enough movement to know she bent her head.

"Do I look grand to you, Miss Chris ?" he asked, embarrassing her further by using the twins' version of her given name, even though he now knew her real one. "I dare not offend my valet or he could dress me in a clown suit, and I would not know."

"Yes, you would," she retorted, although she kept her voice low. "You know how your clothes fit on you, and you know you look good in them. Is that the flattery you seek?"

Actually, it was, he realized. How far would honesty take him? "I cannot see admiration or disgust in your eyes, so I must force you to speak," he admitted. "It would also help if my useless relations would tell me how splendid you look."

"Why?" she demanded. "I will never be more than plain, and even when you are old and gray, you will always look distinguished. I thought you said looks don't matter."

"But my curiosity is never ending. Indigo eyes are not plain," he said.

"Miss Townsend has lovely honey-gold hair, my lord," Aster said in that voice he assumed meant she had a twinkle in her eye. "It's streaked with lighter strands and is quite fetching."

Ash had never seen Theo's wife, but her behavior described her best as a mischief-maker.

"Indigo eyes and honey hair is not boring either," he declared, reaching to test that the lady's hair was actually uncovered for a change. His hand encountered a delightful wisp of curl. "I shall picture you as a proud Viking goddess."

Since she did not strike him, he explored her coiffure, discovering she'd woven it into multiple small braids and wore it in a complicated knot at her nape. Just touching roused his unruly lower parts.

"Have you seen any Viking goddesses lately?" Miss Chris asked dryly.

"Only in my head, which is rather where I live these days," he countered in the same tone.

"You have stacks of invitations on your desk. You could charm women all over London if you so desired," Celeste said in her deceptively charming Jamaican lilt.

"I have already charmed women all over London," Ash answered with a shrug, releasing Miss Christie's hair to ease her discomfort. "The widows and bored wives are particularly welcoming. That pastime grew stale with the passing of youth."

He turned his concentration on the beef consommé set in front of him. He almost wished for a napkin tucked into his neckcloth. Perhaps someday he would become accustomed to going about with food stains on his linen as Theo did.

"You are not old!" Miss Townsend said in shock. "You are in the prime of life. You just grow cynical."

"For that acute observation, I will not molest you again until after dinner."

Theo kicked him under the table. "For a rake, you have a rotten notion of courtship."

"On the contrary." Ash sipped his soup, sensing his guest's nervous stiffness. "My lady wouldn't believe me if I told her she has the voice of angels and the wisdom of the ages. I have to *show* her that she is more perceptive than anyone else at this table."

"We've noticed her perceptiveness," Aster said speculatively. "One would think Miss Townsend knew you for much longer than she has."

"Obviously, we are mates of the soul and understand each other, if I can only persuade her to admit it. A little pepper, my dear? The broth is a trifle bland." He gestured for a servant without waiting for her reply.

"*Pepper* is his way of telling me I am more interesting when I argue with him," his intelligent lady explained, allowing the footman to add pepper. "I am assuming this means Ashford is uncomfortable with softer emotions and would rather be disagreeable."

Even though he couldn't see her, Ash turned an admiring glance on her. "You see? Tell me one other fashionable miss who could make that leap of judgment."

He was actually enjoying himself, and he thought perhaps Miss Chris was too, although she was undoubtedly loathe to admit it. Caged animals did not always know how to behave when released from captivity—and Townsend had obviously kept her magnificent spirit caged in their tiny village too long.

By the time the servants had refilled their glasses several times, the atmosphere at the table had relaxed into one of more comfortable familiarity. Miss Christie had, for the most part, ignored Ash's fumbling with the food delivered to his plate already cut. She rescued his glass a time or two, but that was no more than anyone else would do in the course of an animated conversation.

He didn't detect pity or distaste in her voice, just justifiable annoyance. Once upon a time, he would have anticipated fawning attention, but Miss Chris wouldn't give him that either, even if he'd been whole. For the first time, he understood it might be possible to feel equal to a woman. They were both handicapped in their own ways—she by her lack of experience and uncertainty. But he would swear that Miss Chris was as strong as he in intelligence and fortitude. Amazing!

Of course, they were both adept liars. Since he'd never before given matrimony much thought, Ash wasn't entirely certain if that was good or bad.

By the time the ladies departed in a rustle of skirts and petticoats after dinner, he had made up his mind. He sat back with his brandy and regarded his unseen brothers. "I am asking her to marry me," he told them. "A special license and quickly, so Townsend does not have time to rouse all London against me."

"She has yet to accept, you coxcomb." Theo clinked his glass against his plate in setting it down. "She is in a precarious position. Opportuning her now is not the act of a gentleman."

"We suit," Ash said implacably. "We don't have time for the usual foolishness. Are you upset because you thought your son would inherit and now I may yet have the opportunity to produce a legitimate heir?"

Theo roared in laughter and Erran joined in with snickers.

"As if either of us want anything to do with manipulating Parliament and running a kingdom," Theo said with genuine amusement. "If Miss Townsend is the general who will run your affairs for you, I will tie her up and produce the vicar."

"But if she turns into a placid cow and retires to the country, what will you do?" Erran asked, ever the pragmatic lawyer.

Even knowing that's what Miss Christie had done all her life and what she wished to do now, Ash shrugged. "I'll ask her preferences." He shoved back his chair.

"And then you'll ignore them," Theo said. "That's what *you* do."

"That's how things get done." Ash flung down his napkin and counted the steps to the doorway.

Seventeen

THE NEXT MORNING, AFTER THE MAID brought a summons from Ashford, Christie debated not leaving bed. Then she wondered if she might crawl out a window and run.

Recognizing the impossibility of either feat, she lay there examining the cause of her distress. The intimidatingly grand and arrogant Duncan, Marquess of Ashford, Earl of Ives and Wystan, terrified—and fascinated—her.

He had looked magnificent at dinner last night, utterly striking in black and white. His evening coat and gleaming linen had clung like a second skin to shoulders and chest. He was so broad, she could even imagine her large frame settling comfortably against him. She *wanted* those powerful arms around her. She'd sat next to him practically aching with the need for his kiss . . . and more.

She was a shameless hussy, but Ashford was almost godlike in his superiority to all other men. Oh, of course, his brothers were good looking and capable and all that . . . they simply weren't Ashford.

And it wasn't just the marquess's magnificent exterior that frightened her, she admitted. His quick intelligence and instinctive ability to hone in on others' weaknesses and strengths were almost supernatural.

Supernatural. That was laughable considering the pragmatic disposition of the Ives men she'd met. Still, if she was to believe in the supernatural, it was far more likely that Ashford had weird abilities than that *she* possessed any useful *gifts.* Ashford had Malcolm blood in his veins, too, and his ability to manipulate was positively uncanny.

"He scares me," she told the room's spirits. "He will make me do whatever he wants, without giving me time to think about it."

THEN DECIDE WHAT YOU WANT FIRST, the voice in her head responded. *TAKE THE LEAD.*

Take the lead, indeed!

Harriet had retired to hide in her room last night after dinner, before the marquess could hunt her down. She would be fortunate to climb out of bed.

Christie would have to stand strong against Ashford's domineering personality—especially if she wanted her independence.

Taking the *lead*—well, that was beyond imagination. Ashford had already done that by summoning her. She could not ignore his command if she wished to stay in his house. Which was why she was considering running.

HE NEEDS YOU, the voice said encouragingly.

That foolishness persuaded her out of bed and into clothes, at least. She would really like to be needed by someone, although the marquess had everything and needed no one. She wasn't entirely certain it was a good thing that this house—or it's ghostly occupants—spoke to her as no other had.

Hoping for some insight that might allow her to stay, she anxiously adjusted her silk shawl over her simple day dress, took a second look at her braided hair in the mirror, took a deep breath, and descended the stairs.

To her surprise, the marquess was waiting at his study door instead of hiding behind his desk. He caught her hand, drew her inside, and turned the key.

"That is most improper, my lord," she scolded, turning to release the lock.

He caught her other hand before she could unfasten the door. "I will heave out my entire family and all the servants if we don't have a little privacy. Leave it be." He led her unerringly to a chair and held her hand until she was seated.

Neither of them wore gloves. The contact was exhilarating, catching her by surprise and leaving her even more breathless than before. He was looking particularly aristocratic this morning in a dark blue coat with a casual white neckcloth above his gray waistcoat.

When he gracefully kneeled down on one tightly-trousered gray knee, she nearly keeled over in shock.

"Miss Townsend, I think you are aware of my feelings for you. Your uncommon good sense, modesty, patience, and humor are far more than I merit. But I believe I can offer you the position in society that you deserve, and that we will suit well in all respects. Would you do me the very great honor of becoming my wife?"

While she attempted to catch her breath, he produced a velvet cloth from his coat pocket and unfolded it, revealing a beautiful dark sapphire ring surrounded by glittering diamonds.

"My lord," she whispered, in such astonishment that she was barely able to find her tongue. The magnificent marquess . . . on his knees, in front of *her* . . . She had never ever dreamed of such a fairy-tale scene in all her lonely existence.

And the ghosts expected her to take the lead with a man of action like this? She was in well over her head.

He couldn't see her expression and waited anxiously for her reply, while balancing on his damaged leg. She had to give him an answer *now* and not let him believe she was a foolish miss who would run from his scarred visage. She couldn't dither for long. She had to say *something*.

She longed to say yes, to have him slip that ring on her finger . . . and she would make him a laughingstock of a certainty if she did. He was being honorable for a change. How could she risk his anger if he discovered she was no more than a plain, foolish woman with voices in her head and that he'd thrown his life away?

Besides, independence was far preferable to being bullied or ignored for the rest of her life, her Christie persona thought.

She respected the marquess too much to humiliate him by saying yes, but she wanted what he offered too much to say no. That left with no idea what to say.

"Just say yes, Miss Chris," he said with a hint of his usual impatience and a touch of humor. "Whatever you are mulling around in your over-cautious head can be conquered. Tell me there is someone else, tell me you could never marry a monster, and I will step back and pretend this never happened. But I'm convinced you are the only woman in the world who will be honest with me, and this is one lie you will not speak."

"You are not a *monster*," she said in horror, finding it hard to believe that this confident man hid the same sorts of insidious demons as she did. "That is beyond ludicrous. And if I had Lady Aster's confidence and connections, or even Celeste's beauty and charm, I would happily say yes. But I possess none of those essential qualities. You deserve better, my lord," she said with sadness.

"You have all those qualities and more," he corrected, sliding the ring on her finger. "So I will take that as a yes. I detest formality and cannot have my wife calling me *my lord*. You must call me Duncan or Ash, as the others do. Kiss me, my dear."

Frozen in shock, she wanted to protest. She wanted to kiss him. She wanted to thank him for the most amazing moment of her life. But she was too speechless to manage any of this or the rejection she *ought* to offer.

Instead, she dropped from the chair to kneel with him in some vague hope of convincing him from his level. Besides, she was too humbled by his position to let him remain there alone.

Ashford caught her easily, taking her in his strong arms and claiming her as if she'd actually said yes.

And his kiss . . . she sank into his kiss with all the passion of her lonely heart. Closing her eyes, she let this intimate connection draw her in. He smelled of a masculine soap that tingled all her senses. She had to stroke his jaw to test that his usual dark beard shadow had just been shaved. His kiss deepened and his arms tightened with her caress, and she relished the press of her softness against his hard chest.

She savored the desire and triumph he emanated, just as if he thought he held the most ravishing woman in the world. If she pretended she was what he needed, she could have this exciting man for her own. The possibility shivered through her.

In his arms, with his mouth claiming hers, she could believe anything. If the most desirable man in the world kissed her like this, then she must be dashing and enchanting and all those things she longed to be. She curled her arms around his neck, let the pretense take over, and learned to ravish his mouth as he did hers.

His kisses did not lie. He *wanted* her. *Her*, literally the biggest wall flower in society. Impossible, ridiculous tears of joy rolled down her cheeks, and her lonely heart overruled her head for just this instant. Every woman deserved to live a dream for a moment or two.

"Special license," he gasped, breaking away and cupping her breasts while pressing kisses on her cheek. "I cannot wait another night."

She didn't want reality intruding. She didn't want to make monumental decisions. She wished to cling to this marvelous moment. She drew his head down again and moaned as the heat of his hands mixed with the hungry press of his mouth on hers.

Ashford tumbled her to the floor as if they were two ill-bred servants. He sprawled his great masculine length on top of her so she knew exactly how small—and *strong*—he made her feel. Excitement coursed through her as he parted the wisps of fabric over her breasts and bent eager kisses to her bare skin.

"I'll take you right here if you don't stop me soon," he groaned. "I am trying to be proper for a change. My wife deserves that respect."

She only wanted sensation and for the moment to never end. But a knock at the door warned this tiny slice of heaven had to stop.

Ashford groaned, pressed his big body into hers, and nibbled her neck. "Go away," he shouted at the door.

"Not likely," Pascoe Ives shouted back, still knocking.

The marquess muttered creative obscenities. He propped himself on one elbow and ran the other hand over her breasts and waist. "I want to *see* you," he said in frustration.

"I want many things too, my lord," she said ruefully. "We must be thankful for those we have, I believe."

He actually smiled, a beautiful smile that wrenched the heart right from her chest as she tried to push him away.

"Ash," he corrected. "And now that I have you, I shall be thankful." He pressed another kiss to her cheek and rolled off her with more dignity than she managed in trying to return to her feet.

"You do not have me," Christie said fretfully. So much for being strong and leading the way. She hastily covered her disarranged bodice with her shawl.

"Dammit, Pascoe, go find someone to give you tea," he shouted at his visitor.

"I want whiskey, and I want it now!" his uncle called back.

"It's too early for alcohol," Ashford yelled at the door while helping her to her feet, then whispered for her ears alone, "You will have no choice if Pascoe finds you in here. Slip into my room and out that way after the coast is clear. Or better yet, wait there for me." This last he said in a decidedly lascivious tone.

She ran for the connecting door to his chamber as soon as he released her. She checked over her shoulder to be certain he was able to find the door alone. She shouldn't have bothered. Ashford was straightening his coat and dusting himself off as if he could actually see what he'd done to his impeccable tailoring.

She nearly swooned at the sight. She really was a goosecap. She slipped into his bedchamber and left the door slightly ajar, just in case he might need her. She wanted to be needed—another sign that she was surely demented.

"What the devil brings you here at this hour, demanding whiskey?" the marquess asked, unlocking the door and letting in his uncle.

Christie ducked back out of sight. She knew she should leave, but she couldn't help studying the big bed that had been set up for Ashford's use. This wasn't meant to be a master suite, by any means, but if they married . . .

A man who couldn't see how plain she was . . .

She swallowed hard and listened to the men on the other side.

"You were right," Pascoe Ives said, clinking the crystal decanter.

She peered through the crack to watch.

Ashford returned to his seat behind the desk, showing little sign of what they'd just been doing beyond a slightly askew neckcloth. "Aren't I always right?" he asked.

Pascoe raised his glass. "At least when you're being cynical. Lansdowne has land in Dorset that abuts your heiress's acres. He and Townsend have plans to enclose both properties and raise sheep."

Christie covered her gasp with her hand and remained frozen where she was. She thought maybe Ashford knew she hadn't left, because he looked directly at her, even though she was hidden behind the door.

Her stepfather meant to enclose *her* land? She might be ignorant, but even she knew what that meant—dozens or more families would lose their homes and their only means of making a living. Little children, who now lived in sweet little cottages with gardens out back, would be on the street, forced to go north and work in the manufactories—like the crippled servants Lady Ashford hired.

"Tell me Lansdowne is selling Townsend the sheep from his Northumberland estates," the marquess said, drumming his fingers on the desk. "And that Caldwell and Montfort have both agreed to buy into this monumental stupidity. Enclosures and sheep are not cheap, and none of them have cash."

"Damn, but you're good. How do you know that? You've scarcely given me time to discover details. I've set men to hunting down the investors, but from what little I've put together—it's likely fraud, on Lansdowne's part, at the very least. I have evidence that he's done this before. In the last case, he told the bank he had a thousand acres of land for grazing a thousand sheep—or whatever the number was—and that he needed funds to enclose the land." Fortified by the whiskey, Pascoe took a seat.

"He assembled a consortium of landowners, then took the consortium's deeds to the bank. The bank lent whatever he asked for building fences," Ashford continued for him, tossing an empty inkpot back and forth.

Christie frowned. She'd removed the spilled inkpot after yesterday's flinging incident. Where had he found this one?

She studied Ashford's desk through the crack. While she'd dithered and hidden in her room, he'd set his uncle to investigating her stepfather. And then he had somehow collected an entire array of inkpots—cut glass, crystal, painted metals of some sort, a dozen or more! He must have set servants hunting through every shop in town.

He'd lined the pots up in a neat row across the desk. She prayed he had not yet filled them with ink.

She was thinking of anything but the enormity of the plot wicked men could devise to rob each other. Or the decision he was forcing her to make.

"Lansdowne apparently has found some source of funds stupid or crooked enough to lend him money recently, yes. If he follows his usual path, he will put the proceeds into his own account, go to another source, show he has funds and property, and borrow the funds for sheep. Then he can take the sheep purchase to another source and borrow against them, and so on."

"While his investors are doing what?" Ashford asked with interest.

"Going bankrupt, eventually, as most of Lansdowne's investors do. He'll send them some sheep, hire a few laborers for the fences, show progress, but his hand is on the purse. Next, he'll start selling shares in his new woolen mill to be provided by his nonexistent sheep. The only fleecing that will be done is to his investors."

"Brilliant mind, heart of coal," Ashford said disparagingly. "Will we be able to save Miss Townsend's property from being mortgaged or enclosed? I don't have much sympathy for the others."

He might not be concerned by the other investors, but Christie was concerned about the villagers she had never met. She had neglected them because she'd foolishly thought her stepfather understood property management better than she did!

How could she have been so naïve? Men were no smarter or better informed than she could be, if she only asserted herself! Why should she be the polite, well-behaved miss while men trampled all over her? She was practically shaking with fury—at herself.

"Erran is looking into whether Townsend has the right to mortgage the trust's lands, but as executor, he probably does," Pascoe concluded. "They have not yet done anything illegal, and once they are done, it will be nigh impossible to know who to blame for the disaster."

"Or they could conceivably make money, but Lansdowne will siphon it off before anyone knows of it. I suppose I should warn the parties concerned, although they'll not appreciate the information and will no doubt ignore me. Rumors of my madness will escalate," Ashford said with his usual matter-of-fact pessimism.

"I'll put together the figures when I have copies of documents and written evidence from previous investors," Pascoe said, rising. "I'll let you know the instant I have word that he has formed another consortium. You can decide how to deal with it."

Ashford frowned. "I'll not be satisfied until Lansdowne is behind bars."

"He's an earl. It's unlikely," Pascoe warned. "Destroy his sources of cash, and you'll destroy him just as well."

Ashford set aside the ceramic inkpot he'd been tossing and saluted his advisor as Pascoe let himself out. Then he rose and approached the door where Christie waited.

"Do you have any doubt now about the wisdom of taking charge of your own affairs?" he asked, taking her in his arms again as if she'd never left them.

"No, I have no doubt about taking charge. That doesn't mean I don't have a dozen different doubts." She shoved away, determined to be in charge of her entire life, and not just the property.

Decide what you want, the voice had said. Taking a deep breath, she made her decision. "If we are to wed, I wish you to take me into society and show that you are not ashamed of me, as Townsend was."

Eighteen

TAKE HER INTO SOCIETY? Walk out in public for all to see his helplessness? He nearly panicked until he took in the rest of her statement, and then his fury erupted.

"What the *devil* does that mean?" Ash tried not to roar as his bride-to-be shoved from his arms and seemed prepared to flee. He grabbed for her but missed.

"What does what mean?" she asked in puzzlement, opening the study door as if they'd just been working on correspondence.

"That remark about being *ashamed* of you." He wanted to shout and stomp and shake whoever had put that inane notion in her head. "Why the devil would I be ashamed of you? Are you purple and missing your nose?" He stalked her to check her nose.

He heard her skirts rustle as she dodged him and slapped away his questing hand.

"Purple, indeed! Because I have the appearance of a dowdy rural nonentity, as I've tried to explain to you. It will look as if you are taking your housekeeper into society. Your friends will laugh behind your back. I expect you'll change your mind swiftly after that. I've spent my entire life living in the shadows, and I don't intend to do so for anyone ever again."

"That sounds like a declaration of war," he protested. "I don't give a damn what my so-called friends say."

"If you don't, then there is no reason for you not to leave the house. Shall I go through your invitations?" she asked, the taunt in her voice.

"I don't leave the house because I cannot see!" he roared. "It has nothing to do with what people think."

"Being blind doesn't stop you from living your life in here, in the safety of your family. You are afraid people will point and laugh if you stumble in public."

She patted his arm. "As you manifestly are not, my lord, of course, why did I not see that? So we are at an impasse. I am hampered by being a single female and cannot be introduced to society on my own. Without you, I am nothing and no one. If you will not leave this house, you will have to marry someone already established in society who can go out without you. You need a political wife, and I am very obviously not one. Marry Margaret."

She walked out.

"That's just another excuse," he shouted after her. "Quit hiding, Christie!"

"Harriet hides," she threw back senselessly. "Christie is going shopping."

"Devil take it, you can't go alone." He stomped into the corridor but heard her heading up the stairs. He was pretty certain everyone in the whole damned house was standing about, listening.

"Then if you won't go with me, I'll take the twins," she called back. "Or perhaps Aunt Nessie."

"I'll go," Moira called from the front of the house.

"See? I'll have an entire entourage. I won't need you." Her voice faded as she reached the upper story.

"Smith!" Ash yelled. "Jones! Call the carriage, fetch my coat and hat!"

"You'll need a chaperone, my lord," Moira called, voice filled with mischief. "I'll be ready when you are—unless you want Nessie, of course."

He wanted the whole damned world back in proper alignment, but he wasn't stupid enough to give them that much insight.

He figured the bedeviled women already knew it and merely mocked him with what he couldn't have.

"THAT INDIGO VELVET BODICE is stunning on you," Moira said in genuine admiration. "Simplicity becomes you. Matching a frilled sleeve cuff with the ruffles on the gray taffeta hem adds beauty without marring the sleek line. Complete it with a cashmere shawl in those colors and maybe a jewel tone or two, and it's perfect."

Appreciating Moira's description, Ashford nodded agreement just as if he could see. He intended to get some reward for being dragged from his lair. Following Christie's scent and using his stick, he groped his way through the modiste's cluttered salon to test the quality of the material and fullness of his bride-to-be's sleeve. She wore some fanciful hat that tickled his nose. "I want to test how much the bodice reveals," he murmured for her ears alone. If he was to be stared at like a circus act, at least he'd have some pleasure of the day.

"For evening attire, I've chosen a lingerie bertha with a minimum of lace and no frill, my lord," she retorted. "It will be very respectable."

"And rural," he complained. "If you do not wish to be a *rural nonentity*, as you so crudely put it, drape a bit of silky stuff instead, but don't cover your lovely throat. Neckcloths are for men."

"He's right. A simple surplice crossed over the neckline, possibly in a gray lace," Moira said.

Satisfied he hadn't made a complete spectacle of himself yet, Ashford retreated to a wall of fabric bolts. He didn't dare lean on anything for fear there wasn't enough support for his size.

"Is that Ashford?" he heard a querulous matron ask from a row behind him. "I heard he was dead."

"I heard he was blind and insane," another woman whispered in the rounded tones of nobility. "And who is that with him? I didn't think there were any women in that family. And certainly none so unprepossessing."

He could hear other customers join the whispering, but Ash discovered he truly didn't give a fig for their gossiping. Once upon a time, he'd enjoyed the envy of other men as he'd escorted the most beautiful women in town about. Now that he'd set his sights on marriage, his Miss Chris's happiness was more important than feeding his pride. It helped to know that she didn't care if he looked like an ogre and stumbled over his own feet. Her admiration held him steady.

He hoped the ring on her finger was the reason she'd come out of hiding, that he had given her the same confidence she had given him.

That didn't mean he wasn't wary of being seen in public. If Townsend hoped to steal Christie's land, there would undoubtedly be nasty repercussions if he perceived Ash's courtship as an obstacle. A blind man couldn't easily defend his family against physical assault, so he had to hope Townsend's anger wouldn't come to that.

Still, the whole shopping expedition was unnecessary and asking for trouble. He could summon any modiste in the city to the house. They didn't need to parade in front of tittering foolish females and draw attention to themselves.

Unfortunately, he understood the recognition that his betrothed craved. He had walked these streets in his youth, to see and be seen, to show the town that he had arrived. His Christie had never had that opportunity and she deserved it.

The scent of lilies wafted around him, and he unbent slightly as she took his arm.

"Now that I have a notion of what is available, my lord, I'll have Madame come to the house for the remainder of my wardrobe. May we take a look at shoes and hats, or are you bored?"

There she went again—understanding his discomfort. How the devil did she do that?

For her sake and to stop the whispering biddies, Ash established his proprietary pride in his chosen bride. "I can never be bored in your company, my dear. Your trousseau should be of the finest." He claimed her hand and placed it on his arm, hearing the gasps of the matrons behind him with malicious gratification.

His sharp hearing caught mutters of *madness, insanity* and *why her?* Since he couldn't punch ladies, he covered Christie's hand, squeezed, and indicated with a defiant nod in the direction of the shopkeeper his intention of purchasing everything she'd chosen.

"You do enjoy upsetting apple carts, do you not?" she asked in amusement, understanding his ploy.

"You know me too well." He followed her guidance from the shop. They'd met less than two weeks ago. How could she understand him better than his family?

"You roil with emotion," she said placidly, as if reading his mind. "It's hard not to notice. I gather from the spitefulness emanating from the corner behind you that you were eavesdropping on the gossips?"

"Spite is the general way of gossips," he said, trying to puzzle out how spite might emanate but needing to concentrate on where he put his feet. He could see movement directly in front of him, if he concentrated. "I have been a target of matchmaking mamas since I was in leading strings. It is a relief to let them know I'm off the market again."

Christie laughed. Moira muttered something about an arrogant donkey's posterior, but aloud, she only asked, "Trousseau? I heard that remark. Is there an announcement in the making?"

"Not here," Christie said equably. She added a warning for Ash's benefit. "I think that dapper gentlemen is about to intrude."

"Ashford, good to see you out and about," a bluff familiar voice called from directly in front of him. "Heard you were in town but haven't seen you at the club."

Not being able to recognize people until it was too late to avoid them was one of the many reasons he did not present himself in public. Ash did his best to keep an even demeanor when he wanted to glower at the rake. "Been busy, Whyte, old man, unlike layabouts like you. Miss Townsend, have you met Viscount Whyte? He plays cards, horses, and ladies, in that order. Whyte, my fiancée, Miss Christie Russell Townsend, from Somerset and Dorset. And you know Miss McDowell, of course."

Christie held his arm as she bobbed a brief curtsy. "A pleasure, I'm sure," she murmured.

She didn't *sound* pleased. Recalling Whyte as a young fop, Ash assumed the idiot was looking dumfounded. "Do I punch him in the nose for salivating over your beauty?" he asked into the silence, reminding Whyte that he could not see what was happening.

"'Pologize, stunned and all that," Whyte said hurriedly. "Hadn't heard the announcement. Miss Townsend, it's a delight to meet you, except it means another of us shackled and my mama will be making demands again."

"One will note," Moira said cheerfully, "his lordship is tugging anxiously at his neckcloth and glancing in the direction of his club, where one assumes a wager needs to be paid or amended."

"Perspicacious, Miss McDowell," Whyte grumbled. "I look forward to seeing you at the season's events, Miss Townsend. Congratulations, Ashford, wish you well and all that."

The lout scurried off. Ash stamped his walking stick. "Putting up with donkey's posteriors is one of the reasons I don't go out," he said irritably.

Moira giggled. Christie didn't.

Of course, he'd just declared them betrothed when she hadn't actually agreed, but she was wearing his ring. He could feel it through her glove.

"This is likely to be the most fun I've had since Emilia set fire to her laboratory," Moira declared. "I want to look in this hat shop."

"I cannot comprehend the minds of women without speech," Ash said after he heard Moira pattering off. "Your silence does not speak to me. Did Whyte insult you in some manner I could not see?"

"Of course not," she said stiffly. "His disbelief is insulting, but nothing more than I was expecting."

"Since everyone assumed I would eventually marry Margaret, disbelief is to be expected. If he was actually rude, I will break his nose."

She relaxed and laughed a little. "I'd rather not wrap your fingers every time we go out together. I appreciate that you have taken time from your busy schedule to escort me. I will simply go with Moira next time. We should go home now."

"Not until we have bought you a new hat and some walking boots, unless you wish to send to Townsend for your wardrobe? I thought to wait until the nuptials were set before stirring the hornet's nest."

"Oh, that's already stirred, I'm sure," she said with a sigh. "I've avoided taunting him in public until now, but he'll be on the doorstep when we return."

"Fine. We'll invite him to the ceremony. Erran has gone to purchase the license."

"You presume a great deal, my lord," she chided.

Moira returned in a flurry of petticoats and rose scent. "If you are talking weddings, you will have to wait for Mama and her bag of Malcolm tricks," she said. "Come along, Christie, there is the most exquisite hat in here."

Christie's hand dug into his arm. "Malcolm tricks?"

Ash wanted to ask the same. He wasn't female and didn't need Malcolm witchery. "We'll say our vows in secret," he murmured.

"I don't want them said in secret," Christie said irritably. "That is the whole point. I wish to be acknowledged as an independent lady of good family and wealth, not someone's shameful secret."

"You have bats in your attic. There is nothing shameful about you." He left the bright daylight to enter the crowded dark shop and froze when he could barely see a shadow. "Now who's concerned with what people think?" he retorted, to cover his hesitation.

"I am concerned for you, since you won't care for yourself," she said. "Stand right here, and I'll try on the hat and we'll leave. Smith, order the carriage brought around, will you?"

As Christie abandoned him near the door, a voice at his side added to his annoyance. "Ashford, it's generous of you to take your decorator and her assistant shopping. Or is she your secretary? I have heard both."

Margaret. Town was too damned small this time of year. Ash tried not to sigh in exasperation, but his frustration was building to dangerous proportions. "If you wouldn't wear a different perfume every day, I might know you are there and could greet you without you sneaking up on me."

"You never knew I was there before you were blind," she said resentfully. "Miss McDowell is a relation of Lady Azenor's, isn't she? And is her rather large assistant another cousin? She resembles Lady McDowell."

Ash remembered Moira's mother from before his accident. Viscount McDowell's wife resembled a galleon in full sail when she entered a room—wide prow, thick waist, sailing along on billows of skirts. "That's spiteful, even for you, Margaret."

"If I'm to be a dried-up old maid, I'm allowed to be spiteful. I thought you might appreciate the image. That family is a managing lot. I trust you're not considering marrying into it."

"The McDowells? Hardly. And Miss Townsend is no relation."

Although now he thought on it, his uneasiness increased. Aster had known a little too much about Miss Townsend for comfort. A moment ago, he had believed Moira was jesting about a Malcolm ceremony. Perhaps she knew something he didn't? Was Christie lying to him again? He'd better have a talk with Aster, the little witch.

Margaret returned him to the moment. "*Miss Townsend,* is that who she is? So you have stolen Townsend's missing heiress! That's rich, even for an Ives. How many more votes will you lose your party by encouraging that family of eccentrics? I wish you well, Duncan." She squeezed his arm and drifted out the door, if he was to judge by the cold blast of air.

Why the devil had he ever thought it amusing to visit London?

Christie approached. Taking his hand, she set it on her new hat. "It has lace and roses. That is not too much, is it?"

Absurdly, that she'd asked his opinion lightened his mood. He counted the roses and examined the quality of the lace and nodded approval. "Blue ribbons, to match your eyes?"

"The roses are blue, my lord," she said with laughter. "A blue ribbon is an excellent idea, thank you." She kissed his cheek.

She was tall enough to kiss his cheek. He tried not to beam like a besotted idiot.

Margaret irritated him. Christie made him happy. This marriage business wasn't so difficult to decide after all.

That thought lasted until the carriage arrived at the house and Christie leaned over to whisper, "That's Townsend's carriage across the street. The nest has been stirred."

"As ye sow, so shall ye reap," he quoted philosophically. "Go visit the twins and see what they've been up to. It will keep them from worrying when I start flinging things about."

She laughed, sounding relieved. "Just don't fling Townsend about. You'll strain yourself."

He wasn't about to do that before his wedding night!

Nineteen

"ASHFORD!" TOWNSEND ROARED. His countryman's bellow echoed up and down the city street.

Harriet wanted to cringe, but bold Christie turned and kissed Ashford's cheek as he descended from the carriage. Then she sailed into the townhouse without acknowledging the shouting fool.

She'd had her very first taste of freedom today, and it had been delicious. Arrogant Ashford hadn't even cringed when the gossips had called him mad. And he'd barely acknowledged his beautiful ex-fiancée when she'd whispered whatever poisonous words she'd had to say in his ear. He almost gave her confidence that he meant what he said about not minding her plainness—if only he could see, and she could be sure.

However, her stepfather had humiliated her beyond all redemption yesterday. She refused to let him do so ever again, not when she finally had the power to escape his control. Knowing he meant to invest her holdings in a fraudulent plot added resolution. Her stomach was in knots and her hands were shaking, but she could not, would not, let Townsend know.

"I will fetch mama," Moira told her as Christie hurried toward the stairs to protect the twins. "You're a Malcolm now, and we take care of our own."

"I think Ashford can do that, but he might need to be hauled off the ceiling before day's end." She tried to sound amused and unafraid. "There are only so many inkpots that can be thrown."

It was amazing that others couldn't tell when she was about to boil over like burned soup. Perhaps that was her gift—hiding her emotions from others.

Moira laughed, hearing only what Christie wanted her to hear. "Mama won't like to miss the show. I should stay and watch instead, but I won't. I admire your bravery!"

"No promises have been made," she called after her friend, but she had to admit that she had severely limited her choices by wearing Ashford's ring and appearing in public with him and not correcting his possessive behavior. It had felt so very lovely to feel cherished for a short while, which made her a *self-destructive* goosecap.

Lifting her skirts, she raced up the stairs to the attic. Out on the street, Townsend continued shouting like a coarse peasant.

The twins were sitting at their desks, working, when Christie entered the schoolroom. Steadying herself, she smiled at the startled tutor. "If you would, please, take Hartley and Hugh to the park for a while. Or for a lesson in the abbey."

Hartley looked anxious. "Is Papa in trouble? Shouldn't we stay and help?"

Hugh was already up and aiming for a window. "Father wouldn't want us to desert him if there is to be a fight."

Christie studied them in exasperated amusement. "The two of you are so much like him that I really ought to send you downstairs and let you deal with my stepfather. But your father wouldn't appreciate our interference. There will just be a lot of shouting and improper language, and you shouldn't have to hear it."

"Then you should go with us," Hugh said seriously. "Have you seen Westminster? It is very grand."

"I would like for you to show it to me. Go make notes of what you like best and what you think I'd like best. But I'm expecting visitors and can't go out again. I shall be fine. My stepfather has yelled before, and I've survived, as you can see."

"Can we take Chuckles?" Hartley asked, already donning his coat.

"Not if you're going to the abbey," the tutor said. "We will take our poetry books and you may discuss the poets buried there."

Satisfied the man had the twins in hand, Christie hastened down to her room. She took off her lovely new hat, discarded her pelisse, and checked the mirror. She didn't mean to confront Townsend unless it became necessary, so she prepared herself for Moira's family.

She would leave off her cap. The complicated coif Moira had created for her looked rather elegant. Could she find a maid who could do that for her every day?

Nothing would ever change her size, but knowing Lady McDowell was large—and also the wife of a viscount—seemed to have a steadying effect. Aster had said Christie was a Malcolm, like Lady McDowell. Perhaps her family was *meant* to be large. And gifted. And wouldn't mind the voices in her head if she didn't call them *ghosts*.

Perhaps she could learn to lie to herself as well as everyone else.

She took the back stairs down. The footman stationed at the garden door glanced up in surprise. Pretending she was Ruler of the World, she nodded regally and listened for Ashford's voice.

He'd taken Townsend to his study, of course. She could linger in the anteroom and hear muffled roars. Or she could hide in his bedchamber and hear almost everything.

Even Ruler of the World hesitated at entering the marquess's bedchamber in view of the footman.

She smiled at the servant. "The gentlemen will need tea shortly, if you please."

He bobbed his head and trotted off. She slipped into the chamber—the one she would share with Ashford if she were so crazed as to agree to his proposal.

She was fairly certain she was that crazed. Or desperate. His proposal had melted her mind along with her heart. She knew better, but a lifetime of longing couldn't be dissuaded. Independence sounded even lonelier than being bullied.

The voices in her head laughed. She didn't have time to listen so she shut them out.

The door between the chambers was open slightly. She waited with interest to see how the madman dealt with her stepfather at his worst.

"You were seen with my daughter!" Townsend shouted.

Christie sighed and pulled up a chair so she could see through the crack. If stating the obvious was his idea of argument, then this would be a long fight.

"Stepdaughter," Ash corrected in a bored drawl. "Miss Townsend is of an age to set out on her own without your permission."

"An unmarried lady does not stay under the roof of an unmarried gentleman! You have ruined her. I'll never find her a suitor now."

Townsend sounded apoplectic and used his worst bullying tones. Christie wondered what she thought she could accomplish by eavesdropping. Perhaps she should simply walk in there now and tell her stepfather to go home—not that he'd ever listened to her.

"Miss Townsend is of the legal age of consent and has agreed to be my wife," Ashford stated in what passed for patient tones for him. "She is quite adequately chaperoned by my sister-in-law's family. I would not harm the woman with whom I mean to spend my life. It is you who is causing her grief. Mortgaging her properties was not well done, especially if you are trusting Lansdowne to return your funds."

Oh very good. Even she recognized that tactic—take the offensive. But a thrill shot down her spine at his declaration of protection. Marriage suddenly felt a little more real.

"I am doing what any proper executor must do to maintain his assets!" her stepfather argued. "They cannot be allowed to lie fallow or deteriorate. This is none of your concern. You cannot just appropriate my daughter like so much baggage without consulting me!"

"I can and I have, and if you do not return the funds from the mortgages to her accounts, I will have you drawn up on charges of fraud," Ashford said relentlessly. "As her husband, I will have the power to do that."

Christie frowned. Was there an undercurrent here she hadn't realized? Ashford hated Lansdowne. He wanted to stop the earl and his manipulations. Would forcing her stepfather to back out of his dealings with the earl achieve his goal? And she had conveniently provided the means to destroy Ash's enemy? That took some of the starch out of her newly-discovered backbone.

"Don't be ridiculous," Townsend practically spat out. "It's a very profitable deal. It will make Harriet a fortune."

There was the confirmation Ashford had sought—her stepfather really had mortgaged her properties and spent the money! Christie bit her hand to prevent crying out her rage and despair.

"It will cost Miss Townsend all her property if you continue on this disastrous path," Ashford retorted. "You are gambling on a known thief. In a few days, I shall have the documents to prove that Lansdowne intends siphoning the funds to his own purposes. You will be left holding nothing but a mortgage. Demand the return of your funds, and withdraw from the earl's consortium, and I will provide you with safer investments upon my marriage to your stepdaughter."

"You have robbed me of my daughter and now you would rob me of her property?" Townsend asked. "And you think I should *trust* you?"

"I've robbed you of nothing," Ashford said curtly, in a tone that brooked no argument. "Miss Townsend chose to leave you. And Lansdowne has already robbed you, whereas I am willing to offer you a substantial investment upon my marriage, one with none of the strings I'm certain Lansdowne has attached. You would do well to look to the industrial future of England rather than sheep."

Now she was confused. It didn't sound as if Ashford would need her help for anything—or even that inkpots would be flung. He was very much in control. He didn't need her after all. Disappointed, she thought she might join the boys at the abbey, with a poetry book. That sounded more interesting than this.

"Woolen mills *are* industrial," her stepfather declared belligerently.

"Not profitably," Ashford said implacably. "Cotton is cheaper and superior."

"I don't need the advice of a young whippersnapper!" Townsend shouted, turning purple with fury. "If you actually mean to marry my daughter, then I'll call my solicitor to negotiate her dowry. You needn't give me anything. I'll simply keep the properties."

Nooooo, Christie howled inside her head. Those properties were her independence.

"Under no circumstances," Ashford said, repeating her objection with more erudition. "Those properties are part of Miss Townsend's inheritance, and she does not wish the lands enclosed. They are to remain in her trust for her children."

"And if I refuse?" Townsend asked in an ugly tone.

"Then I will marry her and sue you for fraud, quite simple. My brother is a barrister, so it won't cost me anything but time. You, unfortunately, will be out a fortune in legal fees and bribes to the court. And until the issue is settled, I'll notify the banks that the properties aren't yours to mortgage, and I'll post guards on the land to prevent enclosures."

My word, she thought in awe. For most of her life, she had seen Townsend as the law, as the ultimate ruler of all she owned. The marquess was turning all she'd known on its head—because he had power and knowledge she would never possess.

Ashford's bullying had silenced a tyrant. This was a spectacular new perspective to the concept of privilege, arrogance, and domination. When applied appropriately and for the betterment of others, power might actually be a *good* thing.

Townsend was sitting there speechless, looking for another advantage. Ashford had left him none.

Of course, she would be passing her inheritance from one despot to another if she married. That ought to give her pause. But as a marchioness, she would possess a modicum of that power—

Any immediate explosion in the other room was prevented by the footman scratching at the door with the tea she'd requested. Both men uttered annoyed exclamations at the interruption, but Ashford called for entrance.

She wished she knew for certain that Ashford wasn't marrying her just to spite Lansdowne. She knew she wasn't a prize in any other sense of the word. He certainly didn't need her wealth.

But he did need a woman. His lust could not lie.

Her stepfather stuttered and argued awhile longer, then caved to the marquess's greater power.

When the argument settled into boring details, she got up and wandered the room. Ashford's bedchamber was Spartan, which made sense. Fewer objects gave him less to stumble over. He could no longer see to read or write, so he needed no desk or shelves. His washstand was fastened in place, so even if he bumped into it, it wouldn't tilt and spill the pitcher.

The valet would take care of his wardrobe, so there were no more than a robe and slippers in here. She studied some odd contraptions fastened to the wall and decided the straps were for exercise. He couldn't ride or box any longer, so he had to keep up his powerful build in some manner.

She admired him all the more for overcoming his disability in any way available to him. She should use him as an example of how to surmount her own damaged pride and timidity and be a better person for it.

She smoothed her hand over his covers and tried to imagine herself beneath them. Her imagination wasn't that good. Remembering his heated kisses, she just shivered with anticipation and returned to the door when voices rose again.

"You cannot possibly expect me to sway the votes of Montfort and Caldwell!" Townsend shouted in the other room, coming out of his fugue with what sounded like panic. "They'll despise me for pulling out of the consortium as it is. They are relying on the mill to repay their mortgages!"

"You will be saving them from financial disaster and be a hero," Ashford retorted. "I ask nothing more of you except your votes."

"Damn you, Ashford! You leave me little choice." Townsend said. "What will become of *Harriet* if I do not cooperate?"

There was just enough hesitation for Harriet-Christie to chew her fingernail in anxiety. She ought to go in there and tell Townsend what she thought of him, but Ashford seemed to be enjoying himself. Besides, it wasn't in her to be rude to the man who had cared for her and her mother all these years. She waited to hear what the marquess thought of her worth.

"Miss Townsend will become my wife and worth nothing to you if you vote against me," Ashford finally stated. "However, she is worth a great deal to you and England's future if you work *with* me,"

A pawn, that was how he viewed her. Really, that's all she'd ever been. And she'd *known* he would bully and intimidate her.

As a marchioness, she might work around that—if she kept her independence. She just needed to be brave and stand up for herself and see how he liked it. Ashford could not have it *all* his way.

The voice in her head cackled in delight.

Twenty

ASHFORD ADDED A DOLLOP OF BRANDY to his tea and listened to the confusion outside his study.

The interview with Townsend had been as amusing as it had been appalling. The man was a disgrace to his title to use a gentlewoman like Christie for a bargaining chip. He'd enjoyed running the man into a corner and letting him scrabble about like a trapped rodent.

As soon as her stepfather departed, he waited for Christie to present herself. Instead, she seemed to have disappeared. He assumed the tea had been her way of diverting fisticuffs, adding a layer of civilization he'd forgotten. The servants hadn't delivered it of their own accord, he knew.

So where was she?

He could wander out and ask, but he was fairly certain he heard Moira and her interfering witch of a mother in the salon. How big of a dolt did he wish to make of himself by looking for his misplaced not-quite-a-fiancée?

He detected the low rumble of Erran's voice, so that might be Celeste laughing. Shortly after that, he heard the twins tumble in the front entrance. Miss Chris had blessedly kept them away as he'd asked, although Townsend had been defeated more easily than he'd expected, which had kept his shouting to a minimum.

Overall, he was pretty damned satisfied with his negotiations. He hadn't had anything interesting to cut his teeth on in a long time. He had Pascoe to thank for finding the connections to the Dorset property that he wouldn't have found while he was imprisoned here by his useless eyes.

He needed to persuade Christie to the altar before a duke showed up to fling his weight around.

Restlessly, he waited for Erran to join him in the study. Or he supposed . . . Ashford toyed with his pen. He could go out there and make his announcement about his betrothal to a room full of eager women.

He needed Christie with him to do that.

He probably should have planned ahead for a celebratory dinner . . . except she never really had given him her promise. That brought him out of his chair. Confound it, he couldn't keep hiding in his own damned house. He needed to find the woman and seal the deal he'd just made with Townsend.

If he wanted marriage, women were a necessary nuisance, ergo, he must deal with them. In fact, he could consider it a new challenge—how to keep Christie at his side while scattering all the other birdwits.

Using his stick to detect any stray objects in his path, he counted his steps until he knew he'd reached the foyer. Voices emanated from the front salon, so he walked in, hunting for the scent of lilies.

"Ashford, there you are! We've prepared a proper announcement for the papers. You really should have held a dinner to declare your betrothal. You cannot do it in front of *shopkeepers*! What were you thinking?" Lady McDowell asked in indignation.

"I was thinking that it was my own accursed business how I make my announcements." Well, so much for making a proper declaration with his bride at his side. "Where's Christie?"

"She isn't with you?" Moira asked in concern.

"Of course she's not with me. Do you see her with me?" he asked in disgruntlement. "And it would be highly improper if she were. Hartley, run out back and see if she's in the garden. Check the kitchen on the way."

"Yes, sir. How did you know I was here, sir?"

Ash could hear his son approach and recognized the motion of a short shadow. When the boy came near, he cuffed him on his shoulder. "Because you stink of mangy dog."

"He found a hurt puppy in the bushes at the abbey," Hugh explained as Hartley ran off. "Shall I check Miss Townsend's room?"

"Do that, and I thank you." With the boys out of the way, Ashford glared at what he presumed was a roomful of women if he gauged the variety of scents and shapes correctly. "The rest of you may fly away on your brooms. Erran, do you have the license?"

"I have the license." Erran's deep voice came from near the mantel, where there was no window light to give him shape. "I even have a vicar ready. But you seem to have lost your bride."

Which made Ash extremely uneasy, but he refused to show it. "Is the vicar here already?"

"Of course not," Celeste said in her serene voice. "We needed to consult with Christie first. This salon is too small for a wedding. We need Iveston."

"I don't have time for Iveston or a big hurly burly. The administration is about to fall, and I have meetings every day." And he wouldn't have the support of Townsend's men if he didn't marry his damned stepdaughter and draw up the settlements immediately. If the Duke of Sommersville caught wind of a scandal . . . all bets were off.

Ash maintained a grip on his rising panic. *Where in the devil was the woman?* Christie had known Moira had gone to fetch the wretched viscountess. She should be down here, entertaining the guests.

She wasn't his wife yet. She couldn't be his hostess. He almost groaned in impatience and swung his stick in the direction of the whispering women. "We need the words said and the deed done. I don't need all of you making a circus of it."

"And do *my* wishes matter, my lord?" Christie asked from behind him, in a cool voice unlike the warm, welcoming one he'd come to expect.

He swung around as if he could see her. The foyer was too dark to easily discern her shape. He stepped aside and bowed so she could enter. Once he knew she was close and could see a portion of her silhouette against the front window, he caught her hand and kissed the back of it.

"Your opinion is why I sent for you, my lady. Will you tell these slubber-de-gullions that all we need are the vicar and words? I haven't time for more."

"Insulting my family is probably not the best way to ask that," she said, withdrawing her hand and drifting away.

"Your family? Is Townsend still here?" Irritated that he couldn't tell, Ash glared at the entire company.

"Aster says Christie is a descendant of Christina, the third duchess of Sommersville and is thus a Malcolm, just as we are," Moira said with a hint of triumph. "So we are her family."

"Impossible," Ash said in disgust. "She is much too level-headed to be one of you. But the dukes have always been good, logical men. I suppose we should send them an announcement."

"Exactly what we thought—about the invitation, anyway," Celeste said sweetly. "But the dukes are gifted healers, and their siblings and offspring often have interesting abilities, Aster tells us."

Ash waved this nonsense away. "Christie, tell them you are perfectly normal and harbor no weird abilities to talk with ghosts or whatever foolishness they encourage."

"Actually, my lord," she said, "I've given it some thought lately. I've been hearing my mother's voice in my head ever since she died. Since moving here, I've learned it's possible to *hear* other ghosts. If you wish to cry off, I'll understand." She said this defiantly, as if *expecting* him to cry off.

The other women exclaimed in excitement and all began nattering at once. He wished he could see Miss Chris. She hadn't sounded happy about her announcement. *Ghosts?* She heard *ghosts?* Not saw them—heard them. Irrational, mad . . .

And meant to scare him off.

Fighting a rising panic, Ash pinched the bridge of his nose, wishing he could twist this conversation back to the beginning and start over. "I do *not* wish to cry off, and this is not amusing. What do your voices say?" he asked, because he couldn't think of a more appropriate response.

"The one who calls you her grandson says you need me," she said in what sounded like relief and amusement. "I really haven't heard other people's ancestors until I moved in here."

"Oh, I bet that's Ashford's great-grandmother Ninian," Moira said excitedly. "Aster *told* you this house enhances our abilities!"

"I need a physician to give me a headache powder," Ash muttered. He had proposed to another jingle-brained Malcolm. Perhaps he really was as mad as they.

He had definitely gone soft in the head, because he couldn't find it in himself to cry off, even though she was giving him the opportunity. *That* was what this scene was about. He'd pressured her into accepting his ring, and now she was showing him with her defiance what he hadn't wanted to hear when she'd said she wasn't suitable.

Bloody hell, she *needed* him. And he needed her. They'd muddle along just fine, if they didn't throttle each other in the process of learning to deal with their differences.

"If my ancestors were healers, perhaps I should be a physician," Christie said, with amusement underlying her coolness. "I know how to fetch headache powders, however."

He caught her arm before she could leave. "Don't go, please." To hell with Malcolms and ghosts, he knew he needed this manipulative, elusive female more than he hated the irrationality women brought into his life. "Erran has a license and a vicar. Your stepfather has agreed to return the funds on your property and release your entire trust to me, but only if we marry. Do you really want a duke bearing down on me breathing fire for compromising you? The sooner we do this, the better for all."

CHRISTIE STUDIED THE HANDSOME but flawed aristocrat clutching her upper arm. She had almost choked on terror when she'd forced herself to be honest and mention her ghosts. She had feared he'd take a complete disgust of her—or that he wouldn't.

The idea of spending her life with another man who would control her and who didn't love her was even more daunting than imagining a lonely life of independence. So she had dumped her fear and the decision onto Ashford by trying to scare him with her voices.

She sensed him fighting panic, just as she was, which was comforting in its own way. She couldn't read his mind, however. Did his panic mean she had put him off?

Perhaps the ghosts really had given him a disgust of her. She couldn't imagine he was too worried about a weak man like Townsend. And the idea of a distant duke defending her was almost as ludicrous as Ashford believing she was his only chance at a wife. He could have any woman he liked.

She was the one who could never find a better man, and she desperately wanted a family to love. That was the factor swaying her—even if Ashford couldn't love her, she could hope that their children would.

After overhearing his conversation with Townsend, she'd gone to her room to decide whether to pack and flee—or stay and fight. Harriet had fled, perhaps permanently. *Christie* had chosen to stay and fight for what she wanted. If she was to be more than a pawn, if someday she actually hoped to take the lead as his ghostly great-grandmother had recommended, she had to learn to stand up to a powerful marquess, one accustomed to having everything his way. She swallowed her fear and forged on.

"Can you accept that I might be a Malcolm with ghosts in my head?" she asked, to make herself perfectly clear.

Given a problem to solve, his panic lessened. "As long as you're listening to me and not to them," he said warily.

The other women had fallen silent and waited expectantly.

Christie tilted her head and considered that possibility. "I've never really listened to them until I moved in here. I think I know you better than I know them. What if I just listen to myself instead of you or the ghosts?"

His lips turned up wryly. "I think I can trust your wisdom in that. What's more important is that we keep your stepfather from spreading scandal."

Well, no, there were many other considerations more important in marriage, but he knew that and for whatever reason, was using the political advantage to manipulate her. Keeping her mind open like this, she would soon have his headache, but she needed to know how he truly felt beneath the truth he twisted to his advantage.

"I do not like being rushed on such an important occasion as this," she said frostily, in a voice she'd never ever used to anyone. She ought to be terrified to speak to him in such a way. Correction, she *was* terrified.

But if it came down to living under another man's thumb or being thrown from the house—she'd choose being thrown from the house. Otherwise, her lonely heart would become more involved with these people, and Ashford would own her as Townsend had.

She waited, holding her breath, for his response.

His grip relaxed. "Shall we go in the other room to talk about what you want without all . . ." He hesitated, bit back whatever insult he meant to use, and indicated the women. "Without all your *family* making choices for us?"

She almost smiled at his struggle to offer this concession. Ashford was not accustomed to yielding power.

"I rather like having family to help me, but if we are to marry . . . perhaps we ought to find ways of dealing with each other in private." She took his arm and allowed him to lead her out with a measure of dignity, ignoring the protests rising behind them.

He led her into the anteroom and left the door partially open, so there could be no complaints of impropriety, at least while there was company to notice. Christie knew the arrogant marquess wouldn't observe such niceties otherwise.

He assisted her to a cushioned settle. "You have never actually said yes to my proposal, Miss Townsend."

Her lips quirked at his formality, but he couldn't see her, so she must convey what she felt with care. "I would be more than honored to accept your offer, my lord. I think you know that."

"That was not an enthusiastic acceptance. I sense a 'but . . .'" He took the cushion next to hers. The solid wood held both their weights without sagging. "Do you trust me to return your dowry untouched? I truly do not need more land or funds, and will gladly allow you to do as you wish with them, although I hope that you will set them aside for any children we might have."

She thrilled at the mention of having children—or at the idea of the process leading to them. But if he was offering to let her manage her own property, she must not sound missish about the opportunity.

"I trust you on matters of money, but I wish to be part of the settlement negotiations to determine what is mine to control and to establish that control," she said, threading her fingers together and trying to gather her wits when he loomed so close and spoke of such intimate matters. "I do *not* trust you, however, to treat me as more than an extra appendage to be used as you see fit. I have been nothing for too long to ever wish to be treated as such again. If I am to be *nothing*, I wish to be so on my own."

Which was a huge horrible lie. She *hated* the idea of being alone for the rest of her life. But she hated even worse what would become of her once Ashford grew bored and moved on, as he most certainly would.

To give him credit, he actually took the time to consider what she was saying rather than laughing at her fears or pressuring her to say yes. Unlike Townsend, Ashford always knew when she was lying, which was uncomfortable. But he couldn't know about what part, so he had to stew, just as she did.

Sitting there in his form-fitting coat, his white neckcloth askew, his square, beard-darkened jaw jutting, he clicked his stick against the floor and stared at the empty wall for a while before replying, "I will admit that I have not led a life that gives you reason to trust me in matters of the fairer sex. It's impossible to make promises for the future, but can you trust that I have learned my lesson and take you more seriously than the others?"

Christie bit her lip. This was the crux of the matter. They had no way of knowing if he'd recover his sight. If he did, he wouldn't need her. He might despise looking at her. But by then, might they have learned to rely on each other? Without love, what else could they have?

At her silence, he rubbed her cheek and touched her lips as if she were a precious piece of porcelain, which thrilled her to the marrow.

"I cannot imagine using you as an extra appendage, my dear, wise Miss Chris, except perhaps as my eyes. For that, I would be eternally grateful. I took my eyes for granted before. I'd never be so foolish as that now. So I'm not entirely certain what you ask of me."

"Respect," she said with decision, not daring to ask the impossible. "I know I am not your equal in many things, but I am my own person and not an extension of you. I do not wish you to make my decisions for me, and I would like my preferences to be consulted on matters such as where I'm to be married." She added dry inference to the latter.

He uttered a snort of amusement. "It won't be easy," he warned her. "I'm accustomed to making all the decisions in my life without consulting anyone."

"I gathered that." She relaxed her grip and tried smoothing her skirt. "And I am *not* accustomed to making decisions, having had them taken from me all my life. From here on, I mean to have my voice heard, so it will make me angry if I must fight to have my say. I may not be a pleasant companion."

"I want to kiss you senseless right now and carry you off to make mad, passionate love," he said cheerfully, with apparent relief— although she could no more interpret the source of his feelings than he could her lies. "I think we will manage. Since I cannot seek that prize until after we are wed, how soon can it be done, my dear? I'd like to get on with this business of fighting."

She bit back a grin at his perspective. "And I would rather not," she said as sternly as she could manage. "But I understand if we are to save my property from enclosure, and you are to twist arms for the votes you need, we must wed quickly. Therefore, I must ask that you let me be the final arbiter on the negotiations of my settlements."

"You wish to sit in on a dry meeting even I have no desire to attend?" he asked in amazement. "I meant to set Erran on it, but I will happily agree to you sitting in with him and arguing to your heart's content. Now may I ask Erran to fetch the vicar?"

"You are to tell Lord Erran that I have the final say in the agreement, and then we may ask the vicar if we may use his church.

You may be tired of public spectacle and wish a private life, but I am tired of hiding in the shadows. I want a spectacle."

She practically beamed her defiance and waited for him to start flinging pillows. She even offered him one.

Ashford took her offering and obligingly flung it across the room. Then he hauled her into his arms and kissed her until her head spun.

Twenty-one

THREE DAYS AFTER HIS PROPOSAL, Ashford stood in an unfamiliar space, fighting his panic, while listening to pandemonium echoing through a very large stone chamber. He was still struggling with his decision to marry a woman he'd never seen, one who wanted him to *trust* and *respect* her. He thought he did, far more than he had Margaret, at least. His Miss Chris was a remarkable person. He certainly *relied* on her. But he relied on his brothers and had no desire to marry them.

Desire—ah, there was his motivation. She could be blue with spots, and he wouldn't know. So he was marrying her for her ripe curves and her . . . reliable . . . nature. And maybe because he knew she wasn't marrying him for his wealth and title. That seemed as solid a basis for marriage as any.

"No doves," he said firmly, hoping his hearing was providing the correct details in this echoing chamber.

"We have a cage full," one of the younger females said in disappointment. "Perhaps we can release them when you walk out."

"And have bird cack on their heads," Jacques agreed cheerfully, to Ash's relief. "Here, I'll take charge of the cage. All will be drama, if that's your goal."

"That is quite rude and not our goal," Viscountess McDowell admonished. "This is a spiritual drawing together of two souls into one whole. The doves are for peace."

Ashford winced at hearing this idiocy—peace? Did she really believe marriage made peace? Not in his family.

Rather than remain frozen at the front of a church he couldn't see, he limped his way toward what he prayed was a distant corner. He couldn't hope to find Christie unless he could smell her perfume, and there were so many women fluttering around in here, even smell might confuse him.

He hated churches, he decided. They were dark and gloomy, and he couldn't even see shadows.

"I'm sorry, we should have done this in the park," Christie said from somewhere to his right. "I had no idea the ladies were so . . . fond of nature."

"Are you wearing your crown of thorns yet?" he asked dryly, breathing a sigh of relief at having one sensible head in the room.

How the devil had he been brought to this—marrying a crazed Malcolm?

Because this one wasn't crazed, he was convinced. Christie wouldn't throw pigeons into a church. And even if she thought she heard voices in her head, she didn't regale him with the tales. He'd found a perfectly sensible, intelligent wife who lusted for him as he did her—a most excellent bargain, better than he'd made when he'd had eyes. He allowed his panic to settle. She had a habit of calming his worst side.

"I am wearing a rowan circlet. They have made my hair look almost fashionable, with ribbons and curls and one can hardly see the twigs. I'm also wearing a lovely white cape which unfortunately covers the bodice of the new, silver-blue gown I wore just for you." She took his hand and lifted it to her nearly-bare bosom beneath the cape.

"That is a riveting décolletage," he said in approval, with a surge of relief and gratification that he had chosen his bride so well. He ran his hand over the . . . outstanding . . . bosom holding up the bodice, and down the firm curve of her waistline. She'd allowed him these liberties in the few days while they awaited a time he and the vicar and the church were all available. Being able to caress her lush form and dream of his wedding night might be the only thing saving his sanity. "Have you arranged to send everyone out of the house for the evening?"

"I have, as you requested. Even the twins are on an expedition with one of your cousins. I appreciate everything you have done for me, and will do my very honest best to do whatever you need." She leaned into him and related with glee, "Townsend almost swallowed his tongue when Lord Erran allowed me to approve the settlements giving me full management of my inheritance. There was much storming and frothing. It was very gratifying, and my land remains my land. I am an independently wealthy woman."

Ash wished he could have observed that scene, but her satisfaction was nearly as pleasing. He supposed he ought to be worried that, now she had her own funds, she could walk off and leave him anytime, but he thought his bride was made of sturdier stuff than that. "I'm glad I can amuse you so easily. Erran says the baron was so rattled by your presence and responses that he seemed glad to escape with his reputation intact."

Ash found it hard to believe that any man could have ignored her for all these years. The woman he was holding was built to dominate a room and had the mind to do so. He supposed some men would find that daunting, but he enjoyed the challenge. "Did Townsend never *notice* you before?"

"Not if he . . . or I . . . could help it. Really, it was as much my fault as his. He disliked the sight of me, so I hid. I shouldn't have."

"Absolutely not. Perhaps your milieu is with a more mature crowd than the silly debutantes in a ballroom. I hope you have a large audience here today to observe my pride in my chosen marchioness." He could hear the low murmur of voices and echoing steps as people entered the church, but the space was too huge for the sound to have meaning.

"I believe all of your family and Lady Aster's family are here, plus a number of very proper gentlemen and their ladies who must be known to you. We sent no announcements, but word spread quickly. It was generous of Lady McDowell to hold the wedding breakfast for so many people in her home."

"Did Sommersville send anyone?" he asked gruffly. He'd hate to disregard a duke.

"I think his son is here," she whispered. "Or so Lady McDowell tells me. A tall, distinguished gentleman about your age?"

"Most likely. I ought to speak with him." He clutched his stick in frustration that he could not just stride up and greet guests.

"If I am part of his family, I suppose I should speak with him as well, although I fear there isn't time now. They're coming for us."

"Miss Townsend," a female voice hissed from nearby. "It's almost time. You must stand with Viscount McDowell."

"You will note, Townsend did not show up to give me away. I am grateful to the viscount for taking his place," his bride-to-be said. "Lord Theo is heading your way. Are you sure you do not want to cry off?"

"I am salivating and wondering how quickly we can leave the breakfast," Ash whispered in her ear, feeling her shiver deliciously as he kissed her cheek.

His frustration continued to roil knowing that he could not spirit her away from the festivities anytime he liked. He would have to wait for others to take them from the McDowell's house to his own.

He'd waited over thirty years to marry, and he couldn't do it *his* way. Humbleness did not suit him.

"Patience, my lord," she whispered back. "I hope you will always look on this day with the same fondness as I will. You look magnificent."

Then she was gone in a whisper of lilies and rustle of silk.

"Tell me she's as lovely as she sounds," Ash demanded when Theo arrived.

"You are in serious peril, old man," Theo replied with relish, leading him toward the nave. "You may have met your match. Your bride even stood firm against Lady McDowell over the breakfast details. Her looks are half her success—not only as powerful as a Viking goddess but more. She's stunning, yes, but not in any battle-hardened way. She's all softness over steel, expecting people to do as she says without argument, like any good, formidable marchioness."

"My very own tyrant," Ash said, not entirely certain that's what he wanted but enjoying the idea. If even level-headed Theo was impressed, Christie was already making a difference.

"She filled all your inkpots with water," Theo whispered, releasing Ash's arm.

Ash had a hard time containing his laughter.

CHRISTIE TOOK A DEEP BREATH and released Viscount McDowell's arm. He was a large, gray-blond, older gentleman who tolerated his Malcolm wife's eccentricities without flinching. She'd been told he was working hard on labor laws and supported the various interests of his daughters, so she felt safe on his arm. But she only had eyes for her groom.

His valet had outdone himself today. Ashford's tailored black coat clung lovingly to his broad shoulders and his trousers to his muscled thighs. His silver-blue waistcoat almost matched the color of her gown and was shot through with silver threads to match his buttons. His white linen set off his naturally dark coloring to perfection, and a sapphire as large as the one in her ring sparkled against his neckcloth. Of course, it was nearly concealed by the short black cape Lady McDowell had insisted he wear.

The rowan crown on his dark curls looked as if it belonged there. The vicar hadn't even seemed to notice. Her crown was buried in ringlets and wrapped in a gauzy veil and not as obvious. All around the church, the ladies had lit evergreen scented candles shaped like trees. Lady Aster had told her that the ceremony had been adapted over the years for more modern circumstances, but she was to think of herself as marrying in a forest, surrounded by her Druidic clan. Christie had almost snorted the watered wine they'd given her.

But the final effect was enchanting. The church did smell like a forest, and the cavernous space became warm and inviting in the candlelight. She almost felt as if she were a fairy princess marrying the fairy king in a medieval forest, except they were more likely giants than fairies. She took Ash's arm to let him know she was there, and he squeezed her hand against his side.

The vicar's sonorous voice flowed over her. She was nervous about a thousand and one things, but oddly, she wasn't *afraid*. She felt as if she were finally coming home, to a place that accepted her, where her size and her intelligence weren't bad things that must be concealed at all cost. Since Ashford was blind, he judged her for herself, and that gave her confidence.

She probably ought to be worrying about more than her appearance—her odd voices, for instance—but hiding had been so much a part of her past that she felt as if she'd climbed a mountain and stood overlooking a future beyond her imagination. She didn't know enough to worry. In ways, she was as blind as Ashford.

When the vicar waited for her to repeat her vows, she remembered the very applicable line Lady McDowell had impressed on her. Still clinging to Ash's arm, she repeated with care, "I vow to love, honor, and take thee in *equality* for so long as we both shall live."

Her groom's lips quirked, as if he'd been waiting for that, and he repeated it in his turn, using the deep chocolate voice that thrilled her to the marrow. Obedience would never be part of their vows to each other, and she loved that he accepted that. The *love* part . . . she hoped would come.

Now, if the service had mentioned *lust*, she could vow that wholeheartedly. Shy, frail maiden—she was not. She was eager to see where Ashford's hungry caresses would lead.

When the service ended, and she was pronounced in public as the wife and marchioness of the Marquess of Ashford, Earl of Ives and Wystan, the Malcolm ladies stood and cheered. She half expected them to release the doves she'd seen earlier.

"They should have stayed with forest ceremonies," Ashford whispered, steering her—not toward the main aisle and their guests but toward a side door.

He must have paced off the distance because he aimed unerringly for a courtyard exit where his servants waited to escort them into a carriage.

"We will miss whatever your brothers have prepared for the church entrance," she murmured back. "I could tell they were plotting, probably with my . . . family." She was having difficulty adjusting to the knowledge that she had family who had taken her in as if they'd known her all her life.

"Jacques has the doves," Ashford said with a shrug. "There will be wheat grains involved. The confusion does not suit me. Having you to myself . . . suits me very well." He handed her inside the closed carriage.

Walking down an aisle filled with people he should greet but couldn't see probably didn't suit him either. Christie understood his need to hide. "Ignoring our guests is exceedingly arrogant, but this escape suits me as well," she said, settling in the forward-facing seat, leaving room for him.

The moment the carriage rolled off, her *husband* circled her waist and kissed her the way she longed to be kissed. Thrilled beyond reason, Christie threaded her fingers through his gloriously thick hair and reveled in the passion and hunger with which Ashford claimed her mouth—and more.

She arched into his questing fingers, aching for him to release her from the confining corset, knowing he could not. But his experienced hand slid beneath her bodice, finding the needy nipple beneath the low-cut gown she'd worn for just this purpose.

"If the carriage halts for more than two minutes, I'll tumble you right here," he growled coarsely. "Do you have any idea of how you've haunted my dreams these past nights? I almost considered finding my way up the stairs and hunting down your room." He lifted her breast from confinement and bent to kiss it.

Christie bit back a scream of pure pleasure. "Oh, my—I never knew . . . Please, my lord . . . Ash. We cannot do this here. I cannot put myself back together and all your friends—"

"Will know exactly what we've been doing," he said in satisfaction, nibbling and smoothing his bites with kisses. "In fact, if we did not show up, they would not be surprised."

Christie hastily pulled away from temptation and tucked herself back into her bodice. "No, you *must* introduce me. I must be able to put names to faces if I'm to be of any help to you at all."

She was shivering with desire, embarrassingly wet with need, but she could not let him distract from her purpose. She had to become as valuable to him as his brothers were so he would not set her aside once he grew bored. She needed an occupation so *she* did not grow bored.

"I'm thinking you'll be of best help if you lie naked in my bed, waiting for me, while I sit through tedious meetings in the next room," he said with a lascivious leer. "I'll not even throw inkpots if I know I can throw out my guests, then go straight to your arms."

He punctuated his words with kisses that carried from the tops of her breasts, up her throat, and behind her ear, until she nearly sat on his lap and agreed to anything he asked. The notion excited her beyond reason.

She was understanding the disadvantage of marrying a man with so much more experience than she.

"I think waiting in bed might be a trifle tedious for me," she protested breathily. "Better that I sit in on the meetings and take notes while waiting for them to leave so I may . . ." She murmured her errant thought about sitting on his lap, determined to meet him equally but afraid she may have gone too far when he froze.

"I like the way you think!" he finally said—to her utter delight. He discreetly adjusted himself in his tight trousers. "And now neither of us is respectable for a party."

"Only fair, sir. Shall we sing uplifting songs until we arrive?" She slid her hand up his thigh, not quite daring to go all the way but thrilled that he felt the same as she.

"Why do they insist on weddings in the morning?" he grumbled. "It's foolishness."

"But Earl Grey agreed to be there so that you and a few of the other members could talk in informal circumstances," she reminded him. "So you are not completely wasting this day."

He groaned and leaned his head back against the high seat. His muscled shoulders nearly filled the space beside her, and she longed to see what waited for her beneath the formal clothing.

"Speak to me of labor and electoral reform and freedom for slaves and all those things that keep me going each day," he commanded.

"I fear I cannot do so intelligently," she said with regret. "I'm still learning. But I do know that it's extremely important that your party take over the administration so reform can be had."

"Yes," he said heavily. "Old men, entrenched in the existing state of affairs, cannot see the world is changing. Very good. That helps. I promise to be an irreproachable minister of reform for one hour."

"And then?" she asked, breath catching.

He turned his handsome head and leered at her as if he could actually see her. "And then we fornicate, my dear."

Twenty-two

"YOU NEED TO LEAD THE WAY, ASHFORD," Earl Grey said heatedly. "The Commons is too unpredictable. We have too many factions willing to lean toward whoever speaks loudest. You need to gather your articulate members and push them to speak. When those on the fence see how strong we stand, they can be swayed."

Ash knew he was right. He also knew that the blind leading sheep wasn't effective leadership. Unfortunately, he had no good alternative. "I'll keep Erran on the road, gathering the straying lambs. He'll see they're present. If he wishes to run in the next election, it's good for him to be seen."

"That's not enough," Birchcroft insisted from Ash's side. "At the very least, you must hold a soiree the night before. Line up all those whose votes are still uncertain. Impress them with the importance of standing with us. We'll all stop in during the evening to prove their votes won't be wasted, that we have their backs. You have the industrial interests on your side as well as the agricultural. You're our linchpin."

"And if your new bride is related to Sommersville, we'll pass the word on that," Whyte said. "It would be a coup if you could drag him out of his castle."

"Distant relation," Ash said stiffly. "He stands with us, but I don't expect him to stir himself for us. He's not the political sort."

"Shame. His grandfather was a damned good party supporter," Palmer said.

Ash didn't explain that the distant dukes had been good politicians only until one married into the Malcolm family. After that, the eloquent statesman had a son who became a physician, as had the current duke, and politics had become less important to them. "His Grace's son might join us," was all he could offer.

"They'll come just to see your new bride. Have her help gather and encourage your followers. Once we have the momentum, Wellington will be on his way out," Whyte said.

As if Miss Chris had any notion of how to gather society and feed them at a moment's notice. He'd married her because *he* needed her.

He hadn't considered sharing. Hadn't thought beyond the bedroom, actually.

He tried not to reveal his uneasiness. Even though he knew the real business of government was done at gatherings like the one they suggested, he hadn't planned on entering society. Once the administration was settled, his place was on his estate.

His bride had made it clear that she might have different ideas. Ash tugged at his confining neckcloth.

"We're counting on you, Ashford." The earl pounded his shoulder. "We'll leave you to the wonders of married life for now."

Within moments, the crowd that had surrounded Ash had abandoned him—in a strange room, in a strange house, with no means of knowing what in Hades was in his vicinity.

He could discern no windows and very few shadows. He swung his stick idly, as if in thought, just to determine what obstacles were in his way.

He wanted to rage and heave heavy objects, but he could only do that in the security of his home, where the inhabitants knew him, where he *preferred* to stay. He had appeared in public only for Christie—because his bride deserved the wedding of her choice.

He loathed being an object of pity and wouldn't do this again. The only way he could lead anyone anywhere was if someone led *him*.

The lush scent of lilies filled his nostrils, and Ash relaxed a fraction, although his temper was still on edge. The soft pressure against his chest didn't feel like the breasts he wanted. He grabbed the pillow she thrust at him and tossed it to one side, uncaring if he knocked over a dozen lamps in the process.

"Time to leave?" she asked hopefully.

"How do you always know to be in the right place at the right time?" he asked in exasperation. "You were even there in the park that day when my abominable footman abandoned me. Don't tell me your ghosts told you."

She took his arm and steered him in what he hoped was the direction of the door. "Don't be silly. I hadn't even met you then, so I couldn't have met your great-grandmother's ghost. And my mother's ghost doesn't know you."

"I'm fairly certain that hearing voices in your head is not a sign of sanity," he grumbled. "I wouldn't spread the word about if you wish these people to heed you."

"Oh, I know that," she said cheerfully. "Why do you think I spent so much time hiding? I couldn't very well tell Townsend what my mother thought of him, could I? She wasn't very helpful anyway. Your great-grandmother is much more outspoken."

"I don't think I want to hear about it. Imagining my grandmother in your head while I'm making love to you could be a deterrent to creating heirs," he said dryly, sensing a crowd ahead and keeping his voice down.

She laughed, then whispered as they walked, "Lord Winchester, the duke's son, has already left, but he was most pleasant and promised to call on us soon. I hope that is a good thing?"

"It is an excellent thing for you," Ashford said, hiding his dismay that she had relations as powerful as he and thus didn't *need* a blind recluse. "He's not often in town, so it would be good for you to know that side of your family."

"That's what I thought," she said in relief. "Even if he only sought me out now because I'm married to you."

She'd done it again—settled his anger before he even expressed it. He kissed her hair, relieved to discover the folderol had been removed, and he could run his hand through silken tresses.

They made their farewells, with Christie deliberately using each person's name so he knew who he was greeting. Her performance was astonishing. To him, her ability to say just the right thing at the right time was a far more interesting magic act than speaking to dead grandmothers.

Escaping without being held up by a dozen well-wishers was probably also a magic act, but one many people performed with more grace than he. So that was within the realm of normality.

"I am amazed that someone who has spent her entire life hiding is comfortable in a crowd of strangers like the one we just left," Ash said, assisting her into the waiting carriage once he heard the footman open the door.

"I pretend I am Christie, a bold wench capable of saying what she thinks. And now I can be the Marchioness of Ashford and pretend I'm actually important." She shifted her petticoats out of his way. "Mostly, it's easy because I know to avoid the people who resent or dislike me and to encourage the ones who crave my notice."

"I would ask how the devil you know which is which, but then I'd have to believe you a witch, when all I want to do is this." He turned her soft cheek toward him and located her plush mouth with ease.

She parted her lips hungrily, running her hand over his rough jaw, and pressing closer so he could take advantage of her lavish curves. A moment later, she pushed him back to gasp for air.

"Which witch is which?" she asked in amusement. "Shall we write a nursery rhyme while we wait to reach home?"

"Devil take it, now I understand why men marry stupid women," he grumbled, burying his lips at her nape. "How can *you* think at all when only one part of *me* is functioning?"

"Magic," she whispered as she rubbed the functioning part of him through his trousers.

They had to hastily right their clothes when the carriage stopped and the footman opened the door. Ash felt the carriage tilt as his bride stepped down, so he was able to catch her by the waist and swing her, petticoats and all, into his arms. "Lead on, Smith."

Christie squealed in shock, and he grinned at catching his know-it-all bride by surprise. She was a goodly size, but he'd wrestled heavier. Carrying her, he counted the steps it took to enter his home. This, he could manage, even limping as he did.

"You will break both our necks or strain yourself to incapacitation," she protested as he carried her over the threshold. "Put me down!"

"Is the champagne chilled, Smith?" Ash called upon entering, knowing full well there were more than two footmen in the house and that they weren't all named Smith. It simply saved time and embarrassment for both parties if he didn't have to ask which one was present.

"Someone has gone to fetch it, my lord. May we extend our congratulations to you and the new marchioness?"

"That's the new butler, but he has intelligently not lined up the staff to greet us," his bride whispered in his ear. "Now put me down."

"Thank you, Jessup." He knew the butler's name, even if he hadn't learned to detect his silent presence yet. "Have the wine sent to my chamber, then all of you may have the rest of the day off." Ash carried his bride straight down the hall, trusting the new butler to know to dodge out of his way.

"The staff must have champagne and cake too," Christie called over his shoulder. "This should be a day of celebration for everyone!"

"Thank you, my lady," the butler said from safely behind them.

Ash navigated the doorway of his chamber and the few steps to his bed. Instead of releasing his beautiful burden, he kissed her. Heady with anticipation, he continued kissing her as the servants carried in a bucket of ice and a tray of edibles. Only when they closed the door did he lower her to the mattress.

"It's still daylight," she murmured as he leaned over the mattress and began hunting for her bodice hooks.

"Not in here," he said. "I should have had them light all the lamps so I have some hope of seeing you."

"Seeing me?" Christie squeaked nervously, scooting backward on the covers. "You can *see* me?"

"Not at the moment, no," he said impatiently. "I need sunlight. Then I can see your shadow."

CHRISTIE HAD PLACED HER NEW husband's hands on the cunning fastenings she'd had the seamstress sew over her breasts so she needn't call for a maid at private times like this. Registering his words, her heart pounded erratically, and she stopped his fingers. He could *see* her? "Wait! How much of me can you see?"

"None of you in here," he grumbled, pushing her hands aside to go back to the hooks. "Merely your silhouette and motion when we're outside."

He knew how large she was and had still married her? Of course he knew. It wasn't as if he hadn't touched her every chance he had! Finally accepting that he *really* didn't care about her size, she let warmth and desire spread through her, adding to the surge of lust. For this man, she would risk all. "Instead of this gloomy room, you need sunlight to move about?"

She admired Ashford's massive shoulders as he shrugged. Even though his leg must have been tired, he had *carried* her, as if she were a featherweight. Her marvelous husband could have done nothing better to encourage her desire. She tugged him down to the mattress and began unfastening his waistcoat.

He deftly helped her, then reached for his trouser buttons so she could tug his shirt loose. "It's not as if England provides a vast amount of sunlight," he said deprecatingly. "So it matters little."

"It matters a great deal," she said in astonishment. "I am not entirely certain I am comfortable with you seeing me, but if that is what you want, then we shall go upstairs where there are windows. There are a few more hours of daylight."

He hesitated. "Upstairs?"

She felt his fear and his surge of curiosity. She had to be brave enough to do this, for him. "We'll count the stairs as we go. My room is in the very back, so once you hit a wall, you'll know where you are."

She offered this with her heart in her throat. She had counted a great deal on him not actually seeing her. Still, if all he was seeing was a silhouette, at least he wouldn't be discouraged by her lack of beauty.

"I want to see you," he said in determination, refastening his trousers.

Swallowing her own fear, Christie rang for a maid and ordered the tray and wine carried to her room—and the draperies pulled back.

"This house isn't large enough if you mean to stay in London," she said nervously as she held his arm and steered him toward the wide front stairs. "And if you need sunlight, I'm not entirely certain London is a good idea at all."

"This place is close to Parliament," he said with a shrug. "Unless we wish to rent one of the palaces closer to Westminster, I don't have many choices." He leaned over to nibble her ear. "And there are other things on my mind at the moment."

Since she wasn't at all certain his trousers could contain his rampant masculinity, she hadn't lost sight of that matter. Frock coats really needed fronts. She didn't dare look at him for fear she'd stumble, and they'd both fall backward down the stairs.

The maid would take the back way, out of sight. Christie hoped no one was peering from behind doors as they worked their way up the stairs in near dishabille like a pair of drunks. But the intimacy of sharing this moment shored up her flagging nerves.

Ashford had told her something no one else knew—his eyes still worked! They just didn't work well. She swelled with pride that he'd trusted her with his secret.

"I don't think you could have given me a better wedding gift," she said as they traversed the upper corridor. "Have you talked to your physician about seeing shadows?"

"It hasn't improved," he warned her. "This is why I say nothing. I cannot raise hopes if there is no improvement. It's little better than being completely blind. I am trusting you to keep this quiet. It would be hard on the children."

The children—another matter she must consider, once the election was over. He had at the very least three offspring already. "You are right, I understand. I hoped perhaps your physician might have some thoughts."

"He says it means my eyes aren't damaged but my brain is," he said in a tone as dry as the desert. "All in all, I do not consider that a betterment."

She laughed, feeling his acceptance of what must have been a terrible disappointment. "You have enough brain to spare a little damage. You must have been formidable when you had your sight. I probably would never have dared approach you, and you most certainly would never have noticed me."

"Then I would have been a great dunce," he said, adding wryly, "And I'm aware that I've been a dunce more often than not."

"Being blind has given you wisdom?" she asked in laughter. "Do you think that works with everyone? We could blindfold all Parliament."

At the end of the corridor, two maids darted from her room and ran down the backstairs, eyes averted.

"We've arrived. If you should decide you'd like a suite up here, perhaps we could install gas lamps along the wall and you could count them instead of steps. Or I could place a table outside the door so you know you're in the right place," she suggested.

"Mind no longer functioning," he reminded her, striding through the doorway and closing the panel behind them.

He halted, as if to measure the level of light. It was a southward facing wall, so the sun's rays still fell through the windows, although winter illumination was never strong.

"Now," Ashford said in delight, "show me that front fastening again." He reached for her without a moment's hesitation.

Oh dear Lord, he really could *see* her.

Twenty-three

ASH SAVORED THIS MOMENT OF "SEEING" his bride, now that he knew how easily these rare privileges could be lost. He'd spent years taking women and sex for granted—until he'd lost his sight and realized how much time he had wasted on sating his hunger instead of appreciating moments of sensual beauty like this.

His new bride's silhouette against the window light was all lush, firm young curves, more seductive than any of the blowsy mistresses he'd known. He delighted in the silkiness of her skin as he fumbled with the hook that would release her bodice. He relished her intake of breath as his fingers slid between her breasts. She was Juno come to earth, and she was *his*. The knowledge that she was his alone, the woman who had chosen *him* for partner, was arousing enough even without the amazing gift of Christie's innocent eagerness.

The fastenings came undone, and Ash pushed her bodice off her rounded shoulders. He could *see* how they curved, unlike his squared ones. He squeezed her giving flesh and could almost, *almost* see the movement of her breasts if he tilted his head just right.

She eased her arms from the sleeves while he sought the ribbons of her chemise and released them.

Undressing her was a slow process, but Ash meant to take his time. No matter how starved he was, she was a dish meant to be savored. Where once his fingers had been swift and sure on corset strings, he now fumbled, but inexperienced Christie didn't know the difference. She ran her fingers through his hair and moaned with each new field he conquered.

They fumbled together. In tandem, they pried off his coat. She undid the last of the corset hooks when he could not find them. She tore off his neckcloth. He lifted her breast from her under-chemise and suckled. She muffled a scream.

He could see the outline of the bed and decided it was best to repair there before the light gave out entirely. Still drinking at the fountain of her beauty, he lifted her by her silk-clad waist and dropped her on the mattress.

The bed wasn't as wide as his, but Ash didn't give a groat. Enough light fell over them that he could see the curve of her waist and hip beneath whatever flimsy bit of nothing she still wore. "You are the most exquisite creature I've ever touched," he murmured, kissing her shoulders as he unfastened the last bit of cloth covering her.

"I am no slender sylph whose waist you can encompass in your hands," she countered.

"That's hardly a test that interests me." He wrapped his big hands around her waist and squeezed.

"Your hands are very large," she said, sucking in her breath and laughing when his thumbs didn't touch but dug into her supple belly.

"You are the perfect size," he declared. "I need not fear I'll break you. You must tell me what you like, so I can give you the pleasure you are giving me."

AMAZED THAT ASH'S BIG HANDS could *almost* circle her waist, Christie would have handed him the sun if he'd asked. "I like everything you're doing," she said with certainty, tracing the darker V of skin at his throat where he'd apparently discarded his neckcloth in the sun for too long. "I cannot imagine you doing anything that wouldn't please me . . . in bed," she amended honestly.

He chuckled, and she felt the vibration through her skin, right down into her woman's place. She tugged his shirt upward, wanting more of the crisp hairs she could see beneath the linen.

"You are such a virgin," he said with another chuckle.

Then he ran his hand beneath her chemise, skimming his rough fingers over her naked hip, and she arched into him in surprise at the intimacy.

"I admit ignorance in many things," she agreed, finally freeing his shirt and pulling upward until he threw it off. "But that simply means you may educate me in the manner you prefer."

Awestruck at the rippling musculature revealed, Christie's attention wandered from wherever the conversation had led. "Oh, my," she murmured, stroking heavy muscles, eliciting a moan from the mighty marquess. "You are so very . . . hard."

"You don't even know the beginning of how hard," he muttered, leaning over to kiss her with thrusting tongue and a heated passion that left her mindless and empty.

Not until he'd unfastened his trousers and released the long bulge he'd concealed beneath his civilized façade did she have any inkling of what he meant, and by then, it was far too late to object.

Her husband was a large man in every possible way.

"Swiftly this time. It's been too long a time for me and I need you desperately," he said, returning to her breasts, lavishing them with attention until her womb ached, and she parted her legs of her own accord.

In appreciation, he kissed down her belly and nipped lightly between her thighs until she grabbed his hair and tried to tug him away. She supposed she ought to be embarrassed and wonder if this was proper, but right now, she didn't care. She ached for his possession. "*Now*," she agreed.

"Slower next time." Ash shifted his weight over her, his arms on either side of her head, his magnificent shoulders thrown back as he positioned himself.

Christie gulped, closed her eyes and felt the heaviness pressing into her most private place. "Swiftly, yes," she muttered incoherently, wanting and dreading this moment.

He leaned over and kissed her, then when she wrapped her arms around him and felt her body open, he impaled her . . . swiftly . . . as he'd promised.

She cried out her pain and pleasure, and he halted, letting her adjust to his thickness. And she did—*swiftly*. That he filled her completely seemed to indicate she'd been empty too long. She was designed to be a vessel for his lust.

Ash renewed his kisses to her breasts, and before long, she arched against him, taking him deeper, accepting his thrusts, thrilling when he threw back his head and roared his pleasure.

She was finally a wife. She *belonged*. Satisfaction settled deep inside her.

"I WOULD POUR YOU CHAMPAGNE, if I could see it," Ash said, although he said it with what sounded like contentment instead of his usual bitterness.

Now that she knew her husband admired the large bosom that had always discomfited her, Christie boldly leaned over his chest to reach for the bottle.

He caught one of her breasts and suckled. "The ambrosia here is better."

She nearly dropped the bottle, then pushed it into his hands to occupy them. "I cannot open it."

Propping his bare shoulders against the headboard, he took the bottle and expertly cracked the neck against the bedpost, snapping it off and shooting champagne over the wall. "Neither can I. Glasses?"

Astounded, she laughed and leaned over him again to reach the table. "I prefer not to imagine how you perfected that trick, sir." She grasped the stems of both glasses in one hand, then took the bottle from him with her free hand.

"Being a crude male without a butler, not knowing where the cork remover is, and lacking the patience to fiddle about might have more to do with it than your lewd imaginings," he said, taking the glass she pushed into his hand.

"I did not know how to imagine lewd until now," she said in reprimand. She sipped the effervescent liquid she'd never before tasted. "Ooo, I think the bubbles went up my nose. This may be an acquired taste."

"Assuming we only have this night to ourselves, I mean to make you drunk enough to forget the pain and be ready for that slow round I promised." He pressed the chilled glass to her breast.

Christie nearly snorted out the bubbles as her nipples rose to the occasion and her insatiable insides craved what he suggested. But the place between her thighs was sore, and she wasn't prepared for another assault.

"You mean to do this more than once a night?" she asked in doubt, casting a worried glance to that part of him that seemed to have lost some of its length.

As if he knew where she looked, Ash set his glass on the table, stood up, and removed his trousers entirely.

He was a magnificent animal silhouetted against the dying light from the window. His one thigh seemed more withered than the other, the damage that often caused him to limp—a result of senseless violence, if she understood correctly. She had not questioned the reason for leaving his trousers on until now. Had he tried to conceal his flaw as she had tried to hide hers? She was too new to marriage to ask, but his vulnerability added another warm nugget to her feelings for this indomitable man.

He paced away from the bed, counting off steps until his hand touched the mantel. Then he rooted around until he found coals to throw on the grate.

"This next time, you will share the pleasure. I want you to want our bedplay as much as I do." He fumbled about until he found her water basin and doused a cloth before turning toward the bed.

His manly sword was already rising to the occasion. Christie gulped. "You are very large, sir," she said tentatively. "You did say I was to tell you what I liked. I think I should like to wait."

He sat beside her and dabbed the cool cloth between her thighs. She thought she might expire in embarrassment. She exchanged her glass for the cloth and completed the job herself.

"Thinking is dangerous," he informed her, handing her the champagne once she was done. "It would only give you time to fear. I promise, this next time will be better. Have I ever broken a promise?"

She sipped the sparkling wine, feeling the bubbles stream through her blood. Or perhaps that was the effect of the naked man beside her. She narrowed her eyes in thought, trying to concentrate on words instead of his . . . manliness. "I don't believe you have ever promised me anything."

She glanced at the beautiful ring on her finger. That wasn't quite true, but promising to love in a church was simply a means to an end. As practiced liars, they'd both understood that.

"Perhaps that is why I am a very bad politician," he said with a shrug of his magnificent shoulders. "I must learn to make more promises—except a politician's promises are based on the premise that he can persuade hundreds of wrong-headed people to do what is right. I prefer promises I can make without beating people about the ears with a stick."

She laughed and the bubbles went down wrong. She coughed and Ash pounded her on the back, then handed her a chocolate morsel from the tray. It was almost natural to be sitting in bed, completely nude, and consuming champagne and chocolate beside this marvelously masculine marquess.

It still didn't relieve her concern about having that great weapon of his shoved clear up her middle until he nearly reached her heart.

Compared to him, she was *tiny*. It was a very disconcerting sensation. Was this how the rest of the world felt next to her?

"My lady needs more wine," he said at her silence. He took her glass and poured until the liquid slopped over the brim and down his fingers.

"My lord is a messy pig," she said aimlessly. "The maids must clean that up in the morning."

"People are messy. We are basically animals beneath our veneer of civilization. And we breed just as animals do. There is nothing to be ashamed of in that. Just imagine the king and queen doing as we are about to do. George Three had fifteen children, if I don't mistake." He fingered the morsels on the tray until he found one that apparently squished the way he liked it, and popped it into his mouth.

"I can tell you I do not want fifteen children," she told him as assertively as she knew how. "I wish to have a life of my own, above and beyond children. I don't believe the poor queen had that."

"That's why nurseries were invented. And French envelopes. And other preventives. We'll learn together." He spilled a bit of champagne on her breast and licked it up.

Christie gasped. Deliberately, he repeated the gesture. When he dribbled the liquid down her belly, she threw back the rest of her glass as she'd seen him do with whiskey. She sputtered and coughed as he sucked on her flesh, then gasped again when his fingers slid between her thighs.

"Do you like this?" he asked, penetrating and rubbing at a place that liked it very much.

She moaned in answer.

"I don't think you need much wine," he said wickedly, plying her with two fingers until she arched and begged for more. "You are incredibly responsive. I need only . . ." He tweaked a little more, pushed his fingers a little deeper, and her insides quaked and shivered, and she reached to pull him back.

"Touch me," he demanded, bringing her hand down to the part of him growing longer. "Then I'll be as ready as you are shortly."

"I will accept your bullying tonight, but beware of it on the morrow," she warned. In wonder, she did as he said, wrapping her fingers around his velvet hardness. She stroked as he showed her, and almost yanked away when he groaned and shoved against her, excited by her touch. Which excited her.

"You learn quickly," he muttered, leaning over to kiss her. "I may need more lessons since this," he rubbed her again, "is more pleasurable to learn than undoing the bad habits of a lifetime."

This time, when he pushed into her, it didn't hurt, and she was more than ready.

In fact, she bubbled over much as the heady champagne had, exploding with a triumphant cry of release, followed by a series of frantic bubbles foaming over as pleasure coursed through her.

As promised, Ash took longer, bringing her to shudders over and over again, until he spilled deep inside her, quite possibly planting his heir.

Wife, marchioness, possible mother of an earl . . . it was too much for a country girl. Tomorrow, she would worry about promises and lies and secrets. Christie fell asleep with her new husband still inside her, sheltering her with his big body.

Twenty-four

THE NEXT DAY, REALITY RETURNED with a vengeance.

Wrapped in a warm cocoon of lush woman and soft sheets, Ash was willing to even ignore his waking cock for a few more hours of much-needed sleep. Except Hartley's dog set up a howl of loneliness in the garden, and a maid scratched at the locked door, reminding them of the world awaiting them. The maid distracted Christie, who rolled away and dragged a sheet up to her chin—as if he could actually see her nakedness. At least it was light enough to see where she was, and he kissed her cheek.

"Rise and shine, beloved, before the twins return and Moira decides to redecorate this chamber."

He wished he could see her expression as Christie fought him for the sheet, then grudgingly rolled from the bed without it. Satisfied, satiated, and almost at peace with the world, Ash sat up, resting his bare shoulders against the pillows, and pulling the sheet over his stiff cock. In the dim light of dawn, he watched his wife's shadow flicker back and forth past the window as she washed and dressed. She had the substance so many skinny misses lacked—in more ways than in the flesh.

She leaned over to nibble his ear and tickle his rib. "Twins," she reminded him. "Moira. Visitors."

He sighed and prepared to return to the real world. Without his valet, his robe, or his shaving gear, Ash reluctantly had to let his new bride half dress him and lead him down the stairs to his own chambers before his first visitors arrived.

Ash despised asking for help, but Christie made it easy by knowing what he needed without his having to actually put it into words. And she did it while smelling of lilies and sex and laughing at him and *with* him and making him want to return to bed instead of his office.

This was what it was to be alive again—bliss.

"After this is all over, we'll have a honeymoon," Ash told her, catching her arm before Chris could escape when his valet arrived to shave him. "We'll go to Iveston, order whatever changes you need made there, then travel wherever you'd like to escape family and the demands of the estate."

"You lie," she said without rancor. "You won't leave the house if you can avoid it."

He glowered at her. "You're supposed to believe my promises." Even though he hated the confinement of carriages, and she was probably right.

"Just as you should believe me when I say your great-grandmother just told me I should put a ring through your nose and lead you down the garden path. She is a very strange woman."

"My grandmother is dead, and you're the strange one in this room. Go prepare yourself. The visiting will commence shortly." He kissed her, actually reveling in not seeing the disapproval on his haughty valet's face.

He was probably fortunate that he couldn't see Christie's glare as well. Marriage didn't mean he had to actually change his ways. His wife was clever enough to understand that.

After he'd been made presentable, Ash poked his way to the dining room in hopes of finding his new marchioness waiting, only to be disappointed. Upon inquiry, he learned his ladyship had asked for toast in her room, so he ate in lonely splendor.

Judging by the rush of feet up and down the back stairs, he suspected his bride was taking a bath, which was entirely understandable. She'd been a virgin, and despite her apparent joy in their conjugal union, she was probably feeling a little shy. They needed to retire to Iveston soon so he could show her their decadent Roman-style bathing room—and join her there.

Imagining all the ways he could take his bride, Ash worked his way through the morning's estate business without his usual boredom and irascibility. Even Erran commented.

"We should have found you a bride much sooner," his brother said, taking the papers Ash had just sealed with his signet. "You won't need this collection of inkpots any longer. May I have the crystal one?"

"No, it will shatter nicely when I next throw it at you. How close is the head count?" Ash wiped off his pen nib and tested its sharpness with his finger. He'd had to verify with a footman which pot held ink instead of water.

"They're still closely divided. Trying to persuade some of the more northern Whigs to travel is difficult in this rain. Aster's father claims to be hauling some men down with him, but we can't count on a timely arrival. Grey's idea is a good one—gather the indecisive ones here, feed them a hearty meal, and fill them with ale, so they're eager to see things our way when the speaker calls for a vote of confidence on Monday."

"Promise them manna from heaven, that they'll never die, and all their sons will be dukes," Ash said gloomily. "Nothing I like better than dealing with fools. Couldn't you send me the intelligent ones and let Grey deal with the stupid?"

Erran chuckled. "There's the Ashford we all know and love. Go find your bride before your next visitors arrive."

"Better yet, send her in here and let her play my secretary. That will provide some entertainment," he decided in satisfaction.

"She's decorating the front rooms with Moira so your guests won't have to sit on paint brushes and cat hair for much longer. They're also packing off Aunt Nessie to the next needy cousin. Do you really want me to disturb a nest of Malcolms? And what's this Celeste tells me of your bride hearing our grandmother's voice?"

Ash waved his hand in irritation. "They feed off each other's fantasies. Christie only mentions such things when she's in the company of your wives, so I'd be pleased if you'd tell them to cease and desist their idiocy."

Although she'd dared to mention his great-grandmother just this morning. How far did one have to humor a wife?

He could hear Erran rise and slide the documents into a portfolio.

"I'm thinking your wife is cannier than you are and has learned to hold her tongue to prevent pot throwing. You might encourage her to talk of her *idiocy* someday. It could be meaningful when you least expect it."

"If you think you and Celeste have some magic greater than erudition to lead people when you speak, you have as many attics to let as they do. There is no magic in impassioned speech. You merely fill empty heads and tell them what they wish to hear. And talking to dead grandmothers is a useless habit." Ash re-ordered his inkpots rather than reveal his curiosity about his wife's Malcolm ability.

Sometimes, he was almost convinced that Christie did have some magic ability to understand him where others did not, but he knew that was just his need to believe he'd married the right woman.

"It's not magic in the fantastical sense," Erran argued. "It's just an extra ability that other people don't have or don't recognize, and that Malcolm women have learned to exploit—with the encouragement of all their nattering journals."

"I'm fairly certain that most people who have voices in their heads belong in Bedlam," Ash said disparagingly. "And if you and Celeste wish to mesmerize crowds, don't ask me to bail you out afterward."

"And there, the Beast is back. I'll try to return before your meeting this evening. Give my sympathies to your beautiful wife." The door opened and closed and Erran's breath of fresh air was gone.

Apparently having watched to know when Ash's office was empty, Hartley dashed in a trifle breathlessly. "There's a man in the mews who wants to buy Chuckles. How do I know he'll be kind to him?"

"William usually visits the places where he sends his dogs," Ash explained. "I won't sell a horse unless I know how the man treats his animals. I don't think you're quite old enough to make that judgment. We'll take Chuckles back to the estate after the election is over."

He couldn't see Hartley's expression to judge his reaction. He'd always been too busy to pay attention to his sons when he'd been able to see them, and now he would be unable to watch the changes as they grew into young men. He wouldn't be able to see any babe Christie bore.

He buried the sadness and shut the lid on it.

"I don't think Chuckles will like the other dogs in the country," he heard Hartley say, before the new butler introduced another visitor.

"HE WANTS A SOIREE SUNDAY NIGHT, and then a luncheon buffet on Monday, before the vote," Christie said, attempting to hide her distress.

What if she failed? What if the entire country was doomed to revolution because she could not be the political wife she needed to be?

DON'T BE FOOLISH, the voice in her head said angrily. JUST KEEP MY GRANDSON OUT OF TROUBLE. HE'S BLIND IN MORE WAYS THAN ONE.

That was helpful. Christie rubbed her temple and shut out the voice. She didn't want to be told Ash was in trouble when she was already in over her head.

"The rooms should be ready for guests today," Moira said, straightening the new drapery and completely missing the point. "The dining room is still shabby but cover it in food and silver, and men won't notice."

"I have never even organized a luncheon for *two*," Christie clarified. "I am a marchioness with no social skills whatsoever." Much less any ability to keep a stubborn man like her husband out of trouble, even if she knew where to look for it.

Moira patted the final fold in the drapery and looked up with laughter in her eyes. "You have tamed the Beast of Ashford! How can you doubt your ability to take on society? Tell the servants what you need, approve the menu, order Ash to prepare an invitation list, and have someone to write and address them. Then you simply stand about, looking elegant. That's what my mother does."

Moira's mother was the daughter of an earl and the wife of a viscount. She *knew* the people she was inviting. Christie took a deep breath to steady her racing thoughts. "Would it be terrible to impose on your mother and ask her to help me?" she asked.

"She'd love it!" Moira cried excitedly. "Especially if we're all invited. Marrying off six daughters is an expensive nuisance, but if we can appear at Ashford's affairs, that will be fewer she has to arrange. She'll be ecstatic. What about Aster and Celeste? Will you ask them too? You'll have an army of your own."

Christie nodded in relief—she loved having family. "Anyone who is inclined to help is welcome. I can direct menus and servants, but right now, I honestly do not even know what silver we possess. I had hoped I might have time to learn my way, but this is already Friday and they're planning to vote on Monday. Apparently the fate of the kingdom depends on the outcome, so invitations must go out *immediately*."

"Resting the fate of a kingdom on the shoulders of one woman is about as efficient as depending on a volatile, blind marquess," Moira said with laughter. "Obviously, the times are desperate."

"You are not helping," Christie protested.

Hartley appeared in the doorway, looking uncertain. "My lady," he said formally, "might I have a word with you?"

On top of all else, she was now a *stepmother*. Christie thought she might not have examined this marriage agreement as thoroughly as she should have. Steadying her incipient panic, she said, "Call me Christie or Chris, please. I cannot be your mother, but perhaps I can be like an older sister."

Hartley looked doubtful but nodded agreement. "There is a man in the mews who wishes to buy Chuckles now that he is healed. I don't think Chuckles will like living in a kennel, and I can't take him to school. How do I know if he's a good dog owner?"

"Oh, dear, you really can't, not unless you've seen how he keeps his dogs. Why don't you wait and talk to your Uncle William?" A man she had yet to meet, since he'd been in the north country when she'd so hastily wed. "You won't be returning to school until the first of the year. Can it wait?"

Hartley looked glum and scuffed his feet, but a new assortment of important-looking men arrived and had to be distributed in the anteroom to wait their turn. In the confusion, the boy disappeared.

By evening, Christie had written the invitations for Sunday evening's soiree, consulted with the cook over menus, and inventoried the silver and china with the butler. New plate was obviously needed, but this would be a buffet. She hoped busy men wouldn't notice. Their wives probably would. Perhaps she could find something better for them to think about—like pushing their husbands to support reform.

She waited until Ashford's last visitor had departed that evening to approach her new husband. Looking lordly and grand in his tailored coat and starched linen, Ash was staring peculiarly in the direction of his inkpots, lining them up in some order explicable only to himself.

YOU CAN HELP HIM, DEAR, the voice in her head reminded her. THE FAMILY HAS HEALERS, IF YOU WOULD ONLY ASK.

As Ash certainly wouldn't, she realized. Except she didn't know anything about *healers*, and she doubted if Ash did either. One more lesson on her list to learn.

Out of instinct, feeling his pain, Christie crossed the study to stand behind her new husband and rub his temples. "I fear you do too much and will wear out the only brain you will ever have."

He laughed tiredly and picked up a yellow ceramic inkpot. He seemed to be examining it in the lamplight. "My head is too hard to wear out, ask anyone. Those gentleman who just left—and I use the term loosely—want to be assured that the Whigs will not allow trade unions."

"If I am to speak knowledgeably to these so-called gentlemen, you must teach me the issues," she suggested. "What is a trade union?"

He gestured dismissively. "I will not trouble you to learn my headaches. Are the invitations sent out?"

Christie grabbed a lock of his thick black hair and yanked.

Ash yelped and grabbed her wrist. "What the devil was that for?"

She leaned over and kissed his scarred temple. "I am testing to see if your skull is intact or if brain matter leaks out at night."

She had difficulty believing those words had come from humble Harriet's mouth. But bold Christie had evidently found a home—and meant to shape it for her own.

To her astonishment, a rumble of laughter met her audacity.

"You do not shy away from the difficult, do you? I am sitting here wondering exactly that—how damaged is my head? Is this pot yellow?" He held up the ugly ceramic inkpot he'd been moving about.

"It is, my lord," she cried, forgetting to use his name in her excitement. "You can *see* it?"

"Do not get too excited," he admonished. "I can see that particular yellow. I can't claim more than that. I know it's an inkpot because I can feel it. I have a sense of where my desk is and where it is on the desk, but only the yellow one."

"I have a yellow gown I can try on for you upstairs," she murmured in his ear. "And you can explain trade unions for me while you help me undress."

He shoved back his chair, rose to tower over her, and nipped her ear while caressing her breast. "We'll have supper sent up."

Twenty-five

MARRIED LIFE SUITED HER, Christie decided on Saturday morning. The *bed* part of it suited her, she amended as she nervously watched servants racing about, polishing the newly installed furniture in the salon.

She liked to keep an eye on their activity. Otherwise, the lame scullery maid had been known to haul heavy coalscuttles and the one-handed servant had eagerly balanced enormous bouquets in the crook of her bad arm. Christie admired their zeal, but coal spilled on the new carpet and broken vases only increased the work load.

She had experience with servants and easily ordered them about. When she was calm, she could block out their familiar resentments and jealousies. It was the upcoming festivities and the barrage of emotions from so many strangers at once that nearly paralyzed her with fear.

Straightening out the eager maids and admonishing the new housekeeper to keep their tasks sorted appropriately, Christie caught a kitten escaping from the kitchen and looked around for someone to hand it to. The housekeeper had already bustled off. The new butler was nervously carrying out one of Ash's bellowed commands. The maids had fled upstairs as the footmen introduced the first of the morning visitors.

Christie held up the gray half-grown kitty and admired its blue eyes. "I can have a kitten of my own now, can't I?" The kitten yawned, and pure pleasure seeped through her. *This* was how she'd hoped family life might be. She could be herself in the warm acceptance of familiar surroundings—as long as she could close her mind to the needs of dozens of strangers.

The door knocker rapped imperiously, the kitten clawed its way out of her arms, and no servant appeared to direct the latest arrival.

Well, that was also part of family life, she supposed, especially *this* family.

Knowing marchionesses didn't generally answer knockers, hoping this was the Malcolm ladies come to plan tomorrow's soiree, Christie opened the door.

A tall Gypsy woman in a gown of the latest fashion—except in a vibrant gold and purple no aristocratic matron would wear—waited impatiently on the step. Christie tried not to gawk—or compare her outmoded housekeeping gown and frumpy visage with the dramatic presence of this visitor. She glanced to see if even a maid accompanied this imposing personage, but she saw only a carriage rolling away.

"I am here to see the marchioness," the woman said haughtily, presenting her card as if Christie were a servant.

Hidden Harriet almost emerged to take the card like any good housekeeper. But there was just enough bold Christie attached to see the humor and contemplate saying *of course* and shutting the door in the stranger's face. Or perhaps she should say disdainfully, *she's not at home.*

LET HER IN, CHILD, her inner voice scolded. *USE YOUR EYES. YOU KNOW WHO THIS IS.*

Christie looked at the card. *Mrs. Pamela Weldon.* No husband's name. The name meant nothing. Still, she stepped aside to allow in the stranger while studying her surreptitiously.

The woman was almost as tall as she, but far more dashing. Handsome, not beautiful, Christie decided. She had striking auburn hair rolled into an elaborate coiffure beneath a hat designed to emphasize her theatrically large blue eyes, sharp cheekbones, and wide, red mouth. The woman wore rouge! And kohl.

And even though she'd thought the twins looked just like their father—Christie could see their wide mouths and mobile expressions in this woman. She nearly swallowed her tongue in awkwardness. *This* was the woman Ash had taken to his bed and who had borne his sons.

"Ashford is entertaining visitors today. We can talk upstairs, in the family salon." Uneasily, she gestured toward the stairs.

Miss—or Mrs.—Weldon narrowed her eyes and studied Christie and her old gown. "*You* are the woman he finally married?"

Trying not to wince at the visitor's disbelief, Christie stiffened with the arrogance of the marchioness she must become. "It seems so, Mrs. Weldon." She led the way up the stairs to the shabby family floor. The twins were apparently at their studies. She could hear nothing from the schoolroom above.

"I am almost relieved," her guest said. "I feared Duncan would choose another porcelain figurine like Margaret. Such a creature would never survive in this household. Where are my sons?"

If she hoped to catch Christie by surprise with her familiarity with Ash's household and mention of the twins, she failed—thanks to the voice in her head. "The boys have been sent down from school for objecting to being called useless bastards, I believe," Christie said caustically. She had little sympathy for a woman who had abandoned her children to earn that fashionable gown on her back.

"They'll learn to deal with bullies." Mrs. Weldon's tone echoed Christie's lack of compassion. "What have you done with them?" She scanned the drawing room they entered, as if expecting her sons to materialize.

"If all is as it should be, they're being tutored upstairs. I have not yet taken up boiling little boys in oil." Christie wasn't certain where that comment had come from, although it might have something to do with the anxiety her guest exuded. Despite her proud façade, Mrs. Weldon was treating Christie as if she might turn into a witch and fly off on her broom at any moment.

Christie bit her wayward tongue and more carefully assessed the twins' mother. She'd been reluctant to open herself up to such a strong character, but the woman seemed to be agitated and a little afraid. For her sons? Most likely. She tried to place herself in the visitor's shoes and be more forgiving.

"I had heard you were a Malcolm," her guest said stiffly. "One hears tales."

So much for being forgiving. Rolling her eyes, vowing inwardly to behave herself, Christie gestured at the chair least likely to contain animal hair. "If you'll have a seat, I'll ring for tea. The house is at sixes and sevens until the matter of the administration is decided."

Mrs. Weldon settled on the aging Louis Quinze chair. "Politics," she said disdainfully. "Duncan has this marvelous ability to play Shakespeare, but I always knew he'd end up in politics."

Christie rang the bell and hoped someone was in the kitchen to hear it. "As a marquess, he has little choice. I admire his dedication to steering the kingdom in the proper direction. Not many men of his status would have the understanding of a working man's concerns."

He'd taught her about trade unions last night, in between . . . other things. Her cheeks burned, and she hid the fact by tossing a few coals to engage the embers before the maid arrived.

"I'm glad he found someone who understands him," Mrs. Weldon said. "My concern is my sons. Do I need to take them off your hands?"

Startled, Christie turned back to face Ash's stunning ex-mistress. It was a good thing the man was blind. Christie knew her fair plainness could not begin to compare with that fire and drama, although— With a little paint, she might enhance her best features as the actress had. Interesting to contemplate.

"Your sons are fine here. I think Ash needs them about to be reminded that he is human and not an automaton. Did you *wish* to take the twins?"

"Good heavens, no." The woman waved a gloved hand. "I can arrange my schedule to take them on regular holidays, but if they insist on getting sent down at midterm, they'd have to travel with me. I still play ingénues, and I'd much prefer that my audience not know I'm old enough to have adolescent sons!"

Christie had heard the gossip about the boys' actress mother. Pamela Weldon had grown up in the village near Iveston but apparently wanted to see a larger world. She couldn't blame her entirely, except for the part of earning Ash's support by bearing him sons, then deserting them.

Christie ordered the tea and settled into a rattan settee across from the twins' glamorous mother. "Ask me what you will. I understand your concern for your children and would like to assure you that they are in safe hands."

Mrs. Weldon gestured dramatically. "It is impossible to keep those two safe. I accept that. As we have seen, even Ashford is not safe, and he has more experience. It is the nature of life. But I would see them cared for and if possible, happy."

Having been sheltered every minute of her life, Christie was horrified by this attitude.

SHE IS RIGHT, YOU KNOW, the voice said sadly. WE CANNOT GLUE THEM TO A SHELF IN A LOCKED CABINET.

Christie hid her wince at this description of her own life and focused on Mrs. Weldon's agitation. "I never had siblings," she said slowly, searching for the words to calm her visitor. "So I think of the twins as mischievous younger brothers who must be guided in the right direction. Did you have any particular plans for them?"

Her guest's posture almost imperceptibly relaxed. "I want them to be happy. They seem to be so at Iveston. I'm not so sure about London. It is a dangerous place."

The tea arrived and Christie poured it while pondering her reply. "I agree that they would prefer the country, but right now, Ashford's brother has taken charge of the estate. It is awkward to ask him to look after the children too."

Mrs. Weldon's expression brightened. "Ah, yes, I see. Theo must make a perfectly horrible farmer. And he is newly wed, I hear. My boys would be too much for a new wife. Which brings us back to you—how can you possibly look after them? They are adventurous."

"Only when they are together," Christie said with humor. "Hugh fears nothing, and Hartley is impetuous. Together, they bring out each other's most dangerous traits. At some point, it may be necessary to consider separate schools, or they'll continue to urge each other to greater mischief."

"Exactly." Mrs. Weldon relaxed and sipped her tea. "I had feared you would be too much like Margaret and order them sent to boarding school all year so that you needn't put up with them. I am relieved to see the Great Ass has developed sense with age and chosen a woman with a heart in her chest."

Christie bit back a smile at this appellation. "Ashford loves his sons. He would not let anyone come between them. Shall I send for the boys? I think their studies can be interrupted for this occasion."

"If you would, please," she said eagerly. "We are only passing through London on our way to Bath. I should have a house rented there by mid-December so they may come to me then. I do miss them."

The Malcolm ladies arrived just as the twins raced downstairs to lead their mother to the garden to meet Chuckles. Relieved that the elegant actress didn't object to a filthy hound, Christie returned to the downstairs salon to welcome Aster, along with Moira and her mother, Lady McDowell. Moira's sister, Emilia, had also come to help prepare for the soiree. Slender, tall, and black-haired, Emilia looked every inch an idle, elegant lady in her fashionably billowing sleeves and sweeping skirt.

"We need yellow," Christie told them, sweeping her hand to indicate the newly-decorated chamber. "Ashford can sometimes see yellow."

Moira exclaimed in distress over her delicate design of blue and silver, but glancing around, she instantly rallied. "I have a very large gold decorative fan we can fasten to the mirror. Do you think he might see that?"

"I have a bright yellow shawl we can drape over the chair, if that will help. The house has strong power," Lady Aster declared in satisfaction. "It must be healing him. Emilia, you really should study the herb garden. There may be vital physics that can cure him entirely."

Moira's fashionably bored sister actually appeared interested.

"Emilia is a healer," Aster explained. "She also studies the therapeutic quality of plants, much as Ashford's great-grandmother did."

TELL HER TO LOOK FOR THE RED GINSENG, the voice said with what sounded like excitement.

Christie rubbed her forehead and decided if she must go mad, she was in good company. "I believe that his grandmother just told me to look for . . . red ginseng?"

"*Red* ginseng? That takes years to root and grow!" Emilia exclaimed, already aiming for the door. "It normally grows in a forest. How can there possibly be any here?"

THERE WAS ONCE INDIA SNAKEROOT AT IVESTON, IN THE CONSERVATORY. This was said a little sadly, as if it might not be there any longer.

Christie repeated the message. Emilia looked at her cousin with excitement. "Aster? Have the heathens left anything living in the conservatory? Christie's voice is telling us that fatigue is part of Ashford's problem, as well as possibly something to do with his blood vessels. Snakeroot needs tropical conditions. It won't be in the garden."

"There are a few things still rooted, but I don't know if anything tropical survived," Aster said, following her cousin.

"Moira and I will stay here and prepare the salon for tomorrow," Lady McDowell said, dismissing them with a gesture. "The rest of you go grub in the garden."

"I should have some dried snakeroot at home. If we could just find the ginseng . . ." Emilia was saying eagerly as she called for her pelisse. "We could prepare a potion that might help Ashford's headaches, at the very least."

Before their outerwear could be produced, more visitors were announced. Christie sighed in exasperation at the cards presented. "Lord Palmer has brought his wife and a guest. I know he's important to the vote. I fear I must entertain them."

"Nonsense," Lady McDowell declared. "Lady Palmer is a nosy gossip come to spy on you for her friends, to see whether they should attend the soiree. You go on outside to the garden. I'll have the butler send them out to you. We'll close up the salon so they can't see what we're doing. It's ill-bred of them to show up prior to the event."

"I think I love you," Christie declared happily, kissing the stout lady's powdery cheek. "And if this is Lady Ninian speaking in my head, she says you remind her very much of her Aunt Stella, and she sends her love."

Lady McDowell covered her cheek with her hand and blushed. "Nonsense, go on with you then."

Excited—and terrified—that there might be some possibility of saving Duncan's eyesight with Emilia's herbs, Christie led her excitedly chattering cousins to the rear door.

HEARING CHRISTIE'S VOICE CARRYING ALONG with the babbling of Aster and her cousin toward the back of the house, Ash frowned. Hadn't he just heard the conniving bitch Pamela and her twins head to the garden? Were they having a circus out there on this chilly day? He had to assume it was gray. It was November in London.

Had Pamela already met with Christie? And they hadn't killed each other? He wished he'd been a spider on that wall. He rubbed his pounding head and heard the butler at the door announcing Lord Palmer.

Ash groaned a few minutes later at the sound of *Lady* Palmer's carrying voice—accompanied by *Margaret*? Oddly, they seemed to be strolling down the corridor instead of waiting in the salon.

The twins' mother and Jane Palmer despised each other— probably for good reason since Ash had taken up with Jane while Pamela was carrying the twins. He'd been young. Jane had been newly widowed. Lord Palmer hadn't been on the scene then and probably knew nothing of the liaison now.

Two mistresses, an ex-fiancée, a wife, and her family in that tiny garden . . .

Ash's sins had come back to haunt him with a vengeance. His gut clenched as he imagined the battle ensuing. Could he play invalid if war erupted in his own yard?

Had he possessed eyesight, he would have excused himself, rushed to the garden, and extricated innocent Christie from the mudslinging. She was so much better than the shallow women he'd chosen in the past. Last night, she'd been splendid in her yellow gown, swinging the skirt so he could see the motion, testing him by lowering the bodice. She'd worn it to bed so he could wake up and find her.

The last thing in the world he wanted to do was hurt kind-hearted Christie. In an attempt to extricate her, he called for a footman as Lord Palmer entered.

"Find my wife and tell her I need the letters she was working on," he told the servant, hoping he was providing an excuse for Christie to escape.

While Palmer rattled on, Ash clenched his fists and waited for screams.

Christie didn't appear. The footman merely returned to murmur a message to Erran, who excused himself to seek the documents—leaving Ash terrified that his exes would have his wife packing and gone before he could escape this interminable conference.

Twenty-six

"WHY ON EARTH ARE YOU TAKING calls in this dismal, cold excuse for a garden?" Miss Caldwell asked as she and a lady Christie assumed must be Lady Palmer lingered on the back stairs, unwilling to descend to the muddy gravel.

Recognizing Ashford's former fiancée behind the furred cloak and muff of a grand ice princess, Christie grimaced. The lady beside her was older, as rouged as the twins' actress mother, and radiated bitterness and grim satisfaction as she studied Christie and the muddy scene beneath her.

Both ladies emanated spite and jealousy and—

A footman ran out with a message from Ashford about documents, and enlightenment gradually dawned. Here was her husband's rakehell past. She appreciated his offer of escape, but she didn't think retreat from a battlefield was the best solution. She told the servant to ask Lord Erran, then tried to find a polite way of greeting the uninvited guests.

"Ah, the whore of Babylon has arrived," Mrs. Weldon cried before Christie could find her tongue. "Come to see who won the Great Ass where you could not?"

Oh dear. That was definitely a battle cry. Christie exchanged glances with Aster and a startled Emilia, who had just exclaimed in delight at some discovery among the overgrown weeds. They shrugged and left the situation to her.

The twins looked up in surprise at their mother's operatic challenge. That could not be good.

Did no one care that they were worrying children and distressing her? Apparently not—or they were too wrapped up in themselves to notice others. Christie stoppered her own anger to assess the situation.

"You are the company you keep," the older woman on the step purred maliciously. "And I see Ashford has descended to the very dregs of society."

At this insult, the twins' mother reached past the dog to the mud he'd been wallowing in. The boys lit up like Christmas candles and followed suit, forming their own mud balls.

Jealousy and repressed frustration emanated from the newcomers. Rage at the insults came from the twins and their mother—

And a battle like this was how Ives earned their reputations, through little fault of their own except carelessness.

If Ashford was to emerge as the powerful politician he deserved to be, it would be up to Christie to set limits that Ives men seldom recognized. And as much as she might be inclined to push Margaret and the obnoxious newcomer into the mud as they deserved, she had to provide an example for her new family.

Realizing in wicked relief that she outranked every woman in this scene, she stooped to scratch Chuckles behind the ear and lay a restraining hand on Hartley's shoulder. The twins' paused in their mud ball formation.

"I wasn't aware that I invited callers at all," Christie said. "Miss Caldwell, Lady Palmer, as you can see, I'm much too busy for visitors. If you would like to entertain the twins or help Miss McDowell with her herbs, I'd be delighted to accept your aid. Otherwise, I fear I'll have to forego your charming company. I have a party to plan."

She hugged Hartley, forcing him to drop his mud. Heart pounding in exultation and temerity, she bent her head regally at Ash's ex-mistress, ex-fiancée, and Lady Palmer. Wielding her greater size, Christie sailed past the bevy of beauties, forcing the uninvited to step out of her way, into the garden mud.

Ash's previous women were strikingly lovely, but he'd married *her*. That would have to keep her going strong, not only in the face of adversity, but Ives insanity.

PREPARING FOR BED THAT EVENING, Ash grimaced as he drank the concoction Christie had insisted that he try. "What the devil is this? And can I add brandy?"

She didn't dare explain that his great-grandmother had demanded that Emilia dose him with snakeroot or whatever was in the drink. "I think Emilia added ale with the herbs and milk. I cannot really say. But if there's some chance this might heal your vision, how can we not try?"

"Depends on whether you mean to poison me first." He threw back the last of it and shuddered while Christie unfastened his waistcoat.

"Am I a terrible person if I fear that Emilia's posset will actually work and return your eyesight?" she asked with a shade of weariness.

The day had been exhausting or she would never have asked such an awful question, but having all Ash's women converge on her at once—worse, understanding that hadn't even been *all* of them! She didn't think she could tolerate knowing the rest. She wanted to hide under the bed.

Ash's meeting hadn't been over until all her female visitors had left. He had been tense and anxious ever since. Now that they were alone, he caught her hands and pulled them behind her back so he could tug her closer. "Why would you wish that?" he asked with the formidable intellectual curiosity that hid behind his tantrums.

"All your former lovers are *beautiful*," she said wistfully. "If I thought you could see plain me, I'd have to flee in despair."

He hugged her harder, and she could feel relief pouring off of him.

"You entertained those bitches and did not run screaming in horror?" Amusement laced his voice. "I am more relieved than I can say. The party only needed Olivia's mother to form a witchy coven more treacherous than anything Malcolms can conjure."

"Don't say that," she said, aggrieved. "Your former mistresses looked at me as if I were the witch. It took all my influence to keep them from slinging mud, and not just the verbal sort. The twins ended up taking their mother to the park. Why on earth was Margaret with Lady Palmer?"

"Spite," he said with assurance. "They wanted to mock me through you. That you did not come to blows proves your superior intelligence. I was terrified that you would use that intelligence to run screaming into the night."

She leaned against him, happy to have a man who could support her like this. "As long as you don't mind that I can never be an elegant sophisticate, I'll not run anywhere."

"I will admit that I was once shallow enough to prefer women for how they looked on my arm, but even then, I preferred women who could stand on their own. Margaret was an aberration. I hope I am wise enough to want more than just looks now. They lack your compassion and intellect and selflessness. I never understood the need for tender heartedness until you came along."

Not quite pacified after her eye-opening encounter with three beautiful, self-possessed, theatrical females, but relieved at his response, Christie returned to unfastening his buttons. "I do not mean to sound feeble, my lord, but I have nowhere near their experience. I fear all London will look upon you with pity and sneer at me. I've quite decided that if your eyes magically begin to work, I shall disappear rather than embarrass you further."

"Then I'll not drink anymore of your cousin's foul posset," he declared. "Or, if miracles happen, I will spend the rest of my life chasing after you. Would you rather I wasted my life that way?"

She giggled. "I think we're both very tired to believe in fairy tales. I will be glad to finally see Iveston when this is over."

"So will I," he said fervently. "Pray the weather holds, and we'll leave as soon as the Commons votes on the administration."

"Your sons will enjoy that." She wrapped her arms around his neck and let him carry her to bed. "Tonight, I mean to enjoy you."

He chuckled and fell down on top of her. When he discovered she wore a yellow corset, he laughed out loud and proceeded to tug on the strings.

"My only regret is that I cannot see these beautiful melons," he said, lifting her breasts free. He nipped at a nipple, rendering it exquisitely sensitive to the kisses he lavished next.

"Melons?" she asked archly. "I had never thought of myself quite that way. Am I hard and firm or ripe and smelly?"

"Firm and aromatic and all mine," he said in satisfaction. "No more talk of running away. You are made to be my marchioness."

And he proved it with a vigor that had her biting the pillowcase to keep her cries of pleasure from waking the neighbors.

As long as she didn't have to remind him of the voices in her head, she might hope to build a life on just the basis of their lovemaking. All she had to do was refrain from murdering his mistresses, because this new Christie seemed to be a devilishly malicious wench.

***

"TELL YOUR VALET TO HURRY," his brilliant bride told Ash on Sunday morning as they walked down the stairs. "I have something I wish you to see before your first visitors arrive."

He pressed a kiss to her frown, inhaled her soft scent as she deposited him in his own chamber, then smoothed her worry wrinkles with a finger. "I slept better last night than I can remember doing in months. I don't know what was in that posset, but I'll drink it for that reason alone."

She took his hand, squeezed it, and kissed his stubbly cheek. "I'm glad! Emilia almost expired of joy when she discovered the ginseng growing in that jungle you call a garden. You will need to take more with your meals. Meet me in the salon?"

"What is your hurry? Surely we can have a bite to eat before I tell you the salon smells beautiful or whatever it is you think I need to know." He knew he was hungry enough to clean off the buffet.

"I can't tell you. I need your honest reaction. I've never attended a soiree, and I'm terrified. I know I cannot cling to you in such a function, but—"

Mildly alarmed, Ash held up his hand to stop the flow of words. "You have never attended a soiree? You are planning a function that you know nothing about?"

"Aster's family is helping me," she explained, "but they cannot help me deal with strangers. Sometimes, it is very difficult to block unexpected emotions. I have learned to manage disdain, to some extent, but sometimes people are so angry that they emit . . ."

"Wait, wait!" Ash didn't think he wanted to hear more about *managing disdain*, but unlike his wife, he preferred to face his fears. He set her down on the bed and stood over her, wishing he could see her expression. But he sensed she was being entirely truthful. "Start with disdain. What disdain?"

"When people meet me," his amazing bride said earnestly. "It is the reason I hide behind potted plants and columns. I know it is weak of me, but I cannot bear so much negativity aimed in my direction. It is as if they decide I'm a worthless lump of nothing based on my looks alone. I *know* I'm not, but I lose any interest in knowing someone that shallow. And I retreat from the pain. Once I know what they're like, I can learn how to block them, and . . ."

Alarmed, Ash waved her to a halt again. "How do you know they feel disdain? The voices in your head?"

"No, of course not," she said in puzzlement. "Disdain is a rather blatant feeling, is it not? Not like contentment, which is more like being enveloped in a warm fuzzy blanket. Or anger, which is sharp and painful but might be directed at anyone, and not me. I suppose if I had more confidence, I could do as others do and block everyone, but I don't have enough experience with groups of people and never learned how to behave without understanding how they felt."

Ash rubbed his head. "I think the posset must be muddling my brain. It sounds as if you are telling me you *feel* someone else's disdain. That's not possible, so I must be misunderstanding. I would gladly pinch any old biddy who *looks* on you with disdain, but I cannot see expressions. You will have to tell me."

She sat silent for a moment. Ash thought that might be ominous.

"I think perhaps I should not distract you right now," she said, forming her words with care. "Dress, and we will visit the salon together."

She swept past him in a rustle of petticoats, leaving him wondering if he was as crazed as a woman who heard voices in her head and thought she *felt* disdain.

He supposed no woman could be perfect, but he had hoped this one was at least rational. Surely, he'd just misheard.

He'd be laughed out of town, and rightly so, if his wife announced that disdain and anger were physically painful. He was definitely misunderstanding.

UNEASILY, CHRISTIE PACED the gleaming salon, straightening the yellow shawl pinned to a chair near the sofa, removing a broken flower in the enormous bouquet of yellow chrysanthemums and blue asters. She'd ordered a few red roses interspersed—just in case contrast made a difference.

But it wasn't concern about Ash seeing yellow that had her fidgeting. If he didn't *feel* how people felt—how did he survive at all? To her, that would be even worse than being blind. She could certainly understand his frustration at being deprived of two valuable senses!

Or—as she'd often wondered—did he and other people block these feelings so often that they no longer noticed them? Perhaps she was just more inept than most, or too inexperienced, to manage her response as others did. It might be like controlling temper—something she didn't possess much of and had learned to divert so often that she seldom became angry.

Perhaps Ash had suppressed all empathy until he no longer felt emotion!

If so—she shuddered a little—then it was very possible that he no longer understood feelings. He would never be able to love! Not even his own children.

The possibility that her husband could never be more than an automaton roiled her already churning emotions. That might explain how he could fling his fear and confusion all around as if no one knew it was there. He didn't know the pain it caused!

She needed the Malcolm ladies here. They were the most compassionate people she had ever met. They'd know what she was talking about.

But they would be in church this morning. They weren't scheduled to arrive until this evening, just before the soiree began. She was just overly nervous at being introduced to all London society at once.

Deep breath. So, maybe some people were better at blocking feelings than she was. She would work at this one step at a time. Not right now.

She'd managed a bite of toast and some tea for breakfast before the first business visitor of the day was announced, an industrialist concerned about trade unions. Ash hadn't emerged from his chamber yet. She really needed him to see, *prayed* he could see, what they had done and give him time to grasp it. Drat these early callers.

She heard the footman rap on Duncan's door, then deliver the industrialist to the study. She'd never grab his attention now.

She checked the table settings the servants were laying out. She'd ordered mostly foods that people could eat with their fingers to minimize the problem of china and silverware shortage. She thought Ash and Erran had concocted some conspiracy to ply some of the less reliable voters with drink, so she confirmed that the wine and brandy were fully stocked.

She went upstairs to be certain their few bedrooms had been prepared for any guests who might not be in condition to stumble into a freezing night. Mary had returned to act as her maid and was busy packing clothes to carry down to Ash's chamber in case they needed to use hers.

Mary still hadn't learned to do hair properly. Lady McDowell was bringing over her own maid this evening to help Christie with her limp tresses. The finished gown had been delivered this morning—a rather bold green and pale gold. Christie didn't know if Ash could see gold as well as yellow, but she hoped he might.

She had come a long way since that night hiding in the shadows at the only ball she'd ever attended, watching the company gliding by in gales of excited chatter and laughter. She was no longer the pathetic spinster who had waited an hour for a suitor to call. Tonight was one more step into her future as the woman she wished to become.

She would have to believe she was a help to Ash, not an embarrassment who should be hidden in rural anonymity. She wanted to be strong enough to lock Hidden Harriet in a box where she belonged and never let her out again.

The Malcolm ladies and their husbands began arriving about an hour before the soiree. Christie had persuaded them to stand in the reception line with her and Ashford. Lady McDowell and Aster had both brought maids to help guests repair and refresh their coiffures and gowns as the evening progressed.

The men went looking for Ash while Christie led the others upstairs to the family salon. The twins had been told to stay in the schoolroom, although Christie suspected they were rummaging through the attic, looking for mischief.

"Everything looks spectacular," Moira raved. "The chandelier in the salon must have taken hours to polish!"

"Don't tell the children, but Ashford can see light and shadow if there's enough illumination," Christie explained. "I was hoping the chandelier might help, although I thought half the staff would quit before it was ready."

"He can see light?" Aster exclaimed. "And shadow? Is this new? Might he really be getting better?"

Christie shrugged helplessly. "I probably should have said nothing. He does not explain because he's afraid it will all go away tomorrow."

Aster raised her eyes to the heavens and clasped her hands, as if in prayer.

"More mirrors to reflect the light are needed then," Moira said, more practically.

"Can he see the yellow we set out?" Aster asked, still excited. Ash's recovery would most affect her and Theo.

"I haven't been able to pry him out of his study all day. It's been one visitor after another. I thought surely he's twisted the arms of everyone in the kingdom," Christie replied. "We'll have to explain to him while we wait in the reception line."

"What Ashford and Erran are doing is crucial to the future of the country," Celeste said in her soothing voice. "It's important that we support them in any way we can."

"I understand that and agree, but . . ." Christie hesitated, uncertain how to approach the topic that had fretted at her all day.

"But . . . ?"Aster said in her blunt manner. "What is wrong?"

Christie took a deep breath, closed her eyes, and removed the barriers she erected to keep too many emotions from bombarding her at once. "But you are worrying—about the unborn babe, perhaps? And Celeste is being polite when she speaks of Erran. She's angry, and I assume it's about something he's done. Lady McDowell, you aren't really listening but are anxious about . . . maybe the election? Surely, I am not the only one who feels these things?"

Thunderous silence followed. Squeezing the bridge of her nose, Christie lowered herself into the closest chair. It hurt to let in so much emotion, but she was registering a rising confusion and excitement.

So it wasn't just Ash who was damaged—so was she.

Twenty-seven

THE SILENCE AFTER CHRISTIE'S announcement about her *feelings* erupted into a babble of excitement. Aster waved everyone to silence. Lady McDowell sent for sherry. Christie huddled miserably in her chair, trying to calm herself while surrounded by a storm of emotion she lacked the strength to block.

"It's not the *babe* I'm worried about," Aster said, "but you and Ashford. Mars is transiting Ash's moon, squaring with his Saturn. In his case, that's a direct and immediate threat to his home and family. At the same time, danger points in your family sector could be triggered by the transit. I cannot predict the direction, no matter how deeply I read your charts."

Christie winced. *Danger points* sounded ominous. "How does one go about guarding against cosmic peril?" she asked, a little more sarcastically than she ought.

"One can't, of course." Aster shrugged and added, "Although you are correct that I am also worrying that I won't be able to reach Wystan in the spring if Theo must oversee the planting. You are very good at interpreting emotion. That's an intriguing gift."

"It's called survival," she said a little too tartly, uncomfortable with being the subject of scrutiny. "I observe and surmise."

The ladies nodded as if they understood. Aster smiled in delight. "I suppose that is the reason you deal so well with Ashford and his tantrums. You understand how he's feeling better than we do."

Oh dear. Christie squirmed. Now she felt intrusive. If other people didn't feel strong emotion as she did, then her guessing the reason for their feelings was almost like mind reading. She really could not let others know what she did!

Celeste added to Christie's confusion by confessing, "And I am angry at Erran for spending all his time with Ashford, which is selfish. You can *tell* that? Or is it the ghosts?"

Christie shook her head, trying to sort through her appalled confusion. She'd always felt different but blamed her size . . . . She hadn't realized she was the only person—possibly in the world—crippled by the emotions of others.

"The voices seldom speak to me," she said slowly, too rattled to think clearly, "or if they do, I don't hear them for all the noise of my thoughts. Sensing how people *feel* is different and unavoidable if I'm unprepared. It's something I do like breathing. I have to deliberately hold my breath to not inhale a roomful of hot, stale air. Does that make sense? And you can't open your minds and sense how I'm feeling right now? How is this possible? How does anyone ever understand each other?"

"We can tell how people feel by watching their expressions and gestures or hearing the tone of their voice," Lady McDowell said with interest. "Some people don't pay enough attention to others to care how anyone feels. With his blindness and arrogance, a powerful marquess like Ashford is at a distinct disadvantage in even listening to others, much less understanding them. Is that what has you worried? That marriage with a man who cannot appreciate your feelings will be difficult?"

"I am worried that I am the damaged one here!" Which was selfish, she realized, but right now, she was the only one who understood her horror of being *different*. She'd spent a lifetime hiding her differences! "I thought everyone could feel as I do and just blocked feelings better. I had no notion . . . I don't even know where to begin . . ." Shaken, Christie longed for a moment alone, but shortly, she would have to go downstairs, smile, and pretend all was right with her world.

"It's just your gift," Aster explained. "I'll find appropriate journals for you to read. Your great-grandmother saw ghosts and talked to them. Everyone considered her deranged, but she saved the duke by listening to spirits, so our gifts are good things. We just need to learn how to use them appropriately. You can provide what Ashford is missing. It's ideal!"

"Only, it might not be a good idea to tell Ashford that you can do it," Celeste said in concern. "He thinks Erran and I are demented when we talk about our ability to persuade people to do what we want."

"Ives are like that," Aster said with a shrug. "They have to be convinced that it's scientifically possible. The only reason Erran believes you is because he's gifted too. Theo tries to find excuses for what I do, but at least he listens to me now. He's downstairs setting guards on the doors in case the danger points in our charts involve the house."

She'd already tried to explain to Ashford and he'd looked at her as if she were crazed. Christie winced at her naiveté. "I think I'd like to read those journals," she said weakly. "I've just . . . I've always . . . It's as if I've been told I'm reading minds. I'm *not*."

"Just think of it as a very strong empathy," Lady McDowell said. "You've been isolated and haven't learned to put it to best purposes."

"That's another thing," Christie interrupted. "Is it possible that I was isolated because people were afraid when I told them things I shouldn't know?" She couldn't shake the feeling that her own mother had arranged her isolation.

"Didn't you once say that your mother sometimes speaks inside your head?" Aster asked in curiosity. "Could you try asking her?"

"I've never ascertained what triggers the voices. Maybe I really am damaged," she said sadly.

"Nonsense. This is the reason other people lose their gifts—they fear them," Lady McDowell said with firmness.

"Because they don't want to be different," Christie pointed out with wryness. "People tend to be laughed at if they say they have voices in their head."

Lady McDowell nodded agreement. "But Malcolms are prepared to understand and experiment. It's a shame you had no one to teach you, but we'll help. Try emptying your head. We will be very quiet. Just let everything else fade away and concentrate on what you want to ask."

Christie wrinkled her nose in distaste, but when the other women politely sat on the shabby family furniture and waited, she sighed and closed her eyes. Emptying her head was no easy task. But the possibility of accessing her mother . . . was too wonderful not to try. She just wasn't certain how to form the question.

But the minute she opened her mind, the voice was there without her needing to ask, as if her mother had been waiting for her to listen.

YOU CRIED, the voice said. *YOU WERE ALWAYS A HAPPY CHILD, UNTIL YOUR FATHER DIED. THEN YOU DID NOTHING BUT CRY. I FEARED IT WAS BECAUSE I DID NOTHING BUT CRY, SO I SENT YOU TO STAY WITH YOUR FATHER'S SISTER. YOUR COUSINS WERE OLDER, BUT YOU WERE LARGER, AND YOU TOLD YOUR AUNT THAT EVERYONE HATED YOU. WHEN SHE DIDN'T BELIEVE YOU, YOU FOUGHT THEM—*

EVEN THOUGH NO ONE EVER SAW THEM DO ANYTHING TO YOU. YOU WERE ONLY HAPPY IN THE SCHOOLROOM.

Christie vaguely remembered that summer. Her cousins had made her life miserable in small ways, ways that couldn't easily be traced, but she'd felt their triumph and spite when her favorite doll lost its head or she tripped and fell on objects that disappeared before adults intervened. So she'd *known* who had done it, but she had no proof and couldn't understand why no one else could feel their meanness.

She must have seemed to be a very difficult child when she started fighting for no reason anyone could discern.

IT GREW WORSE WHEN I TRIED TO SEND YOU TO SCHOOL, her mother's voice said sadly. *IT WAS ONLY THEN THAT I COULD ACCEPT THAT YOU SUFFERED MY AFFLICTION OF FEELING TOO MUCH. MY ONLY CHOICE WAS TO DO AS MY PARENTS DID—HIRE A GOVERNESS AND KEEP YOU HOME. I HAD WANTED YOU TO BE BETTER THAN ME. AND NOW YOU ARE! THANK YOUR FRIENDS FOR UNDERSTANDING.*

The voice faded as Christie allowed the buzz of the real world to enter again. Stunned, she simply sat there a moment longer. All this time, she'd had the ability to speak with her mother? And she'd never tried?

YOU WERE NOT READY TO HEAR ME, AND I DID NOT UNDERSTAND HOW TO REACH INTO YOUR MIND WITHOUT FRIGHTENING YOU.

"I am an idiot," Christie said aloud. "My governess used to applaud my superior intellect, but I am an idiot."

"You said your mother died when you were twelve. Did you have anyone else to explain about voices or emotions?" Aster asked. "This is the reason for our journals and for trying to keep track of all our family. I hope your mother said something useful just now."

"She suffered from the same affliction," Christie explained, rubbing a tear from her eye . "That is probably why she was content with rural anonymity. There was no one to teach us how to block spite or hatred. We had to learn it on our own. And hiding from the negative feelings of others made us very strange people. I think she tried to teach me this before she died, but I was too young to understand. Or I didn't want to accept that I was different from everyone else."

"But for a politician's wife, knowing how people feel is ideal," Lady McDowell pointed out. "You will be able to separate friend

from foe and who is teetering on the brink. Come along, let's see
what the men are up to. They're likely to stay in the study drinking if
we don't line them up."

"Oh, and we haven't shown Ashford the salon yet! Let's hurry and
see if he can see the yellows!" Relieved to have something *normal* to
think about, Christie gathered up her skirt and petticoats and led the
way downstairs.

The men, as predicted, were in the study with their brandy.
Refusing to be put off any longer, Christie swept into the room, took
her husband's arm, and insisted that he follow her.

"It's early," he protested. "No one will arrive yet."

"Remember I asked you this morning to come to the salon with
me? And you didn't. Now's the time. The others can drink
themselves under the desk, but I need you for this."

True to form, the ever-curious Ives men and Viscount McDowell
followed them out. Not only were Erran and Theo there, but so was
their half-brother, the blond playwright, Jacques, and their
sophisticated Uncle Pascoe—wearing a monocle today. The large,
bulky gentleman to whom she hadn't been introduced, she assumed
to be half-brother William, the dog trainer. He appeared
uncomfortable in his evening suit, and hadn't shaved yet this
evening, but like most Ives, he had striking cheekbones and thick
dark hair.

Ashford was dressed meticulously in proper black, with gleaming
white linen fastened by a thin black tie. His silver vest was heavily
encrusted with embroidery and the buttons glittered like diamonds.
His valet had recently trimmed his hair and shaved him. Christie
kissed a drop of shaving soap on his jaw as she drew him into the
salon entrance in front of her. He squeezed her hand, then halted in
the doorway.

"By Jove, is that a chandelier?" he asked in amazement. "Or is the
ceiling on fire?"

"You can see it?" Christie asked in excitement. "I'd hoped it
would give you enough shadow to see motion."

"Go twirl about, let me see," he ordered.

Relieved, she did so, letting her green-and-gold striped gown
flare out, revealing her ankles to all and sundry. The other Ives men
whistled. Ash stood there with his walking stick—turning his head to
follow her movement, looking stunned.

"You're flickering," he said. "And what is that yellow blob over there?" He pointed his stick at the mantel.

"Flowers on the mantel," she said in triumph. "Can you see anything else? Look around."

She danced to the back of the room where the large mirror reflected all the candles and lamps placed around the room.

Ash stepped in her direction. "What the devil is that? Light and yellow?"

"A mirror and a gold fan. The light really makes a difference! Now you know where the back of the salon is."

The others began to press into the room behind Ashford, who continued following Christie, obviously able to see her movement. They stayed out of his way, however, as she hurried toward the window. This one was a little more difficult. With the draperies pulled against the night, she only had lamps and the shawl to guide him.

Following her, he smacked the chair with his stick, rubbed the shawl, and settled onto the cushion. He caught Christie's skirt and dragged her down upon his lap. "You are brilliant. I want to marry you again."

She could *feel* his joy and excitement—and despite all her misgivings, it felt good. Kissing his jaw, she leapt from his grasp. "You're crushing the silk, my favorite husband. We'll marry again after the evening is done. If you poke people with your stick to make them move, will you be able to maneuver around the room on your own?"

"I had planned to follow you around. I don't want to talk to these jingle-brains anyway. Do you mean to abandon me?" Despite his words, he rose and crossed the room, using his stick to detect objects. "What did you do with the furniture?"

"Moved it against the walls so you wouldn't stumble over it in the crush. There should be nothing but people around you unless you walk into a wall, and the yellow ought to show you how close you are to those. You may have to go hungry unless you're feeling brave, but you should be able to reign over your salon without need of me," Christie explained.

He frowned and tapped his stick thoughtfully against the floor. "And what will you do all evening?"

"Whatever you need me to do, but I'm fairly certain you won't even notice my presence or absence once the room fills," she said, now understanding his limitations. He couldn't *feel* her as she did him. That made her sad—and more determined to find a way of reaching him.

"Carriages are arriving," Lady McDowell announced. "Take your places, please."

Six tall, black-clad men sauntered in the opposite direction to grab drinks and nibbles from the buffet. Christie huffed in annoyance, but the other women laughed.

"They cannot be tamed, my dear," the viscountess said. "And you wouldn't want them to be. That they have come together for this purpose speaks well of their intentions, if not their manners."

Clinging to the reason for this soiree—the reform that would save the kingdom—Christie prepared herself for the crush of strangers pouring through their front portals. With family there to introduce her and give Ash notice of who was passing down the reception line, she hoped she might endure the worst hour.

The first arrivals were apparently new to society and eager to make the acquaintance of a marquess and his family. Christie merely felt their curiosity and breathed a sigh of relief—or at least as much as her corset would allow.

Then the crush really began. A pair of gentlemen garbed in coats so tight, she thought they might be lined with whalebone, greeted Lady McDowell and the viscount, but she could feel their spite before they reached Erran and Celeste. She tried blocking them, but she only succeeded in muting their rather odd viciousness. She truly needed more experience with people to interpret what she felt. Or more experience at blocking strangers entirely.

"Who are these peculiar gentlemen?" she whispered to Ash, knowing he could hear them greeting his brothers.

"No one you need concern yourself about," he said dismissively. "They're here to gossip. I didn't put them on the invitation list because they hold no vote or influence. We'll need to be sterner with the servants should we do this again. The footmen are too new to know when guests lie."

"My word, Ashford," the older of the spiteful gentlemen said. "You've found a marchioness who can be your equal. How enterprising of you."

"You have utterly no idea how correct you are, Wilford," Ash said in a bored drawl. "Flutter on over to the punch bowl so you might critique the quality of my refreshments."

He didn't even bother making introductions. Christie thought she might splutter in laughter and outrage at his high-handed set-down, but the gentlemen didn't seem to mind. They swaggered off to stare at the salon's eccentric adornments.

Ashford's equal—she was pretty certain they were insulting her size. And because Ash didn't care—she shouldn't either, she decided. He certainly knew she wasn't small. As long as he couldn't see how unprepossessing she actually was—or learn about her other strange disability—they were fine. If her size was all people had to complain about, she could manage.

Half an hour later, her mouth hurt from smiling, but she hadn't fled the room in tears or punched anyone yet. Although she thought she might enjoy punching a nose or two as she had as a child. But the wife of a politician must smile, smile, smile.

And so she did, until she was introduced to a heavy-set older gentleman and his very young wife. He radiated hatred, and the lady . . . had to be another of Ash's former lovers. Christie shifted instinctively toward her husband, who squeezed her hand.

"Good to see you again, Ballmer," Ashford said with only a hint of dryness over his use of the word *see*. "Lady Ballmer, it's a pleasure. Christie, the Ballmers are old acquaintances. My wife, Lady Ashford, of the Dorset Russells and Winchesters, relation of Sommersville's, actually."

The family names must have meant something to the Ballmers. Jealousy and anger spiked higher. Knowing how they felt was useless, Christie realized. She could do nothing about their hatred, and Ashford apparently already knew about it. He was needling them for fun by mentioning a duke she'd never met.

"They may be spiteful, but imitating their conceit is no way to influence votes," she whispered as the Ballmers moved on.

"Erran will offer them what they want," her arrogant husband said with a shrug of his manly shoulders. "What is more interesting is that you realized their general worthlessness as well as the various peculiarities of our other guests."

"I recognized no such thing," she retorted, remembering Celeste warning her not to tell Ash about her gift.

He narrowed his eyes as if he heard the lie in her voice, but he didn't argue. From then on, however, he purposely tested her reactions, like a boy toying with an ants' nest. She should never have told him that she felt disdain.

How could she pretend that she didn't feel a man's anger or sorrow or malice? If he asked her how she thought they'd vote, should she pretend she was an empty-headed idiot? Or lie and say she thought they seemed friendly or unfriendly toward his party?

She hated learning that he did not know what these men felt—and that she could not tell him. How could she assist him if her knowledge would give him a disgust of her?

In frustrated confusion, she lied and smiled and held out her hand to men who emanated distrust and in some cases, open animosity.

Twenty-eight

UNCOMFORTABLE LOOMING OVER the more slender, petite younger ladies, Christie aimed for the company of stout dowagers and matrons after the reception line broke up. Most of these women seemed experienced and jaded enough not to be emitting any emotion stronger than boredom. They were more interested in how she'd met Ashford than in talking politics. Keeping them entertained was easier than dealing with the greed, ambition, and distrust of Ashford's powerful associates.

Mid-evening, deciding no new guests would arrive, and she could shut off her protective scan of the room, she felt the stir of a new arrival in the salon. She halted in filling a plate for Ash and looked around to see why she'd sensed one person in a sea of many. Carrying the plate and a napkin, she wound her way through the eddying crowd to look for her husband's tall, lordly form. Appearing masculine and elegant leaning his wide shoulder against the mantel, Ash had just been joined by two portly rural-looking gentlemen who suffered in comparison.

"You remember Sir George Caldwell, and this is Lord Henry Montfort," Duncan said as she approached—as if he could see her approach. She'd worn her favorite perfume so he'd know when she was near. "These gentlemen will be our neighbors when we remove to Iveston, my dear."

My dear. He never used endearments. She thought it was a warning of sorts. She nudged him with the plate so he could help himself to the bite-size bits she'd chosen, and opened herself to the emanations of these men.

They concealed jealousy, anger, and suspicion behind their polite façades. She knew that Caldwell had hoped to marry his daughter to Ash, so some of his turmoil was understandable. Montfort—she had to shut him out quickly. He was the kind of unpleasant person who harbored grudges that blackened his soul. He must be the person who had just arrived.

"We had the pleasure of Miss Caldwell's company the other day," she said, biding time while she tried to determine what was wrong here. "I hope we can see more of her when we return to Iveston. A Christmas ball, perhaps?"

She sensed an easing of some of Caldwell's tension, but Montfort was still angry.

"The young people welcome entertainment, of course," Caldwell said with caution.

"It's doubtful if I'll ever see my son again," Montfort said. "Not while he's being accused of murderous intent. The estate will fall to rack and ruin, and Grey and his policies won't help. Breaking up Lansdowne's consortium puts an end to us."

Ah, there was the source of the anger. Remembering Aster's warning of dark portents hanging over Ash, Christie shivered. Losing a son and a fortune would anger any reasonable man, and Montfort didn't feel even slightly rational.

And Ashford could not *feel* his neighbor's animosity? How could she warn him without sounding as irrational as Montfort?

"Roderick ran before he could be accused of anything," Ash said with a shrug of his wide shoulders. "I can recommend a good estate manager who knows how to make Grey's reforms work. And Lansdowne is on the verge of bankruptcy. You are well out of that scheme. If you'd like, we could discuss sharing labor once I return to Iveston. There is a great deal we can do to improve profits if we work together."

Uneasily, Christie listened as the men dived into a discussion of farming and politics while Ash consumed a few bites of food to offset the drink he'd consumed earlier. He seemed in good health, not even rubbing his head as he was inclined to do when tired. He appeared content to be arguing with angry men who threw insults and insinuations.

She was the one battered by the tension. Once the plate was empty, she made her excuses and looked for a place to hide.

Unfortunately, every room downstairs was occupied with chattering, arguing, laughing people, except for Ash's bedchamber. She feared it wasn't appropriate for the hostess to go to bed.

"The reformists will be the ruination of England as we know it," one loud voice shouted from the anteroom.

Christie winced and standing in the foyer, looked for a change of direction.

"A man like Grey might give hope to the working man and prevent a bloody revolution. Read your history! Look what happened to the French when the wealthy trampled the common man into the ground and treated them like slaves. Without reform, we will destroy this country."

That sounded like Theo. He made it sound as if the fate of the nation really did ride on tomorrow's session. She supposed it might, but that didn't make her feel any better. Her insides roiled thinking her small soiree might influence history. Ashford could sway the future, though. He had that kind of power.

"Don't trust them," she heard a man whisper at the back of the corridor. "Lansdowne swears that they won't have the votes, and we'll be siding with the losing party if we throw in with the Whigs."

"I don't know how Lansdowne counts votes," a stranger argued. "But I'm seeing the Commons overthrowing Wellington."

"Ashford can't lead his men," the first voice whispered angrily, "and the rest of his family have no influence. Lansdowne owns a dozen pocket boroughs and influences a few dozen more. You'll see."

"Or we can all stay home," the second voice said drunkenly. "Let the others fight it out."

"Just do as you were instructed and we'll be better off." The whisper raised enough to almost sound familiar, but Christie had heard many voices this evening. She couldn't pin a name to this one.

"It had better," the drunken one slurred. "Lansdowne promised to pay off his debts once we're in. The bank will take my house if he doesn't."

Afraid to confront such ugliness, Christie darted into the anteroom where she'd heard Theo. With a whisper, she pointed him in the right direction and let him manage their hostile guests.

The man who had spoken first had done so with such malice that she'd felt it even through her barriers. Someone hated her husband. Well, she already knew that. She could hope it was just Montfort and not a different enemy.

She thought she ought to identify the hostile speaker before he left, but a cluster of departing guests gathered in the anteroom to await their cloaks and carriages, and she had to say her farewells before she could work her way back to the foyer.

By that time, even Theo was gone.

When she couldn't find him in the other rooms, she consulted with Aster.

"Oh, he and Erran are steering the more drunken representatives upstairs. All we need do is feed them tomorrow and let Ashford lead them down the street. You are a saint for enduring this as a newlywed!"

"Ask Theo about the belligerent gentleman I told him about when you have a chance, please," Christie said worriedly. "I sensed violence when he spoke of Ash, but I did not see him and could not recognize his voice."

"Violence? You're certain it wasn't Montfort or Caldwell?" Aster asked, her usual smile disappearing.

"The drunken one, I did not recognize. The hostile one was whispering, so I could not identify his voice. He said Lansdowne swore that Wellington would win, so I'm assuming he's not a reform supporter."

"Let us take it from here," Aster said soothingly. "You need to do whatever it is you're doing with Ashford to keep him rational. He did not once throw a vase or inkpot, which is a miracle of sorts."

Christie offered a tired smiled. "He expresses his frustration physically. And he does so more often if he isn't sleeping well. I'll simply see that he gets his sleep tonight."

Aster laughed. "Yes, and I don't imagine that battering a boxing bag is on his schedule for the evening, but I can see how one might be useful for a man with so much physical energy to expend."

Imagining Ash stripped to the waist for boxing, Christie wandered off in search of the marquess so they might send off the last of their guests and go to bed. Her husband had a way of making the world go away.

Since she could not protect him from dangerous portents or malicious men, she'd have to take one moment at a time for now.

WEARY OF ALL THE LIES EXCHANGED this evening, Ash stood in the salon and accepted the farewell of the last of the guests capable of staggering out on their own. If there were more lingering in corners that he could not see, the servants and his family could toss them out.

He welcomed the oncoming scent of lilies, even though he knew she'd been lying to him as well. Until this evening, he'd thought his wife a fairly uncomplicated woman whose secrets he'd already uncovered. He'd been wrong.

He usually appreciated a good mystery, but not tonight. Dropping his arm over her shoulders, he steered her along the wall and toward the corridor, avoiding the dripping candles overhead.

"I trust the servants don't need your aid in snuffing chandeliers?" he asked, just to gauge her mood.

"I think half the candles have guttered out and the others are on the verge, but the footmen know how to snuff them. You should consider gas someday." She sounded as weary as he was.

"Someday when we're not in residence," he agreed. "I've had enough disruption for a while. I dare not ask if you enjoyed the evening, but how did you fare?"

She hesitated, so he knew she was about to lie again.

"It was . . . interesting," she said. "I am in no hurry to repeat it."

"What did you think of the Ballmers?" he asked, trying to prod more insights from her.

"I'm not sure I remember who they were. I fear I spent most of the evening entertaining dowagers, making certain the food and liquor flowed freely, and sending your brothers to snuff brawls."

"That's one task Ives know how to manage," he said with a wry laugh. "You picked up no interesting information I could use?"

"I'm sure I wouldn't know if it was interesting." She hesitated again, then merely continued, "I am too weary to think. Perhaps in the morning."

"You would not hide things from me, would you?" he asked more directly as he steered her into his chamber.

"Of course I would," she answered airily. "Do you really think I would tell you of the ragged edges on my favorite corset?"

Ash hid his frown. He supposed prevarication was better than outright lies, but now he would spend the night wondering what she wasn't telling him. He glared at the posset waiting for him, but if it had helped him sleep . . . He picked it up and sipped at it.

"Were there red flowers in the bouquet?" he asked rather than argue.

"You saw them?" Genuine excitement lit her voice.

At least he could rely on her enthusiasm for finding ways of helping him—despite her declaration that she would flee if he could see again. "I think I must have, if they were there. Will you wear red for me?" he asked provocatively.

"In the bedroom only," she warned with a laugh. "I'd look a perfect fright in red."

"I doubt that, but if it means only I will ever see you in red, I can live with it."

He didn't want to poke and prod the truth from her as he did the men he wished to manipulate. For now, he was satisfied with teaching his wife more of the pleasures of their marital bed. He'd spent all the spare minutes of his day planning this part of the evening.

MONDAY MORNING, SERVANTS TAPPED at the bedchamber doors before Christie could remember sleeping. With no windows, she couldn't tell the hour, but it was much too early. She yawned and rolled out of bed while Ash snarled and grumbled and told everyone to go to hell.

He'd spent a great deal of time last night pleasing her in ways she could not even think about without blushing. And she'd returned the favor to the best of her limited experience. It was a wonder the servants hadn't come rushing in at his roars of pleasure. Really, they needed a large castle to lose themselves in should they continue to indulge themselves this way.

But the result, despite the posset, was a decided lack of sleep—not healthy for Ash's temper.

Christie washed and dressed herself so she was ready when Ash called for his valet. Sharing a single bedroom on the public floor was awkward.

When Ash dragged himself into an upright position, she lit a lamp so she could admire her husband's broad bare shoulders and chest emerging from the covers. He scrubbed sleepily at his tangled hair and scruffy beard. Without all his elegant clothing—he was still a magnificent marquess but more heart-breakingly human and masculine.

She pinned the fine wisps of her hair into a braided chignon, kissed her husband's bristly jaw, and slipped out.

Aster had sent over extra servants to aid in the cleanup. They were already at work when Christie arrived to sort them out. The new housekeeper hadn't quite learned priorities. Christie ordered the buffet table and dishes cleared before the chandelier wax was scraped, since they had several guests who would need to be fed before they left for Parliament.

Once the servants were efficiently tidying up, she didn't know what to do with herself. Erran arrived bearing papers for Ash to sign and probably with news of the discussion in the Commons since the two of them holed up behind closed doors. It was too early for their few hungover guests to emerge, but the business of the household had started.

She took her tea and toast in Ash's chamber to be out of the way of the servants restoring the public rooms and wished for a window. Should he ever see again . . .

She halted her reflections at a knock on the door. One of the twins stood there in shirtsleeves and waistcoat, looking anxious. His mop of dark curls needed cutting.

"Is Father available?" he asked.

Ah, Hugh, the more responsible one. "I'm not sure he wishes to be disturbed. Could I help?"

The more he scuffled and avoided answering, the more fear balled up in her midsection. The twins had been dangerously quiet lately. "If it's important enough, I can be the one to disturb him. If you can tell me, I can decide, and he can shout at me."

Hugh flashed a brief, grateful smile. "It's Hartley. He went off to see if Mr. Garrett would be a good dog owner. Mr. Garrett left his card and everything. I wanted to tell Father first, but Mr. Garrett said Father knew, and he was in a hurry, and since he was one of our guests, we thought maybe it would be all right. But then, just when he closed the carriage door, he said something that didn't sound amusing . . ."

Perhaps she was simply sensing Hugh's uneasiness, but her toast felt as if it was ready to come back up. "What did he say?" she asked, trying not to react in any way that would frighten the boy.

"He said if we wanted to see Hartley again, we should visit him at this address." He handed over the card.

To see Hartley? Did he mean to keep the boy instead of the dog? Full-blown panic took root at that possibility. She glanced at the card.

The address was in Chelsea. She didn't know how long it would take a carriage to travel that far, but she knew the village was a considerable distance from where they were now.

Today was the day Ash needed to encourage men to save England. She couldn't disturb him with this, if it was some sort of prank.

TROUBLE, Ash's great-grandmother whispered worriedly in her head.

Hidden Harriet whined that this time, Brave Christie may have bitten off more than she could chew.

Christie swallowed hard. Ash had solved all her problems. If she was to learn to be as strong as he . . . She should be able to deal with the twins herself. She fought sheer terror at the responsibility.

Twenty-nine

ASH SEALED THE LAST DOCUMENT and shoved it across the desk at Erran. "I am bored with this game. I'll be happy to hand the Commons over to you."

"You're good at twisting arms in both Houses," Erran insisted. "You're simply bored because you're not juggling two dozen other challenges at the same time. You need to find a trusted carriage driver so you can travel about more. You can do far more talking to the villagers and tenants back home than Theo can. He'll be happy to have you back."

Ash had no intention of being hauled about in a carriage like an aging invalid. Contemplating training his stallion as his eyes, he heard Erran depart and Christie's voice in the corridor. A moment with his wife would be a pleasurable break in his day—he had yet to determine what she hadn't been telling him last night.

He counted the steps to the doorway and searched for her scent. It wasn't as strong as usual—probably because someone was sleeping in her chamber, and she hadn't had access to her perfume this morning.

His hesitation apparently offered the opportunity for her to come to *him*. Ash relished the unexpected pleasure of hearing her pace increase at his appearance, and he more than enjoyed it when she kissed his cheek. He didn't like it quite as much when he realized she was wearing a hat and pelisse.

"Where are you going?" he asked, caressing her silky cheek and wishing the day were over.

"I'll be back in time for whatever madness is planned this afternoon. Do you really mean to lead your lost lambs to slaughter today?"

She was prevaricating again, and trying to distract him. Ash frowned. "I don't mean to lead anyone anywhere, but yes, we intend to arrive *en masse*. What are you and the ladies plotting?"

"You have your plots. Let us have ours. I'm in a bit of a hurry and you have another appointment shortly." She kissed his cheek again and hurried out of his reach.

Ash slammed his fist against the door jamb in frustration at literally and figuratively being kept in the dark. Wincing at the pain, he retreated to his desk and waited for the next obstacle in his path. He wanted to follow Christie. Why would she lie to him when she *knew* he would know she was lying? What was she hiding?

He knew he hadn't misjudged her so badly that she might be out consorting with other men or running away to join a circus or any of a dozen other things his former mistresses had done. Christie was the kind of woman who would help others before she'd help herself.

And she knew how important the outcome of this day was to him.

That thought played in the back of his mind as he cursorily dealt with the next piece of business. He worked himself into a state just imagining the ways Christie could be *helping* him without worrying him. Or would she be helping the twins? They'd been sadly neglected this week.

"Jessup!" he shouted after the next visitor left. "Send for the twins." With luck, some servant would hear his bellow.

Before the butler could appear, one of the boys rapped on his door. "Did you wish to speak with us, sir?"

"There's only one of you, Hugh," he said in irritation. "Where's Hartley?"

A hesitation singularly akin to Christie's warned him that the boy was parsing his words before Hugh spoke a word.

"With Chuckles, sir. Did you need us for something?"

"Shouldn't you be in the schoolroom?" Ash asked in irritation, trying to figure out why his son would be lying—and if it had anything to do with Christie's lies.

"Our tutor has today off. Miss Chris said I was to call for your headache powders if you start yelling. Shall I have someone bring them?"

"Where is Christie?" Ash asked craftily, seeing how far he could test the boy's honesty.

More hesitation. "She asked me not to say, sir. She says you are very busy and must save the kingdom today."

Save the kingdom? Ash rubbed his forehead. Was that what all these papers and arm-twisting amounted to? At this point, if men couldn't figure out the right course without being told, the kingdom might as well go to hell.

"I'm done with saving the kingdom," he lied. "Is Christie with Hartley and Chuckles? We could join them."

"Yes, I'd like that, sir," the boy said with such a huge sigh of relief. "They took the berlin to Chelsea. I know how to drive a gig, so I can probably drive the curricle."

Chelsea? Ash wanted to knock all his inkpots to the floor and roar *What the devil are they doing in Chelsea?* But for a change, remembering his wife's warning about terrifying people with his shouts, he put a curb on his temper so he didn't terrify Hugh. If both Christie and Hugh had to lie about her whereabouts . . . Ash had a really nasty pain in his gut.

His brothers were out martialing the clubs and coffeehouses as Ash could not. If Christie already had the berlin and driver, he had no one to rely on but himself. And Hugh.

If he meant to find out what was happening, he would have to play the part of a damned drooling idiot being driven about by a lad of ten. The mighty marquess of Ashford would make an ass of himself in front of all London—because every important man in the kingdom was in town and right down the street for this session.

He could wallow in his pride or accept Hugh's offer.

Accustomed to having his demands met without having to make uncomfortable choices, he wanted to howl. Howling wouldn't find Christie and Hartley.

Once upon a time, he would have simply dismissed the domestic problem and went on with his work. He'd learned almost too late that life was about paying attention to details—and to family.

"Call for the curricle. I'll handle the horses," he said, nearly tearing his hair out with impatience and irritation. The town horses weren't the placid ponies Hugh had driven in the country, and the curricle was no stable gig. "You tell me where to turn, and we'll meet up with them in no time."

He was officially out of his mind, but it was better than sitting here slowly simmering and yelling at everyone who crossed his threshold.

Action satisfied him far more than fretting. He may have lost his sight and possibly his mind, but he refused to lose his wife and son.

"I CAN ONLY SAY THE SPIRITS IN MY HEAD are restless and worried." Sitting in Aster's colorful parlor, Christie expressed her fears to the Malcolm ladies, who had hastily assembled at her request. "You can only look at your charts and say there is danger. And Celeste can't sing down an enemy holding the boy, even if we are sensing that correctly, and there is no assurance of that. Our gifts are not helpful in protecting the family."

She was failing already. She had thought seeking help would give her some notion of what to do, but the problem only seemed to grow greater.

Weak Harriet wanted to take the coward's way out and worry Ash with her fear that Hartley may have been abducted. The strong marchioness of Ashford she wanted to be suffered agonies at the possibility of failing those she loved.

"Oh, we're correct about Hartley being in danger, no doubt," Aster said, rolling up her chart and frowning. "We're fortunate William is in town to sell some of his dogs. I've sent word to him, and he's said he'll meet us at that Chelsea address with his animals. Theo and Erran need to concentrate on this afternoon's session, so it's best not to disturb them until we know what we're dealing with. Jacques should be joining us shortly. We'll work out something if the situation is as bad as it seems."

A servant knocked at the door of Aster's colorfully-decorated jungle parlor.

All three women glanced up. The servant nervously gestured toward a footman in Ashford's livery in the hall. "Lady Ashford has a message."

"Oh dear. What is it, Smith?" Christie reached for the pelisse she'd simply thrown over the chair arm in her hurry to gather an army to find Hartley.

"It's his lordship, my lady," Smith said, stepping forward. "He and the boy have taken the curricle, and Lord Erran is wondering if you know where."

"Ashford is driving a *curricle*?" Christie gasped, her heart falling to her stomach.

"*Blind* Ashford?" Celeste asked in astonishment. "How is that possible?"

The footman looked uncomfortable and shifted from foot to foot. "I cannot say, my lady."

"My word, that's it!" Aster cried. "Lester, bring my hat and pelisse! Is the berlin outside?" She turned to Christie.

"Do you know how he's driving a curricle?" Christie asked in bewilderment.

"Hugh is his eyes, of course. Even though the team is well trained, this is pure Ives arrogance. They'll kill themselves." Aster gestured at Christie's footman. "I need you to give this address to Erran and Theo." She hurried to her writing desk and jotted down a note. "They must decide what to do about your indecisive guests, but we must tell them that Ashford and the twins are in trouble. The Commons will be voting today, and it is possible someone is trying to distract Ash and his brothers from turning the tide against Wellington."

As the footmen raced to do her hostess's bidding, Christie wanted to shrink under the chair. *This* was what the voices were telling her? That Ash would kill himself driving blindly after his son? Or that the kidnapper meant real harm? And she'd only made it worse by not warning him?

"The guest last night," she whispered. "Did Theo tell you who the man was I warned him about?"

"He only saw Lord Montfort. The baron is always surly." Aster fastened her pelisse and reached for her hat.

"He was with another gentleman, a drunken one." Christie swallowed, trying to remember that furtive meeting. "If it was Montfort speaking, he told his friend to 'do as you were instructed and we'll be better off.' And the gentleman said he'd lose his house if Lansdowne didn't pay his debt to him."

"Bryghtstone," Celeste said worriedly. "Erran mentioned that Bryghtstone loaned Lansdowne a great deal of money and was now unable to pay his mortgage. Lansdowne apparently promised to double his money but the investment hasn't come through."

"Bryghtstone was one of the sots Theo installed in your guest chambers," Aster said in horror. "It all fits. He's lured Hartley to Chelsea in hopes of distracting Ash. Still, I'm sure we can manage a worthless piece of human garbage like that."

IF BRYGHT IS LIKE HIS FATHER, HE WON'T BE ALONE, a new voice in Christie's head said worriedly. Aster's house had ghosts too? She would experiment some other time. Right now, she could just listen and pray, and try not to worry the ladies too much about being haunted by their family's ghosts.

"He won't work alone." Christie spoke the ghost's warning in terms they understood. "Weak men hire thugs. Ash is riding into a trap."

***

"SLOW DOWN," HUGH CRIED. "Farm cart on your right."

Ash gritted his teeth and sought the shadowy motion that would indicate an obstacle in the curricle's path. If only he had his stallion . . . Futile thought.

"Tell me more of this Mr. Garrett," he commanded, trying to make the best use of their infernally slow pace. They would no doubt freeze to death while he drove like a septuagenarian.

"He's the gentleman who offered to buy Chuckles. Watch, there's a dog running in the gutter on your left."

Ash was willing to sacrifice animals if necessary for his son and Christie, but not if it could be avoided. He still didn't know if they were in actual danger, so he moderated his pace even more, clenching his jaw in the process. Had the gas lamps been on, he might have had a better idea of the road. As it was, the gray day offered only limited light and shadow to determine his location. He was relying mostly on the experienced horses and Hugh's warnings. With luck, they were almost out of the worst traffic, and he could pick up their pace.

His gut was roiling that any dastard would even *think* of touching his son. He could not concentrate for the fury infusing him, so he filled his skull with information.

"What is his appearance?" he demanded, knowing the senselessness of asking description from his sons but hoping for some small piece that might identify the culprit.

"Old, sort of skinny, ginger side-whiskers." Hugh's voice indicated how hard he was trying to remember.

Old meant anything from twenty to a hundred to a child. *Ginger*, however, reduced the suspects to one in a hundred. He sought another identifying factor that Hugh might recognize. "Watch fob with a rabbit's foot?"

"Yes, sir," Hugh said eagerly. "Do you know him, sir? Does that mean Hartley is fine?"

Bryghtstone desperately needed money. Brought up as a spoiled only son, Bryght wasn't very bright. He could very well be stupid enough to hold Harley for ransom.

"Watch for the sign post," Ash reminded him, not answering the question. "The turnpike should be approaching. Have our coins ready."

The nodcock probably hadn't counted on a blind marquess coming in person. He no doubt meant to intimidate Christie or a servant into handing over his purse. But Ash had no intention of letting his son suffer in fear while waiting for a ransom demand.

They paid their toll and Ash let the horses have their heads as they traveled the wide, paved turnpike. Early Sunday morning lessened the amount of traffic encountered.

"I need you to stay out of sight once we reach the house," he told Hugh. "Hop out, hide in the bushes, whatever it takes so he doesn't realize I have help. He'll be taken by surprise at seeing me. If you have a chance, sneak around him and find Hartley."

"Yes, sir," Hugh said worriedly. "What if he has a weapon?"

"Bryght may be stupid, but he's a gentleman. He won't shoot a blind man, and he'd be drawn and quartered for killing a lord. He simply wants money and he won't get it if I'm dead."

"That makes sense, sir," Hugh said in relief. "You think he meant for Miss Chris or one of my uncles to come looking for Hartley?"

"I don't think he thinks at all, but we can be certain he didn't expect *me*."

Ash hadn't memorized the winding lanes of Chelsea as he had the city, so it took them several efforts and questioning the locals to find the location. "Tell me where to stop where they can't see us from the house."

"May I have the reins, sir? There's a narrow path . . ."

Ash hated releasing control of the precarious vehicle, but it made sense that the one with eyes handle the tricky parts that didn't require knowing roads or powerful horses. He handed over the reins and tried to determine their surroundings from his limited vision and scents, but he was afraid he was failing badly. That did not improve his fury, but he would not take it out on his son. He had better targets.

"Hedgerow and evergreens?" he guessed as the curricle slowed and turned. "Can you see the house? Are there any carriages or horses in sight?"

"Nothing, sir. The house is a rather large, three-story brick," Hugh said, sounding worried again. "There are several outbuildings. I can't see them all. Hartley could be anywhere."

If there was no carriage, then Christie had not come here. That wasn't exactly a worry off his mind, but her whereabouts could be relegated to later. They need only find his son now and leave. "Look for a dog pen. Hartley may not be in any danger at all."

"How will you proceed, sir?"

"Stay hidden and scout the area for me. Come back and tell me how many buildings, if you see Hartley, and how many others you see. I'm going to find my way into that stand of evergreens, out of sight. I can tell a great deal by just listening. We'll decide what to do once we know what we're up against."

"Yes, sir." Eager for adventure, too inexperienced to know fear, Hugh leaped down and confidently tended the horses.

Moving more tentatively than his son, Ash shuffled through dead leaves and tried to determine markers for his senses. This late in November, there were few flowers to light the darkness, but he smelled rotting apples and felt them crush beneath his boot to the left of the curricle. The evergreens were to the right, closer to the property.

"I'm off, sir," Hugh whispered. "I'll try to be right back."

He couldn't possibly return soon enough. Furious, frustrated, wishing he could ride up to the house with sword and rifle and shoot anyone who moved, Ash recognized his irrationality. This could all be an innocent romp in the country or just a drunken Bryght looking for an easy hand out—nothing worth shooting over.

That Bryght had given an alias to the twins was not promising, but perhaps he was wrong at guessing who this *Mr. Garrett* was. A rabbit's foot fob was not completely unusual, or Bryght would never have adopted one. He wasn't a creative thinker, which made this whole episode unlikely.

Once Hugh was safely on his way, Ash inched forward. His boots trampled a soft bed of needles. Long branches swiped at his clothes and face. He gripped his whip and walking stick, but he hoped his wits would be all he needed for weapons.

Waiting was not one of his many accomplishments. Months of confinement as an invalid and learning to navigate without eyes had taught him to slow down, but they had not taught him patience. He locked his jaw, listened to a squirrel chatter, and stiffened when he heard distant voices. Had Hugh already reached the house?

The horses snuffed and crunched branches. Was that Hugh's shout? Perhaps he'd found Hartley.

Ash forced himself not to step out until he better understood the situation. The sun was higher now. Light and shadow played across what he assumed was a lawn. He couldn't discern the house, so it must be a large yard. He heard more voices from in front of him and slightly to his left. The house and outbuildings were no doubt in that direction. He tightened his grip on his limited weapons.

"Ashford, I know you're out there," cried a jovial voice.

Bryghtstone. He'd given the man a bed in his own damned home last night.

"And what of it?" Ash called back, counting on the cover of the evergreens to disguise him until he knew what the situation required.

"I'm having a Defeat the Revolutionaries party. Come join me."

"You're a moron," Ash said in disgust, tapping the whip against his thigh. "The only revolutionaries in this country are the dunderheads rioting in the streets because they believe machinery will doom their miserable occupations."

"They have a point. The world spins too fast, for the benefit of only a few like you. The old ways work better for the rest of us. Come along, you can't stand there freezing in the hedgerows while your sons huddle with the filthy hounds. I really didn't expect you to care, but now that you're here, we may as well make the best of it."

"Who did you expect to come?" Ash asked out of curiosity, trying to determine how many others were out there.

"Your brothers, of course. But we had other plans if this one didn't work. It was a stroke of brilliance giving out the location, wasn't it?"

Christie would question his absence before his brothers would. The thought of his wife panicking when she discovered his departure churned Ash's innards. He could see only one shadow approaching. Bryght was slightly younger than Ash, but he wasn't large, and he spent his time gambling and wenching, so he wasn't strong. Even blind, Ash could beat the sot into the ground with one hand behind his back—if Bryght had no companions.

Hearing Hartley's shout and a dog's howl in the distance, Ash breathed a sigh of relief. If Hugh had freed Hartley and the dog, his sons would find their way to him. Finally, he could act.

Locating Bryght's shadow approaching, Ash stepped from the cover of the trees.

"There you are," Bryght said, not too brightly since his voice gave Ash better distance and location. "You'll forgive a man for doing what is necessary to save his home, won't you?"

"I won't forgive a man who uses children as his shield." Gauging Bryght's height from memory, Ash swung his fist in the direction of his opponent's soft lower jaw, connecting soundly before the younger man knew the blow was coming.

For good measure, he aimed the solid brass ball of his walking stick into the man's gut. Bryght groaned, bent in two, and from the sounds of it, lost last night's supper into the grass.

One solid whack of the stick across the back of the coward's neck toppled him into the dirt.

Before Ash could even whistle at the boys to come out, another voice spoke from the shadows where he couldn't see him.

"I've been wanting to do that for some time now," Montfort said. "The boy is an idiot. But I'm not. There are three shotguns aimed at your heart and your sons are locked in the dog pen. I think we'll wait in the house for all your brothers to ride up. Without anyone to shore up their courage, the Whig mongrels will go down in defeat."

Thirty

WILLIAM IVES-MADDEN AND A GIANT mastiff waited at the corner of the rural Chelsea lane to which the driver of the berlin had been directed.

Riding their horses beside the carriage, Jacques, Pascoe, and a Cousin Zack, who looked just as big and tough as the other Ives, rode up to consult with the dog trainer. Inside the carriage, Christie twisted her fingers in nervous anxiety. Once upon a time, she had wrung her hands while listening to a ticking clock and waiting for a suitor who never arrived. She hadn't known then how shallow and meaningless the pain of rejection was. The fear for others was much more agonizing.

Aster patted her hands. "You haven't lived with Ives as I have. You did the right thing coming to me. It's a pity your bone-headed husband chose to be the lone hero in this instance, but that's how he was brought up. The others are more civilized."

Celeste laughed. "To a small extent. I wish Erran could have come. He would have terrified the lot into fleeing with just his voice. I'm quite certain he'd be angry enough to bellow them into the next kingdom—which may very well be the reason he stayed to reassure visitors. He thinks it's unethical to bully people with his gift."

"But even if he can persuade Ash's guests that all is well, he can't read Ash's speech in the Lords," Christie fretted. "What are the men saying out there? Perhaps Hartley really is just visiting a dog kennel."

"Judging by their frowns, I'd say not," Aster said. She opened the window and spoke sharply to the one they called Uncle Pascoe. "Speak to us or we'll order the driver to proceed without you."

Garbed in a finely tailored green riding coat and fawn breeches, sporting gleaming knee-high boots, the sophisticated Pascoe Ives kneed his gelding toward the carriage, leaned over, and lifted his hat. "Good morning, my ladies. Looks like it should be a fine day for a ride."

Christie pushed Aster aside and glared out the window. "You will take me to my husband and his sons now. We may discuss the weather later."

Pascoe's thick dark eyebrows shot upward. "Spoken like a true marchioness. William has scouted the grounds. There appears to be a small army present. We need to develop a plan."

"We don't have time for delicacy if we're to return Ash before people start worrying about his disappearance. Tell Zach to take his bucket down from the back, then have the driver let us out and drive the carriage somewhere less conspicuous." Christie shut the window to prevent argument. She was shaking in her shoes. She'd just ordered about a man she'd been told acted as the king's personal envoy. He looked astonished, but unlike Ash, he wasn't beating the door down to rip at her.

Pascoe hadn't denied that Ash was here, which meant Hugh was too. She was relieved that the pair of nodcocks had arrived safely, but she was terrified that they weren't racing down the drive to meet her. Where was the curricle? If she'd only been faster . . .

The carriage door opened and the steps were let down. Wearing the old gown she'd donned to direct the housekeeping, Christie didn't feel like a marchioness as she took a footman's hand and climbed out. But her country gown didn't require yards of stiff petticoats. She could tramp for miles like this.

She checked to see that Zack unloaded the bucket of yellow paint he'd brought over just this morning for her bedchamber. He set it beside the road without questioning her command. She knew the paint was madness, but to her, it was a symbol of hope and courage and defiance. She needed to convey confidence when all looked lost.

Celeste and Aster were also dressed in morning dishabille, although their gowns were of a more frivolous than sturdy nature. Since they were both in the early stages of pregnancy, Christie didn't want them involved at all. But their husbands' futures depended on Ash as much as hers did. She couldn't hold them back.

"William, will you please explain what you have found?" she asked the intimidating giant with his enormous dog.

"Ash's equipment and animals are in the hedgerow," he said in taciturn brevity.

Christie closed her eyes and thanked the heavens they'd arrived in one piece.

"I trust you tended to the animals?" Jacques asked in amusement, climbing up on a stile and using one of Theo's portable telescopes to scan the field.

William scowled. "Yes. The farm has a dog pen full of half-fed hounds, but the boys aren't there."

"We'll rescue the hounds, too," Christie said reassuringly, sensing the man's concern. This was Hartley's hero, a man who loved animals and avoided people. She was grateful for his aid, but she needed to understand the situation. "Guards?"

William nodded while emanating a degree of approval. "None."

"That doesn't mean there aren't men with weapons inside," Pascoe reminded them.

"I do not understand what they hope to accomplish by holding a marquess hostage," Celeste said in puzzlement.

"If Montfort or Lansdowne is behind this, then they mean to either stop the vote or distract enough of Ash's politicians to prevent them from overthrowing Wellington," Aster said with a frown. "It is a very close call as it is. Perhaps they are expecting Theo and Erran to lead a rescue party out here, thus reducing the number of votes as well as creating uncertainty."

No one argued with this assumption, although Christie wondered if there might not be more to this than Aster was seeing—or mentioning. *Danger to family* meant something more personal than an election, didn't it? Neither Theo or Erran had votes—they only helped Ash negotiate deals with voters.

But harming any of Ash's family would drive him mad—and lose the confidence of the Commons he'd worked so hard to gain.

"Let's set fire to the privy," Jacques said, studying the farm's layout through the glass. "That ought to bring a few of the louts out, give us an idea how many there are."

"I can cry out as if I'm in distress," Celeste suggested. "That could draw out a few more."

"You really think men like this care about damsels in distress?" Zack asked cynically.

Aster vigorously nodded her red curls. "She's dispersed rioters and led an entire factory of workers into the street with her voice. It will work. The fire would be fun too. Perhaps they'll believe Celeste's inside."

"Give me a big stick," Christie demanded. "I'll trounce them as they come out. The rest of the men can go in the front door and find Ash and the boys."

All the men except Jacques protested. None of them provided a stick. Jacques returned to studying the house.

Without persuasive words to argue against an experienced diplomat and Ives stubbornness, Christie examined the sycamore branches overhanging the road. Finding what she sought just out of reach, she leaped, caught the dead branch, and snapped it with her weight. Another tug broke it off entirely. Channeling her fury, she decapitated an entire row of weeds, then glared at the stunned men—who had finally quit arguing.

"That's what I do to people who stand in my way. I am a country girl, gentlemen." Actually, she was a terrified shy miss who had spent far too much time hiding. But for Ash, she would be a war goddess. Later, she could hide in her room and fall apart.

"If we take the mastiff through the front, he will scare any left inside," William said, accepting her at her word. "I'll chase them out the back, toward you. But a stick isn't enough. They'll have weapons."

"I have Erran's pistol with four bullets." Delicate Celeste removed a deadly-looking weapon from her bag. "I am a good shot, but if there is someone better . . ."

Pascoe snatched the weapon and placed it in his pocket. He handed his smaller pistol to Cousin Zack. Snapping a trigger, the king's envoy opened a deadly sword in his walking stick. Whistling in admiration, Jacques leapt down from the stile to claim it.

Aster took the whip they'd commandeered from the driver earlier. She looked dubious about its use, but she stuck her jaw out stubbornly. "We don't have much time. Shall we proceed?"

"You do realize this is patently insane?" Pascoe said genially as they traipsed into the woods. He glanced at the bucket Christie carried but courteously didn't question the eccentricity of a marchioness.

Taciturn William merely grunted. Slender Jacques whacked an evergreen branch with the sword stick. Zack—an architect Christie had been told—merely sighted along Pascoe's small pistol before shoving it into a belt containing a collection of tools. He took the heavy bucket from her and swung it easily.

"We will be fine," Celeste said in her sweetest, most reassuring voice.

Christie almost believed her—for a moment. The others nodded as well. And then they began frowning as logic overpowered whatever spell she cast with her voice. If Celeste truly had a siren voice, it did not last long.

"Disbelievers," Celeste scoffed, evidently ascertaining the same. "If you're all so certain we'll fail, why don't we turn back now?"

"No time," Aster said prosaically. "And we're all just smart enough to know nothing is certain, so your voice isn't effective on us. Formulate a call that will convince anyone listening, something no one can argue with."

"Shouting fire should do it," Jacques suggested.

"No, because that won't draw out everyone," Celeste explained. "It must be more like—'fire, I'm trapped. Come help me.' The compulsion is in the call for action."

Explaining magical, *other* abilities to Ives men was much akin to pounding one's head against a wall, Christie decided. Once they smashed out their brains, the men would examine their gray matter for evidence of insanity.

Ignoring male disbelief, she inquired of Celeste, "If they hear your call, will even Ash and the twins try to escape and help you?" She stopped at the edge of the evergreen line to study the house ahead.

"Possibly, although Ashford will catch on faster. He's particularly hard-headed and will be more concerned with escape once he recognizes my voice."

If he was alive or conscious, Christie mentally amended. Or not tied up or locked in a dark room where he couldn't even see the door. Their plans had more holes than a spider web.

Glancing at the location of the sun, she concluded they didn't have time for better. "The boys will be so hungry, they'll gnaw their way out," she said, hoping to lighten the gloom as they studied the fortress of brick.

"Cannibalize their captors?" Jacques suggested. "Well, I'm off. By the time I have a good fire started, you should all have found your battle stations. Celeste, are you going back with me so your voice will carry from the direction of the fire?"

He gathered dry sticks and twigs as he trotted along the hedgerow toward the back of the house. Celeste followed in his path, using the front of her gown to hold the tinder.

"Aster, perhaps you could study the dog pen and see if they might be released if necessary?" Christie asked this diffidently, since Aster was usually the one giving orders.

The shorter woman reached up to hug her. "It will work. You'll see. Be very careful. My chart shows the part of Expected Birth in your family sector this time next year." Stooping low, she hurried along the hedgerow of the drive, toward the far side of the house.

Christie barely had time to recover from the shock of that prediction before Pascoe spoke—ignoring the implications of Aster's usually correct prophesies.

"We can't cross the lawn until we know the guards are running out the back," he said, gauging the distance.

"I'll stand between the front and back," Christie suggested. "I'll signal when the fire is visible. After I signal, storm the front and find Ash and the boys. Does that work?"

"Then you'll run to the back and bash heads as they come out?" Cousin Zack asked, eyeing her stout stick. "This wrench is sturdier than that stick."

"I need the bucket and the brush," she insisted. "But I can tuck the wrench into my skirt band." The paint made her feel as if she was competent and in charge. She wanted Ash to *see* what they were doing.

Stupid foolish thought, but madness kept her going. Carrying the bucket, awkwardly wrapping her pelisse tighter, as if that would hold her together, Christie trudged between the evergreens until she had a good view of the outbuildings in the rear. A kind of peace settled on her as she regarded the house where her husband—her *family*—was held.

She had family. If they survived this, she might bear Ash a babe by this time next year. She had been so busy trying to learn so many fascinating things at once that she hadn't had time to consider a child or how she felt about carrying Ashford's heir.

With the peace of the forest around her, she let the knowledge of her new life seep in. For one who was so quick to identify emotion in others, she was slow to understand herself. But understanding that she could lose Ash and the twins forced her to recognize the source of the anxiety eating at her confidence.

She loved Ash—with all her heart and soul and every breath she took. She even loved the devilish twins. She adored her new family—a family that accepted her as she was, weirdness and all. It didn't matter if they might never love her back. Her fear was that she would lose the only people who made her life worth living.

She would rather die protecting them than to lose them.

Breathing deeply of this knowledge, she felt courage rise within her, and she clenched her weapons with assurance. Ash and the twins were worth whatever happened next.

At the first flicker of fire near the privy's base, she signaled the men waiting in front. Then lifting her skirt, she gracelessly ran to the back as if she were Boudicca heading to war—if war goddesses carried large paint buckets.

Celeste's voice rose in a compelling scream just as Christie reached the rear yard and set down her paint pail. Determinedly holding her branch ready, she braced herself.

Moments later, a rough looking man clattered out the back door. With no compunction whatsoever, Christie stepped out of the shadows and bashed the branch over the back of his head, then slapped him with a brush full of paint.

"Take that, you blackguard!" she cried as he staggered and hit the ground.

Thirty-one

SNAPPING OFF A PIECE OF THE ROTTED window frame with his bare hands, Ash halted his demolition at a feminine voice crying for help in the yard several stories below. "Who is that?" he demanded, gut clenching and panic rising.

The twins stopped sweeping the shattered glass aside with their feet to listen.

"A lady is in trouble." Hartley said anxiously. "We need to help her."

His boots hit the bare wood floor in the direction of the locked door.

Ash already knew the door couldn't be budged. His shoulder was sore from trying. Hartley pounded and kicked at it anyway, irrationally consumed by the need to help a lady he didn't know and couldn't see.

Hearing the sound of breaking glass, Ash hoped Hugh was using his coat sleeve to clear the glass clinging to the frame. "It sounds like Aunt Celeste. She's in trouble. I can get out now—"

Celeste—and her damned haunting voice. He'd have to start believing in her compulsion if she could drive the twins to irrationality. Even he had almost fallen for that cry. Now that he listened, he could hear the lie in her call.

Ash grabbed his son's coat and yanked him back into the room. "If she's here, then so are the others. Look before you leap. What do you see?"

"The privy is on fire! Hart, come see." Hugh leaned past Ash, apparently shaking off his need to leap from tall windows with this new distraction. "Look, isn't that Miss Chris mashing the smelly man on the head?" He laughed in delight as if watching clowns at a circus. "She got him good. Look, he's out for the count!"

Ash sensed that Hugh was nearly jumping up and down with excitement. Ash, on the other hand, thought he might swallow his tongue in terror, and his gut turned to stone. What the devil was *Christie* doing out there? And Celeste. He was almost glad he couldn't watch.

"Do you see anyone else?" he asked, praying the women weren't alone. He'd counted at least six hired thugs, plus Bryght, Montfort, and of course, the dastard Lansdowne. Nine armed men against two defenseless women would be bad, but he hoped Christie wouldn't be that foolish.

"Uncle Jacques is swinging a swordstick at the bald one," Hartley cried gleefully, pressing up to the broken window. "Can we climb down now?"

Ah, if Jacques was here, then Christie had been smart enough to seek aid.

Angry voices erupted in the rooms below—followed by a pistol shot.

"Damnation." Now that he needn't be quiet, Ash booted out the remainder of the frame. He didn't want any of his family shot by anyone other than himself. "Climb onto the porch roof and guide me when I come out. I can tell where the edge is but not what's below."

The boys scrambled out, disturbing old roof tiles and sending them clattering to the ground. More shouts erupted. A hound—or a mastiff?—howled. Heavy feet, accompanied by shouts, thudded through the downstairs.

Christie's triumphant voice yelling, "For England!" offered some relief. He would have laughed, but if he climbed out this window, he was in serious danger of breaking his fool neck.

"Uncle William!" Hartley crowed. "He has a ladder. We don't need to jump."

A ladder was marginally better than jumping. He'd still prefer stairs and a wall to guide him.

"What is that yellow I'm seeing?" Ash leaned over the sill to follow the motion. Thank all the heavens, the sun was actually shining for a change.

Hugh laughed in delight. "Miss Chris is smacking them with a yellow paint brush—after she bashes them with a wrench. She broke her stick on the fat man. No one can come near her."

She was marking the culprits so Ash could find them—he laughed at her ingenuity. His remarkable bride was making a cake of herself while risking her neck for *him*. Despite his fear of falling and cracking his head again, his heart swelled two sizes, and he couldn't prevent a grin from splitting his face.

"Isn't that Baron Montfort?" Hartley cried. "Look, Miss Chris is so mad, she can't stop slapping him with the brush! He's waving his arms and shouting at her, and she keeps dipping the brush in the pail and smacking him again. He's all over yellow and spitting paint, the coward!"

"One should not hit an unarmed gentleman with a brush," Ash intoned formally, holding back his laughter at the image conjured. This, he really wished he could see.

"What light in yonder window breaks?" Jacques called from below, slapping the ladder against the roof loud enough for Ash to hear him.

"Ladder is up. Let's go. You first, Father," Hugh said in concern.

Ash rumpled his unruly curls. "Go down and help Christie. I hear a key in the lock and prefer a more civilized exit."

He lied. Only one person had that key, and he fully intended to throttle him, earl or not. Ash located the piece of window frame he'd set aside. They'd taken his other weapons, but even his fists would do once he had Lansdowne in range. He hadn't spent a lifetime boxing out his frustrations for nothing.

The boys scampered down the ladder. Groping his way across the small room to stand beside the door as it opened, Ash smelled the earl's sweat through the deteriorating scent of last night's brandy and pipe smoke. Lansdowne evidently had never gone to bed in his effort to build this trap.

Waiting until he could see the shadowy motion entering, Ash swung the broken frame as hard as he could. He connected with a skull and cracked the rotten wood.

A body sprawled across his boots.

From the hall, Zack called, "Thanks, Cuz. I didn't think a peasant was allowed to hit a lord, and I wasn't about to step through that door first."

"Peasant." Ash snorted at this description of his educated cousin, son of a viscount. He shoved Lansdowne with his toe. "The stick was rotten, Pill-Face. Get up and fight like a man."

"Not with a gun at my back," the earl said furiously. "I'll see all of you hang for assault and invasion of my property."

A gun? If Zack was armed, that gave Ash a nice wide safety net.

"I'm surmising the bank owns the property now." He reached down to grab the earl's collar, contemplating strangling the bastard. "And by the time I have you held on kidnapping and assault, you won't have a lawyer to stand on."

"That wasn't me! That was Montfort!" With a lunge, Lansdowne twisted free to tackle Ash's legs.

Ash toppled like a felled tree, cracking his head on the floor.

A PISTOL SHOT REVERBERATED from the open window above Christie's head, the one the twins had emerged from—the one where Ash was no longer standing. Gripped by terror, she shouted a warning that brought everyone running.

A moment later, a stranger garbed in gentleman's clothes scrambled out of the window over the porch roof.

Where was Ash? Terror clutched her heart. She set down the useless paint brush and wrapped both hands around the deadly wrench. The man on the roof had the distinguished mien and expensive attire of an aristocrat but was clambering precariously down the roof without an ounce of dignity. Did she dare strike him when he came down the ladder? Should she?

"Lansdowne," Aster murmured beside her in a tone of horror. "He must be—"

Her scream joined Christie's as the earl tripped on a broken tile and lost his balance. He slid toward the edge of the slanted roof, flailing his arms in search of support. Finding none, he tumbled off the edge, falling head over foot to the crushed gravel drive. He landed with a bone-crushing thud.

Christie screamed her horror, but panic had her searching the empty window above. *Where was Ash?*

If this was the earl who had caused her family so much grief, she could easily disregard his pain. Remembering the gunshot, hysteria set in. If Ash was up there and *alive*, he'd be at the window right now. He had to know she was here. The twins would have told him.

"Ash!" she shouted frantically. When he didn't appear, she couldn't contain herself any longer. Letting others tend to the earl, she ran for the ladder.

Zack's broad frame filled the broken window. "He's been injured. I need help carrying him out."

Oh God, oh my Lord, help her in this hour of need. Injured? But alive.

Realizing it was safe to go inside now, Christie lifted her skirt and raced for the back door with the twins on her heels. The men were still tying up or chasing the earl's hired thugs, but Aster and Celeste joined her.

Zack met them at the top of the stairs. "Women can't carry him," he cried, appalled. "Fetch the berlin and the driver."

Christie shoved past. The twins dodged around. Aster and Celeste turned about to do as commanded.

Ash lay sprawled, spread-eagle, on the barren floor. His tailored frock coat was torn, dirty, and exhibited other signs of struggle. Christie ached at how he must have bravely fought to protect his sons, even though he couldn't see his assailants. Terrified, she fell down on her knees beside him and slid her hand beneath his waistcoat, hoping for a heartbeat.

Sighing in relief that he breathed normally and his heart still pounded, she lifted his poor head to see if he'd cracked it again.

Dark eyes snapped open, and a slow, dazed smile spread across his face. "Viking goddess," he murmured in satisfaction, before grimacing and closing them again.

"Oh, thank all the heavens!" Weeping, Christie fell across his broad chest. "I thought I'd lost you. Don't ever do this to me again, you beast, or I shall beat you senseless. I swear I will."

Ash's strong arms wrapped around her, and she was almost certain she felt a chuckle rumble.

"She means it, old fellow," Zack said with amusement. "I've never seen a more ferocious woman. Don't ever teach her to use a pistol or you're a dead duck."

"Do I look like a simpleton?" Ash grumbled, not moving. "Having a Valkyrie at my back is dangerous enough without arming her."

Terror turned to fury that he'd risk his neck so stupidly. Christie sat up and smacked his shoulder. "You arrogant monster! You didn't tell anyone you were *driving a curricle!*" She almost screamed this last. "You didn't even stop to ask for help. Do you think you are a god? I ought to . . ." She stopped to think of something bad enough.

"Kiss me?" he suggested.

"Kick you," she said firmly. "In the shins. As soon as you are up again."

"Make it my left leg, please," he said, almost penitently. "That one still aches when it's damp. It's easier to limp on only one leg."

Zack laughed, and Christie nearly wept at his humor when she could feel his pain. "You will not ever, *ever* do anything so arrogantly insane ever again, promise!"

"I promise I will try not to crack my head again," he agreed, deliberately missing the point. "Hartley, Hugh, come here a minute."

Christie was reluctant to release him, but the boys needed reassurance. Now that she knew he was whole and not the least bit addled—or no more so than usual—she sat back so Ash could hug his sons.

He ran his big hand over their faces in wonder, as if memorizing them, then hugged them both at once. "I'm proud of both of you. Now go feed the dogs and let me talk to Christie. You, too, Zack, begone."

"We need to take you to a physician," Christie protested, wiping her eyes. "Can you stand?"

"Out!" Ash roared when the others heeded her and not him.

"At your command, lord and master," Zack said wryly. "C'mon, boys. Your father's hard head has overcome worse knocks."

"The vote," Christie whispered anxiously. "We must return in time for you to lead your guests and friends."

"The Commons won't give up speechifying and shouting at each other until they're all starved and ready for bed," Ash predicted after the others left. Opening his eyes, he ran his hand over her cheek. "Before anything else happens, it's more important to say what I've never said to another. You are a woman above all others, my beautiful Miss Chris, and I worship and adore you beyond measure. I have little experience at love, but if what I feel now is anything at all like love, it terrifies me. My heart feels as if it might explode. You make such a splendid marchioness that I'm afraid that I don't deserve you, and you'll realize that sooner rather than later. Don't ever leave me, or I think I shall perish of a broken heart. That's a rather daunting admission for me, so don't expect to hear it often."

Tears poured down Christie's cheeks, even as she choked back laughter at the erudite marquess's impatient—not impassioned—speech. She yanked his ear in retaliation, then rained kisses on his bristled jaw. "I've nearly suffocated my heart trying not to love a man I know will make me miserable. I have to accept that you'll trample me into the dust as you race about, saving and exploring worlds I can never imagine. But if there is any hope that you might love me back, I'll love and admire you even when you're flinging inkpots and behaving like an arrogant . . . donkey. You are so strong in the face of adversity . . ." She choked on all the emotion attempting to pour out at once—words she almost hadn't had a chance to say.

"I have been a miserable tyrant." He pulled her down to kiss her again. "But if a woman as indomitable as you can love me, I know I'll learn to be a better person."

She covered his face in laughing kisses at this foolishness. "Don't pretend to be what you are not. I know you don't understand and probably can't accept that I can *feel* your love right now. It's pouring out, as if it's been imprisoned for too long. So even when you're at your worst, I won't doubt you, as long as your love runs true. No one but my mother has ever loved me, but I remember what it feels like, and it's glorious."

"Then I shall try very hard never to look at another woman," he said fervently, "Or I'll expect to be murdered in my sleep. You are the only woman I shall ever love, and the only person I'll allow to see me flopping around like a babe." The towering marquess wrapped his arm around her shoulders. "Now that the others are gone, help me up, my love. I feel weak as a newborn lamb."

Laughing with joy, she helped him to regain his feet.

HE COULD SEE HIS WIFE.

Ash held his breath as he struggled to stand, terrified his narrow bit of vision would disappear when he shifted position and all the blood rushed from his head. It was rather like looking through a crack in the wall. He had to tilt his gaze to see anything more than her nose, but he could *see* Christie!

His head pounded worse than he could remember, feeling as if his brain matter sloshed around inside his skull. Only Christie's words of love held the frayed strands of his hope together. For this goddess he'd been granted, he would climb mountains naked. He was well aware that he'd played the part of fool—and she not only forgave him, but loved him for the selfish arrogance that had driven every other woman away.

She understood that was who he was —and still claimed to love him.

He clung to her soft shoulders, studying each perfect feature that appeared in his limited vision as he painfully found his feet.

His wife had hair the color of ripe wheat. Fine strands had escaped the confinement of her braided chignon to tumble around a complexion of pale rose and cream. And her eyes . . . Ash fell into the depths of the blue sky over his fields in summer. She was the embodiment of the rich, fertile land he loved, all sunshine and roses and promise.

No, she wasn't dramatic. She didn't use cosmetics, so her lush pink lips matched the faint blush in her cheeks. And her lashes were as light as her hair, which made him wonder about lower parts. He hid his grin as he staggered upright and kept her possessively in his grip. His life contained enough drama for a dozen people. He needed Christie to be just as she was—a thorny English rose all his own.

He was terrified of telling her he could see her. She had threatened to run away if she thought he could see again.

She had deliberately *lied* about the danger his sons were in—to protect him. A woman as independent and courageous as that might think it necessary to leave—so he wouldn't have to look at her supposedly plain, statuesque self.

Women took insane notions that he had little chance of comprehending, especially with his head pounding torturously. So he limped along beside her and down the stairs without saying another word. The stairs were dark. It strained his narrow glimpse of the world to see where to place his foot . . . but if he concentrated, he could see the motion of his boot as he set it down. He couldn't see anything else while doing so. In another time and place, he'd roar his frustration, but for this moment . . . seeing the dirt on his boot pleased him enormously.

She led him outside where the winter sun opened the world to him again. Ash could hardly keep from falling to his knees in gratitude as he carefully turned his pounding head and saw the concerned expressions of his brothers, cousin, and uncle, one by one. He refrained from wincing at the glimpse of Lansdowne's body sprawled face first in the drive, his neck at an angle that left no doubt of his condition.

Earlier, Zack had attempted to block the earl's escape, and in the struggle, Zack's pistol had gone off. Worried that a magistrate would have to be called if an earl had been shot, Ash steered Christie closer so he could see more. He couldn't see blood or bullet wounds. The dastard had effectively killed himself.

Hiding his limited sight would be difficult. Ash let the others speak first while he decided how much he dared reveal.

"I'll clean up here," Pascoe said briskly, hiding the concern in his voice as he laid a reassuring hand on Ash's shoulder. "You need to lead your men to battle."

"Montfort?" Ash asked about the cad who had held a gun to his head and locked him up with the boys.

"Your wife put him to shame. We've tied him up, and he's whimpering like a baby. I don't think it's safe to leave him as your neighbor," Pascoe warned. "But he's a baron. Putting him on trial will be messy."

"I'll leave the decision in your hands." Ash leaned against Christie, grateful for her support since he was fairly certain his head would roll off at any minute. "I have no idea exactly what happened here today, but my thanks to all of you. I owe you."

"Put the Whigs in office, and you've repaid us all," Aster declared.

Aster. And Celeste. Ash shook his head in amazement. His brothers would kill him for endangering their lives. Theo and Erran had only married since his accident, so Ash had never seen them before. He turned toward the sound of their voices.

He tilted his head to better study the one who had to be Aster. She was almost as he'd imagined her—a carrot-red riot of curls, laughing eyes, short and well-rounded. She would lead staid Theo a merry dance.

Celeste—Ash tried not to stare as she entered his narrow line of vision. He'd known she was Jamaican and different. He hadn't known that meant her complexion was more brown than he became after a summer in the sun. Tall, thin, with lustrous dark hair falling loose from her hair pins, she was the sensuous dessert hard-working Erran deserved.

If his eyesight disappeared again, at least he'd had these few moments to see his family. Sighing with pleasure, he finally released Christie to let William take his weight and lead him toward the waiting carriage.

With a sensation akin to awe, Ash kept stealing glances at his magnificent wife. She was wearing a dowdy blue gown with a single petticoat. Her lack of fashion didn't deter him so much as fascinate him—he could watch the sway of her sturdy hips as she hurried ahead of them. No vaporish female, this! Instead of uselessly smothering him with worry or weeping over what couldn't be changed, she was already shepherding her flock. Any other female of his acquaintance would, at the very least, be demanding smelling salts and wilting all over the scenery.

Instead of hysterically scolding the troublemakers, Christie hugged the twins as they ran up, surrounded by half-starved hounds. She ordered the driver to help Ash into the berlin so William could take care of the dogs. Hoping to stall the inevitable, Ash refused to climb in until she did. He leaned against the berlin, arms crossed, and kept angling his head so he could watch his wife command her troops like a good general. She ushered in Aster and Celeste, then verified his brothers would find the curricle and look after the twins while Pascoe sought out the local authorities.

And even disheveled and distraught, she looked the part of a ripe Venus. Ash thought his heart would swell with pride and explode. He prayed his eyesight would last long enough to see her naked and with her hair down.

That was the image that got him through the humiliating carriage ride back to town, fighting nausea and the demons pounding on his skull. For Christie, he even endured the torture of a cramped carriage populated with nattering women.

He might possibly die for Christie, and he would die happy. He circled her shoulders with his arm, she rested against him, and the world blissfully went away.

Thirty-two

"TWO TUBS, IN MY CHAMBERS, immediately," Ash commanded as they entered the house. "All hands to hauling hot water," he told the footman on duty, who stared at their disheveled states, then rushed off to do as bid.

Christie shook her head in amazement at the arrogance of her lordly husband. He could barely hold his head up for the pain, yet he entered the house as a king would his stateroom, shoulders thrown back, chin up, and shouting orders.

"Our guests will be calling for their hot water if they're just now rising," Christie reminded him. "I'll use a basin until everyone is gone." She didn't even know if the house contained two tubs, and she blushed at the thought of bathing in the same room with Ash.

Which was foolish of her, admittedly, given what they'd done in bed these last nights. It was just... she was having difficulty adjusting to the notion that the magnificent marquess actually *loved* her. It was a little too much to believe after a lifetime of neglect. Perhaps all this time, she had been wrong about her ability to feel emotion, and it was all in her head. She needed time to absorb so very much . . . .

"The layabouts can wait," Ash said rudely, giving her no time for romantic fancies. "You come first. And if they expect me to lead them anywhere, I need to be rid of this headache. Or we could share a tub," he suggested wickedly.

There was the arrogant monster she knew and loved.

"I doubt one tub would hold us both," she said dryly, letting him drag her into his chamber. Now that he was home, he seemed better able to move about. He wasn't even using his stick. Had he lost it? "I'll have someone fetch your headache powder."

"The tub at Iveston will hold us," he said with a leer that almost convinced her he could see her state of dishabille. Her morning gown was very thin. "We'll head there directly tomorrow," he continued, "and I'll show you the wonders of sharing a tub."

"Then we can wait until tomorrow. Today, you bathe alone, and I'll just wash and change and see to your guests. After you have all marched off, I can have a bath."

She tried to slip away, but he held her tight, and she had a hard time telling him *no* after almost losing him. She was still feeling weepy and longed to cling to him. She loved that Ash was big enough to hold her so easily. He found the fastenings of her gown and began undoing them.

"I can do that myself." Gathering her hard-won courage, she pushed him away to work on her bodice. "It's too complicated to undress each other, especially if you want to go out there and talk to your guests anytime soon."

"I don't, really," he said with blunt honesty. He focused on her undressing with avid scrutiny, as if he could actually see her, while tearing blindly at his own buttons. "Tell me why you didn't let me know where you were going. You worried me past redemption."

Surprised at this tack, she took a moment to understand what he was feeling. He was brimming over with lust, so it was difficult. "Because I must learn to manage family matters on my own," she finally asserted.

"Only if I'm not available!" He wrestled out of his frock coat, his eyes still following her as she undid her skirt. "I didn't marry you so you could treat me like an invalid."

"I am treating you like a busy marquess," she responded, surprised at her own tartness. "Your children were being children. If you don't wish me to interfere with their upbringing, then say so."

"You are deflecting the argument. There is a very real danger of haring off on your own."

"Just as there was a very real danger in driving a *curricle* while blind," she cried in outrage. "If I thought it would work, I'd take a stick to your head for that. I had the sense to look for *help*. You stubbornly struck out on your own!"

"Because you weren't there." Her arrogant husband jutted his stubborn jaw and cast aside his waistcoat, but he didn't yank off his shirt while the servants rushed in. They carried in two tubs and buckets of steaming water. Christie darted behind the dressing screen.

"Just build up the fire," Ash told his valet, his frustration obviously mounting.

"Jones, bring his headache powder, please," Christie called.

"Yes, my lady. I'll lay out fresh clothes in the dressing room. Shall I have your maid fetch fresh linen?"

"Fresh everything," Christie agreed with a sigh, glancing down at her paint-splattered gown. "Afternoon attire, please."

"Yes, my lady."

She discarded the rest of her clothing while Ash stomped about, ordering servants. After his morning's exertions, he ought to just collapse in bed and groan, but he seemed to be in full martial mode. His eagerness was so great, she could feel it across the room. She didn't know what he was eager about. Earlier, he'd been beyond surly about leading a parade down Pall Mall to Parliament as he'd been ordered to do. She surmised it wasn't the election he was thinking about.

She heard a bolt slamming home. When had a bolt been installed? Since the chamber had three doors, that was fairly useless.

She heard two more bolts slamming shut. My heavens!

"All clear, my love. You may come out of hiding."

She was down to her linen shift and nothing more. She peered around the screen to see Ash alone, lowering his splendid nakedness into a steaming tub. Entranced by the sight, forgetting the argument, she stepped out of hiding. His broad back rippled with muscle and his arms bulged as he gingerly held himself above the hot water.

"Shall I wash your back?" she asked, daringly walking up to the tub to admire the front of him. He had a taut belly and not an ounce of fat marred his waist.

He was partially aroused. At the sound of her voice, he stiffened more, she noticed with fascination.

"By all means," he said gruffly, settling into the water. He seemed to study her as she reached for the soap the servants had left within his reach. "If that's one way of keeping you from haring off on wild escapades."

At his blatant stare, her nipples rubbed at her linen, even though she knew he could see next to nothing in the dim lamplight.

"I no longer wish to be a hermit hiding inside houses," she said stiffly. "I shall hare about as I deem necessary." She leaned over to scrub his shoulder.

"Then I shall have to arrange it so I go with you." Ash grabbed her waist and hauled her half over the tub to kiss her. She squealed and struggled, but finally finding a comfortable purchase, she eagerly returned his kisses. She was still in desperate need of reassurance that he was home, safe and unharmed.

He massaged her breast until she was as wet inside as out. He lifted her higher so he could cover her nipple with his mouth, soaking the linen between them even more. It didn't take further persuasion to step into the tub.

"There can't be room," she protested faintly as he tried to pull her down, and she resisted, holding the tub sides.

In answer, he unerringly grabbed the hem of her shift and yanked until he ripped the ribbons loose. He tugged the wet linen down, parted her thighs, and licked between them as she gingerly balanced above him.

Christie muffled a scream and quickly figured out how to drop down and kneel in place. Her husband was not a small man in any way. Even when she kneeled, his arousal brushed against her.

Ash eyed her as a starving man might study a feast, as if he might actually be *seeing* her. Uneasily, she edged back, but he pushed her breasts up and together and kissed them both. The place between her legs opened and ached.

"You are more luscious than words could ever say," he said reverently. "I knew you would be, but this . . ." He sighed and took her bare nipple in his mouth until Christie nearly shrieked with need.

She wanted to question his words, explore the excitement he exuded, but he captured her buttocks in his large hands and eased her over him, and she couldn't think at all as he filled her.

He pumped into her until they were both sweaty and frantic with need, then bit her shoulder to muffle his moans of pleasure. Expertly, he fingered sensitive tissues just as he drove deep and achieved his own release. It was Christie's turn to bury her cries in his shoulder while she writhed with muscles clenching, milking him until pleasure satiated them.

"Yes," Ash said in satisfaction, pulling out what was left of her pins to fill his hands with her hair. "If I never see another day, I'll have this moment in my head forever. I wish I could paint you like this. You have no idea . . . Someday, I'll take you to the Continent to see the masters. Even they could not replicate your beauty."

Hunger momentarily slaked, unable to move despite the awkwardness of the tub, Christie leaned her head against his brow and tried to translate his declaration. He must be speaking in metaphors. "You cannot touch the old masters to see them," she

said, although the notion of visiting the Continent enthralled her.
"They are paint and canvas."

"Which is why you are so much better." He caressed her breasts.
"But I wish *you* to see your beauty as I do. It's a damned shame
Lawrence died. I'd hire him to paint you."

Horrified at the thought of a giant *her* on the wall, Christie finally
discovered the energy to push away. "You would subject your family
and guests to staring at what they can already see. That's foolish.
Now hurry, I can hear people in the dining room."

He caught her hands against his chest and wouldn't let go. "You
have an intriguing freckle just below your left breast, and your eyes
are the color of summer skies. And if you run away, I will follow you
forever."

Christie froze. She studied his sightless dark eyes. She watched as
he tore his gaze from hers, deliberately dropped it to her breasts,
then kissed the freckle hiding below her over-plump breast.

"You can see?" she whispered, not sure whether she felt horror or
joy. Most likely both. His joy filled her, and she could scarcely resist
his ballooning excitement—but if he could *see* the roll of flesh at her
waist . . . "How much can you see?" she asked in horror. "When did
you start seeing?"

"After the knock on my head. I don't know if it's the result of
Emilia's potions or the blow or just another stage of the problem. I
still need a lot of light to see clearly in just the narrow band in front
of me," he admitted. "I have to turn my head to see anything else.
But to be able to finally admire your lovely skin and the beauty of
your lips—" He slid his fingers through her hair and steadied her
jaw. "I cannot get enough. It's like being handed heaven. I need to
know every detail that I've missed."

Confused, she hastily scrambled from the tub and grabbed for a
towel. "I . . ." She looked down at her very large and unstylish self
and back to his magnificent muscled form and ran for the screen.

"I will find old masters right here in London," Ash declared. "You
will not run until you see what I see."

"You are mad," she cried, scrambling for the clean clothes her
maid had left. "Your mind is still addled. Wait until you see me next
to Celeste and Aster—"

"I've seen you next to them," he said, splashing in what water
remained. "Celeste is skinny and brown. Aster is short and her

mouth is too wide. Erran and Theo think them beautiful. Have you never heard that beauty is in the eyes of the beholder?"

She didn't know whether to trounce him for not telling her about his eyes sooner or preen that he thought her prettier than beautiful Celeste or . . . just scream. "That's for old people," she said scornfully. "We'll all be gray and fat someday. We must hope to be known for kindness or wisdom by then so people will see those traits instead of wrinkles."

"Christie, my beloved, I have been *seeing* those traits in you for weeks now. Do you think I can see anything other than your patience with a tyrant, your kindness to my sons, your command of my unruly household? I have held your voluptuous beauty in my arms and imagined every lovely curve to perfection. You could have warts on your nose, and I would love them."

She swallowed a giggle at the image and clung to her outrage. "You got me naked before you told me!" She knew she was being ridiculous in the face of his brave declaration. She'd spent a lifetime with her unlovely self. He couldn't change her mind so easily with pretty words.

"Of course I did," he admitted cheerfully. "I'm not a fool. You should remember that the next time you lie to me. I always know it when you do."

"Then you know I'm not lying when I say I'm no beauty," she said darkly, struggling with her bodice. Realizing he could help her now, she came out from behind the screen.

He stood naked and dripping, towel in hand, looking like an Adonis. She'd spent a lot of time studying illustrations in her stepfather's library. Her husband was Greek god material.

"Your definition of beauty and mine differ. That's opinion and not fact. I have an ugly scar down my face, a withered thigh, a big nose, and I'm not exactly of a gentlemanly build or coloring."

Outraged at this description of perfection, she pinched his patrician nose. "You are looking for compliments. Have you even seen the scar? It merely emphasizes your handsomeness. Perfection would be boring."

He snorted and studied the blue and white striped gown she'd donned. "I have wondered how you dressed. I like the simplicity. It suits you."

Still roiling with so many emotions that she couldn't think straight, she presented her unfastened back to him rather than gawk in awe at his nudity. "For my new gowns, I intend to order lace and ribbons and those lovely billowing sleeves," she said spitefully.

"You're lying. Try again." He accurately pulled her bodice hooks together until it fit snugly, then kissed her shoulder.

He could see. He really could see. Christie shivered. "I'm a terrible liar."

"That's a lie," he said with a laugh. "You do it all the time and no one notices except me."

"That's a lie," she countered. "I told you your valet's choice of wallpaper was excellent so you'd leave poor Zack alone. Take a good look."

He glanced around the unlit walls. "Too dark to see it well. And I didn't believe you. I was just intrigued that you'd settle for walls you didn't like and wondered why. Now I know. You were saving my cousin from my bullying."

She was finally calming down enough to realize he truly believed what he was saying—that he was a human lie detector. If she wasn't so upset, she'd have to ponder that, but anything seemed possible these days. "People must lie to you all the time. You cannot possibly always know the truth unless you have a gossip monger on your shoulder."

He shrugged. "I collect information, admittedly." Finished with her bodice, he returned to drying off. "But I only do so after I hear the lies. I like to know why people do what they do."

She sensed his conviction and shook her head. If he would insist on this nonsensity, then he had to listen to hers. "If I am to believe that, then you must believe that I can tell what the people around me feel. You're feeling rather smug right now."

He stopped toweling off to stare. "Is that part of hearing ghosts in your head?"

"No, the voices didn't start until I heard my mother after she died. The *feelings* have always been there." She looked around for a mirror to fix her hair, but of course, Ash had none. When they'd remodeled a public room for his private chamber, they'd had no reason to install mirrors for a blind man. With a sigh, she borrowed his brush to start braiding.

"And I can tell that you aren't lying, that you really believe you hear your mother," he said. "That doesn't mean it's true, just that you believe it. But if I'm to believe that you know how I feel, then you must know that I love you, and I think you're beautiful. So you can't run away." He took the brush to stroke the damp strands of her hair.

"I can't read minds," she said irritably, not understanding how the conversation had gone so far off topic. "I can *feel* love, yes. I don't feel distaste when you look at me, which is a pleasant change, but feelings can change at any minute."

"Mine won't," he said reassuringly, stroking her hair, then braiding it. "We can argue this tomorrow, on our way to Iveston. For now, I would very much like to rest my aching head for an hour before confronting our guests. I need time to consider how and if I should let them know about my recovering sight."

Immediately concerned, she let the confusing conversation drop. She caught his big, competent hand and kissed it. "You are worried. You're afraid your sight will go away."

"Perspicacious." He carefully stuck the pins she handed him into the circle of braids he'd created at her nape. "Would it be better if a blind marquess marched through the streets and spoke extemporaneously in front of the Lords, or a half-blind one?"

"Be yourself. Say nothing of your sight. And I dare say you've already memorized a perfectly ringing speech."

"Not so ringing if I can see them yawning and nodding off," he said dryly, applying the final pin.

She turned and kissed his rough cheek. "If I must believe you see me as beautiful, you must believe that you can command men to do what is right. Rest. I'll see that your guests are entertained."

Still so unsettled she didn't know whether to stay or hide, Christie swept out of the room. She could only hope all the traitors had been caught or had gone home. She might knife the next man who touched her family. She never wanted to suffer another day like this again.

And she still had the longest part to go.

Thirty-three

HEAD NO LONGER POUNDING after his nap, Ash let his valet straighten his tie and tuck his neckcloth into his waistcoat. If his vision continued to improve, he would have to order a mirror brought in here so he could arrange his own damned linen.

He was thrilled that his narrow view of the world hadn't left while he slept.

At a knock on his door, he commanded entrance, knowing it wouldn't be Christie. She wouldn't knock. He hadn't seen her since he'd fallen asleep for half the day.

Theo and Erran entered, both garbed in afternoon attire. Ash had ordered lamps lit around the room so he could better see as he moved about. Now, he tilted his head back to observe as much of his brothers as he could. Theo's tie had already come undone and his waistcoat was unbuttoned. A sheaf of paper bulged in one of his coat pockets, and a hank of brown hair fell across his brow. Ash was rather relieved to see his heir hadn't changed much over these past months.

Erran, on the other hand, looked like a vanity plate. If he cocked his head just right, Ash could finally admire one of the pleated shirts Celeste produced. His younger brother had recently had his hair trimmed and his beard shaved and appeared more polished than any lord. Erran would make a fine representative in the Commons when the time came. It was good to know that blindness hadn't deceived him in that.

Ash still didn't know what to tell his brothers. He was terrified even this limited scope would vanish at a moment's notice.

"Your bride told us we are to admire your attire and ask if ours is up to snuff. What the devil does that mean?" Theo asked, attacking the fire in the grate so the flames added to the room's light.

Apparently everyone had developed the habit of ignoring the lamps around him. Ash could see the point. "I want my sword stick. Anyone know where it's got to?"

"From the sounds of it, the boys probably used your walking stick to herd dogs this morning while you were lying about being coddled by your wife. You have another in your office," Erran said, crossing to the study door.

"That's not the one I mean. The one with a horse head is a sword," Ash called after him. "I didn't have that one because I couldn't find it."

"Pascoe stole that one, unless the one he was carrying was identical." Theo paced. "Why do I need to be here? I'm no good at politicking."

Erran returned with an assortment of sticks. "No horse head."

"Tell Pascoe I'll whack him for stealing my favorite stick when I couldn't see his thievery." Ash chose one with a silver knob, studied it for the latch, then opened it to reveal a flask inside. "This will suffice. Where's my brandy bottle?"

His brothers gawked. Jones scurried to fetch the brandy.

"What do you mean, when you *couldn't* see," Erran inquired, eyeing the tricky knob in suspicion.

Rather than ask, Theo stepped in front of Ash and met his eyes. He raised a finger and passed it back and forth between them. Ash followed it by turning his head.

"You can see." Theo continued holding his finger to the right but swatted Ash on the left, a blow Ash hadn't seen coming while focusing on the finger. "You can *almost* see."

Ash cuffed him back. "For now. For this minute. Let's not be hasty." Ash held out the stick for his valet to fill, waiting out the stunned silence.

"Enough to ride a horse?" Theo demanded.

Leave it to his heir to pinpoint Ash's major concern—returning to riding the fields Theo hated. "Maybe. Do I tell those men out there?" He nodded to the corridor where laughter and rising voices carried.

"You're asking us?" Erran asked. "That's a first. My vote is to just walk out there, say nothing, and let them judge for themselves. Your eyes are really none of their concern."

Until recently, Ash had not been inclined to listen to his younger brothers. After these past months of relying on them for almost everything, he couldn't be so . . . blind. His brothers had intelligence and strengths that multiplied his own. Better yet, he could trust them to be honest.

"You're right," he agreed, catching Erran's look of surprise with chagrin. It was a wonder they hadn't locked him in the attic and thrown away the key when they had the chance. "Let's go out there, raise a cup of punch, and send them off like a conquering army."

"Oh, we'll be an army, all right," Theo said with dryness.

Ash raised an eyebrow.

Erran shrugged. "We'll leave it as a surprise. Marriage is a unique institution and we have a *lot* to learn."

Considering they hadn't had a woman in the household for twenty-five years before Aster arrived, Ash could appreciate that. He was anticipating whatever madness their wives had spun this time.

"THE WHIGS FOR THE WORKING MAN!" Celeste called from her platform near the park. "Show your support for the party that will give all men the vote!"

Wearing the tri-color sash sewed on Erran's new sewing machine, Christie handed out small flags to anyone who held up a hand. A small crowd was forming in the cold November gloom.

"Ash will kill us," Aster said cheerfully at Christie's back, handing out more flags on that side.

"Ash won't have time to kill us," Christie said in satisfaction. "He has messages from the king to answer. Under his suggestion, the Civil List is about to become a point of contention on which the current administration shall fail."

From her higher perch on the bench, Celeste considered the group of gentlemen gathered to enter Westminster. "Some of the representatives actually look determined."

"Finally." Aster made a moue of disgust. "How fast did Erran have to talk to convince them that reform is necessary?"

"Probably not too fast after they learned of Lansdowne and Montfort's misdeeds." Christie handed out the last of her flags. "Any left lingering on the fence are now in Whig pockets."

"And how did they learn of that?" Celeste asked, climbing down from her perch now that the mob at their feet had surged, shouting, toward the group of representatives entering the hallowed halls of Parliament, urging them to vote reform. "I thought a gentleman's code of honor prevented speaking ill of their own."

"Women gossip," Christie said in satisfaction.

Aster laughed. "Malcolm women especially. There will be an entire army of outraged members speechifying. Did you really tell your guests what happened, Christie?"

Christie smiled. "No, I told Ash's valet, who told the other servants, who told everyone in St. James, apparently. Malcolm women cannot compare to the gossip of loyal hired help. Shall we repair to tea and wait for the results?"

"Happily, but you're the one who has to listen to the bellows of the Mad Marquess tonight," Celeste said in her lilting accent, taking Christie's arm. "Your outrageous gossip may have forced the king's involvement."

"Ash won't have time to bellow at me," Christie said in satisfaction. "He'll have so many other things to bellow about that he'll find a better use of his time."

Her sisters-in-law laughed, and Christie basked in the warmth of understanding. For the first time since childhood, she felt as if she *belonged*.

ASH STOOD BEFORE THE MOST AUGUST BODY in the kingdom, trying not to squint into the candlelit shadows. This small chamber in the medieval Palace of Westminster was not designed for six hundred plus men who had gathered to hear the outcome of the debate in the Commons. Given the way the members slouched and lay about the hard wooden benches, snoring and gambling and occasionally punching each other into responding, Ash thought it a good thing that they didn't have room for an audience.

It was also a good thing that he mostly saw the chamber from memory. It was too dark to see beyond the first bench as he preached his sermon of reform or revolution. He understood why it had been so hard for the leadership to give up the wooden tally sticks they'd once used to count the vote. He'd often been tempted to throw them to wake up the drunkards. His marksmanship currently wouldn't allow throwing anything, however.

Shouting to wake the dead, and those in the back row, he finished his speech. "And I tell you now is the time for all true Englishmen to stand up and be counted, to ensure our future, to encourage an *industrial* revolution and not a revolution of the people we are sworn to protect, a revolution that will make us leaders of the world.

Electoral reform will move us forward into an era of prosperity for all!"

When he finished, Ash was gratified to hear more than his small crowd of supporters clapping. His family had pushed hard for this moment. He wished they could be here now to savor it. That would come if the king heeded his words about a choice in a new prime minister to lead them out of the past. He used his stick to find his way to his seat.

When the Lords finally received news of the vote in the Commons, the result was not a surprise. Without Lansdowne and Montfort, the other side had fallen apart—just as Ash's enemies had hoped to shred his faction by removing him.

As word leaked outside, a great roar rose in the square.

"I'm told that one of my great-nieces is out there raising the rabble." The Duke of Sommersville fell into step with Ash as they attempted to push through the mob to the exit.

"My wife, your grace, although shouting isn't Christie's style," Ash said. "She is more likely encouraging others to do so."

The duke pounded his shoulder. "Good to know that the family tradition of sensible matches marches on. My son told me of your accident. I'd like to have a look at your eyes someday, if you don't mind. I have a particular fascination with injuries of the head. I've been told I have a healing touch. Do you believe in magic?"

Given that his wife and her family's magic potions and a blow on the head had started sorting out his vision, Ash snorted. "No, not in magic, but in things that we can't explain. I'd be honored, but I'm already seeing better, although that was more likely the knock on the head and not Christie's influence, if you're hinting that she has supernatural talents."

The duke nodded. "It's good enough to know that you have an open mind and are willing to experiment. Give my regards to your lady and tell her I'll call before I leave town."

If Christie wanted family, she'd have more than she knew what to do with shortly. But Ash had other plans for his wife, and they had little to do with dukes. "We'll be leaving for Iveston in the morning, your grace, but we'll be happy to have you visit us any time you wish to travel that way. My estate has been neglected too long."

"Understood. We should keep in touch. There's a lot of work ahead if we're to make reform happen." The duke sauntered off as they broke through the throng in the old palace and onto the crowded street.

Ash swallowed hard at the solid mass of humanity ahead. The gas lamps merely showed him a swirling mass. He would have to hope he remembered his direction and hold on to his purse. Fighting pickpockets wouldn't happen easily when he could scarcely move or see.

Before he had waded ten feet into the throng, the scent of lilies reached him. Ash waited, and his astonishing wife shoved her way to his side. Hugging her, he kissed her cheek. "Tell Celeste to dissolve this mob and let us go home."

"You believe she can dissolve a mob?" Christie asked with interest, raising her hand to signal someone he couldn't see in the darkness.

"I currently believe in miracles. Let us go home and create a few more. We have an early start on the morrow. It is a good thing the boys went with William. I'm not inclined to share the carriage."

"You radiate triumph," she declared. "And lust, but that seems to be a given."

Ash laughed and watched the mob part as Celeste's magical voice called for dispersal. "How was I so fortunate to find you?"

"I found *you*, remember? How could I ignore such a ferocious blind man? You didn't even have the sense to be afraid until the thief fled. I knew then that I had to meet you, even if you laughed in my face. I had never met any genuine heroes."

"So you lied to me. That makes complete sense. I'm happy to have that explained. Come along, wife, the waters part and even I can see the way." Offering his arm as if they were out for an evening's stroll, Ash led his bride home. Or she led him. He didn't trouble to work it out.

Thirty-four

"I AM HALF TERRIFIED TO TAKE YOU to Iveston," Ash declared as the carriage departed busy city streets for the rural roads of Surrey. "Until Aster arrived, women were in the habit of fleeing our abode."

Christie had heard enough about Iveston to feel a degree of apprehension. "Is that why Theo and Aster chose to stay in London?" she asked. "They fear I'll run screaming from the house and not return?"

"No, if they'd thought that, they would have come to laugh at me. Theo had a paper to present to the Astronomical Society, and Aster is hoping to found her own Astrological Society. Now that the harvest is done and I'm on my way back, they're probably plotting a mad escape to Aster's home—or Wystan, where there is an observation tower for Theo and a Malcolm library for Aster."

Christie studied the quiet winter fields rolling past their window. "So far, everything looks very ordinary. Are we close yet?"

"Those are my fields." He nodded to the right. "I've been dreading seeing them from inside a carriage, but it is good to catch glimpses of them, even if I cannot view the whole hillside. I can't abide sitting still, but having you to talk to has prevented me from beating the walls of this cage."

To her surprise, Ash had spent this journey watching out windows, eagerly soaking up the sight of places of interest he hadn't been able to see since spring. He'd related stories about the various clubs they'd passed on Pall Mall, pointed out new construction, and when reminded by familiar views, told her tales of his youth in London.

She was thrilled that his vision was improving. She loved hearing him speak with her as she'd always imagined a husband might. She basked joyously in his conscientiousness in seeing to her comfort and allowing her to observe a side of him that wasn't immediately apparent in the authoritarian persona he presented to the world.

"Does the household know we're coming?" she asked, trying to hide her anxiety.

"I sent word. They'll be down on their knees in gratitude. William is no disciplinarian when it comes to the twins. They'll be running amuck. Our housekeeper is inclined to tipple in the afternoons, so the servants pick up bad habits. I'm hoping the new butler won't quit once he sees what's in store. I suspect Pascoe and Jacques are still dealing with Montfort's situation, so they'll be about, encouraging chaos. I told Zack to hang around if he could. There are undoubtedly repairs you'd like him to undertake."

"Me?" she squeaked. "You've lived there all your life. Why haven't you made them?"

He shrugged. "There were always other more important things."

"Like a fiancée and a mistress or two," Christie said wickedly, remembering Aster's warnings and sensing her husband's uneasiness.

He hugged her close. "I now have a distracting wife to take care of the household for me. And the former fiancée is in London and the mistresses are no more, so you are saddled with the full responsibility for me as well as the house."

His tone sent a shiver of need straight through her, but with the daunting prospect of meeting his entire household ahead, she refused to act on her baser nature. "Perhaps we should stay in London," she murmured.

"You prefer the city?" he asked, turning his attention entirely on her.

She adored the way he treated her as someone of importance whose opinions mattered, just as he believed that she was fully qualified to run his household. "I have only been in the city a month or so. I could not even say if I like it. I'm simply terrified of running an immense household. My stepfather's house was only a little larger than your London home. We were very rural and quiet and entertained little."

Ash chuckled. "I'm not concerned. We muddled along all these years without burning it down. That's all you need do, if that's your choice. Watch, you should see the dome and towers shortly."

With fascination, Christie surveyed the sprawling Hall emerging from the trees. Mostly, it was bleak blocks of stone with four towers at the end of wings built around a tall center structure, almost medieval in its simplicity. Not even a single rose bush adorned the walls.

MY ROSES ARE STILL THERE, the voice said. *YOU NEED ONLY FIND THE ROOTS TO BRING THEM BACK TO LIFE.*

"Are your gardeners in the habit of chopping down roses?" she asked, wondering how to find roots of what didn't seem to exist.

"If they're too much work, probably. The goats eat everything else. And the dogs and horses trample anything the goats leave. Why do you ask?" He ran his finger under the neck of her pelisse and kissed her forehead. "Roses are not where my mind travels upon seeing that fortress."

"Your great-grandmother wishes to see her roses returned," Christie explained. "I should think dogs and goats could be penned and gardeners could be taught to tend instead of cutting."

He rubbed up and down her nape and neck, sending more shivers of desire coursing through her. "Roses? I do seem to remember them from childhood. If you must listen to orders from ghosts, you will have a very busy time."

"That fortress needs roses," she said firmly, watching in horror as the carriage drew up the drive and black-and-white uniformed servants formed a line down the broad front steps. "And flowering shrubs and trees instead of a barnyard for a lawn."

"It's all yours to command, my general," he said sympathetically, before turning his head to see the servants. "And I wish you well of it. They've all been trained only recently, except Mrs. Smith, the housekeeper."

"The stout one who keeps tilting?" Christie asked faintly, studying the retinue.

"That's the one. The stress of preparing for this moment must have sent her to the bottle early," he said in amusement. "She's the only staff member who has never deserted us. She knows where all the bodies are buried."

"Family retainer, of course." Christie took a deep breath as the carriage rolled to a stop.

Garbed in a bottle-green riding coat and fine white linen, Ash stepped from the carriage looking every inch the marquess he was. Christie could almost feel the tension of the staff as she took his gloved hand and emerged from the carriage. She'd worn her most elegant traveling gown in hopes that fashionable grandeur would be enough to impress.

She opened her mind and sensed nothing but curiosity and nervousness at her arrival. She was one step closer to feeling like Christie the Marchioness, and not Harriet the Hidden. Breathing a little easier, she took Ash's arm. Feeling ridiculously regal, she lifted her trailing skirt with her other hand.

Apparently comfortable with familiar stairs, Ash didn't use his walking stick as he strode up, introducing her to the beaming Mrs. Smith, giving the terrified new maids the opportunity to bob their curtsies.

A raw young footman opened the door to give them entrance.

With only a howl of warning, a pack of hounds and a herd of goats raced out of the opening, followed by the shouting twins. Ash managed to avoid being tumbled down the steps. Christie caught his arm, but a tiny kid ran into her skirts and bleated in terror at being blinded by acres of fabric.

Without a second thought, Christie crouched down and hugged the crying baby.

She had no understanding as Ash roared in laughter. Following the pack, shirt-sleeved William appeared equally startled and halted his chase. Pascoe and Jacques ambled out to the wide portico to watch the servants scatter. They, too, laughed when Christie stood with the bawling kid in her arms.

"Honestly, the lot of you ought to be ashamed of yourselves," she scolded. "You did this on purpose, and after all these good people probably spent hours scouring the halls." She shoved the goat at the sophisticated London gentleman draped in monocles and watch fobs. Pascoe caught it gingerly. "Take this poor baby back to its mother and grow up."

Lifting her skirt, she sailed past the stupidly grinning men and into the wide foyer that was to be her new home. Ash promptly followed her.

"How did you know they did that on purpose?" he demanded, still laughing. "Theo once had a fiancée who fainted on the doorstep when they pulled that trick."

"I could feel their amusement, of course. Male humor is very strange, but I think that's their way of welcoming me. I felt no malice in them." In relief that she'd not only survived the grand entrance, but didn't feel a bit of negativity, she swung around to admire the towering domed foyer. Oddly, she felt more comfortable that his family had accepted her enough to pull one of their foolish stunts.

Emanating so much satisfaction and love that she couldn't help smile, her husband swung her around to face him. "You are the most amazing female I have ever encountered." Ash kissed her with such enthusiasm, her knees nearly gave out.

In the doorway, staff and family applauded.

"This your new home," he whispered against her ear. "We are all yours to command, my love. Be gentle with us."

Unable to speak her happiness, she pulled his head back down to hers so she might kiss him even more thoroughly.

THAT EVENING, ASH INTRODUCED her to their own private bathing room, complete with a sunken marble tub so large and decadent that they could both easily fit into it. Despite Christie's protests, he lit candles all around the tub.

"I have no desire to return to darkness, my pet," he told her in that deep voice of authority that aroused her as much as the sight of his muscled nakedness. "I wish to spend the rest of my life basking in your beauty and all the marvelous changes that life makes." Laughing, he leaned over and kissed the furrow over her nose.

"Perhaps I'll grow thinner chasing goats and little boys," she suggested.

"Or plumper carrying my children," he corrected, with so much satisfaction and pleasure that she had to believe he wouldn't mind.

She'd found the one man in a million who could love her as she was, and her heart expanded with joy. "My love for you is so great, my arrogant lord, that it will even encompass goats and pigs and tippling housekeepers."

"And to think, I only need to accept meddling magical women and their eccentric families. Fair enough." He pulled her into him and kissed her until all the ghosts scattered and left them alone.

Even the stone walls sighed in happiness.

Historical Notes

IN 1830 ENGLAND, ELECTIONS WERE NOT anything similar to what the modern reader understands. After King George IV died, the new king called for a "general" election that took place over the summer for all the United Kingdom. Google **history of parliament.** That should give you some idea of the wildly differing views, topics, and maneuverings that occurred at the time. There weren't just two political "parties" but a variety of oddly-named factions. I have used my creative license to reduce their numbers to the two most widely understood since the others aren't important to the story.

My purpose was not to write the history of the election, but the result. In actuality, the general election produced a reform-oriented Commons which did not support the prime minister at the time—the Duke of Wellington—who had blatantly rejected any notion of parliamentary reform. Wellington resigned because the Commons would not support the Civil List he'd proposed—a political boondoggle all civilly carried out without public fanfare. Within the week, the king appointed Earl Grey, who took office on November 22, 1830—all very boringly polite and not story fodder.

Earl Grey is a fascinating man in his own right. He had fifteen children, lived four days from London, and seldom made the sessions on time. Right or wrong, he eventually, not immediately, led Parliament past all the stumbling blocks to open up the election process so aristocrats didn't control the government any longer.

The point is, Grey was *appointed*, not elected. I'm sure arm-twisting occurred behind the scenes, but history does not record it. So rather than write about one tiny local election or a boring petition to the king (and they did love their petitions), I tweaked history a tiny bit to add some fun.

Acknowledgments

As ever, it takes a village to create a book. Book View Café Publishing Co-op is one of the best villages I've ever occupied. Kudos to everyone involved for all the advice and encouragement and hard work. In particular, editorial advice from Mindy Klasky and Jen Stevenson, proofreading from Sherwood Smith, and above-and-beyond-the-call of duty formatting from Vonda McIntyre, and the tireless efforts of Pati Nagle for keeping us all organized!

And much gratitude to the newest edition to my group of tireless, hardworking associates, Ryan Zitofsky, who helps me find readers, wherever they may be.

GET A FREE STARTER SET OF PATRICIA RICE BOOKS

Thank you for reading *Theory of Magic*.

Would you like to know when my next book is available? I occasionally send newsletters with details on new releases, special offers and other bits of fun news. If you sign up for the mailing list I'll send you a free copy of the Patricia Rice starter kit. **The books average 4.4 out of 5 stars and together usually retail over $15.00** Just sign up at **http://patriciarice.com/sign-up**

Would you review my book?

I am an independent author, so getting the word out about my book is vital to its success. If you liked this book, please consider telling your friends, and writing a review at the store where you purchased it. Reviews help other readers find books. I appreciate all reviews, whether positive or negative.

About the Author

With several million books in print and *New York Times* and *USA Today's* bestseller lists under her belt, former CPA Patricia Rice is one of romance's hottest authors. Her emotionally-charged contemporary and historical romances have won numerous awards, including the *RT Book Reviews* Reviewers Choice and Career Achievement Awards. Her books have been honored as Romance Writers of America RITA® finalists in the historical, regency and contemporary categories.

A firm believer in happily-ever-after, Patricia Rice is married to her high school sweetheart and has two children. A native of Kentucky and New York, a past resident of North Carolina and Missouri, she currently resides in Southern California, and now does accounting only for herself. She is a member of Romance Writers of America, the Authors Guild, and Novelists, Inc.

For further information, visit Patricia's network:

http://www.patriciarice.com
http://www.facebook.com/OfficialPatriciaRice
https://twitter.com/Patricia_Rice
http://wordwenches.typepad.com/word_wenches/

ALSO BY PATRICIA RICE

The World of Magic:

The Unexpected Magic Series
MAGIC IN THE STARS
WHISPER OF MAGIC
THEORY OF MAGIC
The Magical Malcolms Series
MERELY MAGIC
MUST BE MAGIC
THE TROUBLE WITH MAGIC
THIS MAGIC MOMENT
MUCH ADO ABOUT MAGIC
MAGIC MAN
The California Malcolms Series
THE LURE OF SONG AND MAGIC
TROUBLE WITH AIR AND MAGIC
THE RISK OF LOVE AND MAGIC

Historical Romance:

The Rebellious Sons
WICKED WYCKERLY
DEVILISH MONTAGUE
NOTORIOUS ATHERTON
FORMIDABLE LORD QUENTIN
The Regency Nobles Series
THE GENUINE ARTICLE
THE MARQUESS
ENGLISH HEIRESS
IRISH DUCHESS

Mysteries: ***Family Genius series***
EVIL GENIUS
UNDERCOVER GENIUS
CYBER GENIUS

About Book View Café

Book View Café is a professional authors' cooperative offering DRM-free ebooks in multiple formats to readers around the world. With authors in a variety of genres including fantasy, romance, mystery, and science fiction, Book View Café has something for everyone.

Book View Café is good for readers because you can enjoy high-quality DRM-free ebooks from your favorite authors at a reasonable price.

Book View Café is good for writers because 95% of the profits goes directly to the book's author.

Book View Café authors include NY Times bestsellers and notable book authors (Madeleine Robins, Patricia Rice, Maya Kaathryn Bohnhoff, and Sarah Zettel), Nebula and Hugo Award winners (Ursula K. Le Guin, Vonda N. McIntyre, Linda Nagata), and a multiple Rita award nominee (Patricia Rice).

bookviewcafe.com

Praise for Patricia Rice's novels

FORMIDABLE LORD QUENTIN

"another gem . . .with touches of whimsy, astute dialogue, a bit of poignancy, passion and sensuality —fast-paced tale of love and laughter." –Joan Hammond, *RT Reviews*

"Rice has crafted her novel with plenty of witty, engaging characters and a healthy dose of romance. Clever Bell is a splendid protagonist, and readers will cheer her efforts to get men to take her seriously and treat her as an equal." –*Publishers Weekly*

MERELY MAGIC

"Like Julie Garwood, Patricia Rice employs wicked wit and sizzling sensuality to turn the battle of the sexes into a magical romp." Mary Jo Putney, *NYT* Bestselling author

MUST BE MAGIC

"Rice has created a mystical masterpiece full of enchanting characters, a spellbinding plot, and the sweetest of romances." *Booklist* (starred review)

THE TROUBLE WITH MAGIC

"Rice is a marvelously talented author who skillfully combines pathos with humor in a stirring, sensual romance that shows the power of love is the most wondrous gift of all. Think of this memorable story as a gift you can open again and again." *Romantic Times*

THIS MAGIC MOMENT

"This charming and immensely entertaining tale . . .takes a smart, determined heroine who will accept nothing less than true love and an honorable hero who eventually realizes what love is and sets them on course to solve a mystery, save an entire estate, and find the magic of love." –*Library Journal*

MUCH ADO ABOUT MAGIC

"The magical Rice takes Trev and Lucinda, along with her readers, on a passionate, sensual, and romantic adventure in this fast-paced, witty, poignant, and magical tale of love." *Romantic Times* (Top Pick, 4 ½ stars)

MAGIC MAN

"In this delightful conclusion to the Magic series, Rice gives readers a thoughtful giant of a man who can bring down mountains, but with gentle touches can make the earth tremble for the woman he loves. This is a sensual, poignant, humorous and magical read." *Romantic Times*

Made in the USA
Coppell, TX
28 December 2020